"I'm Not Wrong. I've Seen It All Before.

You'll call it love. Traver will call it another successsful seduction."

Mitch had moved terribly close. She smelled his clean scent, and the softness of his silky sideburns brushed her cheek. Struggling to get her arms through the long sleeves, she asked, "Are you going to kiss me? What are you trying to prove? Is this some contest between you and Traver—like the fight on the dock? Whatever one of you has, the other one wants?"

She hoped her accusations would divert him. But they didn't. While her hands were still tangled in the sleeves, he simply gathered her into his arms. He looked arrogantly resplendent in the last rays of twilight, the glow of thick golden hair melting into the fair skin and limpid blue eyes. She realized he could no more keep from kissing her than he could keep from breathing. . . .

Dear Reader:

We trust you will enjoy this Richard Gallen romance. We plan to bring you more of the best in both contemporary and historical romantic fiction with four exciting new titles each month.

We'd like your help.

We value your suggestions and opinions. They will help us to publish the kind of romances you want to read. Please send us your comments, or just let us know which Richard Gallen romances you have especially enjoyed. Write to the address below. We're looking forward to hearing from you!

Happy reading!

Judy Sullivan
Richard Gallen Books
8-10 West 36th St.
New York, N.Y. 10018

Sunrise Temptation

LYNN LE MON

Q

PUBLISHED BY RICHARD GALLEN BOOKS
Distributed by POCKET BOOKS

Books by Lynn LeMon

Sunrise Temptation
This Rebel Hunger

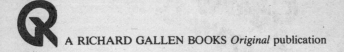

A RICHARD GALLEN BOOKS *Original* publication

Distributed by
POCKET BOOKS, a Simon & Schuster division of
GULF & WESTERN CORPORATION
1230 Avenue of the Americas, New York, N.Y. 10020

Copyright © 1982 by L. L. Wert

ISBN: 0-671-43930-8

First Pocket Books printing January, 1982

10 9 8 7 6 5 4 3 2 1

RICHARD GALLEN and colophon are trademarks of Simon & Schuster and Richard Gallen & Co., Inc.

Printed in the U.S.A.

To
A.L.W., K.K.W., D.H.W.
"Individuals"

"It seems to be a law inflexible
and inexorable that he who will
not risk cannot win."

John Paul Jones

positioned guards and strung heavy, woven nets at the narrows."

Chapter 1

Ariel Cortland closed her chocolate brown eyes, ran long fingers across the golden braid of hair which lay across her shoulder, then confided in a husky, dramatic whisper, "And there we were—after the bed collapsed—hot, damp and sticky, but gloriously happy!"

The dormitory room of Honolulu Academy rang with girlish giggles of approval. "You win, Ariel!" cried one of her classmates. "Yours is the best prediction of what we'll be doing a year from today's graduation." She lowered her eyes, smiling. "I hope!"

Ariel joined the laughter and farewells of the spring class of 1869. A year from today? Ariel hoped by the time 1870 rolled around, she'd be on the mainland of America, investigating a legacy of California friends and a Nevada mining claim willed to her by her mother. It seemed a distant dream. In less than an hour she'd board the inter-island steamer at the merchant pier. Tomorrow she'd be home on tiny Lanavi Island. Her plan was to teach the children who attended her father's school. Ariel loved children and wanted to teach. But not forever, she promised herself.

She pinned her braid atop her head and reached for the required uniform hat. The navy straw, grosgrain ribbon ties and ugly button in the center had annoyed her for the entire eight years she'd boarded at Honolulu Academy. "One thing I won't miss is this dumb bonnet!" she complained. Her laughter was tinged with sadness at leaving her friends. This was home! Ariel had grown up in the cosmopolitan city of Honolulu. At twenty she was granted privileges the younger classmates were denied. Ariel had visited the royal court, the opera house and the embassy balls, always entertaining her wide-eyed classmates with stories of her adventures.

Ariel suspected she'd been kept in school until age twenty and tutored in every subject the Academy offered simply because her father, Elijah Cortland, had no idea what to do with a grown daughter. His life was books, and the quiet, orderly cloisters of the library on Lanavi. All lively, talkative Ariel had in common with Elijah was a love of reading in bed at night.

Now Ariel wiggled the last pin into the hat. "Come and see me off, girls! My trunks are already at the wharf." She hugged her classmates, one by one. "Promise not to forget me!"

"How could we ever forget *you?*" laughed her friends.

Ariel wondered what they'd remember. Her deep, husky laugh? The way her hands fluttered when she talked?—which was rapidly and often. Undoubtedly they'd remember all the times she'd broken curfew and the scandal she'd caused at the conclave by kissing a missionary's son. She hoped when they thought of Ariel Cortland they'd think of a girl who loved life, who liked to make people laugh, who tried to express the spontaneity and joy she felt.

A classmate giggled. "Mostly we'll remember your spirit! Didn't we elect you the girl most likely to uphold tradition *and* cause trouble?"

Tradition and trouble. Ariel's energy radiated in both directions. Her love and respect for tradition meant she sincerely hoped to be useful in the Polynesian outpost of Lanavi. How proud she was of her teaching certificate in the teak frame! Again she thought of her mother, Leah, and wished she had lived to see this happy day. Teaching would be a link with her mother, who had once been tutor to the children of famous California tycoon Sonny Staidlaw. One of the mysteries of Leah's life was why she had given up residence in an elegant Nob Hill mansion to marry dour Elijah Cortland and move to the genteel poverty of thatched huts and a one-room tropical school. When Leah had talked of California, it had been with animation and delight. Once she'd suddenly stopped, touched Ariel's cheek and smiled. "We're both distinctive with our light hair and dark eyes. Someday, if you go to San Francisco, perhaps you'll find that an asset."

Now Ariel shook off the trance of the past and turned her attention to the future. "Hurry, everyone! I want time to dispose of my hat properly."

It was an Academy tradition for graduating girls to toss their bonnets into the Pacific. "Personally, I intend to go a few notches better!" Ariel hinted suspiciously.

The girls scurried for their hats and purses, not doubting her ability for scandal. In minutes the group had moved down Fort Street, stopping long enough to buy the traditional green garlands given to departing travelers. Along the Oceanic Steamship Wharf sat a forest of full-masted clippers, Spanish sandalwood schooners, Yankee whalers, outriggers from the royal boathouse and the small inter-island ferry. Ariel had made many crossings on the boat. It hauled copra from Caledonia, cotton from Fiji and vanilla in trade for Lanavi's one crop—sugar.

Ariel smelled spicy foreign crates as she moved across the pier. A sultry haze from the green mountainsides shone like a silver shawl, wrapping warmth over the island. Ahead an aquamarine world blended ocean and sky. Far off clouds swelled and a distant rain flew downward like a drooping sail. Breakers curled and pranced over the reef. Closer to shore white sea birds circled, squawking as they dived. Far down the beach she saw the banyans and willows which choked the stagnant Waikiki swamp. Sometimes she wondered how, in such a delicate climate, she'd grown so strong. This wet, warm world had sickened her mother and wrapped her father in silence. Yet she'd thrived, growing tall, with full cheeks, lips and breasts.

A classmate nudged her back to the moment. "All the sailors and dockhands are watching you. As usual."

Ariel knew she attracted attention. Any slim, pale woman stood out among the short, round, brown Polynesian girls. With a natural flair for dramatics, Ariel smiled and untied her bonnet. With a flourish she whisked it from her head and sailed it far out over the water. The sinking of the hat was accompanied by laughter and applause. The lounging sailors moved closer.

Ariel bent down, popped loose the side buttons of her shoes and kicked the footwear off. Amid surprised questions of, "What are you doing now?" she held the shoes over the end of the log block pier. "To the bottom of Fair Haven!" she cried, calling Honolulu Harbor by its English name. She heard commotion on the pier behind her. The shoes splashed into oblivion. Wait until the crowd saw her next surprise!

She untied the sash of her prim blue daydress and loosened the collar tabs. Several classmates stifled shocked giggles. She heard a hearty whistle from a dockhand. Then, as she lifted the flounce of hem above her ankles, there was a horrified plea of, "Oh, Ariel! Stop!"

Ariel knew every head now turned her way. She pulled the dress upward, hearing the shocked sighs turn to a relieved, "Thank goodness!" as she revealed the long-sleeved, high-necked Polynesian *holoku* she wore beneath. But when she'd tossed away the daydress, she reached for the top button of the shapeless gown. A classmate squealed, "No more! Oh, dear!"

She laughed and unfastened the second neck button. Suddenly the fun was interrupted. A hoarse cry rang along the pier. "Over here, mateys! A fight! Come quick."

Instantly the sailors converged toward the new excitement. Ariel was a bit annoyed that her surprise had been disrupted, but she joined the others to see what the commotion was about.

In seconds Ariel was fascinated by the two strong, muscular men she saw. She wondered if she enjoyed rowdy men simply because her father was small in stature and never raised either his voice or fists. She distrusted the way he avoided the world with his books. Ariel esteemed men—and women—who met life's challenges and opportunities headlong.

The two fighters stripped to the waist. Coins from all over the world jangled as a cap was passed around for bets. She watched the shorter man pull his sailor's tunic over a medium, compact frame. He was about thirty years old, golden and sturdy, with long, bright sideburns and a strong, square jawline.

But the other man seemed the better bet. He was a giant, over six feet tall and probably no more than twenty-eight years old. Stronger, younger and taller than his opponent, this man was darkly bronzed to the waist, with obvious muscles in his arms and chest. He had a dark, clever face framed by vivid auburn hair.

The crowd pressed around the men, exhorting them in Russian, French, Italian and clipped Australian English.

Ariel was good at languages and could translate most of what she heard. "A kroner on the Scottish lion," called a strong Swedish voice. She stood on tiptoe, trying to decide which fighter bore the nickname. "Two shillings says the Irish bulldog can take him!" She laughed aloud. An Irishman and a Scotsman! Certainly there was no love lost between those two.

The whistle of the Lanavi ferry seared the air. Time to go aboard. Reluctantly Ariel realized she wouldn't have time to see the fight or finish her surprise. She ran a few steps down the pier, then raised the long *holoku* skirt above her knees— revealing bare legs. Most heads turned in her direction. "Over here!" chuckled a sailor. "This girl's giving the fisti- cuffs some competition."

Ariel slid the skirt further upward, exposing more of her slim, bare legs. Finally she pulled the dress completely over her head. Her classmates' cries of alarm echoed down the dock. In a deft movement she let the gown flutter behind her as she stood revealed in a tightly tucked, brightly colored sarong.

The insistent whistle screeched again. Ariel dropped the long dress on the pier and ran up the gangway to the steamer. Her friends' applause blended with her farewell cries. She flung out both hands, tossing kisses to her classmates. "I'll miss you all! Be sure to write! I love you!"

The roustabouts strained to lift the anchor ropes. She heard new shouts from the direction of the sailors' fight. Had the red-haired Scottish lion finished pummeling the sturdy Irish bulldog into submission? Unable to see, she moved toward her trunks. She must put on a skirt and blouse before Mrs. Feddy, the ferryboat captain's wife and self-appointed chaperone, discovered the tropical, makeshift costume.

Suddenly she heard the clatter of running feet. As she turned, the two fighters from the dock came racing toward the ferry. They reached the gangway as it was swung aside. Without hesitation the two men leaped across the three-foot chasm onto the deck of the Lanavi steamer.

Ariel was confused. Did the two men intend to finish their mayhem on board? Then she saw the angry crowd rush along the dock as the ferryboat backed away. The Scottish lion called, "Thank you, gentlemen!" The golden rogue held up the cap full of money. Then the two turned to each other, shook hands and laughed outrageously.

Ariel blurted, "You weren't fighting at all!"

They looked toward her and, although out of breath, both men took a deep breath of surprise.

"Pardon me, ma'am," replied the Irishman, his chubby cheeks glowing with effort. "But we were fightin' to kill! That's all! Traver Loch is a wild-haired Scotsman and a hell-raising Presbyterian—"

"And Mitch Galway's a bastard and a Catholic," interrupted the man with the dark face and luminous green eyes. "That's reason enough to beat any man six feet into the ground!"

They glared at each other and raised their fists as if to go at each other anew. They danced and circled, coming closer to Ariel. She caught their healthy, hot, animal smell and saw their tense, glistening bodies. They seemed overwhelmingly close, and she was glad their eyes were full of laughter. She turned away slightly, fearing they'd show off simply to impress her. At least she now had proper names to go with the nicknames. The Scottish lion with the charming lilt in his voice, red hair and green eyes, was Traver Loch. Mitch Galway was the older, sturdy, blue-eyed man, whose aristocratic accent said he was only masquerading as a brawler.

"Staging a fight and then running away with the money is cheating," she pointed out.

"Cheating?" Traver's voice curled around the word. "Nay! Them gents gave coin of the realm of their own free will!" His arm and shoulder muscles rippled as he held the cap with fingers widespread. "Don't begrudge us a few pennies, lass. Mitch and I are both so far in debt we'll not get out in this lifetime." He poured the coins into his hand, eyes sparkling sea green, an excellent specimen of a healthy, handsome sailor.

Mitch Galway, the Irishman, tensed. He took a step toward Traver and pushed his shoulder. "Keep the coins yourself! I have faith in my own fortunes! Just wait and watch. When we reach America, I'll build myself a railroad, while you'll do nothing more than spout off that mouth of yours!"

Ariel noticed the intensity of Mitch's vow. She sensed great pride in his ambition. Then she saw Traver's face redden like his hair. Obviously Mitch had hit a tender spot with his remarks.

Traver growled. "Talk big, do I? By jingo, I'm not the one who left Dublin with an empty stomach and empty hands—"

"You left Edinburgh empty-headed!" retorted Mitch.

Once again he raised his fists and sparred menacingly, hurling shouts of, "Ox! Fool! Numskull!"

"Stop this!" cried Ariel. "For goodness' sake, I don't care about your fortunes. But I am wondering why you're on this boat to Lanavi."

"We were wondering the same thing about you," said Traver, edging closer. "I was keeping an eye on that peeling act you performed on dock." He let his eyes appraise her sarong, which barely concealed high breasts, sleek hips and a slender waist. "Up close, I can see what all the fuss was about! Say, are you headed to Lanavi as a wife for that native chief?"

"A bride for Chief Kanoa?" Ariel laughed heartily, surprised he knew of the last of the native rulers not under control of the Sandwich Islands royalty. Kanoa was another reason Ariel had been kept in school in Honolulu. He had offered to buy her on every birthday since she turned twelve.

Suddenly embarrassed by Traver's direct question, Ariel decided it was time to find her cabin and change into more discreet clothing.

As she moved toward her trunks, Mitch directed the conversation away from her, as if he, too, disapproved of Traver's openly lusty interest. "To answer your question, miss, we're heading to Lanavi to rejoin our ship, the *Pallas Maru*."

"A ship at Lanavi? That's been rare these past years. Whalers always bypass Lanavi for the port at Lahaina Roads. Clippers avoid Chief Kanoa's island because he tries to collect taxes."

"The *Pallas Maru* didn't put in of her own accord," explained Traver. He again edged closer to Ariel, smiling and eager to talk. "We'd hardly been storm-tossed onto the beach before Kanoa showed up, decked out in feathers and gourds. He blew a conch shell and announced we'd have to stay in Lanavi until we paid his unusual port tax. Know what he wants?"

"Of course," answered Ariel, well aware of Kanoa's interests. "He'll charge you a round of competition in his mele games, plus scarlet cloth for all his wives."

Traver tied his sailor's jumper around his waist, letting the sleeves dangle like floppy ropes. "The price has gone up a bit," he commented, again watching Ariel closely. "This time Kanoa wants a new bride as well. Something about a tradition of three nights of desire." He smiled at her, running his tongue across his teeth. "That's why I thought you might be cargo for the chief. You'd make any man a tasty dish."

Ariel ignored his bold remark, half-scandalized to be talking with strangers of such things as the three nights of desire. She knew of the island tradition in which the chief satisfied himself with sports competitions, a feast and a new wife. But she hadn't realized he obtained the necessities by force from visiting ships. "How will your ship meet such a demand?"

Mitch Galway shrugged. "Not our affair. Traver and I have done our job by spending a couple of days in an outrigger canoe carrying the *Pallas Maru*'s rudder to Honolulu for welding. Now we're headed back on the ferry, with the rudder in the cargo hold. Brides and games aren't our department. That's Ricket Putnam's worry."

There was startling, intense dislike in the way Mitch said the name, "Ricket Putnam."

"Who is he? Does he own the *Pallas Maru?*" Ariel questioned.

Traver Loch swung his lean, hairy arms and frowned. "Bloody Putnam!" he blurted. "Owns the ship and the cargo and me and Mitch as well." He pointed a finger at Mitch. "Him, especially. Mister Mitchell Regis Galway must work for Putnam till hell freezes over, thaws and refreezes!"

Again Ariel saw a fierce anger in Mitch's eyes. But being an underling didn't seem to weigh so heavily on Traver, perhaps because he was younger. She liked Traver's eagerness to do battle with the world. "After your ship pays Kanoa's taxes, you'll be bound for the China trade?" she asked.

"Other way around," answered Mitch, obviously relieved to have the conversation turn away from Ricket Putnam. "Bound for California. The *Pallas Maru* makes the great lopsided triangle route. England to Australia with whiskey and machinery, then sheep to Hong Kong. Takes on a load of Chinamen and heads for San Francisco. I signed Traver on while we were in Sydney."

She turned to Traver, startled. "Then you're *not* from Scotland? I heard them call you the Scottish lion."

He gave a mock bow. "Edinburgh, by way of holiday in Van Dieman's Land, honey lass."

Van Dieman's Land. The British prison colony. Uncertain, she took a step away from him. This laughing, brawling giant was a convict? This was another subject unsuitable for conversation. It was safer to talk to Mitch. "Mr. Galway, are you direct from Ireland?"

"From Dublin, but not direct. I've spent so much time in the American states the past years, I almost think of myself as a citizen. Mean to stay put this time. I'm a railroad engineer by trade, and God knows America is going to be laying track for the next few years."

Traver teased Mitch. "Don't act like laying track is your great passion. It's laying wagers—especially on horses."

Mitch ignored him a moment, then murmured, "I only take risks when I have faith." He grinned. "I'd be a fool not to have faith in my own stallion, now, wouldn't I? Why else would I transport a damned horse along on this voyage?" Mitch shifted position, barricading Traver out of the conversation. He smiled at Ariel. "I've sailed the double horn route twice now in the employ of Ricket Putnam. But this trip I'm dry land bound, along with our cargo of Chinese workers. Putnam has a contract to build the Virginia and Truckee Rail Line across a place called Nevada."

"Nevada! Oh, yes, I know all about it. Wild and wealthy, tall mountains, wide deserts, deep mines and fabulous riches." Ariel was anxious to tell all she knew. "I know about Nevada—and Virginia City in particular—because my mother willed me shares in a mining claim there."

Suddenly Traver barged back into the talk. He moved back between Mitch and Ariel, his muscular upper arm brushing against her bare shoulder. He held up his fists and then spread the fingers. "See these paws of mine? I'll start with no stake but these and dig myself a fortune from the bare earth!" He leaned closer, his breath warm in Ariel's ear. "What's the name of your mine, honey lass?"

"I've not seen it." She hesitated. "I know nothing of it. It could be worthless."

"The name," insisted Traver. "What's it called?"

Ariel knew she would blush when she spoke the indecent words. "Hell's Candy," she murmured and turned her face aside.

"Hell's Candy!" Traver repeated the words loudly, without flinching. "Ah, a sweet and devilish delight, for sure!" He came around to face her directly. "Like a beautiful woman."

Ariel didn't mind being teased. She knew how to flirt. But this was too blatant. "Why, I thought it was Irishmen, not Scotsmen, who had the talent for blarney," she said with brittle sarcasm.

Traver was not chastised. "For sure now, I can't hold a candle to Mitch when he's in the mood for song, dance, women or cards."

Mitch shot Traver a dark look, but he goodnaturedly refused to be bullied. Ariel couldn't help admiring Traver's spirit as much as his physique. So hale and hearty and laughing, and without a care for the future. She smiled at him as he said, "Now, honey lass, you've found out Mitch is a gambler and a rail man. I'm a street boxer and a tin miner. What about you? What's for you on Lanavi Island? And have you a name?"

She knew better than to tell these two rogues her name. "Lanavi's my home. I'm a teacher."

Traver suddenly looked taken aback, as if he had no use for books or slates. He was a man who prided himself on living by his wits and hands. Mitch smiled arrogantly. "You could teach me a few things if you want." He winked at her. "But from the looks of your rosy cheeks and innocent brown eyes, I'd say it's you who needs the instructor."

It was the first time Mitch had looked directly at her body. When she looked at his eyes, she was shocked to find a lingering caress which was so unexpected and intense it took her breath away. She felt herself turn hot under his gaze and was relieved to see Mrs. Feddy coming along the deck. "I must see to my trunks," Ariel said hastily, and turned away.

At the sound of footsteps behind her, Ariel turned, half-expecting to see Mitch Galway and his cool blue eyes. Instead it was Traver, trotting along like a patient dog. "I'll heave them trunks for you," he volunteered.

He hoisted one on each shoulder. She admired his strength as he moved easily along the passageway. When they reached her cabin, he stowed the trunks, then stretched out his hand. "How about a sixpence for hard labor, honey lass?"

She hadn't thought of paying him! She felt her face flush as she fumbled for her travel bag. Then she saw he was laughing again. Flustered and off guard, she was unprepared as he swung his hands tight around her waist and brought his face close to hers. "That's all right. A pert and saucy smile will help pay, and I'll settle your debt for a kiss." He brought his lips down over hers. She was amazed, first at his strength and boldness, then by the hot earthiness he exuded. It was astonishing to be held tight, her bare shoulders against his naked chest, the tight sinews of his long legs pressed hard against her thighs.

She had barely savored his kiss when, suddenly, he went flying backwards, knocked askew by Mitch Galway. Mitch grabbed Traver's shoulders and pushed, sending him sprawling backward over Ariel's trunks.

Ariel gasped and covered her cheeks with her hands. Traver leaped to his feet, fists cocked. "A bit of a skirmish for real, Galway?" he challenged Mitch. "You want to fight because I was doing what you were only thinking of!"

At that moment Mrs. Feddy appeared in the cabin doorway. A thin, serene woman, she had a tanned, small face like a cheerful little bird and a crown of gently gray hair. She raised her tiny hands in a shooing motion at Traver and Mitch while she chirped, "Gentlemen! Gentlemen, please! It's not necessary to kill each other while toting a lady's baggage. Go below, both of you!" She cushioned the order with a quick smile. "You'll be more comfortable there."

Traver and Mitch straightened up, taken back by her gentle, no-nonsense tone. They departed quietly.

Ariel was glad they were gone—but they *had* been interesting! She liked Traver's dark, handsome manner and rambunctious strength. And Mitch—when had she ever seen such thick golden hair and long eyelashes? His cerulean blue eyes were as appealing as a vivid seascape. She turned to Mrs. Feddy, giving her a quick greeting and hug. The two had traveled together many times on the crossing from Honolulu to Lanavi.

"Ariel, you look wonderful, but a bit underclad," Mrs. Feddy greeted her. She nodded toward the passageway where Traver and Mitch had gone. "Do you know those two husky gents?"

"No," answered Ariel. Not yet, she added silently.

"Well, you will. The look on your face says so. I saw you studying them as they left. Which one were you gazing at? The red-haired fellow? Or is the laughing Irishman the one who takes your fancy?"

Ariel didn't answer. She wasn't going to tell everything to Mrs. Feddy, who might feel duty-bound to report to her father. Then, too, Ariel wasn't certain which man intrigued her most.

Mrs. Feddy perched daintily on one of the trunks. "Ariel, this last year in Honolulu seems to have agreed with you. You look very grown up. I like the way you're braiding your hair, and your movements are as graceful as a dancer's. Does this mean you've finally given up your tomboy ways?"

Ariel laughed. "Oh, Mrs. Feddy, you know I'll never give up horseback riding. Or diving from the cliffs on the Lanavi headlands. Or wearing as little as possible! I'm so glad to be done with bonnets and belts and button-up shoes."

Mrs. Feddy's face glowed with pleasure at having another woman to talk to. "I'll miss our trips back and forth, Ariel. I've enjoyed watching you blossom. What did you study this last year?"

"A lot of useless things, as usual. Italian, tile-painting, astronomy, algebra, piano, harpsichord, Latin, geometry and Chinese!"

"Most women don't need that much education," Mrs. Feddy agreed wistfully. "But it suits you, Ariel. And the Academy's a fine school. So fancy that even mainland families send their daughters there, I understand."

"Oh, yes. Some of my best friends were from California. Do you know they say 'at the Bay' for living in San Francisco? And 'upon the Sierras' for going to the mountains. And when they want an extra piece of dessert, they help themselves but always politely murmur, 'Why, I don't mind if I do!'"

Mrs. Feddy cocked her little finger and tried out the fine phrase, "Why, I don't mind if I do!" Then the bright tones of her laughter filled the cabin. "What else did you learn?"

"Bad habits! I learned about chewing gum. And waterfall hairdos. And that hoop skirts are out and bustles are in for fashion."

"Speaking of fashions, Ariel, I don't have to tell you your father won't approve of your coming home in a sarong." Mrs. Feddy had resumed her chaperone's role.

Ariel pulled a long cotton dimity dress from her other trunk. "I know. He still believes all the women on Lanavi should go around wrapped like Egyptian mummies. Oh, I'll hate wearing those shapeless dresses again!"

"And Elijah won't approve of your flirting with a couple of raw sailors from the *Pallas Maru*. You'd best stay in the pilothouse in the morning while we put those two ashore in the south lagoon."

Ariel lifted the dress over her head. Sighing, she said, "I'll never see those two again." Changing the subject, she added, "How is father?"

"Still studying. I never met a man more dedicated to book learning. We have three crates of new books for him in the cargo."

"Oh, poor father! All the things he needs, and he orders

more books! The leather bindings mildew and termites eat the glue. Such a waste! He's been ordering books for his library for twenty years, and there aren't more than fifty that are usable."

Mrs. Feddy nodded primly, clasping small hands together. "And for twenty years he's been trying to convert Chief Kanoa. Again without notable success."

Ariel knew a lot of her father's dreams hadn't come true. He was diligent and steadfast, but so removed from the real world that he was gullible to every far-fetched island tale, every dishonest housekeeper, every rice-bowl convert. If only he'd been stronger, she thought—physically strong like Traver Loch, or proud-strong like Mitch Galway.

Ariel realized that Mrs. Feddy was staring at her. "I'd be willing to bet money . . ." began the woman slowly.

"On what?" asked Ariel.

"I'd be willing to wager when the ferryboat makes its run to Lanavi six months from now, you won't be on the island."

"Where else would I be?"

Mrs. Feddy laughed as she left the cabin. "If I were a gambler, I'd put money on the idea that when those two fellows sail for California, you'll be with them."

Ariel closed the compartment door and turned the idea over in her mind. California. The *Pallas Maru*. Traver and Mitch. She thought about the exciting prospect the rest of the afternoon and most of the night, sleeping only three hours. California! Surely Elijah could take leave after all his years of service at the school.

She rose early and dressed in a demure yellow lisle sundress. She wound its matching scarf into her braid. Her plan was to be on deck early, to find either Traver or Mitch and ask if there were passenger space aboard the *Pallas Maru*. Standing at the bow railing, she watched Lanavi's silhouette rise through the morning mist. The tiny island consisted of a purple volcano sticking its head through towering white clouds. Terraces of sugar cane ran in triangles down to the sea. A wall of sheer cliffs sat along the north shore. On the south shore stood Chief Kanoa's long hut palace, the tiny village of Lanavi Town and the protected leeward lagoon.

As she breathed the fragrant, sharp air, she was surprised how glad she was to be home. Ariel thrilled to the glorious colors of the cane fields, the heady perfume of plumeria, and the whistling of tiny, brightly feathered birds. The Polynesian myths and legends she knew so well flooded her mind. In sophisticated Honolulu they had seemed archaic and silly, but on Lanavi they were as natural as the landscape she looked out on. She watched the mountain shadows—the *ma'u*, the mist zone, the *ilima* where the shrubs grew and the *apa'a*, the windy place.

Then, as the ferry rounded the lee shore, she saw the *Pallas Maru*. So huge! And new. She'd expected a regularly rigged, black-hulled clipper ship. Instead, the *Pallas Maru* was a full-rigged merchantman, made of iron and probably not over five years old.

She spotted Traver Loch on the lower deck and immediately called to him, "Good morning!"

He grabbed a winch rope and climbed it as easily as if it had been a swing toy. Hand over hand, shoulder muscles bulging, green eyes twinkling and auburn hair tossed by the wind, he scrambled to where she waited. Pointing to the *Pallas Maru*, he asked, "Ain't she prettier than heather in bloom?"

"I daresay she's a beauty," Ariel praised. She admitted privately that Traver was also a gorgeous sight, with his flashing grin, bronzed face and daring manner. He leaned close to her, not touching, but she could feel the heat radiating from his inner arm as it lay casually close to her back.

Traver talked of his ship. "She's fast as streak-lightning on the high seas. Made twenty-one trips around the world in six years. But since Ricket Putnam took over, she's a bad place to be, whether she's hauling salmon from Russia, immigrants to Australia or coolies to America. She's known mutiny and death because of Ricket Putnam."

"That man's name sets you and Mitch both to shivering."

"And rightly it should! The Devil take him," snapped Traver grimly.

Curious, she asked, "What, exactly, is it about the man that sets grown men's teeth to chattering?"

But Traver only looked away, apprehensive and moody, darkness settling into his green eyes. Then he pointed to activity near the landing. "Here come the catamarans to meet the ferryboat! Listen to that music! Hot enough to set any redblooded man's brain on fire." He took a long, frank, amiable look in her direction. "It's too bad you have so many clothes today. We could kick up our heels in a round dance to that rhythm."

"I might have liked that," she admitted. She was fond of

the Polynesian music made with gourds, flutes and drums accompanied by the pulsating whines of slack-key guitars. But dancing with Traver would have meant European-style, she imagined, though she couldn't picture him in a stiff collar or cutaway jacket. When she smiled at him, she again saw his frank, intimate glance. *He's too bold*, she thought, not altogether disapproving. She felt warm, remembering the quick kiss he'd stolen yesterday. *He's the kind who sets his mind on something and doesn't back off*, she thought.

"Traver, I want to ask about passenger space aboard—"

She was interrupted as Mitch Galway appeared on the lower deck, shouting for Traver. "Where are you, Traver Loch? Get to the hold! Let's get this rudder ashore." He looked up, spotted Traver and waved him back to the lower deck. Ariel was disappointed when Mitch didn't acknowledge her with a smile or a hello.

Traver explained. "Mitch will be a grouch all day. Ricket Putnam casts a long shadow over Mr. Galway." Traver looked toward the *Pallas Maru* and sighed as if he, too, hated to return. He swung down the winch rope, agile as a panther, supple as a strong vine. "So long, honey lass!"

She followed him to the railing and blew him a kiss. Disappointed, she realized she hadn't finished asking about sailing on the *Pallas Maru*. She watched as the two men moved into the shadows. Then she went to the pilothouse.

Ariel took the prismatic telescoping spyglass from the leather sidepocket. Focusing the long lens, she watched Traver and Mitch lower their crate into a tender and row toward the *Pallas Maru*. On the bow of the ship she spotted a thin, pale man, elegantly dressed, with lean, curved hands locked over the line. Ricket Putnam? His eyes were pale gray and his wisps of gray hair were smoothed back over an oblong skull. Bushy black eyebrows stood out on pallid skin. Although he was expensively dressed, his stance and features had something degenerate about them. "He looks scary," she murmured aloud. "Even from a distance." The thin, fixed lips were those of a man who would never yield to mercy or compassion.

A young Oriental girl came to Putnam's side. She was so young—barely thirteen, Ariel guessed—that at first Ariel assumed she was a serving girl. Then Ricket Putnam made a simple gesture, raising his right hand index finger and barely touching the back of the girl's bare neck. At his touch the girl bowed her dark head and trembled. In that single view of domination and submission, Ariel grew to fear Putnam.

She lowered the glass. Had she really considered traveling to California under this dreadful man's authority? Hadn't she seen Mitch and Traver, two strong men, sullenly resent having to work for him? She hoped Mitch would make good on his promise to reach Nevada and make his fortune in railroading, apart from Putnam.

She took a final long look as Mitch and Traver climbed the deck ladder of the *Pallas Maru*. The Scottish lion looked tamer today. Mitch seemed subdued. His stance as he spoke to Putnam indicated a reserved defiance.

Ariel tried to scorn them, saying to no one, "Oh, they're simply adventurers! The kind of men who have plagued the Pacific ever since Captain Cook stumbled onto the islands." But even as she turned her back, she knew in her heart she'd find a way to join Traver Loch and Mitch Galway aboard the *Pallas Maru*.

Chapter 2

Pious, frowning, his nose in a book, Elijah Cortland looked cantankerous in a heavy, three-piece black wool suit and severely starched, high-collared white shirt. Ariel waved to him on the mission dock. The hair atop his lean head made a scanty arch, his eyebrows met in a fierce angle over his nose and little sun scars of red, purple and brown dotted his forehead. She could never remember a time she'd thought him robust. Now advancing age—wasn't he past sixty?— made him appear stooped and tired.

She called to him in greeting. He barely raised spectacled eyes from the book. Crossing the gangway, she wondered how she could have changed so much and he so little.

Lanavi had changed not at all. The school compound remained settled in the clearing with sandalwood trees. Starflowers still dripped into the courtyard. The trim house remained intact with its outside stairways, balcony and over-grown trellis of maile vines, their scent like sweet, warm oil. The garden, protected by whitewashed pickets, held sweet potatoes and taro, a plot of sugar cane and Ieie shrubs, whose sturdy roots were used to weave baskets. To the side stood the school with its roof of palm and walls of wood and straw.

After unpacking, Ariel went to the parlor where Elijah

fussed with his crates of new books. From the window she saw the volcano slopes where old lava flows reflected incandescently on the bottom of the clouds. Her senses were pleasantly aroused. The moist earth smelled of freedom. The pink hibiscus flamed like a rainbow dropped into a green sea.

Far across on the headlands the Kalo Cliffs, her favorite *pali,* rose like green velvet. How many times she'd dived from their perches high above the marbled tidal strait.

"Lanavi seems timeless," she mused as she turned to help Elijah unpack. "The mist patterns by the blowhole, the cane scent, the crescent leaves of the koa tree, the tiny, scarlet birds by the palms. It's hard to remember Honolulu is full of traffic jams and women wearing the latest European-designed clothes." She looked at Elijah, still wearing the heavy suit. "Father, aren't you hot as blazes in that ridiculous winter outfit?"

He didn't seem to hear. She moved to the teakwood pigeonhole desk where he was cataloging the new library acquisitions. She wanted to be gentle, but she wanted to be heard. "Father, I'm not certain I can remain on Lanavi."

"You must stay here." He spoke in a thin, emotionless voice, as if he'd read the line from a book. He reached to place a dictionary in the glass-front case with fingers that were gnarled and curved under with rheumatism. Ariel was frightened; here was an old man who lived for nothing more than leather bindings and card files! Perhaps he was happy with his choice. But she must be free to make another.

"Father, did you know there's a ship bound for California in Lanavi lagoon?"

"I'm quite busy, Ariel."

She realized from his curt response that he *did* know of the *Pallas Maru.*

She and Elijah had always spoken directly to one another. "Father, I realize you know about the *Pallas Maru.* If it has passenger space, do you think—"

"No."

A one-word refusal before she'd even finished her question! She saw Elijah's hands shake as he shut the book crate. The color rose in his cheeks, blotting out his yellowish complexion. His eyes seemed somber, yet fearful. Was he afraid she'd leave Lanavi? Or, more specifically, did he fear she'd leave on the *Pallas Maru?* "Father, how long have you been on Lanavi?"

"Some twenty years—and I've accomplished nothing."

She pointed out some of his practical advances. "You don't think the irrigation sluices for cane have helped the farmers? What about the hundreds of children you've taught to read and write? Father, you've done so much good! If we went to California, you could continue—"

He interrupted. "I'll not leave here. And you'll not leave either."

Dismayed, she asked, "Not ever?"

"Not until your wicked flesh is tamed and your unclean soul is saved."

Shocked at such abrupt, hurtful words, she remained silent a moment. Then she smiled. "Are those words from one of your sermons, father? Or fine phrases from a book? Wicked flesh? Unclean souls! My goodness!"

He turned to her with pleading eyes. "Don't leave Lanavi. The world can hurt you."

She wondered if hurt was all the world would offer. "Don't you remember I've been living in Honolulu? The city is the crossroads of the Pacific. I've seen every kind of custom from every continent. There's nothing to fear."

"Leaving is too big a risk."

Her answer began tentatively, but grew angrily forceful. "An island—any island—is too small for me. Here I can hike *mauka*—to the mountains—and again *makai*—to the sea—in an afternoon. I don't even have to think about existence here. The sky brings water, the sun brings health, the earth brings food. Life drifts along too smoothly, without a change of seasons, without change at all!"

Elijah's thin voice rose to a crescendo. "You'll not leave!" It was the closest he had ever come to yelling at her.

"Go back to your books, father," she said sadly. "I'm going to my room." She executed a swift turn and marched up the outside stairs. Ariel tried to clear her head with a breath of fresh air, but the smell from the dingy library had followed her, the odor of the whale-oil lamp like gray weather.

Inside her room, she locked the door. The image of Elijah with his gnarled hands raised in anger frustrated her. Why should he be so obstinate? Why should he make her feel grimy with accusations about body and soul? I'll go to the cliffs, she decided. I'll dive! Free and clear! Swim in the clear, cold Pacific.

She exchanged her dress for a *paruha,* which could be wrapped for swimming. She took along a *holoku,* knowing she should come home looking presentable.

Outdoors, she raced along the plateau, following the spine of mountains. Ricegrass grew waist high, singing in the wind. Pumice precipices, black and sheer, hung like sentry towers above the sea. She felt at home among the wild, natural swirl of wind and salt spray as she rushed to the headlands.

Alone on the pinnacle, she let the wind waft silky caresses against her cheeks. She reknotted and tucked the *paruha* against her firm, high breasts. The sun shone softly through the giant ferns. She unwound her braid and let her honey-colored hair hang across her shoulders. As the rising wind blew the strands back over her naked skin, Ariel thought of the Polynesian legend which said the tradewinds and the alternate southern Kona winds were the breaths of dueling ocean dragons.

She started toward the diving cliff, stopping to pick a star-shaped blossom from the red passion-vine. Brushing away a striped shadow spider, she crushed the flower to her skin, creating fragrance. Another Lanavi myth said the perfume of red passion-vine and music from the ocean surf could make young women recall past lives. She laughed. "More happening in my *present* life will suffice!" She stepped around the guava and 'ulu trees, following the narrow path where the monkey-grass bent back upon itself. Logical people said the wind carved the grass, but legend said it was the work of *menehunes*, the little tricksters.

Now the coastline spread below like white sugar heaped in little dunes. The height of the cliffs always thrilled her, the silvery water so clear and deep she could see every rock and reef. Purely from habit she looked for sharks—or, as the Polynesians said, the *Hi'u*, the shark-god. It was from this cliff, legend said, that a maiden had once been sacrificed to *Hi'u*. But he found her so beautiful that instead of devouring her, they swam all night in the moonlight. At sunrise he carried her to shore on his back, then swam away on the path to Tahiti.

Giggling at the romantic story, Ariel swore aloud, "If a shark offered *me* a ride away from here, I'd go!"

"Would you, now?" The man's voice, then his shadow fell across the pathway.

"Who's there?" Ariel challenged as the trees rustled.

Traver Loch stepped from the shadows, attired all in white, making his auburn hair and tanned face seem doubly bright. Curly dark hair shone at the neck of his jumper. The way he looked at her with calculating eyes and half-smiling mouth alarmed her. Already embarrassed that he'd heard her silly remark, Ariel turned and ran for the cliff edge.

"Don't! You'll fall!" he called in alarm.

She was pleasantly surprised to hear the obvious concern in his voice. Fall? How funny! She'd come here purposely to dive. As she reached the edge, she pirouetted, raising her arms in slow motion.

"Get away from the cliff," he ordered.

"I'm quite all right," she insisted.

When Traver abruptly reached out his arms as if to make a grab for her, she lithely dodged his grasp. Quickly checking the pool below for depth, position of boulders and any telltale white flash of the shark-god, she raised on tiptoes and extended her arms in the diving position.

Traver rushed forward, shouting, "No!"

She dived. Arching her body through the air in a practiced, fluid manner, she caught a momentary glimpse of Traver. She had expected to see him shaking his head in confusion, or even secretly admiring her skill and courage. Instead, he was frantically kicking off his shoes and pulling the jumper over his head.

A bubble of laughter caught in her throat. He was going to rescue her! When she hadn't the slightest need for a rescuer! She was so tickled she delayed a split second too long in realigning her body as she hit the water. Damn! Hitting at an angle and making a trail of bubbles were marks of an amateur.

She gave herself over to the ocean, feeling as comfortable as a fish in the salt water. The tangy brine stung her nostrils and the waves slapped at her legs as the current sucked her downward. She sank, exhaling and gliding deeply through the cold, clear water. She was annoyed with herself for not making a perfect dive. Why had she let a burly, red-haired Scotsman distract her?

When she finally swam back to the surface, she raised her hand to wave, meaning to show him she'd been in no danger. He was now stripped to the waist and poised to dive. "No, no!" she called, and waved more forcefully.

"Hang on!" he yelled. Obviously her waving had given him the impression she needed help.

"I'm fine!" she cried, but the words were blown away in the surf and wind. Now she was anxious about *him*. The Kalo Cliffs were no spot for strangers to test their wings.

Then he was flying from the rugged rocks, like a bright star shooting toward the sea from the sky. His dive was not as deft as hers, but he was surprisingly graceful. His neat body exuded strength as well as precision. He cut the water with a half-twist of his muscled torso.

She felt a tickle of pride in his rash action. Watching carefully, ready to go to *his* aid if it appeared he needed help, Ariel lounged in the current, treading water. She could see him perfectly, swimming clockwise about ten feet below the surface, using his large hands to scatter angelfish. His body moved easily, sending silver streams of bubbles upward through the sunlit water. All at once she thought of the shark and the maiden swimming till dawn.

Traver broke the surface of the sea, flinging back his glistening red-brown hair. "For godsake, are you all right?"

She was indignant. "For godsake, yes! Your heroics were for nothing! Or do you always try to rescue maidens who *aren't* in distress?"

Her flippancy seemed to anger him. A sulky thrust of his lean jaw obscured his normally mischievous features. "So I've played the fool, have I?" A sudden boil of temper reddened his face. Then he dived toward her, rippling the water into foamy cascades, hands spread as if to fasten about her throat. She cringed, knowing he would be able to control her with his strength.

Moving with the current, she kept her distance. Perhaps she could lessen the tension with a compliment. "Calm down, Traver! I'm sure you'd be able to rescue anyone who needed it! Why, with those fists of yours, you could even be one of Chief Kanoa's longhouse warriors."

She was relieved, as well as a trifle disappointed, when he stopped twenty feet away, watching her intently. He raised his hands. "It was these fists that got me my walking papers from the British empire," he admitted.

She remembered the mention of Van Dieman's Land. "Are you a criminal, Traver Loch?"

"Not any more." He laughed. "Strange to tell, but it was after I gave up street fighting and marched myself off to learn the tin trade that I was booted out for being undesirable."

"They threw you out of England for fighting, then? Surely not for learning the tin trade—that sounds honest enough."

"Honest it was. Honest enough for two thugs to follow me down an alley on payday, thinking to take my wages. I beat 'em, each manjack of them, with my bare hands. Laid 'em up permanent. And for that, my peers made me an unwilling emigrant to Van Dieman's colony. But I served my three years proper and straight, then signed on the *Pallas Maru*. Christ, I didn't care where that ship was heading, as long as it wasn't part of Queen Victoria's empire."

Ariel considered the story as well as the spirit in which Traver had told it. He'd disabled two men over a pay envelope. Fists and temper, yes. But courage and a sense of right too. Curious, she asked, "What about Mitch Galway? Is he a convict too?"

"No, indeed. Mitch is first chop! Proper aristocracy not two generations back. But the famine of forty-seven made potato foragers and mackerel snappers out of fine lords aplenty, all the way from Cork to Kerry to Tralee. Mitch's pa died in debtor's prison. That's one reason Mitch ended up in Putnam's employ. They've made a bargain. Mitch is to work for him three more years. Mitch rears back and bridles about it now and then, but it's his ticket to America for keeps. As for me, I don't mind what continent I wash ashore on, as long as there's plenty of space and bonny gals."

Traver chuckled to himself and swam closer, his smile charming and suave. "Here now, don't look so serious. Mitch and I can both stay out of trouble if there's a good enough reason." He splashed water at her, playful and grinning. "You look like a pretty good reason. I've played the fool over you long enough. Let me see you safely to shore, fair mermaid. Can you swim that far?"

Of course she could. But when he put out his hand, beckoning her, she didn't dive away or ignore him. Slowly she extended her fingers, wanting to recapture the warmth of yesterday's embrace. He waited as she floated toward him. As his hand clasped hers, she felt a deep trembling. Then he was pulling her gently toward him, the pressure of his touch insistent, the tugging of the water resistant. Inside, she began to tighten, her muscles drawing up in a new pattern of anticipation.

As she flexed her legs, there was tension in her thighs, and a tingling sensation which moved upward and centered in her breasts. Her pulse raced as he boldly maneuvered her against him. Was it the cold water through the thin silk which made her nipples harden? "Can you carry me to shore on your back?" she asked suddenly, remembering the legend.

"Aye." He put both hands around her waist, swung her lightly upward as he lowered himself in the sea. The waves positioned them together, her legs wound slightly around his.

Barely touching his shoulders, she let her fingers rest on his throat. He tensed; she felt him shiver like a caged animal when it's touched. Then he bent forward, neck and back straining, and pushed off toward shore.

They swam with a magical sense of rhythm, he stroking with powerful motion, lifting and releasing her momentarily, then reuniting their bodies in the water. As the sea buoyed her, she felt she was almost hovering above him. Then the downward pressure of the current would send her breasts and stomach hard against his spine. A wave threatened to pry her completely away from him. Quickly she tightened her arms around his neck.

Now he was swimming more slowly, as if he intended to prolong their time in the bay. She rested her cheek against the back of his head, liking the scent of his hair mixed with sea water. The first hint of tropical twilight spread dark oranges and reds across the sky behind the headlands. The legend said they would swim until dawn. Oh, what was she thinking! In a few minutes she'd be late for evening prayers. The thought of Elijah's wrath sent her rolling off Traver's back. She swam frantically for shore.

She hadn't taken two strokes before Traver caught her. Standing in waist-deep water, she faced him, seeking words to explain. As his hands came forward, she thought he meant to scoop her up and place her on his back again. But his fingers stopped at her shoulders, rounding, pressing gently, then traveled over her wet skin to her face. He took one step forward and their bodies met in ardent embrace.

Now it seemed natural to raise her arms around his neck, to feel his hand glide across the small of her back. The cave of his shoulders was warm, and when his other hand came upward to touch her breast, she put out her hand to touch his face, stroking his eyelids, touching the tiny oblong cleft in his chin. In his neck vein she saw his heartbeat pulsing like a tiny hammer. His breath was ragged and excited.

She broke the spell by pointing at the sea. "A legend says that a maiden and the shark-god swam together all night. Then he swam away through that channel between the rocks—the path to Tahiti."

He glanced at the boulders and the rough riptides beyond. Sensing the joke, he grabbed her arm. "Come! We'll go see Tahiti together!"

"No, no! The story says you leave me here."

"Then I'll have no more nonsense about sharks or mermaids, for I have no intention of leaving until I find out more about you. I don't even know your name, my white ocean dove."

"I'm Ariel Cortland. Elijah Cortland is my—"

"Holy faith, no! You're not his wife, are you?"

"Wife?" She gave a startled jump at the assumption. "Indeed not! But I'm his daughter. Why do you recognize his name? Do you know him?"

"I do not. But I've heard his name spoken on the *Pallas Maru*."

"Who from the ship would know my father?"

"Ricket Putnam." Traver grimaced. "Damned, dirty Ricket Putnam."

"Putnam!" She shivered, remembering the pale stare and evil eyes of the man. "My father knows Ricket Putnam?" She searched the past, wondering if Putnam had visited the islands before. "Would he have been in the South Seas in other years?"

"I don't know. There's rumor he was once a physician, but barred from practice. For certain Putnam's a man without a thought of humanity. He's packed the *Pallas Maru* so full of human cargo he's likely to have either a mutiny or a mass funeral before he makes the mainland."

Ariel was always appalled to hear of such inhumanity. "How many Chinese are aboard?"

"Some two thousand. Wedged below decks like a herd of sheep. Putnam plans to use coolie labor to build that railroad and Iron Mitch Galway to oversee it. I'm not sure who I feel sorriest for."

"Iron Mitch." She tried out the nickname and found it as hard as the man. "I'm glad you're friends." She laughed. "Either one of you would be a formidable enemy."

"Oh, we're typical Irish and Scots—first fight the world, then turn on each other. But Mitch and I aren't a team. Don't confuse us as such. We came from different pasts and are bound for different futures. Mitch will stay put after he builds that rail line. I'll try my luck wherever I land. Mitch has an urge for permanence, while my idea of heaven is to see all seven continents and owe allegiance to none."

"What will you do in Nevada while Mitch is pounding spikes?"

"Whatever Putnam tells me to do. I've done many things in my twenty-eight years, and plan to try several more before kicking thirty. I've been a roisterer in Edinburgh. A peasant by the firth. A boxer at the gates of Holyrood House. A tin miner. And I admit to my share of the drinking and wenching. But in Nevada I've a mind to take what wages are due me in land claims."

"Excellent!" she encouraged him.

"Strong I am and luck I'll need, but I've some grand dreams. I've sharpened my wits on the outback and hardened my body under the Tasmanian sun. I think I'll do well enough."

"I'm proud of your dreams, Traver—all of them! I want to go to Nevada, too. My only link with my mother is there. The mine may be worthless, but I must find out for myself. Traver, do you think I could go with you on the *Pallas Maru?*"

He appeared shocked, but recovered quickly enough to seize the opportunity to pull her close. He wrapped his arms tightly around her waist, nuzzling her hair and throat. "Do you want me as a meal ticket for passage?" he asked. "Or as fare to California? Or do you want to be with me as a man?" Then he kissed her deeply, trying to conquer her with lips that burned against hers. His force caused her lips to part and she felt a rising urgency in the way he molded his legs and chest against her. His kiss became more passionate, tongue advancing, hands caressing, mouth greedily dominating. Huskily he asked again, "Do you want me as a man?"

Confused, she felt her heart beating rapidly in her chest. "I want to learn. About love. From a man who doesn't believe flesh is wicked and souls are sinful."

"That just means you need a man. That's quite different from wanting *me.*" His eyes flashed anger and the fading sunlight illuminated the salt crystals which clung to his lashes.

She felt drawn to him, yet afraid. There was sweetness and exuberance between them, yet something doubtful as well. She could feel a fire building deep inside, like the lava heating up in the volcano's cone. Another kiss and she feared she'd be swept away by the fire's strength and consumed by its savagery.

Abruptly Traver asked, "How old are you?" When she didn't answer, he repeated more loudly, "How old?"

Suddenly a reply came from shore. "Not old enough!"

Ariel and Traver turned to face the sandy beach where Mitch Galway cantered a fine black stallion.

"Mitch!" spat Traver, obviously upset at being interrupted. "On that damned racehorse he's lugging around the world!"

Ariel was determined not to let Iron Mitch spoil the moment. She put her hand on Traver's arm and answered his question. "I'm twenty," she said. "And my own free woman!" She reached for Traver's embrace again, but Mitch urged the horse into the water and interposed his riding crop between them.

"Get back aboard the *Pallas Maru*, Traver," Mitch ordered coldly, "before Putnam discovers you're absent without leave."

Traver sighed and stepped back from Ariel. "Hell, I always get caught!" He looked at Mitch in an unfriendly manner. "All right. But you see this missionary's daughter back to her home before her father comes after all of us with a hangman's noose." He took Ariel's hand and helped her to shore, making introductions as they walked. "Mitch, this is Ariel Cortland."

"I know who she is. And why you've followed her down here to the beach at twilight!" Mitch's disapproval bristled his golden sideburns and turned his blue eyes to navy.

"You know nothing, Mitch Galway!" Ariel blurted. "Except how to appear when you're not needed and interfere where you're not wanted!"

Mitch spoke to her directly, as if she were an errant child. "Quit shrieking and carrying on."

"I am not much given to shrieking, sir. Nor, as you put it, to carrying on. But I do have opinions and—"

Putting up both large hands as signals to stop, Traver refereed. "Shut up, Mitch." To Ariel he said, "Despite Mitch's bad manners, you do need to go home. And I have to hightail it back into Putnam's purgatory. So—" He circled her waist and lifted her as if she weighed no more than a wet feather. He perched her sidesaddle behind Mitch on the stallion.

There were no goodbyes. Mitch spurred the Arabian and the horse took off galloping, causing Ariel to grab instinctively for his waist. "We must go up the cliffside," she shouted. "I have to get my dress."

Mitch nodded and turned the horse. The stallion made the climb effortlessly. He was really a wonderful animal, broad and sleek, without a touch of white anywhere on his jet black flanks. Ariel leaned forward, breathlessly delighted by the horse's increased pace across the ricegrass plateau. He plunged through the twilight with the speed of a bird and the strength of a ship, mane standing nearly upright, breath like a desert wind. No wonder Mitch loved this animal and had faith in him to win races. No wonder he'd brought him on the *Pallas Maru*.

As the sugar cane cartways flattened out ahead, Ariel was jostled against Mitch's back. The wet *paruha* silk rubbed against him, causing her skin to ripple and her breasts to harden. She couldn't avoid the contact, so she tried to ignore it. She attempted to sit erect, but her legs trembled with unbidden warmth. This current of sensation in her inner thighs transmitted itself upward as she tightened her knees and threw back her head. "Please, slow down!" she shouted against the wind.

Mitch pulled the reins; reluctantly it seemed. Equally impatient, the animal responded, slowing to a trot, then walking. Ariel slid backward, trying to diminish contact, but Mitch reached around silently and held her.

It was nearly dark now, only magenta stripes on an aquamarine horizon. Mitch spoke for the first time. "So you're twenty, eh? But hardly a free woman." The way he cocked his head and bit into the word "woman" gave it unmistakable emphasis. "Oh, you're free to dive from the cliff and swim in the narrows and trade hot kisses in the cool sand—"

"You were spying on Traver and me!"

"I was looking for Traver. He's my responsibility. When his work isn't done, it's my back Putnam brings the lash down on."

Ariel tried to restrain her anger. Was Mitch upset because Traver had neglected his duties? Or was he raging because of what he'd seen happening between her and Traver?

Her thinking was interrupted as he continued, "As for all that blabber about being a free woman—pure blarney! The fact is, you're not a woman at all."

Ariel felt unbalanced by his wrath. "And you've made it your self-appointed duty to see Traver Loch has no part in changing my status?" she charged.

"Get your dress." He let her down from the stallion by draping an arm diagonally from her waist to her shoulder, letting it slide up her bare back and linger on her neck. To her dismay, little bumps of sensation stood out along her arms and throat. Hurriedly she bent down and grabbed the *holoku*, flinging it around her shoulders like a cape.

She looked at him defiantly. "Mitch, there's anger and anxiety written all over your face. I don't understand it. I'd much prefer to have you for a friend. Traver would, too. How have we made you unhappy? What have I done wrong?"

He swung off the horse in an easy motion, slapping the reins against his open palm. "You've done nothing wrong by your innocence," he muttered. "Indeed, it is the things you've *not* done which alarm me." He moved to face her directly and his hand came forward as if to touch hers, then dropped away. "Oh, Ariel, I see in you the makings of a vibrant and passionate woman. But I also see a little girl who instinctively takes in stray cats and dogs. And a motherly side to your nature that likes to corral children on rainy days and make sure they have hot soup."

She smiled at his insights. "Guilty," she admitted.

"Don't you see that Traver Loch is simply a big, wandering stray? A man who'll take whatever handout you offer, then move on for a warmer bed and a fuller bowl."

"You're wrong about Traver," she defended him rashly. "And you may be wrong about me!" she added.

"I'm not wrong. I've seen it all before. You'll call it love. Traver will call it another successful seduction."

She turned her back and lifted the voluminous *holoku* skirt over her damp *paruha*. When she found the neck opening, she saw Mitch had moved terribly close. She smelled his clean scent, and the softness of his silky sideburns brushed her cheek. Struggling to get her arms through the long sleeves, she asked, "Are you going to kiss me? What are you trying to prove? Is this some contest between you and Traver—like the fight on the dock? Whatever one of you has, the other one wants?"

She hoped her accusations would divert him. But they didn't. While her hands were still tangled in the sleeves, he simply gathered her into his arms. He looked arrogantly resplendent in the last rays of twilight, the glow of thick golden hair melting into the fair skin and limpid blue eyes. She realized he could no more keep from kissing her than he could keep from breathing. His mouth touched her eyelids, then the hollow of her throat, her earlobes, then moved aggressively over her mouth.

She inhaled sharply as he bit at her tender lips. His sturdy, sculptured body seemed like the iron of his nickname. The blue eyes burned with delighted exultation as he buried his tongue between her lips. It seemed as if his entire soul concentrated on eliciting a response from her. Then he drew back and chuckled. "Oh, I'm not wrong about you, Ariel!

You made a charming effort to mislead me. But the innocence shines in your brown eyes like the moon at midnight. And I saw it in the curious unconcern you had for your body when you dived from the cliff. I felt it in the shock of your skin when your breast rubbed against my back when we rode. And right now I feel it in the lack of pretense you have, the surprise I read in your face at my kiss."

The surprise was real. Mitch's kiss had stirred her in a different way from Traver's. Traver's excited every sinew, Mitch's embrace seemed to enwrap her very soul.

He took her face in both hands, a tender and compelling fire in his eyes. "My dear, you are captivating. Twice beautiful because you do not realize your body's power." He stepped away, releasing her completely. "Don't waste yourself on Traver Loch! He'll only spurn you and walk away after he's used you!"

"What makes you say such hateful things? Are you thinking I should save myself for a flaming Irish gambler with a jealous heart?"

"Ariel, you know so little of love. Don't mistake passion—or even affection—for what there can ultimately be between a man and a woman. Don't sell yourself for mere passage on the *Pallas Maru*."

"Isn't that what you did?" She had finally gotten the dress to hang properly and fastened the neck tabs.

Mitch spoke honestly, sounding terribly vulnerable. "It was the best I could do. You can do better." He shook his head. "Do you know that when I held you in my arms, I felt nothing but dismay?"

"That's because I love Traver Loch," she said boldly, hoping to convince herself.

"Damn you, woman! You're so hellbent on going to Nevada, you'd convince yourself you were in love with anything that wore pants!"

She searched for a spiteful answer to his accurate assessment. If Mitch saw her as conniving, she'd turn that to her advantage. Mitch would be precisely the right man to argue her case before Elijah. "Mitch, you are exactly half-right. I do want passage on the *Pallas Maru*. Will you talk to my father? You've a fine way with words. Ask him to let me sail."

"You don't know what you're asking! The *Pallas Maru* is crammed with mutinous Chinese and bossed by Ricket Putnam! I'd not wish you anywhere near that combination, especially Putnam. And, by the way, I don't have the credentials for dusting your father's shoes. My speaking terms with religion lapsed years ago, and my only faith is wagering on my own horses."

Ariel laughed. The way Mitch used his eyes was subtle and superb, one moment letting them soften like an appealingly helpless puppy, the next moment as full of flash as the boldest hero. "You won't help me?" she asked. "Only put obstacles in my way?"

They were nearly at the compound gate. "I'll neither aid nor oppose," he answered. She hesitated before reaching for the latch. In that second he seized her, crushing her against him but not seeking her mouth or breasts. "I'll not help you destroy yourself. But I'll not interfere again, either. God knows, I've no right. Traver's fast, crude ways are not mine. I'd not make a woman of you too soon. So from now on, I'll bide my time. But remember this: any time I take a risk, it's because I have faith. Dammit, Ariel, for you I'd risk—Oh, hell! Let's just say I'm betting that someday you'll learn to love *me*."

Chapter 3

On Sunday mornings Ariel performed two time-worn rituals. She brought out her mother's faded picture, and she helped Elijah into his hot, formal church robes.

This morning, as Ariel pulled the calotype of Leah from its cotton batting bag, she stared hard at the gray image. There's no doubt I'm my mother's child, she thought. She liked the resemblance—the tall, slim figure, the hair the color of ashes mixed with candlelight, the chocolate brown eyes. There was nothing of Elijah in her—nothing physical at least—and she often wondered just what it was that she had inherited from her father.

It was time to help Elijah into the robes. She hurried to his room, hoping to speak to him again about the *Pallas Maru*. "Good morning, father." She smoothed out the black vest and held it for him. Trying to sound nonchalant, she asked, "Is that merchant ship still in the south lagoon?"

"She's there," Elijah replied, "pretty near repaired, but not likely to leave."

Ariel stifled a sigh of relief. "Why the delay?"

"Chief Kanoa and his port taxes. Kanoa has fashioned a six-foot-deep chain of logs across the harbor entrance. He's positioned guards and strung heavy, woven nets at the narrows."

So far, so good. Elijah hadn't exploded or retreated at the mention of the ship. She would test her ground carefully. Working diligently at brushing his suit coat, she questioned casually, "Was there much activity on the docks?"

"The usual brawling. And the Chinese are quite restless, confined in the hold. I counted six fights on the pier in the space of twenty minutes."

"I can well imagine one of the fighters was a red-haired Scotsman." She hoped she hadn't given herself away by the pride in her voice.

"I saw him. That's not authority, Ariel, as your tone indicates. It was only temper I saw, no brain or feeling. He fights like a hotheaded bear."

"Father, that man is my friend. They call him the Scottish lion. I want to sail with him on the *Pallas Maru!*" Damn, she'd blurted out the whole story, knowing instantly how naïve she sounded.

Elijah gave a frightened laugh. "What! You've taken up with the ship's stableboy and all-around troublemaker? Ariel, you can't be serious. You're not the type to take up residence with pigs and chickens for a two-thousand-mile journey. Nor are you likely to take up with a man who has no future to offer you."

"He's a strong man and full of dreams! He won't stay a roustabout and stablekeeper!"

Elijah was surprisingly patient. "Perhaps not. But from what I saw of him yesterday, I think I can safely predict he'll stay a brawler. A man who has no concept of living beyond the moment."

She thought of Traver saying how he hoped to see all continents and owe allegiance to none. She turned to Elijah's vestments, hoping her friendship with Traver would not become the main focus of the conversation. "Father, *you* have a friend on the *Pallas Maru*. Ricket Putnam."

She held her breath for his reaction. There was none. Elijah's eyes watered and wavered, seeking the floor. So he *did* know Ricket Putnam! After thirty seconds of total silence, she blurted, "Well, am I wrong? You act terrified! Or are you simply overcome with joy at finding a friend after many years?" She liked the scenario of a friendship. "Why don't we invite him to supper? Hear the news of the world. Wouldn't you like to renew your ties?"

Breath exploded Elijah's cheeks, then his leathery skin sunk inward like pouches. He whispered the name Ricket

Putnam like a curse, then reached to unbutton his collar as if choking.

Confounded anew, Ariel wondered what was so sinister about Ricket Putnam that every man who heard his name turned angry and defensive. Neither Traver nor Mitch had a good word for their employer. Now the name had sent Elijah reeling.

She helped him finish robing, reaching up tenderly to refasten the tight collar button. They left the house and moved along the path toward the stark stone church. "Ariel, you must never again have anything to do with *anyone* from the *Pallas Maru*."

She understood. As long as she'd simply flirted with Traver and Mitch, there had been no sin. But for some reason knowing Ricket Putnam was specifically forbidden. "Why are you so afraid? What does Putnam know about you? Can't you tell me, father?"

"Putnam is a part of my past I had hoped never to reveal to you, Ariel. A past that even now can unleash havoc, jealousy and betrayal. Ricket Putnam is a man who stops at nothing to gain the evil ends he chooses. He is clever. Ingenious. He binds men—and women—to him in ways far worse than indenture." Elijah hurried along the path as if to outrun his past and the hold Putnam had on him. "Believe me, child. Even after a generation, Putnam has the power to open old wounds and claim old debts."

"From you?"

"And from your mother, God rest her soul."

"*Mother* knew Ricket Putnam? How? When? I'm certain he was never on this island before!"

"No, thank God. Our paths never crossed after Leah and I left San Francisco."

"So she knew him there."

"She knew a great many important and influential people."

"And Ricket Putnam was important and influential?"

"In those days, yes. He'd finished medical school—"

"So he *is* a physician!"

"Disbarred from practice early in his career. Oh, Ariel, I always thought if this day of confession ever came, it would kill me."

She pointed to the wooden bench beneath the koa tree. "We're early, as always. Rest here, father. I'm not afraid of whatever you must tell me." She was concerned about his redfaced, shaky appearance. She'd change the subject until he recovered his bearings. "Father, where are the stocks willed to me by mother? The ones for the Hell's Candy with the drawings of craggy mountains and the seal of Nevada territory on them."

"They're in the strongbox at Castle Factor's office in Lanavi Town. Buried in steel. And I pray that's where you leave them. Please, daughter . . . I have enough set by so you need never touch those shares. Or if they're worthless, so much the better."

Ariel had a sudden inspiration. "Let's take those stocks and travel to Nevada *together*. Not with Ricket Putnam if he worries you. On some other ship." She smiled. "That's probably a better idea anyway, since Chief Kanoa will keep the *Pallas Maru* penned up until doomsday. You need a vacation, father. You certainly deserve one! Why, you haven't taken leave in twenty years, have you?"

"No," he admitted, looking away.

"Then it's high time."

"I can't leave here."

"Why not? The library and school will go on. Someone from Honolulu can come out and—"

"Ariel, haven't you ever wondered why I was never transferred from Lanavi? Why, year after year, we were left outside the Sandwich Island jurisdiction? Why we never had sufficient materials to do a proper job?" He folded his hands together and bowed his head. "I cannot return to the mainland."

She was stunned. "Cannot? Or will not? If you came here of your own free will, then surely—"

"I neither chose to come nor asked to stay." His lips turned gray with the bitter admission.

Now it was her turn to tremble in disbelief. It had never entered her mind that Lanavi and a life of books wasn't Elijah's idea of heaven. But the sadness and despair she saw in his eyes said otherwise. This remote outpost was some sort of private hell for him, not paradise. "I'm so sorry," she began. "Truly, I never knew you were a prisoner here. Can you tell me about it?"

He looked at his watch as if hoping there would not be sufficient time. Then he sighed. "You'll find this hard to believe, but at one time ambition burned in me like a torch. I hoped to build the finest and mightiest church school in San Francisco. In all California! In the world! And more for my own glory than any higher power's. Ricket Putnam offered me his help."

"How?"

"It was not at all unusual in those days for congregations to invest church funds in the China trade. Usually a handsome profit was returned to all parties. But what the venture returned me was a cargo of opium with my name on the bill of lading."

"Opium! Putnam was responsible for contraband?"

"He violates more than the laws of commerce. He actually indulges in the secret vice of the tongmasters. Ricket Putnam is an opium addict."

Ariel gasped. She had known of the narrow streets of the Aala triangle in Honolulu where tiny parlors with red lamps were filled with somnolent old Orientals. "And Putnam is a doctor! You'd think he would have known the dangers."

"I'm sure he did, as well as the pleasures. Perhaps it began as a medical school experiment. And then perhaps he found he could make a great profit importing both Chinese labor and contraband, and also insure himself a steady supply of premium opium."

It was the sordid story of a decadent man, but Ariel did not understand why this had kept Elijah on Lanavi for twenty years. "Was there a public scandal when your name and school were linked to the opium trade?"

"More than that. The contraband was confiscated, naturally, and the investment lost. I became both the laughing-stock and outrage of my congregation. Losing a denomination's money is far more serious than infidelity or blasphemy. Mind you, it was not enough to see me kicked out of service. Merely booted into oblivion. All these years I've sought penance in Polynesia by building a library and school."

"And my mother? Did she want to come to the islands?"

"The choice was hers. She was as determined to leave San Francisco as I was, although for different reasons."

"But did she want to *stay* here?" There were things in Ariel's memory which didn't jibe. Her vivacious, spirited, beautiful mother had slowly turned somber and succumbed to malaria. Ariel looked to Elijah for the answer, and he averted his eyes. She knew Leah had not been happy.

Before she could ask more, Elijah startled her with a confession. "Yesterday I went to see Ricket Putnam. I begged him to leave Lanavi. I begged him not to harm you."

"Me? How could Putnam harm me? How can he harm either of us now that I know your story? He can't blackmail you when I know the truth!"

"There is a more serious matter here than mere truth. Putnam is smart. Nefarious. And he always uses men to his own benefit. It is not enough for him to cheat a man; he must ruin him. He thrives on humiliation. There are wounds he would not hesitate to inflict on you. Wounds that began with your mother and me. Wounds that have not healed with time."

Elijah rose and paced solemnly toward the church. Ariel could do nothing but follow. She barely caught his anguished whisper. "Ariel, there are things in life we cannot excuse. Even people who love us deeply do things which can never be excused. These things we must then forgive. What cannot be excused must simply be forgiven. My dearest daughter, I beg your forgiveness in advance." He made his way to the altar.

Ariel seated herself in the back pew and looked around the Spartan building. Starkly Presbyterian, there was one round stained-glass window at the front. A tattered tapa cloth adorned the altar. Chalice cups were carved of monkeypod wood. The candles were tiki torches. All so impoverished, when her father had been capable of building cathedrals!

And now came the momentarily faithful. Chief Kanoa led the line, grinning and joking as if this were more a party than a service. He wore a flowered shirt and a loincloth, the feathered cloak and the shells and beads which were a native chief's royal trappings. He worshiped whatever he considered sacred at the moment—bright plumage of the *o'o* bird, a shark's cleansed jawbone, a dark-haired, dark-skinned bride from a neighboring island or, occasionally, Elijah's God.

Behind the fat, middle-aged chief trooped his wives. It was a great honor to attend services with Kanoa, one he bestowed only on wives in current favor. Today Ariel counted fourteen barefoot women. They squatted in the aisle while Kanoa lounged in a whole pew. His intelligent but pompous face was perched above a mound of stomachs acquired from years of undisciplined eating. His face was jolly, the color of *kukui* nuts. His eyes lit up when he spotted Ariel. He seemed surprised to see her.

Ariel squirmed in her seat, trying to pay attention to Elijah's sermon. He was telling them that certain feelings and desires must be stifled. How out of touch with his congregation! How out of tune with his daughter!

She was supposed to guard the back door and keep youngsters from slipping out before the service was completed. But there would be no holding the children this morning. Soon they'd wiggle, shift their gaze to the windows, then slip away to dive for coins tossed from the decks of the *Pallas Maru*. Today she wouldn't even try to keep them from their pleasures. Ariel settled back and let her thoughts wander, her reverie broken by Elijah's final amen.

"Amama ua noa." Kanoa responded with the Polynesian equivalent, which meant that the prayer was ended or freed. Prince and pastor shook hands.

"Kanoa, you must send the ship in the harbor away. At once," Elijah said sternly.

"Without holding the mele games?" Kanoa questioned jovially. "Without scarlet cloth for my wives? Without a new bride?" He pouted his fat lips. "No, it won't sail until I have my happiness."

"Be reasonable, sir! The *Pallas Maru* is not equipped for sports. Or for supplying you with more wives!"

Kanoa chuckled. "You could make up the difference, Elijah. Give me Ariel, and I'll send the ship on its way."

Elijah was properly scandalized and genuinely fatherly in his wide-eyed refusal. Ariel chuckled along with the chief. He'd tried to buy her so often it was more a longstanding joke than serious bargaining now. Yet she was aware of the way Kanoa's dark eyes lingered on her hips and breasts. An uneasiness remained even after he'd marched away with his entourage.

As she and Elijah returned to the compound for their meal, she thought how her father, Kanoa and Ricket Putnam were three men engaged in a tug of war. Elijah devoutly wanted the *Pallas Maru* gone. Kanoa intended for it to stay. The key was Ricket Putnam.

And that would be her chance! Suddenly she knew the situation called for direct action. She put her fear of Ricket Putnam aside. This was silly—two middle-aged men bearing grudges from many years ago. They must say their apologies and clear the air. No one should bear guilt for twenty years! She must arrange a meeting where social amenities would be observed and difficulties resolved. Surely she would be safe in her own parlor with her father present.

The moment she was in her room, she composed a handwritten note, then dispatched it with a Polynesian boy. "Dear Mr. Putnam," it read. "Ariel Cortland requests the pleasure of your company at high tea today at four in the afternoon."

"No, father! Please don't go!" Ariel was panicky as Elijah took his walking stick from the hook. "Please don't visit the sick this Sunday afternoon!" She had forgotten her father's routine of parish calls. Now her carefully laid plans were going awry. Ricket Putnam was due for tea in thirty minutes. She could not receive him alone.

Elijah put three books into his basket of supplies and went out the door. "I'll be back before suppertime," he called, blissfully unaware of Ariel's arrangements.

Promptly at four the late afternoon torpor of lulled tradewinds and singing crickets was broken by the sound of crisp footfalls. Ariel bolted from the highback chair, peeking through the curtains. Putnam had arrived.

Her heart skipped fearful beats as the man stood on the porch, ready to knock on the doorframe. Up close he was as sinister as he'd appeared through the spyglass: thin, hawklike nose, Satanic black eyebrows, a haughty stare from eyes which didn't seem to be looking at anything. The skin of his forehead worked up and down, but the eyes held motionless. Despite his expensive trousers and well-cut jacket, his skin and fingertips revealed a jaundiced degeneracy.

She answered his brisk knock. He stood silent, appraising her. His voice was low, controlled and snakelike. "You're Ariel, of course. You look exactly as your mother did."

Putnam had given her a tactful opening. She ignored the fear in her stomach and plunged ahead into conversation with him. "Yes, my father mentioned you knew her in San Francisco."

"Indeed I did. In fact, it was I who introduced Leah to Elijah." He spoke slowly but with confidence, his enunciation impeccable, each word calculated to put him in control of the situation. "A fine young couple they made—the idealistic preacher and the beautiful young tutor. A perfect pair."

A perfect pair? Even as a child, she'd known the vibrant Leah and bookish Elijah hadn't been a perfect match.

Putnam moved to the leather chair as he spoke again. "I doubt Elijah has spoken any good words on my behalf. Is that why he's absent? I suppose he still disapproves of me because I trafficked in opium."

"You have done more than traffic in opium. I know you also *use* it," she returned boldly.

"No worse than a glass of wine for the stomach's sake." He shrugged nonchalantly. "And I have other moderate vices. For example, I like young ladies."

She remembered the morning she'd seen him on deck with the Chinese girl. "Yes, I saw you using a mere child. You laid a finger on her neck and she whimpered and bowed." The memory still upset Ariel. She quickly served the tea.

"I am fond of *young* women," he repeated, contemptuously indicating she was too old for his interest.

She knew it unwise to discuss his decadence, yet she could not help but continue. "In my thinking, your transporting of human cargo is as immoral as your worst vices."

Now she'd riled him. "Please be advised that delivering Celestials from the Flowery Kingdom to the Land of Golden Hills is neither illegal nor immoral. And I have the say-so of the consul general of Imperial China and a contract with the six companies to back me up." Putnam slammed his fist onto the tea tray, jostling cups.

Ariel retreated. She must not fight with this devious man. She must be polite, ask courteous questions. "From what province are your immigrants? I've learned a bit of Cantonese at Honolulu Academy."

"Jesus! I don't know what dialect they babble! They simply jabber and fight. And eat! That's all coolies are good for until I get them to the railhead. They're costing me money every day we stay laid up on this two-bit island. This local chief must be brought to his senses!" Suddenly calm, he leaned toward her. "Miss Ariel, have you any influence with Kanoa?"

She smiled to think Putnam considered her a power. "Short of selling myself into Kanoa's household, I have no influence at all with him." She hated the cat-and-mouse game they were playing, and decided to change the subject. "Tell me about the railroad contract you hold. Will you build clear across Nevada?"

"No, the Virginia and Truckee will only connect the transcontinental route south to Virginia City."

"I've read Virginia City is the wildest and richest spot on earth." Instinct said to go slowly in revealing her interest, but enthusiasm and curiosity overwhelmed her judgment. "Have you been there?"

"Many times."

"Have you heard of the Hell's Candy silver mine?"

Putnam started slightly and tried to cover his reaction by

placing his teacup and spoon back onto the tray. Ariel refilled his cup from the large silver pot on the far serving cart. She saw he was studying her in the pier mirror, taking in her sunstreaked hair, walnut eyes, high breasts and slim ankles. His glance was studious, but not lustful. Calculating. His mouth stayed sealed, nostrils tight together as if they'd collapsed. She checked to see if he was breathing. Such a cold viper of a man!

Suddenly his manner became all smooth charm. His voice was like velvet ice. "Ariel, please sit down. Why, you seem as nervous as a child at her first party. Please think of me as your friend. An old family friend. A benefactor. You'll find me astute in business matters and reticent in personal ones, my dear. Now, how may I be of service to you concerning the Hell's Candy?"

He fired a brisk barrage of questions at her, and she answered truthfully. The stocks were in her name, there was no agent, the certificates were in the Castle Factor's office at Lanavi Town. "The stocks could be worthless, I realize. My mother received them as a gift from Sonny Staidlaw. She was tutor to his children in San Francisco many years ago."

"Yes, that's correct. Mr. Staidlaw was very fond of Leah." Putnam gave his first smile, a calculated upturn of the lips, quickly replaced by rapid speech. "You've no idea of the value?"

"Mother never investigated the worth of the claim, to my knowledge. But those shares are my hope for the future as well as my link with her past. I've promised myself to see Nevada and the Hell's Candy, even if it turns out to be nothing more than a hole in the ground."

Putnam stood abruptly. "That's precisely what it is. Nothing of value. I can save you the trouble of any misguided investigation, Ariel. I can tell you flatly your claim is worthless."

She gasped with disappointment, then realized suddenly that his reply had been too quick. She searched his pale eyes, and saw in them a sudden fever of greed. She stood, moving toward the doorway to indicate their meeting was over. "I think you are lying. You do believe my stocks to be of value," she said defiantly. "I will put them up as collateral if you will allow me passage to California on the *Pallas Maru.*"

He stood and gave an eerie laugh, but made no move toward the door. "So you want to leave this Eden for the Devil's playground and a bittersweet taste of Hell's Candy?"

She was not at all sure. "I have alternatives," she boasted.

"Alternatives! One of my favorite words. Perhaps we will form a partnership. I always have alternate plans. Substitutes. Options. Perhaps we *can* arrange for you to travel with me."

She took a daring risk. "I will not travel aboard the *Pallas Maru* unless I'm guaranteed the protection of Traver Loch."

Surprise was hers. Putnam's mouth twitched. He took a full minute to regain his poise. Then he bristled with anger. "A man like Traver Loch wouldn't protect you! He'd tear you apart for sport. Bed you for a moment's pleasure, then cast you aside like a used rag."

"He's not like that!" she defended Traver hotly.

Putnam met her outburst with a cool smile. "You'll have problems enough without attempting to tame the Scottish lion. Understand me clearly, Ariel. If you travel on the *Pallas Maru*, it will be under *my* protection. Only I have the authority or power to govern what goes on aboard that ship!" He brusquely pushed at the screen door and she followed him onto the porch. He turned in profile, narrowing his slitted eyes in the bright sunlight. "Men aboard a ship will kill for a woman. Men in the minefields kill for even less—tattered pieces of worthless paper, pyrites dipped in quartz powder. The sooner you realize your natural alliance is with me, the better for you."

Silently she retreated. Closing the door, she locked the inside bolt. Ally herself with Ricket Putnam? No. Tomorrow she would send for Traver Loch. Ask his protection. And if he agreed? She remembered the quick bond of desire that had welded them together in the bay, the feel of his hand across her breast, his lips salty and hot. If he agreed, then she would find a suitable way to thank him.

Chapter 4

Ariel ran through the koa trees on her way to the sea cave to meet Traver. The wind cried tumultuously through the palms as she neared the headlands. Would Traver come? Would he risk leaving the ship during working hours? If he comes to meet me, she thought, it will mean he cares deeply.

She scampered along the sandy slope where the lava and stone had been weathered by centuries of water and wind. Ducking into the cave, she caught her breath at its damp, dark beauty. Sparkling salt crystals reflected from the ceiling, casting diamond prism shapes on the walls. Feathery vines grew downward over the entrance, with white and fuchsia blossoms trailing into the shadows. The floor was soft and sandy, cool beneath her thin sandals.

"Traver? Are you here?" she called, tense with excitement.

"Aye, honey lass. That I am."

She traced his curling voice to the back of the cave. As her eyes adjusted to the dimness she spotted his jaunty leather cap atop the bright, thick hair. The sheen of his eyes was like emerald fire. She ran to him.

"Did you send for me to tell me goodbye?" he asked frankly.

"Tell you goodbye? Oh, I could not!" She relaxed into his

outstretched arms, eager for the touch of his cheek against hers, the taste of his lips and power of his embrace.

He kissed her gently, gazing at her softly. "Ah, Ariel," he sighed. "Let me memorize you against the day I'll see you no more!"

She pressed against him as he kissed the fluttering hollow of her throat. "Take me with you, Traver!"

There was instant response in the flexing of his thighs. His lips brushed against her forehead. She repeated, "Please take me with you! I need a protector, Traver."

When he didn't offer an outright no, she went on boldly. "I must go to California. Now. With you!" Then, although she hadn't meant to utter such words and couldn't vouch that she meant them, she cried, "I love you!"

This vow brought a torrent of response. Traver's red hair tossed in the shaft of sunlight. His mouth came down over hers in relentless pursuit. His body burned against her like a fire long held in check and then fanned to brilliance.

"I wanted you to reach out to me. . . . I never had that before," he murmured. His hands came downward to cradle her hips. Then he touched her throat, trailing his fingers lower across the soft material. When he touched her breasts, she felt an instant response. How green his eyes were, like sweet clover. His hair had the bold, lovely colors of autumn, all the russets and golds and browns, colors she had only read about, never known on Lanavi.

Something sweetly incredible was happening, shooting little sparks of anticipation through her body. What was it that exploded when they were together? A power, mysterious and overwhelming.

Aware of every sense and every word, Ariel felt suspended. She could feel his lips and tongue against her ear. She listened to the rustling sounds of her dress as he loosened the belt and buttons.

Next they were kneeling together, pale skin against bronzed. He lifted the dress from her, covering her breasts with kisses instead. She reveled in the exquisite sensation. When he stroked her stomach and thighs, she knew they had crossed an invisible hurdle and there was no turning back. "Then it's settled! We'll be together," she whispered.

He pulled back uneasily. "You're quite as interested in being on that ship as you are in being my woman."

He had spoken the truth. But he saved her having to lie to him. "Never mind," he laughed. "Only understand this—in me, you'll be finding a protector who has no way to protect you except by the strength of his hands."

"You have much more, Traver! More than you realize."

"I hope so. I can only promise that I won't be intimidated. What I fight for, I keep. If I make you mine now, there is no turning back."

"Oh, Traver!" How fine and natural it was that this man should want her. A hush of expectancy settled between them. Anticipation left her apprehensive but not confused.

She sought his lips eagerly, inviting his tongue to explore her mouth. A warm blush spread from her cheeks across her chest. Inside, she felt as pliable as melted wax. She murmured words she hadn't dreamed of speaking. "Oh, yes, Traver! I will have you for my true and wedded husband!" Instantly she hid her face in her hands. Now she'd done it! Gone and proposed! She peeked out at the bewildered look on his face. Then he began to laugh, not in shock, but as if he'd received hundreds of such propositions and found them all funny.

Tenderly but defensively, he held her hands. "Hold on, honey lass. Merely thinking of a preacher man in a black suit and a girl holding a bouquet of day lilies sends me into spasms of despair. Why, even the sniff of a leather-bound Bible is sufficient to set my heart in a panic."

She wanted only to savor the tender feelings between them, and not worry about the future. But he persisted. "I ain't the marrying kind," he said flatly.

There was a moment of strained silence. Then he lifted her chin, cupping her face upward. "Is it vows you want, Ariel? Then by all that's holy, let me tell you I'll cherish you. I'll keep you safe. Protect you. Dig us a fortune from the bare earth!"

"Then perhaps we'll marry later?"

He gazed at her steadfastly without speaking. With a wanton smile and an eager sheen in his eyes, he pulled off his remaining clothes.

There were terrible questions brushing at the corners of her mind, but it was like tearing down cobwebs to form the words. It's quite simple, she promised herself. We'll marry on the mainland. It *sounded* simple. Or was she merely simple for thinking it so?

He gave her no more time for thought, but drew her down to the floor of the cave, positioning her atop the discarded clothing. She felt eager but shy, rolling against him hesitantly. The dress beneath her made a soft rustle, and the warmth of their bodies gave off a radiant heat. His kisses were sure, exquisitely sensitive. He possessed every inch of her flesh with hands and kisses.

Now he cupped her to him as his dark body dictated, crouching as he bent to suck at her nipples. He moved against her firmly, legs atop her thighs, a hand stretched across her taut abdomen. He spread her glossy hair like a cushion behind her head, then spread her legs. She felt an instant of freedom as if she were standing on the Kalo Cliffs, about to dive. Then, from a faraway corner of her mind, came the unbidden cry: this is wrong.

She struggled to sit up. He shoved her roughly backward. Yet his words were gentle. "There now, you're doing fine. Come now, let me touch you." He rubbed against her, causing shooting sparks deep within her womb. She could hold back nothing. And she liked the feel of their lips together, the bodies linked breast to chest. But when he abruptly nudged her thighs further apart, she tried to pull away.

His breathing grew harsh and frightening fierceness overwhelmed his features. Forehead lines creased together. Eyes turned to jade as the pupils contracted. His arm muscles bulged as he pinned her wrists flat.

"What's wrong?" she asked him, then realized, for him, nothing was wrong. He was unrestrained in seeking her now. He was atop her, prying her legs apart and thrusting.

"Stop!"

He tried valiantly. She shoved and he moved half-astraddle, wedged too firmly to withdraw. A heaving breath racked his chest. He raised his head, but not his body. "A steady diet of briars and thistles! That's what I've had! And here you are, all honeysuckle and heather." He choked as she tightened her legs against further intrusion. "I can't stop, Ariel! I fight to the finish."

He groaned, brought his lips down over hers with mastering force, and cut off her protests. The rest of his body was beyond his control. First a tiny, rippling movement spread outward from the core, then he began unrestrained pounding.

Now she felt pain. Involuntarily she flexed and tightened. But something had given way. The sharp pain burned through toward her back, then smoldered and subsided. The tensing of her body seemed to force more movement from him.

Oh, this wasn't what she'd imagined at all! It was like a ship thrashing and foundering in the sea. She shut her eyes, feeling suffocated. The hurt continued to rampage with every thrust. He lifted her hips, leaned back, rammed again and again.

Now she wanted only to get away. He tightened his grasp. She could feel him bound to an involuntary rhythm she had no way of matching. His thumbs ground into her shoulderblades like staves. Each tiny movement from her seemed to inflame him further. As she started to cry out, he covered her mouth with his palm. She tossed her head backward, arching her back and neck. At that moment he broke into spasms, slackened and fell forward limply.

She lay still, wondering. Then she heard his hot, muttered curses by her ear. His forehead, damp and heated, lay against her cheek. Both their hearts were thudding, emphasized by the quiet of the cave. She felt terribly alone in that instant, too angry to cry, too hurt to complain. Using all her strength, she shoved him aside. "Never again!"

"Ariel, it's not meant to be that way." The touch of his fingertips against her cheek was as delicate as soft lace. When he encountered a single teardrop, his hand trembled, brushed it away.

She curled up, her back toward him. "Don't touch me! *Now* is not the time for tender ways and soothing words."

"It's my fault," he apologized again. "Ariel, I promise. It's not meant to be like this. Don't turn against me. Don't wall me off before I can teach you pleasure."

"*You* were the wall! Come crashing down on me!"

"Come, darling. Sit up. Surely you don't believe I'm a man who enjoys hurting."

"Yet you did enjoy it!" Now angry tears brimmed on her lashes. "You can't deny that!"

He held her tenderly, remorse carved into his tanned face. His damp hair made corkscrew wisps at the nape of his neck. "I've always had to fight the world. Sometimes I forget and think love has to be taken by force as well."

She blinked rapidly, trying to stifle the tears. She could not think logically. This wasn't anything she'd read about in books! The Polynesian legends said that kisses were dreams of the soul and love was the union of seawater and sunshine. She felt angry with herself as well as with Traver. She supposed some of the fault was hers. She'd certainly been willing enough in the beginning. She tried to smile. "I once heard it's best to get it over with fast the first time."

"I doubt this disaster would win any medals *except* for speed." He laughed. She saw a tinge of pink in his face, as if he were bragging as well as apologizing. But when he touched her lips gently, she did not flinch. "Oh, Ariel, Ariel . . . I promise we'll do better. Love's not supposed to be one person breaking the other. It's meant to be so complete we won't be able to tell where one stops and the other begins."

"Was it awful for you?" she wondered aloud. "All that bucking and thrashing and moaning . . ."

"No, no. You simply astonished me, darling. I could make you some fancy excuses. Tell you that's the way a man is with a new woman. Or after a long abstinence. But the truth is I had no more control than a clipper ship in a tempest!"

She sat up, reaching for her clothes. She even began to feel a bit of pride in the obviously powerful effect she'd had on him.

"Don't worry, honey lass. It won't be long till I'll have my wits about me again. There's plenty more where that came from. Then, I'll teach you proper!"

His swaggering tone roused her anger anew. "I'll not be taught by a man who can't control himself!"

Her cold reproach stirred his fighting reflexes. The jaw tensed along with his hands, his lips tightened and his shoulders flexed. "By Saint Kilda!" he swore. "I'll make one last apology and no more. I am sorry that my strength hurt you when I promised to protect you! But, my God, woman! Few things in the world scare me more than a girl who'd put herself totally in my power."

"You're afraid? Of me? You who are so strong and sure of yourself?"

"Don't mock me until you understand me better. It doesn't scare me to have my body beaten in the boxer's ring. I could even hold still to be spear-bait in some misbegotten war. But I'm frightened of the challenge you've set me. Settling down. Forever. I've always set my sights on being rich enough to keep a fast team harnessed day and night in case wanderlust struck."

"I'd not bind you like that, Traver," she consoled him. "But, truthfully, your hurry gave me misgivings. I don't want to be some kind of sacrifice—something you take by force. I want to come to you freely, of my own will."

"And so you shall, my sweet ocean dove." He kissed her softly, with warm, hovering lips. She reached out to him, the turmoil of the previous hurt fading away. She must forget the first time and try again.

She heard a dim noise from outside the cave, but paid no attention. In the next moment the sound was louder, then the pounding of horse's hooves sounded clearly near the entrance. Mitch Galway's angry voice cut the darkness. "Traver Loch, damn you! Are you in there? They said you were ditching for the sea caves! And you've left the stable deck open and the Chinese have poured out like a herd of goats!"

Traver and Ariel looked at each other, then he motioned her deeper into the shadows. Straightening his jumper, he scrambled to the opening. "What's the trouble, Galway?" Traver jumped the sandstone ledge to the sand.

Ariel crept to the front of the cave. Traver and Mitch were talking rapidly, Mitch on the stallion, Traver with hands on hips and feet planted obstinately wide.

"Jumping ship!" accused Mitch. "Taken fat leave of your senses, you dumb ox! Sneaking off and leaving the gate down behind you!"

"I had business to attend to," replied Traver.

"In the sea caves? What the hell kind of business—" Mitch's eyes flared with sudden suspicion. He smacked the riding crop across the horse's saddle. Anger, jealousy, fury all competed for dominance in his fair face. "Is *she* in there?"

Traver's masculine taunt stunned Ariel. "What if she is? And what if she's not the same girl she was an hour ago? Admit it, Mitch. You're not mad I ditched the *Pallas Maru* for a spell. Or even that the Chinese have taken a well-deserved break from the hold. They'll be back when it's time to fill their rice bowls. You're just not man enough to admit she favored me."

"You fool!" shouted Mitch. "I ought to break your damned knuckles with this riding crop! Oh, hell, get on back to the ship. Help us round up the coolies. Putnam is threatening murder and mayhem."

Mitch's voice was full of hatred. Ariel knew she'd come between the two friends as nothing ever had before. She moved outside the cave and stood on the ledge, afraid the two might resort to fisticuffs to settle their quarrel over her.

Mitch glanced up at her, curiously at first, then with disappointment. He gritted his teeth as if satisfied Traver hadn't simply been boasting. "Well," he growled, "you look gloriously radiant—and radiantly guilty!"

Ariel felt a sudden hot shame at Mitch's inspection, but she concealed it behind a mask of disdain. As she moved down the hillside, she felt tenderness in her loins and she took small, cautious steps down to the sand rather than jumping as she normally would have.

Noise from the cartway to the left caused Mitch to turn his horse. There were shouts, then two Polynesian runners broke into the beach clearing. "Fire!" they shrieked. "Fire! Fire in the cane fields!"

Both Traver and Mitch jerked as if touched by a brand. A knowing look passed between them as they cried together, "Putnam!"

"He'd fire the cane?" questioned Ariel.

"To recapture the Chinese," shouted Mitch. "He doesn't give a damn about the crop. Just his cargo."

Ariel now believed the man capable of any depravity, but she knew the danger of a cane fire better than Traver or Mitch. "It will burn out of control and devastate the entire island! I must get to father. Warn him."

"I'll take you to the compound," offered Mitch.

"No! Go back to the ship. The Polynesians have a bucket system for fire. They'll gather at Lanavi Town. By then I can be at the school!"

For a second both Mitch and Traver looked uncertain about leaving her. Then Mitch offered his hand and Traver swung up behind him. They dashed for the south lagoon, while she ran toward the compound on the north shore.

As she emerged from the fern forest onto the plateau, she saw the thick white smoke of the burning cane hanging low across the horizon. She knew that even in carefully controlled harvest fires, the sizzling vapors could overcome a man forty feet away. She shuddered to think of the Chinese seeking refuge in the tall fields, only to find themselves in the midst of fire. What a fiend Ricket Putnam was! The fields would make a flaming maze. No one would know which way to run.

At the turn in the main path she saw the fire line. Oh, God, it was worse than she'd feared. Lanavi Town was already a smoldering ruin. The cane fields uphill were ablaze in white, smoky fury. She wondered how Putnam could be so stupid. Kanoa would never let the *Pallas Maru* leave without paying damages! She found herself weak in the knees and shaking with fright as she saw Chinese rushing pell-mell from the fields, wearing long black pajamas, their blood-curdling screams filling the air. Sailors from the ship were rounding up the Chinese like cattle, herding them into groups with their hands high in the air.

Panting with exertion, she crested the last hill to the compound. A sudden puff of wind in her face and she knew fresh horror. The wind had changed! There would be downdrafts. The wind would now feed the fire straight across the mountain's spine and spill it onto the northern headlands. Already a rain of ashes and sparks trailed into the palms at the compound.

Ariel ran faster, forcing her legs to move when they attempted to freeze in terror. A whirlwind of fire moved into the koa trees, igniting them in an explosive instant. By the time she rounded the mango grove where the honeycreeper and finch birds were shrieking, she spotted double plumes of smoke coming from the thatched roofs of the church and school.

Fifty yards away, she saw Elijah moving in and out of the school, boxes of books in his arms. His figure hunched as he stacked the crates on the ground, then turned to re-enter the burning library. "No!" she cried. "Don't try to save those useless, moth-eaten books!" But Elijah didn't seem to hear. He rushed back inside, leaving the door open behind him.

Perhaps it was the rush of air through the open entrance which made the entire structure explode outward. Timbers fell. Torches of thatch careened downward and the flame spread like a wall of rushing tidal water.

Ariel sank down by the fence, forced back from the intense heat. She grabbed a loose picket and beat at the flames. It was like using a toothpick. She knew she'd failed as the smoke rose up and engulfed her. She fell to the ground and beat the earth with her fists.

Ariel awoke to the sound of wailing chants. The Polynesians were mourning the misfortune which had befallen their island. They would not be alone in their mourning tonight. She had lost her father, she remembered with a hollow ache.

Her eyes burned horribly and her lungs were bursting with acrid smoke. She tried to speak, but her throat was raw and only a hoarse rasp emerged.

"Don't try to speak, Ariel," a compassionate voice told her.

She looked up into the blue eyes of Mitch Galway. "I came as soon as I could. I can only stay a moment. Putnam has put a curfew on the crew and thrown Traver in the ship's brig."

Mitch helped Ariel to sit up. Through red, tear-filled eyes

she could see the foundation of the schoolbuilding where her father had perished. The stark stone walls of the church stood, but the garden was only rubble. Miraculously the trim house stood intact, though the outside stairs were charred.

"Oh, Mitch," she cried. "This was father's life. This school. These books. Now they've become his funeral pyre."

"Another victim of Ricket Putnam."

"My poor father," she said softly. She stiffened and clutched Mitch's hand. "Oh, I vow to kill Ricket Putnam for this!"

"I'd help you, if I could!" He echoed her vehement threat. "Is there anything I can do to help, Ariel? I must start back or Putnam will turn on me, too. I won't do anyone any good in the brig with Traver."

She was aware of the risk Mitch had taken in coming. Appreciative of his concern for her, she nodded—he should leave now. He patted her hand, then made his way through the crowd, shaking his head in dismay.

Now Chief Kanoa came straggling up the hill, his plump brown face seething with anger and sorrow. He pointed to the school, then faced Ariel. "Your father was a good man. We will honor him with a sunset chant of mourning." He waved his hand at the smoky sky and the direction of the *Pallas Maru.* "Already that ship owed me games and cloth and a woman. Now the cane and damage to the town must be added to their debts."

She shook her head. "For me, they have destroyed things that cannot be replaced. A debt that cannot be repaid."

"We will have revenge," Kanoa assured her. "Their ship will not leave until they pay. We will collect. They must also return the things they took from Lanavi Town—the whiskey from the trading post and the safe and strongboxes from Castle Factor's—"

"What! Castle Factor's office was looted?"

"Yes. My warriors saw sailors carting away the metal boxes to the ship."

Suddenly she understood. Even beyond the personal sorrows, *she'd* been a victim of Ricket Putnam's plunder. He'd used the Chinese escape as a reason to set the fire. But the flames had been a cover to steal her stock from Castle Factor's. A man who'd thieve behind fire and murder! She turned away from the blackened debris. "I swear it. I shall kill Ricket Putnam!"

Chapter 5

During the week, burial services were held for Elijah. Ariel took the ashes of burned library books and scattered them from the headlands into the sea. The books had brought Elijah no peace in life. Perhaps symbolically he and they would be at rest in the sea.

Kanoa sent an honor guard for the ceremony, then a private message that she would be welcome in his longhouse. She declined, knowing that Kanoa would welcome her sincerely, but he might also attempt to take advantage of her. Alone she would be unable to prevent him from performing the marriage ceremony he had desired for so long.

Repair began in the cane fields. The *Pallas Maru* lay stranded in a tangle of nets, logs and intricate chains woven of seaweeds which fouled the rudder and anchor. Kanoa allowed no one to come or go from the ship to the shore. Ariel worried about Traver. Was he still held prisoner?

Then there was the matter of retrieving her Hell's Candy certificates. At the end of three weeks, when she felt tempers had cooled, Ariel sent word to Chief Kanoa that she would like to board the *Pallas Maru* to speak to Ricket Putnam. Kanoa sent a scroll of approval, plus two burly, dark-skinned Polynesian guards to escort her.

To her surprise she was readily admitted aboard the ship,

and received with all the courtesies—as if she'd come calling from a pleasure schooner. Ariel had dressed simply, as befitted her state of mourning. She wore a loose gray shift and had wound her single thick braid atop her head.

But how could she reason with a man without principles? Certainly it was easy enough to get a man's attention. In Honolulu she'd attended state affairs, picnics, royal beach parties and court. Her flair for languages had made her the delight of embassy balls. She'd captured the attentions of the Portuguese ambassador, an Italian count and the French consul. But she was quite insecure when it came to confronting Ricket Putnam.

She was directed to his cabin on the stern. He met her on the afterdeck. "Good morning," he said politely, executing a brief bow. "I've been expecting you. I had hoped to call on you to express my sympathy. But my activities have been restricted these past weeks." He didn't sound concerned with either restrictions or sympathy. He ushered her into the cabin. Kanoa's guards took up positions outside the door.

What a bold liar Putnam is, thought Ariel. She focused her attention on the cabin. Luxurious. Teakwood and mahogany fittings. A wicker basket filled with dried plumes. Medical books with gold-stamped titles. On the main salon table, an opium lamp. Why was she shocked to find it displayed so openly? She looked at Putnam himself, his angular, thin face scraped clean of whiskers except for the beginnings of a dark mustache. He was pale, as if he never went into the sunshine. A dark stain blotted his fingertips. A yellowish tinge crept beneath his skin, making him appear shadowy.

The young Chinese girl entered the cabin docilely, bowing silently. She picked up a palm leaf fan and moved it back and forth to provide a breeze. Putnam seated himself in a swivel desk chair, leaning back in his frock coat as if he were a visiting merchant trader. "Ariel, I have been so saddened by these last weeks' events. Sailors can be so rash and foolish! I send Mitch and Traver to round up the escaped coolies and what do they do? Fire the cane!"

"Neither man fired the cane. Both were with me."

He didn't argue, merely arched his thick black brows together, then moved on to new lies. "And those reckless Polynesians—looting their own town. Stealing everything that wasn't tied down."

"It was you, Ricket Putnam, who stole my Hell's Candy

certificates," she challenged him briskly. "I have come to get them back."

"You seem certain I have them. Well, then, consider them in my safekeeping." Thin laughter, hard as sea stones, escaped his pallid lips. "In fact, consider yourself my ward as well as my guest."

"I am not interested in being your ward. Not any more than I was interested in being Kanoa's orphan."

"Aha! So Kanoa has put in his bid for you? You'd be better off with me, I assure you." He lifted his eyebrows and sneered. "You're too old for *my* tastes."

A knock at the door interrupted their strained conversation.

"Enter," commanded Putnam, his hollow cheeks blousing outward, then sinking.

Mitch Galway stalked in, his stride double quick. When he saw Ariel, he stopped completely, then looked away. She tried to smile at Mitch, to reassure him she could hold her own against Putnam's deviousness. Mitch only half-glanced at her, glared and kept his eyes averted. Oh, those blue, blue eyes!

"Chief Kanoa is rowing toward the *Pallas Maru*," Mitch said to Putnam. "Shall we man the guns and call general quarters?"

Putnam was amused. "You'd have natives crawling all over this ship with firebrands! Can't you learn patience, man?" He mused for a moment and then spoke to Ariel. "Give this Irish bulldog one of your frosty looks, my dear. See if you can turn his temperature down a notch." He rose and attempted to touch her shoulder, but she moved to avoid his hand. "Come closer, boy," he baited Mitch. "You're an excellent judge of horseflesh. What do you think of this girl? Here, Ariel, show your teeth."

Ariel remained cool. "You cannot embarrass me with your bad manners, Putnam."

When it became apparent she would not be lured into any arguments, Putnam turned his attention to the business at hand. "When Kanoa arrives, send him in at once. We must not keep royalty waiting." He motioned Mitch to leave, adding, "Dismissed, Galway!" as if proud to be able to order the man around.

A few minutes later Kanoa arrived. Two train-bearers carried the hem of his feather cloak. Another orderly carried a long parchment scroll. Kanoa stood erect, bare from the waist up except for a necklace of seed pods and shark's teeth. A helmet of shellwork perched atop his curly dark hair. "This is my list of charges against your ship," he stated, and gestured the aide to unroll the scroll.

Putnam watched the procedure, desultorily scanning the long list. His voice was lazy. "Yes, yes, those silly games. Scarlet cloth. A bride. And now the price of the cane." His voice trailed off. Suddenly Putnam's gray eyes narrowed with flashing excitement. He pointed to Ariel. She flinched, wishing she could fade into the shadows.

Kanoa seemed to sense a bargain in the making. He squatted on his haunches, getting comfortable for a long barter session. "Games. Cloth. Money. And a woman. When you provide these, your ship can go *wiki-wiki*. Till then, no more rice for the hungry men in the hold. And no more *lau-lau* girls for your sailors." He laughed lasciviously. "I have upped the stakes!"

Patient and sly, Putnam approached Kanoa and deftly imitated the squatting position favored for negotiations. Ariel tensed. Something had changed. Putnam had a new plan—an alternative. "Our disagreements are unfortunate," he said. "Let's see if there aren't substitutions to be made." He rocked on his haunches. "For example, perhaps we can arrange some athletic competition between the ship's crew and your warriors."

"The mele games," grunted Kanoa. "Good."

"And for the cane and the cloth, some financial arrangement could be worked out. Do you understand?"

"I understand money," replied Kanoa with dignity. He thought a moment, then asked, "But what about the bride? Money won't substitute for a woman in my bed."

Putnam executed a brisk jump as he rose and grabbed Ariel by the arm. "What if a tall, fair-skinned, dark-eyed girl—"

Ariel pulled her arm away. "I am not for sale or trade, sir! And keep your hands off me!"

Kanoa now stood up, eyes gleaming with delight, obviously eager to pursue Putnam's idea.

"Enough of this charade," insisted Ariel. She attempted to walk toward the door, but Putnam's strong hand grasped her shoulder, while Kanoa's bulk blocked her way. "Let me go," she ordered.

Neither man moved. Putnam spoke quietly to Kanoa. "Pay no mind to her protests. A little spirit makes her attractive, don't you think?" With his free hand, he rummaged in his desk drawer. Withdrawing a printed blue sheet of foolscap, he held it toward Kanoa. "Look here, friend. This is a legal document. Elijah asked me to act as Ariel's ward—"

"Lies! Lies!" cried Ariel. She saw the blue paper was merely a list of ships of British registry. But Kanoa was nodding at the impressive-looking sheet, even though he was unable to read it.

Kanoa hitched up his waistband. The lure of Ariel was obviously overwhelming whatever judgment he possessed. He'd believe anything Putnam told him.

Ariel was damned if she'd stand still between the two rascals, penned in and inspected like a calf for slaughter. Putnam urged Kanoa to examine her further. "She has some good points—even though she's awfully old," he drawled. "Her teeth are straight. Sweet breath. High tits. Tight buttocks. A sharp fork."

Kanoa put out a hand to touch her hair. She ducked her head, and bit him. A shrill call in Polynesian brought the two guards leaping into the cabin. They pinned her between their burly arms. She decided there was more dignity in standing erect than in screaming and struggling.

"No more biting," scolded Putnam. "It's bad manners. No way at all to treat your prospective bridegroom."

Kanoa wasn't alarmed. He chuckled. "Oh, I've had biters, slappers and scratchers enough. But none like this golden-skinned virgin."

Putnam and Kanoa continued to speak about her as if she weren't there. "She's too tall for me," Putnam acknowledged. "And personally I like them on the skinny side. But mainly I like them young. I want them to tremble when I touch them, and open up compliantly." He glanced toward the Chinese girl with the palm fan and she ducked her head submissively.

Putnam put out a hand to show the bargain was official. Kanoa kissed his cheek in return. The chief laid down conditions. "The nets and logs will stay across the bay until the three nights of desire have proved this woman acceptable."

Ariel's alarm sharpened. What could she do to avoid playing into this conspiracy? It seemed she had no vote at all in the matter. But then she thought of something. "Despite your carefully laid plans, Kanoa would find me useless. I am not a virgin!"

Kanoa snorted, nostrils flaring. He glared at Putnam. A wave of dismay swept over Putnam's angular features and sent his heavy black brows crashing together. Kanoa moaned angrily, "I would have sworn . . ." Then he stopped, leaning toward Putnam. "You are a *kahuna?* A medical man?"

"Yes, by training. But I cannot restore what is lost once and forever."

"No, no," muttered Kanoa. He circled Ariel twice as if to tell, by looking, her status. He rubbed his hands across his stomach and fiddled with the tiger-shell armband. "I think her claim is only her *wish.*"

Kanoa squatted. "Doctor Putnam, you examine her medically. We will find out."

"Certify her a virgin?" Putnam seemed willing, but unsure how to proceed.

"Make certain you rupture no veils," instructed Kanoa.

I must escape, Ariel thought. She pinned her hopes on the cabin exit, managed to lurch away from the startled guards and ran. They caught her as she reached the passageway. Dragged back, she was forced to her knees before Kanoa.

He leaned toward her. His voice was soft, almost compassionate, as if he hated to cause her trouble. "Are you lying, Ariel?"

She realized that her situation was, for the moment, hopeless. She must bide her time and look for another opportunity to escape Kanoa, later. Now she uttered the words he wanted to hear. "I was lying. I am a virgin."

"Aha!" Putnam's relief was obvious.

Kanoa wasted no time. He grabbed Ariel, yanking her wrists together and slinging her body across his shoulders as if she were a sack of taro flour. In moments Kanoa had traversed the cabin and stern. "Traver! Mitch! Anyone!" She shouted. Her cries went unheard, covered by whistles and catcalls from the crewmen and cheers from Kanoa's rowers in the barge. Putnam followed, chortling. "Prepare the feast!" Kanoa shouted to the whole world. "Lay out the grounds for the games! The three nights of desire shall begin tomorrow at sunset!"

Locked in the women's longhouse, Ariel found herself a pampered prisoner. The wives' pavilion was built of mud, pumice and thatch. It captured the cooling tradewinds from the sea and the refreshing rains from the volcano slope. The fifty-foot-long building was divided into cubicles. As Ariel paced the length, a dozen young Polynesian women clustered around her. Watching every move she made, they seemed afraid to speak, and equally afraid to get in her way.

"This is all so silly!" Ariel announced. She stood at a mud-rimmed window laced with bars, gazing at the seawall path. The sheer drop was blanketed with vines. Below, the black sand beach sparkled. In the narrows of the harbor the *Pallas Maru* lay stranded.

She paced the narrow hallway. The tiny rooms were hung with silk, contained simple bedsteads and basins. Most had comfortable floor cushions, incense burners and tiny silvered mirrors. In one a young woman busily worked with coral powder, resin and charcoal, making herself attractive.

Ariel knew the women would not challenge her. I must get out of here, she thought. Her courage, however, was useless without an escape plan.

In the afternoon a slim, dark-skinned Polynesian woman approached Ariel. Smiling, about thirty years old and dimpled, she bowed and introduced herself. "I am Loki—head wife to Kanoa." Her hands were delicately graceful and moved in rhythm with her slow speech. Although Loki's English was not perfect, Ariel understood the gestures and much of the Polynesian.

"Try to understand," said the pretty, amiable Polynesian woman. "The needs of a chief are three—food, challenge and love."

"I know about the three nights of desire," Ariel responded.

Loki smiled approval. "Then you understand it is an honor to be Kanoa's wife. The first night you will preside over the great luau feasting. The second night we hold the mele games. The third night you must join the chief on his lauhala mats. We will prepare you at twilight for the feast."

Ariel knew she had no cause for distress on the first night of the ritual.

At twilight the Polynesian girls gathered around her again, pointing and smiling. They offered scented water for bathing, oleander perfume and a long garment of orange, purple and fuchsia silk which wrapped three times around the body and tucked above the breasts.

When Loki held a sliver of mirror, Ariel was surprised at how pretty she looked. She had always favored pastel colors. Now the bright silk fabric brought out the coloring of her pale hair and rosy cheeks. And at the feast, she was shocked at how hungry she was! She was seated apart from Kanoa on a mat of woven bamboo. She served herself from platters made of ti leaves. *Mahi-mahi* fish. Pork. Rice. Coconut milk. She avoided the fermented *okolehao* drink.

In accordance with tradition Kanoa rose from his pedestal seat and toasted her. "Ariel, tonight you are my child. We welcome you! We share this feast as many in a household. Welcome, my daughter!"

She conceded she'd have no trouble playing the role of a daughter. But what happened to brides who didn't live up to expectations on the third night?

The feast ended. The heated stones were taken from the *imu*, the underground oven. Kanoa waved his royal standard —a *kahili* brush made of feathers tied to a long stick. To Ariel it resembled a feather duster. The chief then escorted the women to the longhouse. After installing each wife in her cubicle, he took Ariel's hand. "Come with me."

"No, no! This is only the first night!"

He laughed with obvious delight. "Tonight, despite your eagerness, we only present you the gifts of a maiden."

She was seated on the woven mat on the terrace. Kanoa sipped from a cup of intoxicating, bitter *awa* drink. A procession of gift-bearers arrived, astonishing her with the lovely presents: a caged *koae* bird, very rare with its two scarlet feathers among pure white; a set of sleeping tapas, bed coverings woven together; handsome red berries from the lama tree—wood so hard it was used to build houses for the gods. Ariel knew these were given to favored guests who were expected to take them with them when they left.

"Now, let me escort you inside, my daughter," offered Kanoa, extending a swarthy hand. When she held back, he asked, mystified, "Why are you afraid? I can sense it."

She respected his island traditions just as she loved the legends. But it could not alter her dream of a far different future. "The presents are lovely. And well meant, I know. But this is all deception, Kanoa! I refuse these gifts. And I can't preside over the mele games tomorrow night! Certainly there can be no third night when I'm supposed to—" She broke off, embarrassed.

Kanoa took a torch from the bamboo holder and held it close to her face. "How prettily your white skin turns shades of gold and pink." He gestured toward the seawall at the top of the cliff. "Ariel, why not relax? You will find our Polynesian ways are not wrong. We make no iron or cloth, but we share happiness and music. We revere trees and sea and brothers and sisters. Why not enjoy life like we do?"

Ariel spoke thoughtfully. "Certainly your offer is generous. And your island is beautiful. But there are other islands in the world I find more attractive."

"And are there *men* more attractive than a chief?"

She did not answer. He pulled her close to his chest. "Tell me, girl. What do you find is my attractiveness?"

She attempted to ignore his many faults. She did admire his jolly sense of humor. And he ran his kingdom with justice. Yet she knew she must flatter his vanity and compliment his appearance. "You have lovely hair," she decided. "The dark curls against your brown skin are strikingly handsome."

"Ah, yes! Come and touch my hair."

She did as ordered, then stepped away.

With a sudden, unexpected motion, he swept aside his loincloth, exposing himself. Startled, she viewed him before realizing what she was seeing. "And this?" he asked calmly. "Do you find this attractive?" He pranced forward, holding himself for inspection.

Ariel looked past Kanoa, keeping her eyes fixed on the night stars.

Laughing low, he asked, "You do not care to pet my snake? You have no touch for his handsomeness? Look, girl! See the trick he performs? Watch him grow in his little nest!"

Ariel knew Kanoa would not break the rules of the three nights of desire. Tonight she was safe. Keeping her eyes high and her voice steady, she changed the subject. "The rich food of the feast has left me tired. And the fine gifts have pleased me greatly. I should like to rest now."

"Very well. The games begin in the morning, when the sunrise strikes the waterfall. The children play their contests by day. At twilight I will fight the ship's challenger."

"Whom has the *Pallas Maru* sent to oppose you?"

Kanoa snorted with disgust. "No one!" He pouted, honestly disturbed by the lack of cooperation. "Challengers are always welcome at the first night's feast. Yet no one came." He shrugged. "They have missed a fine meal." Then he grew solemn and angry. "If no one comes forth to answer tomorrow's challenge, then I shall take two of their young men by force and let them kill each other with *ao-dai*."

"Not the poisoned sticks! Mele games are supposed to be tests of skill—throwing, climbing, diving, wrestling." She waited a moment before taking her gamble. All evening she

had thought of the suggestion, but had not found the right
time to make it. "Kanoa, there is a certain man aboard the
Pallas Maru who could provide fine competition for you."

"Let him come forth."

"He is in the lower decks, held prisoner."

"Why is he kept there? Surely not to be hidden from me! It
is an honor to fight a chief!"

"Ricket Putnam has forced him into the ship's brig."

Kanoa nodded; there was no love lost between him and
Putnam. "Then the matter is simple. I will send for this man."
He took the torch from the holder to light his way along the
path. "What is the name of this fighter?"

Her voice shook when she answered and she wondered if
she were putting them all in worse danger. "His name is
Traver Loch."

Ariel could see nothing, but she heard the laughter of the
children's games the next day. Loki explained the evening's
ritual. "Tonight you are deferred to as Kanoa's sister. He will
escort you to the games. You must cheer for his victory."

Ariel nodded. She did not resist in the evening as she was
given a sedate ruffled gown to wear. The patterned material
was made from the bark of the paper mulberry tree and felt
pleasant against her skin. A wreath of scarlet, orange and
yellow lehua blossoms roped her neck.

When Kanoa came to call for her, he admired her silently,
then offered his arm to escort her. She couldn't contain her
questions. "Did the *Pallas Maru* answer your demand? Is
Traver Loch here? Did anyone come with him?"

Kanoa smiled, but gave no answer. He led her along the
path in a roundabout way, taking a junction which diverted
them away from the longhouses. They passed the gaming
fields where she saw the boundary lines for *mai-bolo*, cricket
and *jai-to*. Kanoa had collected games from every culture—
pente from Egypt, boomerangs from Australia, and the limbo
stick from the West Indies. The children's games of turtle
racing, chess and tops were in full swing.

"Where are we going?" Ariel asked as he led her further
into the jungle.

"We must visit the sacred waterfall."

"Why?"

"Tradition, Ariel. I thought you revered traditions."

She smiled wryly. "I've broken more than I've revered."

They passed a narrow, rocky turn. Springeri fern grew

overhead like lace. Kanoa smiled, "Dear sister Ariel, it is my privilege to take you into one of my six houses. My private *heiau*—sacred place—in the waterfall's path." He pushed aside banyan branches and escorted her to the side of a towering, misty double waterfall.

Ariel wondered if she might overpower Kanoa and flee. But she suspected palace guards were lurking within quick range. Sitting on a broad lava rock, she watched Kanoa capture mist from the falls between his palms. He bent and touched the ground, then dipped his hand into the pool and finally lifted his fingers open toward the sky. Ariel knew he was saluting the three principal gods, Ku of the land, Lono of the sea, and Kane, the supreme.

Twenty years of Elijah's books and preaching haven't changed Kanoa a jot, thought Ariel. He would have no trouble sending me to gather seaweed or weave braided nets to hold the calabash.

A conch-trumpet sounded through the twilight. "Aha, the games!" cried Ariel, anxious to return from the waterfall.

"Perhaps the ship's challenger has arrived," cried Kanoa, his excitement building.

"Yes, perhaps he has!" repeated Ariel, trying hard not to give away her hope.

They hurried back along the mossy path. Her fear for Traver renewed itself. What if he couldn't hold his own in this no-holds-barred, Lanavi-style fighting? What if he *wouldn't* compete?

At the edge of the game field, she scanned the area for him. He was nowhere to be seen. Perhaps he was still on the way. She took her place on the raised platform, sitting on the edge of the wicker chair. A Lanavi-style wrestling match was taking place on woven reed mats. In another game young palace warriors chased wild pigs.

Suddenly the conch shells were blown again and the gates to the longhouse grounds were thrown open. Every eye was turned to witness the entrance of the challenger from the *Pallas Maru*. Ariel stood breathlessly. Kanoa flung off his patterned shirt and hurried to the center of the main ring.

Traver! He was escorted into the ring by two tall guards. But no! Traver looked disoriented. Weak. Tired. He could barely drag himself along. The guards were having to support him, nearly forcing him forward and upright.

Ariel bolted from the wicker chair and ran to Traver. "No! Don't do this!" She realized she'd put him in danger needlessly. Certainly he'd try to defend her. His youth, strength and natural combativeness would lead him to try. But this was senseless. "Don't do it, Traver! You'll be killed."

His green eyes implored her to be silent. Before he could speak, Kanoa sauntered over, apparently having sized up the opposition. Kanoa jeered, "Is this the strong man from the *Pallas Maru?* This tired wreck?" Kanoa raised his eyebrows at Ariel, clearly implying she'd tricked him.

Ariel was nearly as upset as Kanoa. "This fight is not a fair challenge, Kanoa! Look—Traver is weak and hungry. He's been held below decks for weeks! His muscles are limp."

Kanoa questioned Traver. "Why would you attempt to fight me?"

"I took a vow to protect this woman!" Traver growled like a hungry tiger. A hesitant smile cleared his face and his green eyes twinkled momentarily. "There are times men do things they don't understand."

Ariel felt a fierce pride in Traver. Even under ridiculously unfair conditions, he'd make a try!

Kanoa's sense of honor demanded fairness. "Traver Loch, you must rest. Eat. We will fight tomorrow night." Kanoa glanced at Ariel. "It will be proper to have the contest and the taking of the bride on the same night."

Traver straightened his shoulders and flexed his legs. "I didn't come here to be mincemeat for your games. She's my reason for fighting. Make her the prize."

Ariel flushed with pride at Traver's boldness.

Kanoa laughed goodnaturedly. "So Ariel is your reason? And a pretty one, too. But you can sail away and find yourself another yellow-haired female." He scratched his belly, then leaned toward Traver, confiding, "I must keep Ariel for myself. But if you fight well, perhaps I will share her with you." It was the ultimate gesture of camaraderie in a society which shared fish, shell charms and wives. Kanoa laughed again. "Take Traver away. Ariel, too. See they rest. *Separately.*"

At the next evening's twilight Ariel heard noises on the seawall path. She ran to the cubicle window. Three men were on the narrow pathway, laughing, joking. Soon she could distinguish voices. Kanoa's. And Traver's curling burr. And Mitch's aristocratic lilt. They turned the last curve and came into full sight. Kanoa wore a brilliant cloak and helmet. Traver towered above the chief, looking well rested. And what was Mitch Galway doing here, striding along so sturdy and golden, his white gambler's shirt tied up with a black armband? Never mind; she was glad to see him. Perhaps he had some scheme in mind.

Kanoa stopped outside her window. "Woman! Prepare yourself."

"You sound like I'm a pig about to be baked!" she shot back.

The women gathered around Ariel, chattering and giggling. "Come along," urged Loki. They led Ariel along the path to the vapor spring where the mineral waters seeped upward through the lava, forming pools lined with sparkling obsidian and green olivine. "Soak and relax," advised Loki. "We will bring anthuriums for your hair. And a sheepskin to dry you. Would you like cocoa butter for scent? It is Kanoa's favorite."

Ariel demurred, trying to be tactful, for she rather liked the delicate, pretty Loki.

Loki sensed her hesitation. "You seem unwilling, Ariel. It is best to return a chief's desire." She beckoned the other dark-skinned women to gather around. "We will help you, Ariel. This, too, is meant in kindness."

Loki nodded. The women seized Ariel. Many hands, although soft, held her like steel bands. Twisting her downward, they dragged her through the water, flipped her onto her back on the spread sheepskin. Her arms and legs were spread apart. A scented cloth was held firmly over her mouth and nose. She held her breath as long as possible, but faded into a daze. Through the confusion, she could tell many hands were massaging her body.

Soft, unhurried, gentle fingers plucked at her, tensing her nipples until they budded tightly. The women spread the lips between her thighs. A cream was applied, smelling strongly of woodrose. She began to feel sticky, then hot. It seemed all the pulse beats of her body concentrated within her womb. Moisture stood out in sensitive areas of her throat, skin and breasts.

And the women's hands continued to knead, unrelenting, circling every inch of her body. They tied little amulets of spice and flower petals around her ankles. The smell of the cloth over her face changed to a honeyed odor. She was forced to a sitting position. White powder was applied to her cheeks and forehead. The scent of cinnamon, cloves, plumeria and ginger emanated from a large garland of flowers placed around her neck.

Now her head was clearing as they dressed her. But a languid, damp feeling remained. She rubbed at the white face powder. The women laughed and shook their heads, amazed that Ariel did not want to look her best. When she stood, she felt slightly dizzy. "I may fall asleep," she complained docilely as they led her back along the path. She breathed deeply, trying to fight her senses back to full activity.

"Sit here," decreed Loki, directing her to a rattan fan-chair. Ariel obeyed weakly. Then Kanoa, Traver and Mitch all entered the gaming ring. They bowed in her direction.

She tried to stand, could not, and settled for calling, "Be safe!"

Traver grinned. "Safe? Don't be ridiculous, honey lass! I intend to step in there and fight like hell!"

Kanoa and Traver stripped to loincloths. They stood in the center of the ring with the firelight torches shining on their bodies, a mismatched pair of opponents. Traver was tall, lean and muscular. But Kanoa, for his age and weight, had an aura of determination which made him formidable. Traver would have the advantage of quickness. But Kanoa had the power of experience.

The drums hushed. A far-off screech of a mynah bird broke the expectancy in the compound. The tradewinds wafted cooking odors of bananas and curry powder from the firepits. Kanoa planted his feet wide apart and ordered, "So, let the challenge be answered!"

What were the rules? Ariel could detect none. Traver and Kanoa ran at each other like rams, heads down, butting together. They fell to the ground, rolling over in the soft gray dirt, arm-wrestling one moment, jabbing with legs the next. Traver, as she'd hoped, was more daring. He darted and attacked at full speed. Kanoa held back as if gathering strength for a final, brutal blow to his opponent.

Suddenly she sensed someone behind her rattan chair. "Don't turn around," whispered Mitch. "Watch the fight. But while all attention is on Traver and Kanoa, escape."

"Escape?" It was a subject which had been on her mind constantly, but she'd been unable to work out a logical plan. "Where will I go? Back to the women's longhouse to await the victor's pleasure? Into the jungle? Into the clutches of Ricket Putnam on the *Pallas Maru?*"

Mitch whispered back, "Traver and I have a plan. You—"

His words were cut off by shouts which rose from the far side of the fields. The clamor of the danger gong suddenly filled the night air. A runner broke into the open, shouting. "The ship is leaving! The *Pallas Maru* is trying to escape. Sailors have cut the tidal net!"

"Blimey!" roared Mitch, forgetting all pretense of being quiet. "Putnam will leave us all!"

There was instant confusion. Ariel started to run toward Traver. How clever Putnam had been to take this opportunity for escape; all the islanders' attention diverted to the games, only a few guards at dockside. The fields were now full of racing men. "Traver!" she cried, losing sight of him in the melee. He jumped above the tangle of warriors. His mouth formed a single word, "Dive!" Then he whirled, raising his fists to do battle.

She ran for the seawall, dodging into the sheltering darkness of the heavy foliage along the precipice. Her body behaved badly; whether from fear or the earlier drugging, she couldn't tell. Clinging to a monkeypod treetrunk, she scanned the dark lagoon below, unable to make out boulders, currents or night creatures. This was twice as high as the Kalo Cliffs! And at night! She crept downward a few steps to a small ledge. Huddling, she listened for pursuers. No footsteps.

From far below she could hear the crash of surf against sand. Dive? She couldn't bring herself to risk it. But she would jump. Placing a hand behind her neck to protect her spinal joint, she bent her legs and leaped. The rush of air pulled at the folds of silk wrapped around her body. Then the crack of the water pounded at her ears. The ocean slapped, then sucked, opening up and pulling her downward as if to crush her. She slid beneath the dark waves, somersaulted and clawed her way to the top. Wide-eyed, she spotted dark boulders only ten feet to her left. Cold fear rushed through her with a tingle, instantly replaced by shocked heat in her cheeks. She must swim to the *Pallas Maru*. Surely that was what Mitch and Traver's plan involved.

The ship stood engaged in battle. Small boats surrounded the larger dark silhouette in the bay. Men with saws and axes were clearing the logs and nets from the *Pallas Maru*'s path. Fires burned at water's edge near the longhouse compound. She could see Kanoa's warriors putting into the water in outriggers. Terrible, high-pitched yells emanated from the hold of the main ship where the frightened Chinese blended their voices with the cries of the animals in the stable deck. There were bursts of gunfire, and smoke billowed near the stern. Already several of the anchor ropes were ablaze.

She kept to the darkness, swimming silently, diving beneath the surface at any unusual noise. Most of the fighting was confined to the starboard side, so she made for the overhanging stern near the port side. As soon as she was concealed she wondered how to get aboard. The davits were too high to reach. There were no convenient ladders. She noticed the open garbage chute, a rope trailing in the water for sluicing buckets. Climb through a garbage duct?

She took a deep breath and grabbed the rope, pulling herself hand over hand into the narrow passageway. She could tell it had recently been doused with dishwater. The smell was slightly sour. Rats? She moved on hands and knees, timidly. But she encountered nothing worse than a cabbage leaf.

Peering into the empty galley deck, she reached for a cook's apron to dry herself. A sudden jolt of the ship sent her toppling toward the pan rack. She steadied herself to avoid clanging the pots. Motion! Did that mean the log chain and netting had been shoved aside? Oh, hurry, Traver! Get aboard, Mitch!

The ship lurched again as she made her way to the descending ladder. The way of safety lay deep in the ship. The stable where Traver would come to do his chores would provide her shelter and security. She could hear fierce shouting from all quarters—Polynesian and English from above decks, Chinese from below. It sounded as if boats were being winched aboard the *Pallas Maru* as men struggled to get back aboard. She could only pray Mitch and Traver had reached the ship.

There was a rumble of machinery as she climbed downward from the galley. Engines? She knew, without doubt, Putnam would rush through the narrows, never giving a thought to anyone left behind.

Now the ship eased into steady movement. Men in the water screamed, "Wait!" Their shouts turned to curses as the ship gained speed. She scrambled down a second ladder. The stable smells told her she was close to her destination. A horse's loud whinny guided her around stanchions. Ducking through a narrow opening between bulkheads, she fell against the warm safety of hay. Slumping forward as the ship sailed into the narrows, she was torn between exaltation at having safely escaped Kanoa and horror that Mitch and Traver might still be ashore. The ship rocked as it moved faster. We're beyond the nets and the breakwater, she thought. There's no hope that anyone will catch the *Pallas Maru*.

Chapter 6

By morning's first light Ariel had finished her tears and was able to take stock of her situation. Traver and Mitch must have been left on Lanavi, or one of them would have found her by now. Two weeks to San Francisco! She looked around the stable deck. There'd be a lot of making-do for her to spend the voyage below decks. But she'd not throw herself at the mercy of Ricket Putnam.

She found the feed bins, lifting the round lids from casks of oats, barley, rice and wheat. They gave off a pleasant, dry smell, like a bakery. Perhaps she could boil the brown, husked rice for food. Moving carefully, so as not to alarm the animals, she passed the pens of ducks and sheep. Two gray and white stable cats mewed softly from the mountain of hay. She stopped and petted them. And there was Mitch's beautiful black Arabian stallion! She smiled as if she'd found a friend, stroking the horse's velvet nose, remembering the way she'd ridden behind Mitch that day on the headlands. Unbidden, the memory of Mitch's demanding kiss haunted her, too.

She turned away from the stallion, passed the cattle stalls, noticing she could have fresh milk to supplement the rice. In a tiny compartment she found a cot with a straw-filled mattress, a reading lamp in a brass bracket and an apple-barrel stool. Traver's living quarters? She rummaged through the sea chest. His basin, comb, razor. Clean sets of flannel shirts and white sailor's trousers. She clutched a set of garments to her face, hoping to recapture his scent. Then she put on the practical clothing, hitching up the waist with a length of hemp and turning the trouser legs into cuffs.

A sudden squeak of hinges alerted her to someone else in the stable. She hid behind slats. Peeking out, she saw a dim shaft of sunlight at the ladder opening. She held her breath in anticipation. Could it be Traver?

Then Mitch's black stallion nickered a soft greeting. Mitch's booming baritone echoed through the deck. Loud. And angry. His voice carried curses and dark threats as he issued violent orders to someone she couldn't see. Then a singsong, high-pitched voice answered. She started to reveal herself, delighted to know Mitch was aboard, then decided for the time being to wait, unsettled by his foul mood. She remained in hiding as he came into view—frowning angrily, his blue eyes harassed and ugly. His anger frightened her. This was a Mitch she had not seen before. An Oriental boy followed, nodding his head and chirping fearfully.

Mitch grabbed the boy by the shoulders. "Now, do these chores proper! Understand?" The boy nodded. Mitch continued to shout. "Hay for the horses! See? This is a pitchfork. Use it like this. Always stir and raise the hay from the bottom of the pile." Mitch went on shouting instructions. The boy nodded in nervous assent. Mitch seemed in a terrible hurry, barely brushing his hand across his cherished horse's nose. The stallion immediately sensed the tension and whinnied nervously.

Ariel felt new disappointment as Mitch bounded up the ladder. If Mitch had sent a Chinese boy to do the stable chores, Traver had not made it aboard! Ariel's hopes sank. Traver had risked everything to protect her. Now she would have to face California without him. She had only begun to love him—to know him—and now she was alone again.

She waited until she was certain the Chinese boy was alone, then edged out of hiding. This would test her skill with languages! She started safely, with sign language, motioning quiet. He looked up, startled. "Please! Don't run away!" she began in English, then attempted a bit of Cantonese, hoping it matched his dialect. *"Jo sun!* Good morning!"

He was surprised, but seemed to understand. She tried the all purpose cry for help, *"Gow manah!"* Then she panto-mimed hunger.

The boy giggled in shock, then spewed forth a torrent of language, much too fast for her to catch. He was quite young, perhaps eleven or twelve, with thin arms, bony face and a sweetly shy smile. He motioned her to stay hidden, then climbed the ladder. Surely he hadn't gone to report her! A few suspenseful minutes later she heard him return. Food! She smelled it first, then saw his offering of dried apricots, raw fish strips and a bowl of thick white rice. Barely murmuring the Cantonese for thanks, she gobbled ravenously. The boy stood by, looking proud, alternately smiling and bowing.

He motioned she should eat more slowly, but she couldn't stop. Now she'd be able to make the voyage to California without aid from Mitch or Putnam! Impulsively she hugged her new friend. *"Aw jung yee nei!* I love you!" He giggled with embarrassed surprise.

She helped the boy finish his chores. His name was Po Fan. His village was Wang Toi and he knew a smattering of English phrases, learned from village wall posters which recruited immigrants. Ariel asked him, "Are you going to work on the railroad?" She couldn't believe this frail child of twelve could lift a sledgehammer.

He nodded yes. "But also have sister go America." Slowly the story came out. His sister's name was Su Lin. She was a dancer—good enough to be recruited to perform at the Chinese pavilion of the Chicago World's Fair. "But she write no letter home," worried Po Fan. So he'd signed on with Putnam to go to America and look for Su Lin. "It is a brother's duty," he said solemnly.

"The United States is a huge land," counseled Ariel. She didn't have the heart to explain just how large the continent was and how small and frail one Chinese boy would be. She patted his arm. "I hope you find her."

When Po Fan left, Ariel went to the little compartment to brood. She had a small, stubborn hope that Traver might still appear. Then she remembered the anguished shouts of the men left behind, the burning ropes and the dark waters. She would cling to her hope that he was aboard, but it grew more shallow as each hour passed. For two days she told herself he'd turn up at any moment, but at the end of a week her thread of hope had frayed to a single strand. She resigned herself sadly to the fact that Traver was on Lanavi. Now she'd turn her hopes to California, finding a way to contact him when she arrived. She occupied several hours each day devising a plan to search Ricket Putnam's stateroom for her Hell's Candy certificates. Sometimes she hoped Mitch Galway would come back below decks, but then she remembered his dark anger and feared he might turn her over to Putnam.

As the days grew cooler and the ocean rougher, Ariel contented herself with her single friend, Po Fan. She tried to warn him, "California is a very large land."

"But no mandarin place," answered Po Fan, setting a supper dish of bean curd before her.

"That's true," she agreed.

Po Fan struggled to tell his story with his hands. "In Wang Toi, many mandarins. I have—" He gave up and hung his head, reverting to Cantonese, "—mien tzu."

She struggled with translation. Finally the little boy drew down his chin and turned his eyes sorrowful and submissive.

"Loss of face!" she guessed.

He agreed, "In California is no loss of face!"

Ariel was shocked that a twelve-year-old child was concerned with loss of face and mandarins. She worried anew how he'd survive the long hours and crushing labor of a rail gang. Putnam and his human cargo! Poor Po Fan probably wouldn't find Su Lin; after a month in Nevada's searing sun he'd be a carcass.

As she lay on her cot that night, she wondered what she could do to help Po Fan. Nothing. She was as much a hostage of Ricket Putnam as the Chinese. For several days she planned to ask Po Fan to help her search Putnam's cabin. But that would only put the child in more danger. Her quarrel was with Putnam. He'd denied her a father, stolen her certificates and abandoned Traver. She must have her revenge—she would not be denied.

By the twelfth day of the voyage she was aware that the creaking noises of the ship had increased with the swells of the ocean. The smell of salt and the cold air made her shiver. She pulled extra blankets from the sea chest to protect her against the night vapors. Huddled in the tiny cabin, she longed for the gentle warmth of Lanavi.

Abruptly she was awake. Someone was looming over her in the dark. She stifled a cry and scooted into a crouch. The man was bent over, his back to her. She heard him sigh. Then he sank onto the cot, bumping against her as she scrambled to get out of the way. In the next confused instant, he grabbed at her. One hand stifled her outcry, the other lifted her arm as he yanked her upward. Then there was silence. A whisper. "By the firth of Kee! Is that you, Ariel? Is that you, honey lass?"

Her astonishment was complete as she grabbed at him. "Traver? Traver! Is that *you?*"

There was a flurry of movement, then a gleam of tallow candle illuminated the cubicle. The flicker confirmed her greatest hope and surprise. "Traver! Where have you been? I thought you'd been left behind!" She stopped as she caught sight of a bandage on his wrists. "What happened to you?"

"That night we left Lanavi, I took a nasty scrape from the burning ropes as I hauled myself aboard."

She studied him with delight and concern. His coppery hair gleamed in the candle's reflective glow. The green of his eyes seemed almost black, the skin near his wrists as pink and tender as a baby's. She touched his hands. "But where have you been all this time? I was convinced you'd been left on Lanavi."

"And I was equally convinced *you* were back with Kanoa, honey lass. They've kept me penned in sickbay, out of my head at first, then to prevent infection." He flexed his fists. "But I'm fine now. I think they've kept me there the last few days just to keep me out of trouble! But I couldn't sleep there tonight. Too cold!" He smiled and pulled her toward him in a gentle embrace. "That first night, I considered jumping overboard and swimming back to find you." He laughed. "Not such a good plan for a fellow who swears he always wants to head away from wherever he's been!"

She wound her arms around his neck. "Oh, Traver! We *do* care for each other!" A sense of tender relief swept through her. "It doesn't matter how close we've come to disaster. We're together now!" She smiled at him with a new determination. She would never lose him again. "Is this what love is, Traver? This sense of risking everything and then being able to laugh?"

"Love?" The word always startled him. But he didn't cringe. "I suppose it has something to do with taking a chance. But this is more like . . ." He glanced at his wrists, then deeply into her eyes. "This is more like healing, what I feel for you, Ariel."

She raised her lips, eager for his kiss. "Darling, I have the feeling that together we can dare anything!"

He laid his cheek against hers, his scent strong and

masculine. "It's still a big risk you're taking with me, honey lass."

She felt like a child who had played too long in the ocean's chill current. Goosebumps sprouted along her arms and the nape of her neck. Cocooned in his strong arms, she nestled into the warmth of his chest. Again she felt his protectiveness, the basic goodness and simplicity in his nature. Her desire for him built like a fast-blooming tropical blossom. "Oh Traver, we're so lucky! We've cheated death!"

"This is our beginning," he agreed. "That day in the sea caves you were cheated of the best that can happen between partners." His arm encircled her waist like an iron band, lifting her against him until her feet left the deck. Curved together, he stood taut and tall, she slim and soft, as they drank of each other's kisses. She knew he wanted her, but not with greedy lust as in the sea caves. Now there was mutual understanding as well as desire in their ardent bodies.

As they lay down on the tiny cot, she felt the ship pitching instead of rolling. Suddenly there was a flash of white light. A noise split the sky. She clutched Traver in alarm. The rafters were creaking and she was afraid that the ship was breaking.

The streak of light was followed by an ominous noise. "What is it? Are the masts splintering?" She watched the ceiling overhead, waiting for something to sway and fall.

Using one arm to shield her and the other to steady the cot, Traver asked, "Have you never heard thunder?"

"Thunder! And the flash was lightning? I've only read of such things. The Sandwich Islands have silent rains that come straight down, noiseless and misty. Thunder! Oh, this is wonderful!" She clapped her hands, imitating the new sounds. Her ears strained to capture more of the strange experience. "There are so many things I've only read about! Deserts, snow, thunder and lightning— Oh, I hope there will always be new things for me to learn!"

He kissed her warmly, delighting in her adventurous spirit. "You've a wild heart, Ariel." He drew her to him again. "Let me hold you," he urged, snuggling alongside her on the cot. His heart hammered as they drew together. She felt him struggle for patience. "Now you will have to talk to me, Ariel. Tell me with your hands and lips and voice the things that please you."

He sounded so knowledgeable she was taken aback. "Traver, have you had many, many women?"

His laugh was hearty, as if he intended to boast like a common rounder. "Are numbers important to you?" There was a hint of defensiveness in his tone, as if she shouldn't hope to be privy to all his affairs. "You already know I'm not the settling-down type. No one-and-only steady lass for me. But which do you think is worse? Me leaving behind a string of one-night companions whose names I can't remember? Or a man who abandons a broken-hearted mistress? What about husbands who offer naught to a wife and keep a missy in splendor?"

She tried to understand Traver's philosophy. Numbers didn't matter? But how could she hope to compete with his past memories of such experiences?

While she was worrying, he stroked her hair and cheeks. "Now, Ariel, when I said you'd have to talk to me, I didn't mean a quiz on what's behind me. But there's no wife and wee ones hiding in the heather, if that's what's worrying you."

At that moment there was a rumble of thunder. She threw back her head and laughed. She returned his kiss and explored his magnificent body with her hands. Surprised, she heard her own breathing become heavy. She lay balanced against him like a fulcrum as he let his hands roam her curves. Pale sheets of lightning lit up his face. The bright hair. Deep green eyes. Tanned, lean face. The sensation of his lithe hips as they rocked against her thighs.

"What would you like?" he insisted as he removed their clothes and drew the blankets over them.

"I don't know," she admitted. "But I want to be able to move. Don't pin me down like—" She made an effort to shed all memories of the sea cave. She must be prodigal in her love. Lose all consciousness except that of the senses. She must learn to be shameless; the mating of a man and a woman was a part of nature. She would dedicate herself to surrender.

Her lips were waiting for his as he bent over her. His tongue tested her mouth, slipping in and out temptingly, sliding slowly across her lower lip. His hands cupped her hips. A flash of lightning showed his skin dappled ivory. "Let go," he urged her. "Act like the woman you really are."

His reassurance made her quicken. A softening and unexplained tensing swept through her. "Come with me, my pet," he said, rolling over swiftly so that he took her with him. He positioned her above him so she sat straddling his stomach, the blanket heaped around her naked shoulders. He leaned upward to kiss each breast, then her neck and throat.

She contracted her thighs around his middle, bent forward and let her breasts swing against his chest. She lifted herself completely above him, waiting.

"I'm not made of endurance," he urged. "Please . . . let me have you."

She quivered, then settled herself slowly over him. She felt her soft flesh collide against hardness, but this time, instead of sparks of pain, there was a rush of sensation like shooting stars. Suddenly she felt able to envelop him. Pliant as rain-smoothed grass, she was aware of pressure on all sides, insistent and softly throbbing. "Oh, this is a fine storm," he whispered, reaching up to trace circles around her nipples.

Moving slightly, she let her inner nature direct her. Her senses began to focus on her own delight. He pulled her forward to kiss her, and more comets of feeling exploded within her. Her breasts tingled as his hands kneaded her buttocks. Without realizing it, she began gently rocking to and fro, imitating the motion of the ship. She felt wonderful, all warmth and glow.

A crash of thunder urged her to move faster. His strong hands held her tightly to him, as if to keep them both in check, yet he whispered, "Aye, darling. Let your own storm break!" She strained for harder, surer strokes.

Then, swept beyond her own volition, she understood his lack of restraint in the sea caves. Now it was *her* hands which clawed his shoulders. *Her* kisses that demanded response. Her intensity which racked them both with torchlight heat. She saw his face beaming up at her as proudly as if he'd sung her praises. He pleaded with her again. "Let go! It'll be fine, darling!"

A last barrier dissolved. Lying on top of his glorious body, she rested a moment, then slammed down against him, tightening and sucking in her breath. There was a hint of explosion within her loins. "Oh!" Then she moved convulsively. A series of sharp spasms gripped her, sudden, unexpected, and overwhelming. His crescendo came close on hers.

She lay spent against him. She hadn't known such an experience existed, but she understood it perfectly. "It was like being hurled over a rainbow."

"Aye, you were a fine port in a storm." He laughed, hugging her tightly.

She was terribly pleased with herself. "Now I know why you couldn't hold back! It's like a bullet, spinning deeper and deeper and then passing clear through you! I felt blinded. Deafened. Like I'd been cut off from the world and was falling only into you."

He was delighted. "Now you know how good it can be."

She was thrilled, exultant. "Oh, Traver, it was like coming out of darkness and then washing away into brightness." She clapped her hands. "Like thunder! And lightning! Tonight I've learned that something else is as wonderful as thunder and lightning."

"As marvelous as all that?" He laughed without sounding conceited.

She giggled and stretched full length atop him, hugging him playfully. "Better than thunder!" she vowed. "Even better."

It was sheer folly which led Ariel to dance around the stable deck the next morning. Traver had returned to sickbay to have his bandages changed. Still full of joy at having experienced such a storm of passion, she darted over to caress Mitch's racehorse, petted the gray and white cats and quacked at a friendly duck. Wearing only Traver's soft white shirt, she stretched and yawned, feeling warm as a ray of tropical sun despite the chill of the morning.

She stopped at the stallion's stall again, leaned against him and stroked his flanks. She remembered how riding behind Mitch had stirred her. Now her knowledge was more complete. She now knew the origins of those tiny tinglings.

Suddenly there was the sound of heavy boots on the hold ladder. Traver back so soon? She couldn't take a chance. Darting behind the haypile, she dropped to her knees. She saw Mitch's glossy black boots drop the last two rungs. What was he doing here? He had not returned to the stable deck since that first day.

He seemed to have come to check his horse. He stood at the railing, talking to the animal. His voice was soft and his demeanor gentle. She crouched deeper in the hay, listening as Mitch murmured silly compliments to his fine stallion.

Then he suddenly leaned down as if to sniff the horse. "Hey, you smell as good as . . ." He swatted the horse's head playfully. "That was some ride, eh?" Mitch shook his head, then shrugged as if to put away a painful memory.

Suddenly he grabbed up the pitchfork. It clanged against the water cask as he grabbed the tool. Ariel panicked. She should have gone further back into the secure area. There was nothing to do now but burrow deeper into the hay.

She curled herself into a tight ball as the tines of the pitchfork whizzed through the air in front of her. A scoop of straw was lifted from the haypile. Stifling her fear, she went rigid against the dark, scratchy hay. Don't move, she warned herself. Don't shift one muscle. Don't cry out.

Despite her resolve she almost screamed when the thrust of the pitchfork just missed her foot. The tines tossed the hay, stirred and retreated. Damn Mitch and his orderly ways! She huddled deeper. The pitchfork sliced again. Her heartbeat echoed loudly in her ear. If the sharp prongs hit her, she'd be pierced belly to backbone by Mitch's sure strength.

Then the battle was over in an instant. The whiz of metal. A rush of air. An abrupt ripping of her hair from the scalp. A scream as the tines tangled against her skull. Mitch felt the resistance, heard the noise and pulled slightly on his pitchfork.

He cursed impatiently, then bent down to examine the hindrance. As he leaned forward on the handle, the pull against her scalp turned to burning agony. She reached out with both hands, grabbed the wooden handle and shoved. She jumped out of the hay, crying with fright. Through the flying straw she saw total surprise on Mitch's face. Then he tossed the pitchfork away and caught her with both hands. She threw her arms around him, instinctively grabbing for help in any form.

He recovered his voice. "The saints preserve us!" Mitch uttered a string of colorful curses, damning the harm he'd nearly caused, not Ariel herself. "Thank the Lord I've not harmed you." He let out an audible sigh.

Ariel clutched the sides of Traver's shirt, pulling it down over her thighs. She was still trembling with fright.

He muttered aloud, shaking his head while his hands soothed her shoulders. "You! On the ship! Down here in the stable deck. All this time! Hiding. Or—" A tiny line of anger creased the spot between his blue eyes. "Or has Traver been keeping you hidden? Has he been sneaking down here?"

"No, no! He didn't know until—"

"You with Traver!" Mitch roared. His face blanched a golden-white, and his eyes traveled over her with accusation and jealousy.

"Stop inspecting me as if I were your stallion," she ordered. She attempted to pull the shirt tighter over her breasts. Damn these long legs of hers! She tried to slip down inside the flimsy garment.

"No, no. Leave it loose," he teased. "I like it."

"Don't touch me," she said, with as much dignity as she could muster.

Mitch looked at her with chagrin. Gently he touched the sore, grainy spot behind her left ear. "Oh, Ariel, I'm sorry! Truly. My God, woman! How could you just lie there? I could have punched your throat as easily as your cornsilk hair."

"Now, what should I do with you, my pretty stowaway? I could keep you in *my* cabin, I suppose. Leave Traver to wonder why you disappeared so suddenly. All these days he left me to believe you were back on Lanavi!"

"He didn't know," she told him again.

She watched his eyes to see if he believed her. But they were cold as stones. Clearly he thought she and Traver had tricked him. Now she saw that same strange, complicated desire she'd seen the night he'd kissed her. The look that combined anger, passion and a need to avenge himself by hurting her.

She held his gaze. "Mitch, please. Whatever you believe, don't belittle yourself. Remember your friendship with Traver. With me. We must be close to the coast by now. Surely there'd be no harm in secrecy for a little while longer."

"If Putnam finds you here, my head will roll along with yours. But if I haul you up to Putnam, then—" He leaned back, thinking. With a cocky tilt of his head that sent golden hair dipping across his forehead, he said, "Let me find out if you're worth the trouble to hide. Come here. Give me a kiss."

She shied away, taut with wariness.

He sighed. "The kiss I took from you on Lanavi was like trying to tame a filly who still needed bridling." Suddenly he pushed her down in the hay. She lay sprawled at his feet. He stood towering and strong above her. "Oh, don't worry, Ariel. I'll not play in the haystack with you like some jack out to tumble a serving maid." He reached across the stable rack and picked up a small leather stinger. "When I buy a new horse, I always visit the stable that first night. I stroke the new mount firmly, lash him with this leather stinger, rub salt into his mouth and musk into his nose."

She stared. "What are you saying?"

"I merely let the animal know who commands him." Mitch

paused, passing a small, excited stream of air through his lips. "My actions are not cruel, but the horse knows who is in charge."

"I'll not call you 'master,' if that's what you're insinuating."

"A moot point if you wish to argue physical strength with me, Ariel."

She appealed to him. "Mitch, you're not a bad man. Leave me here!"

"What about my kiss? The one I *asked* for a few minutes ago. Will it be freely given? Or shall I take it by force?"

She stood up primly, stepped towards him and planted a sisterly kiss on his fair cheek. When she ran her tongue over her lips, she detected the faint taste of salt and ships.

He chuckled. "Making comparisons?" Before she could deny or affirm, he seized her, forcing her head back and lips open. "Then compare this!" he said huskily. He kissed her with coiled eagerness, as if to invade and choke her. She felt a dark confusion and, for an instant, she yielded to his overpowering sweetness.

Then she broke away and struck him. It was no more than a glancing slap, but his face gaped in amazement, as if this were the first blow ever to fall upon his flesh. He rounded his shoulders forward, bowed his head and shut his eyes, like a child on the verge of tears. She was totally unprepared for such a reaction.

As quickly as the unexpected hurt had assailed him, it passed. He pinned her against him savagely. "All right! We'll see who breaks first—in spirit or in body!"

She knew screaming was the worst thing she could do, but could not help herself. Her mouth opened and frantic cries for help poured out.

"Stop it!"

She screamed louder, oblivious to the slap across her cheeks. Po Fan and two other Chinese boys came scrambling down the stable ladder.

"Now you've done it!" Mitch shouted furiously. "You bloody fool! While I might have bedded you, I'd also have kept you hidden! Now you give me no option but to toss you to Putnam!"

She used her eyes to implore his mercy. But while Po Fan and the others chattered wildly in Cantonese, Mitch hustled her toward the ladder. "Please! At least let me dress!" she begged. He ignored her, boosting her up the rungs. He dragged her across deck, through the cloudy, windy open air, straight to Putnam's cabin.

Putnam leaned back in his swivel chair, taking in the spectacle of Mitch's barely concealed fury and Ariel's barely concealed body. If Putnam was shocked, he controlled it. With icy disdain in his voice, he asked, "Well, Galway, did you have her?"

Mitch's provoked baritone shot through the cabin, "I did not!"

"But you'd like to—that much is clear enough. Don't bother denying it, Galway." Putnam folded his hands, his black brows inching toward each other. "And how much will you give me for her?"

Mitch made an effort at disinterest. He shrugged. "What's a stowaway? She's mine by rights of finding her."

Putnam came toward her, pincer fingers working and sour breath hot in her ear. He slapped lightly at her barely concealed buttocks. "She's not sprung very wide, Mitch. She'll make a fine mount once or twice. But then she'll end up saddlesore and broke. Judicious use of a whip might prolong her usefulness."

Ariel salvaged her dignity by holding herself erect, eyes rigidly ahead. She abhorred the way Putnam was cruelly baiting Mitch. Yet she could tell Mitch was too smart to be trapped by Putnam's crude ploys. He braced his feet apart and folded his arms as if to defy the situation.

Putnam snorted, "We'll settle up about this chit's services later. For the moment I'm interested in that damned roustabout, Traver Loch. No wonder he was happy to loll all day in sickbay—creeping down at night to be nursed by this whore!"

Ariel defended Traver rather than herself. "He didn't know I was aboard! No more than you or Mitch!"

"Officer of the deck!" Putnam growled. "Have Traver Loch brought to my stateroom at once—in handcuffs."

Ariel tried to remain impassive, but felt the tears building up like an ache. Mitch's broad face glowered with dismay.

At the moment Traver was hustled into the cabin, Mitch stepped forward. "Enough of this, Putnam. Take the cuffs off this man. He's done nothing to warrant such treatment."

"Giving orders to *me*, Galway?" roared Putnam. "Don't forget whose employ you are in—and for how long."

Ariel saw Mitch's fists clench at his sides. Traver's tense gaze ricocheted from Ariel in the scanty shirt to Putnam's gloating features and back to Mitch's angry face. Traver confronted Putnam. "Whatever quarrel you have with me, leave her out of it."

"For the moment," agreed Putnam. "Traver Loch, you've cost me wages, you've been insubordinate and harbored a stowaway."

Ariel tried again. "He didn't harbor me! I swear it."

"Silence!" ordered Putnam, threatening her with a paper-weight from his desk. Suddenly he noticed she was shivering in the cold. "Cover this woman! Officer of the deck, give her your cloak."

The man complied, leaving Traver long enough to shed the gray woolen cape. Ariel accepted the coat gratefully, glad to be covered clear down to her ankles.

Putnam drummed his long stained fingers against the polished mahogany surface of his desk. He directed a haughty index finger at Mitch. "You, Galway—for your part in this charade, I assess a penalty. You're the blasted fool who signed Traver Loch on for this voyage. He's proved worse than useless. I'll have the sum of his wages back from you. You can pay it in gold or add it to the time you must work for me."

Mitch stood up to Putnam. "You vermin! I don't give a damn about wages or serving time, but I'll not see you unfairly use either Traver or Ariel. The affair is finished— she's aboard and we're twenty-four hours from land. Save your tirades and let us all get back to work."

Putnam ignored Mitch's outburst. "I intend to be done with Traver Loch as of now. I'll not have him in my employ even another twenty-four hours."

Ariel caught the brief, unmistakable flicker of warning that passed between Mitch and Traver. How would Putnam get rid of Traver?

Traver was quick to challenge Putnam. "You want a fight, Putnam? I'd be happy to oblige. I used to make twenty bob knocking men half-loony. But I'd beat you to a bloody pulp for free."

Putnam smiled menacingly. "You're a fine one for shouts and challenges. But it's your bold recklessness that's already sealed your fate." Putnam stood and motioned to the officer of the deck. "Call the quartermaster. Have a rowboat lowered. Set Traver Loch adrift in precisely fifteen minutes."

Ariel cried out in shock. Traver gave a startled gasp. Mitch managed an outraged oath, then added, "Putnam, you're a bloodsucking bastard. Setting a man adrift is the same as killing him."

The words drifted over Putnam like a wisp of smoke. Ariel sensed the futility of argument. The way to save Traver was not with threats or defiance. She must use cunning. "Wait," she said, stepping toward Putnam. "I'll admit everything."

She steadied her voice as everyone turned their attention to her. "It's true," she lied smoothly. "Traver Loch kept me hidden below decks."

Mitch jolted. "Just as I thought!" he muttered. Traver did not give away the story, though a look of puzzlement narrowed his green eyes.

"I was below decks—but not as a stowaway." Ariel raised her voice in accusatory tones. "I was a prisoner! Traver held me captive! Today Mitch found me and rescued me."

There were sharp whistles of surprise from Mitch, but no contradiction. Traver stared in total disbelief, as if unable to fathom why she would turn on him. Ariel turned to face Putnam directly.

He licked his lips and let his voice rise to a falsetto. "So Traver held you prisoner? And Mitch rescued you! What an imaginative story!"

Mitch tried to take control of the worsening situation. "Back down, Putnam. You can't throw Traver to the sharks. Besides, think about it. He's able-bodied now that his wrists have healed. He'll be able to work as hard as two men. Look at the strength in his hands and shoulders. Save him for the rail gang."

Ariel quickly moved to retain the advantage. "Yes! Work him to death for all I care. I don't care a whit for this Scottish stableboy." She brazenly moved to Mitch's side and took his hand. "I much prefer Mitch Galway."

She kept her eyes lowered as she heard Traver's sigh of desolation. He seemed to believe every lie she told! How could he doubt her so easily?

"You faithless tart! So it was Galway you preferred all along? You let me champion you at Kanoa's games! You urged me to protect you! And now you abandon me without the decency a sparrow-hawk gives its prey."

Traver's words cut her to the quick. She glanced up and saw the look of betrayal which clouded his face. He fully believed she'd turned on him. How could she tell him this was a gamble to save him? She was defending him with cunning the way he'd defended her with his fists. Perhaps he was acting his part? She consoled herself with this hope.

Now Putnam put a stop to all the games. "No more dramatics, Ariel. No more pleas and alternate plans, Mitch." He turned to the officer of the deck. "Take this man below. Cast him off."

The guards dragged Traver away as he spat angry curses—first at Putnam, then at Ariel and Mitch. Suddenly Mitch braced himself at attention. "I'll see to getting him gone. Treachery's best done with in a hurry!" He scowled at Putnam and strode from the cabin.

Ariel started to follow, but Putnam motioned the door guard to halt her. She caught a last agonized look at Traver being trundled down the ladder. How useless her speeches had been! How faulty her cunning! She strained her ears and heard wood creaking and the metallic grating of winches. The smell of rust and disuse wafted into the cabin as the lifeboat was sprung loose. She moved to the porthole. Her view was incomplete, but she took heart as she thought she saw Mitch hurrying along deck with oars and water. At least Traver would have a chance!

Then, from far off, she heard the plop as the boat became part of the foggy sky and swirling gray ocean. Clutching the latches of the window with both hands, she braced herself not to swoon. Sailors cast adrift might live for days, suffering deaths far worse than mere drowning. Hunger, thirst, seasickness, isolation—all took a toll until, crazed, the man attempted to drink sea water.

Putnam's dry voice sounded remote and unconcerned. "Are you a betting woman, Ariel? Care to wager which way he'll drift?"

As she stood silently horrified, Putnam answered his own questions. "The current will attempt to send him back to the South Seas. But we're within fifty miles of California. Even if he bucks the outbound current and hails land, he'll end up wrecked on the rocky coast."

Ariel let the tears trickle down her cheeks, no longer able to stop the swirling behind her eyelids. She blinked again and again, staring through the porthole at the murky water. Traver alone. In a tiny boat. Perhaps an oar and a bit of water. She spoke quietly. "I hate you, Ricket Putnam. Twice you have killed a man I loved." To herself she renewed her vow: *Someday I shall kill you.*

Chapter 7

Ariel was locked in Mitch's cabin. When Po Fan appeared with a supper tray, she and the Chinese boy whispered together. "Mitch man try to fix up the big red-haired fellow," Po Fan told her.

"The oars and water? Did he get them to Traver?"

Po Fan nodded. She felt gratitude to Mitch for easing Traver's plight. Perhaps there remained a chance for Traver!

Po Fan whispered again. "Tomorrow we go land-ho. But tonight—big trouble."

"Isn't everyone glad the voyage is ending?"

"They fear *Gum San Ta Fow*—the big city in the Land of Golden Hills. Must burn joss sticks to Queen of Heaven. Sailors no permit." He shook his head solemnly, again predicting big trouble below decks.

When he'd gone, Ariel wondered which was more frightening: trouble in the hold or facing a strange land.

Turning attention to her own survival, she rummaged through Mitch's belongings. His cabin told a lot about the man. He was practical. The sea chest held ropes, pin and bolt assemblies, engineering books, hinges and fittings. "And he's vain about his clothes," she murmured, inspecting fine woolen sweaters, jaunty striped neckerchiefs and silk shirts.

She borrowed a pair of straight-cut black trousers and a jumper with string tie as more useful attire than her nightshirt and woolen cloak. As a finishing touch, she tied Mitch's striped scarf around her hair, leaving the shoulder-length tresses loose.

Beneath the clothing, she found two items which intrigued her. One was a racing form from a Dublin track showing Mitch's black stallion the winner in the five furlongs. No wonder he had faith in that horse. The other was a daguerreotype of a woman and child. Mitch and his mother? The slim, haughty woman had Mitch's proud eyes. The young Mitch had a bowl-style haircut partially hidden by a jaunty hat with a feather. Even as a youngster he appeared dashing and impatient in knickers and vest. "Oh, Mitch!" She smiled. "What kind of man carries a picture of his mother to sea? A sentimental one, that's who!"

She jumped up as the door opened. It was Ricket Putnam. She couldn't bear to look at the man, afraid she'd lose her composure.

Putnam's voice chided her as if she were a servant. "Things are working out well for both of us, Ariel. I see you've finished sobbing over that worthless Scotsman. And taken to purloining gentlemen's clothes. Now, have you eaten?"

"I wasn't hungry."

"You must keep your strength. No one will bid for a sparrow who is all beak and bones."

She questioned him with her eyes, well aware he could do as he pleased with her. Her only salvation lay in not antagonizing him.

"I've decided," he began slowly, "that you're too valuable to let Mitch make a fool of himself over you. He's much too dangerous, thinking himself half in love with you! No, I shall dispose of you properly. I shall sell you on the Dupont Gai."

"What is that?" she asked, deliberately calm.

"Dupont Gai is the main street of San Francisco's Chinatown. An avenue of brothels, gambling basements, opium dens and barracks known as barracoons. A barbaric place, actually."

"Quite your style."

"There is always a ready market for girls on the Dupont Gai. With your light hair, dark eyes and silvery skin, you'll fetch me a handsome price, plus several singsong girls in trade."

"Singsong girls?"

"Chinese whores. I'll need several dozen tarts to service my railroad gangs. I try to keep Chinese girls for the coolies. Irish for the potato diggers. And a few Spanish, kanakas, Chileños, whatever. They say my crew of bastards can lay five miles of track and five kinds of whores in the same day!"

Ariel stood still, with nothing to say.

"Let me explain simple economics to you, Ariel," he continued. "I made an investment in Traver Loch and I lost. I have alternatives of course—collecting from Mitch Galway is one. Another is selling you to the tongmasters."

"I'd walk the streets of the Barbary Shore before I'd consent to anything you or a tongmaster have in mind."

"You will find the tongs have ways of forcing obedience," he told her harshly.

There was no knock at the door as Mitch burst into his cabin. "Trouble!" he shouted. His golden hair was flung back in waves, the blue eyes wild with distraction. "Trouble on deck. The Chinese are spilling out!"

From outside, Ariel could hear shouting and scuffling. Highpitched yells competed with frenzied calls from the crew for order.

Putnam started for the exit. "Mutiny? On the last night out?" He sounded offended, as if such behavior were unthinkable.

The shouting grew uncontrolled. From the jumble of shrieking and chanting, Ariel made out a few words. Trouble. Tongs. Great trouble. She remembered Po Fan's warning of difficulty below decks. She edged to the cabin doorway to watch.

Putnam and Mitch charged on deck. "Make a stand on the forecastle," shouted Putnam. "Galway, break out the weapons! Sound the alarm! Ariel! Take cover!"

This was the moment she'd been waiting for. She ran for Putnam's stern cabin, anxious to ransack the stateroom for her Hell's Candy certificates. Quickly she locked herself in the small room. Where to begin? She rushed to the desk, flinging open doors and drawers. Nothing. His sea chest? Bolted shut securely. The medicine cabinets? Improbable. She grabbed the handle of the drawers built beneath the bunk. The first held only clothing. The second was more promising. Papers. Packets sealed with wax. Books. Opium apparatus—poppy capsules, globular, egg-shaped dried buds, a small knife for incising and obtaining the oil. Pieces of the smoking lamp for boiling, straining, filtering and evaporating the product. A fragrant, gingerlike smell permeated the entire drawer. She shut it quickly.

The final drawer yielded more books, most of them stamped with medical titles. Then, deep in the leatherbound volumes, she spotted the Castle Factor's strongbox. There it was, intact and unlocked! She pulled open the lid, hardly daring to hope her papers would be inside. Yet there they lay, neatly stashed between layers of gauze paper. She lifted them out carefully.

Now that she had them, how could she hide them? Stuff them in her trousers? The heavy paper would crinkle with every step she took. Concealing them in the starchy jumper was equally unwise. It would be the first place Putnam would look if he became suspicious. She snatched the striped neckerchief from her hair, rolled the certificates into it, then quickly braided her hair, weaving the long tube into the plait as a fourth strand.

With the certificates securely pinned into her hairdo, she wrecked Putnam's cabin. Overturning tables, desk, chair, everything that wasn't pinned to the decking, she gave the stateroom the appearance of having been ransacked by the Chinese. She smashed the unlit whale-oil lamp against the bulkhead, then ran back on deck where Putnam and Mitch were shouting at each other. Neither knew what to do with the throngs of Chinese pouring onto the deck. Mitch fired a pistol into the air. It had no effect.

Ariel felt sorry for the Chinese, shouting and flailing, but with nowhere to go. She caught snatches of Cantonese phrases through the cacophony. "I could interpret, perhaps," she offered. "They sound scared—not mutinous. Let me find out."

Putnam whirled toward Ariel. "Do you think you can talk to them? Damned fool coolies!"

Mitch broke in, "You can't send her down there. She'd never get out alive." He shoved Ariel behind him.

The shouting grew harried and deafening. "Tell them to shut up," ordered Putnam. "Tell them I'll listen to their grievances." He offered her a hand to hoist her onto the rigging where she could be seen and heard.

Mitch fired three shots into the air as she gestured for quiet. Even as she explained in halting Cantonese that Putnam would hear their troubles, she knew she was engaged in duplicity. All Putnam wanted was peace and quiet aboard his ship until he could get his cargo to shore! She translated slowly. "They are afraid."

"Of what?"

"Chinatown. *Gum San Ta Fow*—the big city in the Land of Golden Hills." She repeated the words as Po Fan had accented them.

"Chinese afraid of Chinatown?" sneered Putnam. "Tell them not to worry! Most of them are going straight to Nevada—straight to hell!" He turned his back. "Damned coolies!" He spat at the deck.

"Do you know what the word 'coolie' means, Putnam?" she asked. "It means bitter work. That's the civilized translation."

"Find out what caused the riot."

The story was told in pantomime and shrieking. It was necessary to burn joss sticks to placate the Queen of Heaven before landing in the New World.

Putnam interrupted her. "Why do they keep yelling *'fan kwei'*? Why do they point at me and holler *'fan kwei'*?"

"It is the worst thing they can think of to call you—foreign devil."

For a moment Putnam reacted with terrible, unreasoning fury. "Rig the hoses! Wash these bastards into the sea!" Then he remembered his investment. "Oh, hell! They want to burn incense? For godsake, let them!" He paced in a tight circle. "But keep them quiet. Leave them on deck! All night. This cold air will take the heat out of the beasts. I'll offload them at first light. I'll not pay dockage fees for a load of swine." He smiled grimly, thin lips pressed hard together. "Master, make course for the harbor at once."

Despite objections of the sailingmaster to attempting landfall at night, Putnam persisted. The sailingmaster was overruled.

Putnam's next order was to Mitch. "Send for packing crates. Everything in my cabin must be secured tonight. Have coolies pack my furniture, books, personal items. Supervise it yourself, understand?"

Mitch gave a curt nod of assent. As he strode away, he cast a glance at Ariel. The sharp look said, "Be careful." She barely nodded in return. She was only beginning to understand Mitch Galway. He opposed Putnam when it could make a real difference, as when he'd given oars and water to Traver. Now, when it warranted nothing to defy Putnam, he'd been businesslike and obedient. She must learn cleverness from Mitch. Hadn't he said, "I only take a risk when I have faith"? A good lesson for the future.

She realized Putnam was speaking to her. "Get below. Stay in the quartermaster's office out of the way."

She nodded, marched away briskly and smiled. Putnam had no idea she'd searched his cabin. She touched her braid lightly. The secret was looped and knotted securely.

"The mainland! California!" Ariel strained her eyes through the hazy dawn to distinguish the jutting cliffs. Her eyes felt fevered from lack of sleep. But the view was rewarding as the fog rolled back from the soft green shoulders of the hillsides. The ship traveled through a turkey-neck narrows into a goose-egg-shaped bay. Perhaps Traver will drift into this very harbor, she prayed.

The city lay draped on hills to starboard. On the port side sat barren Yerba Buena Island. She studied the waterfront. Huts. Makeshift warehouses. Everything was made of wood. An old wrecked steamer was pulled up on land and renamed a hotel. Further inland she spotted houses of unpainted gray lumber or beige adobe. But on the highest hills she could see church spires, château-like mansions and brownstone offices.

The entire city seemed to march over the hillsides like a parade of wooden soldiers, each peeking over the other's shoulders. Perhaps one of those impressive granite homes on the high hills was Sonny Staidlaw's. She felt a shiver of excitement as she thought of nearing her destination.

The *Pallas Maru* sailed past the crowded docks, past the Hudson Bay pier, the Russian ships loaded with sea otter furs, the nests of clippers with marvelous names such as *Sea Witch*, *Stag-Hound* and *Flying Cloud*.

At eight in the morning the ship was tied alongside pier four on the Embarcadero. The Chinese, herded off the decks, were penned in a fenced palisade. The healthy men would be sent to Chinatown for rice, tea and a day's rest before going overland to the rail head in Nevada. Those who were ill would be booted out on the Barbary Shore to fend for themselves, easy prey for roving gangs such as the Sydney Ducks. Already, Ariel could see a crowd of men pressed against the palisade fence. They eyed the newcomers and issued taunts. "Go home, ye heathens! Paddy don't want ye here!" The voices were thick with brogues, an example of the recently arrived Irish displaying no love for those who came after them.

A policeman mounted on a bay horse patrolled casually. She ran to the bow of the ship, waved her arms and called to the officer. "Sir! You, there!" She cupped her hands around her mouth, hoping to be heard over the pier noises. "I want to report a missing man. He was set adrift in a rowboat!"

The policeman laughed. He made a great show of producing a yellow notebook and stub of red pencil. "Righty, miss. Now then, I'm set. Question number one: which way did the poor devil go?" The crowd roared with delight. The officer grinned, put away his notebook and rode off.

The first group of Chinese were herded up the street. Many tottered on unused, sea-weary legs. The crowd ran alongside, some using lassos to knock the feet out from under the stumblers. Again the Irish policeman looked the other way.

Mitch and Putnam moved onto deck, talking together with serious faces. Mitch nodded as Putnam pointed at Ariel, then gave further directions. Despite the activities of the previous night, Mitch looked surprisingly clean and dapper. His fancy broadcloth shirt was a bit too tight for his robust shoulders, but looked elegant with his navy blue trousers. He sported his pipe like a man-about-town. The harbor breeze ruffled his wavy golden hair like wheat in a field.

Putnam looked gray and sullen. He spoke sharply. "Ariel, I am not up to fighting with you this morning. Accompany Mitch without a word of protest, or I shall drop you into the bay for shark food."

She nodded yes and stepped to Mitch's side. Putnam's thin, impatient voice told her he'd make good on his threats.

Mitch and Ariel left the ship. Putnam shouted a last imperative. "Galway, don't forget your orders. Fix her up. See she looks healthy and ladylike. Then take her to barracoon number six on the Dupont Gai."

Mitch ducked his head in assent, then dragged Ariel by the hand across the dock. He seemed brimming with energy and eager to get away from the *Pallas Maru*. He set a pace along Front Street which she could hardly match. She complained, "Slow down! I'm not as fast as your racehorse."

"Keep up, Ariel! We must hurry. I've got plans for you."

Suddenly she was afraid he meant to take advantage of her. But she wanted to stay in his good graces long enough to enlist his cooperation. No one, including Mitch, was going to send her to the Dupont Gai! She must find Sonny Staidlaw.

She tried to match Mitch's fast pace along the wooden sidewalks. They passed a marine hardware store, a scrimshaw shop, an open-air fish market and a brass fittings maker. "Please, slow down," she begged again. "There's so much to see!"

He slackened his pace. "That's for sure! The town's grown into a city since I was here a year ago." He flexed his arm muscles inside the broadcloth shirt. "Bought this shirt last time I was ashore in San Francisco."

"And you've outgrown it," she pointed out. She urged him to look in the window of Roos Brothers Haberdashery shop. "Look at those elegant silk shirts, Mitch! Oh, let's go in and buy you a proper one."

He pondered, bulging arm muscles working up and down in his forearms as he rolled back the cuffs on the plain broadcloth. "You think I need some better duds?" He struck a pose of dignity, pipe in mouth. Behind his joking, she could see an aristocratic profile and poised manner. Mitch could easily be a man of grace and leisure.

"You'd be more of a gent with a proper fitting shirt," she answered. "One that covers your chest without tugging at the buttons. And a new vest would help."

He looked shyly pleased as well as vain. "What about my boots? Should I have new?"

"How much money do you have?"

He handed her his wallet. "It's bulging!" To her shock, she counted out three hundred dollars. "Mitch! Where did you get so much money?"

He hesitated. "Some's wages. Some's poker winnings. And some's Putnam's—to spend on you." Smiling, he took her arm as if they were about to enter a church. "I have to keep some to put my plan in effect. But we can each have a new outfit."

With almost maternal pride Ariel followed Mitch through the aisles of the haberdashery. He stood meekly, hands in pockets, nodding approval as she selected a white linen shirt with scrimshaw studs, a vest of patterned red hopsacking, black leather Wellington boots and gray trousers of good wool.

Mitch disappeared into the back room, returning minutes later with a beaming smile on his face and the clothes displayed handsomely on his body. Now he wanted every trinket in sight. "A flat-brimmed Alta California hat? Maybe a ruffled collar? What about a gold pocket watch on a striped fob?"

He purchased them all and Ariel could only giggle at his childlike decorations. "We want to make you a gentleman, not a swashbuckling conquistador." But, my-oh-yes, he was gorgeous! He strutted like a bird with new plumage, adjusting the watch ribbon, smoothing his golden sideburns, posing with half-narrowed eyes by the mirror.

When they were back on the street, he continued to admire his reflection in every window glass. When he spotted a women's ready-to-wear store, they repeated the fun by outfitting Ariel. New clothes! All the way from a lacy chemise of spun Egyptian cotton to a double-breasted blue taffeta gown with peplum and neck sash.

The sales clerk hesitantly offered the latest fashion contrivance: a bustle. Ariel and Mitch laughed together and she quickly rejected the cumbersome apparatus of wire and horsehair.

Again on the sidewalk Ariel was as silly as Mitch. They promenaded arm in arm, strolling slowly, turning their heads to catch every glimpse of themselves. Ariel bragged, "Oh, Mitch, we're a fancy pair for sure now! Beautiful clothes. A gold watch for you."

"No fish and cabbage for food! No Chinese chatter for noise." Mitch breathed deeply of the fresh air.

Her delight in the day was marred only by the circumstances which had befallen Traver. She pressed Mitch's arm. "I want to thank you for giving Traver oars and water. I understand what a gamble it was for you to buck Putnam. Not many men would even try."

In reply he put his hand over hers and nodded.

"Mitch, you are a fine man."

"Don't wager on that!" He laughed.

"But you must get away from Putnam! We all must!"

He squeezed her hand with power like a vise. "Don't make it worse for me, Ariel. I needed work. I wanted to come to America and stay. Like I've told you, I take a risk when I have faith—and I have faith I can work for Putnam and not lose my self-respect."

"But Putnam will try to keep you indebted to him forever. Adding to your time because of Traver is an example. Can he do that?"

"Probably," Mitch grimaced. "Serves me right, I suppose." He stopped walking and moved his hands to cover both of hers. "Ariel, all I did was try to befriend Traver. Remember that. And remember, that's what you did, too. You *befriended* Traver. You didn't love him."

Before she could demur, Mitch went on. "Traver got kicked around too much, too young. While I was sitting proper in church, or with my mother teaching me Irish airs or riding ponies across flowery meadows, Traver was fending for himself in alleys. A man must learn to take things, but Traver took too much. It was natural for you to befriend him. But you don't love him."

"Oh, but I do!" she protested.

"No. You wanted a man. Now you're trying desperately to believe Traver was the *right* man."

Ariel realized how her love for Traver threatened Mitch. She patted his hand. "Someday you'll find a woman who can match you—or at least one who can handle you. Then you'll settle down and be the proper gentleman I see lurking beneath your wicked grin and little-boy eyes."

"You're the woman who could work those changes in me, Ariel."

"What makes you say that? Why, we'd make each other miserable, Mitch."

"Don't you remember me saying I'd wait until you *learned* to love me?"

"An idle boast on your part," she teased, trying to return to the lighter mood. She removed her hands from his and proceeded along the street. His glum expression made her try to explain. "You and I made a wrong start, Mitch. Things happened on Lanavi I'll not be able to excuse. Or forgive."

Mitch seemed chastened as they made their way through the wide boulevards, up and down the tilting walks. Foreign voices and clothing of every continent made a gaudy spectacle.

"It seems there's no one in this land but immigrants," Mitch remarked. "For the moment I suppose I'm not much better off than those coolies we packed on the *Pallas Maru*. But I intend to stay put this trip." He grabbed a tethering rail and pointed at the hills with his free hand. "Look at all this! Someday I'd like to have a home here. Winters stay mild. Grass stays green for my stallion. More than that, this city has lots of work that needs doing. Railroads, bridges, buildings to be built. This land is new enough to risk body and brain putting down roots."

The thought of permanence lured Ariel. She could tell Iron Mitch Galway's roots would go clear down to bedrock in America. Not only would he take root, he'd thrive, pounding civilization as well as spikes into the continent. She felt buoyant again, as affectionate as if Mitch were her brother.

They walked three more blocks in an easterly direction. She realized Mitch had a sure sense of where they were going. "You're not taking me to the Dupont Gai to sell me, are you?"

His blue eyes flickered anger. "How could you even think such a thing!"

"No, of course not." Not for a moment would Mitch follow Putnam's orders about Ariel. This was one of the serious times when he'd defy Putnam. "Mitch, I need a favor. Help me find the house of Sonny Staidlaw."

He frowned. "Not a good idea. Not safe. There's only one place you'll be safe." He paused at the corner. "Right here."

Mitch stopped in front of a locked iron gate. The double barred entry stood between red brick columns two stories high. She shrank back. "What's in there? What kind of place has walls with spiked rods? And sharp spokes on the gates." She leaned closer to peer beyond the forbidding gates. "I'll not go in this gate! Not at all!"

Mitch grabbed her wrist as she turned away. "Steady, girl."

"Don't talk to me like a horse!"

"You don't listen when I talk to you as a woman!"

"Where are we?" Ariel stood on tiptoe, taking in the gray granite exterior of a large house. It was styled like a fort: square sides, a single row of barred windows at ground level, turrets at the corners. A lawn of gravel stretched to the gate like a parade ground.

Mitch pulled the bell rope.

Ariel panicked. "What is this place? A poorhouse? A work camp? An asylum? Mitch, for godsake, don't put me in jail!"

"This is Cleo Burney's home for wayward girls."

"No! I'm not a wayward girl!" She thrashed and squirmed, trying to pull away from his grasp. "I'll not be trundled into such a horrid-looking place!"

"It's only for a year."

"A year! God in heaven, Mitch! What are you thinking?"

"I'm thinking you'll be safe. Cleo Burney will take good care of you. And no one goes in or out of here except with her permission. I'll tell Putnam you ditched me and ran away."

A rotund, middle-aged woman appeared at the entry,

moved smoothly across the gravel, the wind billowing her black dress like a sail. She wore sturdy black shoes, a starched white widow's cap and a tiny white cameo as a breastpin. A long ring of keys jangled at her ample waistline. In her left hand, she clutched a billy club. Ariel moaned. "Oh, Mitch! Please! No!"

"Stay quiet, woman! I've gone to considerable expense and trouble to provide for you. Don't act hysterical!"

"I'm not acting."

Suddenly Mitch put his arms on her shoulders, not in restraint but in embrace. He pulled her to him in a swift motion and held her tightly against his chest. She could feel his heart beating wildly. His lips touched hers with the warmth of live coals. In that instant of seeking, she felt his heart leap as if to dance. When he lifted his mouth, he stared at her as if she had satisfied some deep-etched longing.

The key clanked in the lock. Cleo Burney's strong arm pushed the gates open only far enough for Mitch to shove Ariel inside. Cleo grabbed the roll of currency Mitch offered. "A year," insisted Mitch.

"A year," affirmed Cleo.

"A year!" wailed Ariel.

"Goodbye, Ariel," called Mitch.

"How could you do this to me, you Irish bastard!"

Mitch leaned through the bars, laughing. "Put your time to good use, darling. Learn to love me!"

"I'm learning to hate you! And I'm learning faster every minute."

Chapter 8

Ariel explained to Cleo for the hundredth time. "I spent years and years in boarding schools! I can't waste any more time. I'm of legal age. You must let me leave here."

Cleo Burney was equally insistent. She spoke as logically as a lawyer. "Your keep is paid for a full year. Therefore, it is a full year you must stay. You know by now I am scrupulously honest when I take a man's money."

Ariel nodded. Honesty was only one of Cleo's many good points. In the past month Ariel had come to see that Cleo was also goodhearted. She was a wealthy widow who had never had a family. Now in her fifties, she'd opened an efficient, benevolent home for orphans.

Cleo did not trust outsiders to help her. Instead, she assigned chores to the girls and did much of the work herself. Ariel noticed the strain lines in Cleo's forehead, the extra weight around the middle, the tiredness in her stance. Ariel liked Cleo—she just didn't want to live with her!

At first Ariel had been amused. A woman maternal enough to indulge herself in a ready-made family, Cleo hovered over her brood as if they were a flock of ducklings.

Despite the fact that the orphanage was called Cleo Burney's Home for Wayward Girls, most of the young ladies were much too young to have ever lived scarlet lives. A few had worked the streets or begged, but most were abandoned children. Ariel was the oldest; she'd been put in charge of music lessons. It was all too much like being the eldest scholar at Honolulu Academy.

Ariel followed Cleo as they walked around the courtyard during the afternoon exercise period. Cleo had divided the days into orderly periods of lessons, rest, exercise and recreation. Between times came seated meals with thick-crust pies, meat with fat and whole milk. Ariel had nicknamed her "Capable Cleo." And capable of keeping me here forever, thought Ariel. It was time for a new strategy.

"Cleo, if you went with me as chaperone, could I pay a call in the city?"

Cleo fiddled with the cameo she always wore on her simple black gown. "Upon whom would you wish to call?" She made a point of always using correct grammar.

"Sonny Staidlaw."

The mistress of the orphanage frowned. "Staidlaw? My child, he's the type of man who makes wayward girls wayward!"

"Then you recognize the name? You've at least heard of Sonny Staidlaw?"

"All California knows him." Cleo sniffed the air, looking like a plump blackbird with its head thrown back. "Staidlaw and scandal are synonymous in this town. He made a fortune in mining, and used it to build an empire of ranches and polo ponies. Now he's in his sixties, still going strong. He's building a tall building over on Montgomery Street. Bank of the West, he calls it. Oh, Staidlaw is a well-known name west of the Rockies. Nearly as widely known as Stanford, Crocker and Huntington."

"Then why can't I pay a call on him?"

"His name is well known, but it is not a proper one for a young lady to be bandying about!" Cleo concluded, "Your chances of visiting Mr. Staidlaw are exactly the same as your chances of leaving my care. Nil. The only time you'll set foot outside these gates is when it's your turn to help me fetch supplies from the auction house. When I bid on flour and lard, someone has to go with me. Those fifty-pound bags are heavier than they used to be." She fanned herself, red in the face from talking about the exertion. "If you stay on your good behavior, you can earn the chance to come."

"You really should hire someone to haul lard and sack flour for you," advised Ariel. "You work too hard."

Cleo shook her head; nothing could stop her from mothering her flock. "When it's your turn to go with me, perhaps you can see Staidlaw's house. But that's as close as you'll come, I promise."

Ariel appealed to Cleo's sense of fairness. "I also need to visit the harbor police. I know of a man who is missing from a ship. It's possible he made the California coast in a small boat."

"A lost sailor?" Cleo's face lit up with happiness, abundantly ready to help anyone in distress.

"He is someone I'm very fond of," Ariel said. "Please let me go to the port authorities and file a report."

Cleo considered, then jangled her ever-present wad of keys. "I'm sorry, Ariel. But it's a man's world. He will have to make his own way."

"Man's world!" Ariel flared with indignation. "Oh, Cleo, you can't imagine the things women could do—if they could get loose from places like this!"

Cleo laughed. "I know, child. Every generation's impatient. I won't hold you past the year's term."

The supper bell summoned the girls from the courtyard. Cleo hurried to supervise. Ariel lingered outside. When she heard noise outside the wall, she paid little attention. Then a man's shout erupted, followed by a woman's highpitched objection. The top rungs of a ladder appeared above the fence spokes. Ariel ran toward the commotion. The man's face poked over the fence, a shaggy, distraught, sweaty, middle-aged face. Thick arms followed. He was gripping an immense gunny sack. The burden wiggled and shrieked as if a dozen cats were tied inside. The man steadied himself, then heaved the bundle over the wall into Cleo Burney's territory. The sack landed, yelling all the while, on some prickly pyracantha bushes. With a loud curse, the bag toppled to the ground. The man disappeared, ladder clattering against the outside wall.

Ariel almost laughed. Someone had been thrown over the wall! She ran to the bag. "Are you all right?"

"Get me the hell out of here! Be quick about it!"

"Hold still. The rope is knotted."

The wiggling and cursing abated but did not stop. Ariel picked at the hemp, making slow progress until she used a braid pin. The rope finally popped and the top of the bag fell open.

Like Venus rising from the sea, a woman scrambled out,

holding her arms over her head and flailing her fists. Ariel's first impression was of a vivid painting with the colors all mixed together. Then she distinguished individual hues: purple shirt, yellow apron, green skirt, black boots, dingy white cloth purse and matted gray collar. The girl herself, perhaps in her mid-twenties, seemed equally colorful. Her eyes were violet flecked with opal. Cheeks of purply-pink clashed with bright red lips. Her shaggy hair was ebony here, tan there, and orange around the frayed ends. This total mess of girl reminded Ariel of a ragged patchwork quilt.

The girl jumped to her feet and ran toward the gate, bellowing, "Let me out of here!"

Ariel laughed as she ran after her. Another woman who wanted to leave! Now she'd have a partner—and a friend. She tried to calm the new arrival. "My name's Ariel Cortland. Welcome. I think we can be friends—"

"What do I want with a friend like you? I don't care if you're the Queen of Spain! Let me out of here! No one treats Nedra Timbergale like a sack of garbage! I'm a lady! A fancy and very grand lady!"

Ariel smiled, bewildered but amused. Nedra Timbergale more nearly resembled a sack of garbage than any grand gentlewoman. "Don't bother shaking those gates and screaming," confided Ariel. "I've tried that. Nothing opens those gates but the keys tied to Cleo's midriff. We'll have to find another way out."

"We?"

"Of course. Whoever you are, Nedra Timbergale, we have a common goal of leaving here."

Nedra disregarded the offer, bending over to swat dust from her boots in a most unladylike manner.

Ariel continued. "Together, we'd be almost tall enough to scale this fence."

Before Ariel could say anything else, Cleo bustled forward, delighted to have a new charge. "You poor dear-o," fussed Cleo. "Tossed over the wall like a dead rabbit!"

"I ain't a carcass! I'm a grand and highborn lady!"

Cheerful, compassionate Cleo tactfully refrained from laughing. "Oh, ladies are most welcome."

Ariel added a personal, heartfelt, "We're delighted you're here!"

During the next month Ariel and Nedra became good friends, though confidences about the past were all on Ariel's part. While Nedra stuck to her story of being a highborn lady, Ariel related her story of falling in love with Traver Loch, and the way Mitch Galway kept saying she would learn to love him. "Mitch has a lot to learn himself!" Ariel complained. "Especially if he thinks locking me up in Cleo's care will make me love him!"

"Then you still love Traver?" asked Nedra. The two were sitting in the music room where Ariel had finished the younger girls' choir lessons. "And you don't believe he was lost at sea?"

Ariel turned around on the rotating piano stool. To her surprise, she saw the sparkle of tears brimming in Nedra's flashy violet eyes. Why, I'm finally getting through to her, thought Ariel. This sad story of a person adrift moves her to tears.

But Nedra only stifled her emotion and blinked her eyes. "I have a lot of feeling for anyone lost," she commented.

Ariel didn't pry. She played a few chords on the piano, then improvised soft Polynesian tunes she remembered from Lanavi. "Hawaii seems so far away now. I miss its warmth and greenery—and music."

Nedra smiled, as if she, too, remembered a faraway time and place. "That's the first real music I've heard in years. Play some more."

Ariel pursued the clue. "This is South Seas' rhythm. Where did you know such music?"

"Not that song. But similar. With deep chords and a kind of sad excitement." Nedra hummed an eerie, melancholy tune, clicking her fingers in rhythm.

Ariel was fascinated. The music was romantic and spirited, but she couldn't identify it. Neither could she imitate it on the piano. "It sounds to me like it should be played on a violin," Ariel said to Nedra. She went to the storage cabinet and produced a violin. "Try this," she said, presenting violin and bow to Nedra.

Nedra pushed the instrument away. "I can't play this," she cried. Then, like a sudden torrent of rain, Nedra poured out her story. A child cast out of a decorated wagon. A little girl, ten years old, left behind at a river crossing. "There were always campfires. And at night the men played fiddles. What I remember most clearly is the music and the wagons rolling away across the river. That sound! Music and wagon wheels! I'll never forget that sound."

Ariel took a guess. "Nedra, you're a gypsy!"

"No! I'm a highborn lady!"

"Oh, yes, I forgot." Ariel shook her head, dismayed at the story of the lost child. "How did you survive?"

"I begged at a farmhouse. They let me stay a while. Booted me out when it came winter. I moved on to another family. And another. And another." She smiled as if she'd made peace with her past. "Actually, I like moving around. If I had me a proper wagon and friends, I'd tackle any new road. Oh, that's why I can't stay cooped up in this place!"

"We'll find a way out," promised Ariel. She handed the violin and bow to Nedra. "Take this and practice."

Nedra feigned indifference as she picked up the fiddle. But the next morning she burst into Ariel's room able to play a few simple melodies. With two weeks' practice she was playing quite unholy rhapsodies.

"It's gypsy music through and through," gloated Ariel. "And just look at you. Wavy, dark hair. Violet eyes. And the way you love to dress in every color of the rainbow."

Nedra put down the violin. "Let me see your hand, Ariel."

"Why?"

"I've wanted to, ever since you told me the story of Traver Loch lost at sea."

Ariel spread her hands. "My fingers are quite ordinary."

"No, turn your palm upward. The right one. Let me see the lines and shadows. I will tell your fortune."

Ariel held out her palm, fervently wanting to believe in Nedra's powers. "What can you see, Nedra? Is Traver all right? Did he make it to shore? Will I see him again?"

Nedra's bright eyes glinted with concentration as she perused the shadings in Ariel's hand. "Your first love was lost at sea."

"I told you that!"

"Don't interrupt. But he is alive. You will see him soon, although—"

"Although what? Hurry up!"

"Although he is your first love, he is not your true love."

Ariel ignored the cryptic statement and hugged Nedra exuberantly. "He's alive! I'll see him soon. Why didn't you read my palm sooner?"

"It was looking at the truth in hands that got me thrown over the wall into this jailhouse," laughed Nedra. "I told a man's fortune. And told him true enough that he had one wife on Russian Hill and another across the Bay in Oakland. He didn't care for my powers. Sacked me up and dumped me like trash!" Nedra arched her neck and stiffened her shoulders. "I ain't trash!"

"Of course not," comforted Ariel. "You're a wonderful friend. And if you truly want to be a grand lady, then I'll teach you more graces than the Queens of England, Spain and Timbuktu!"

To Ariel's shock, Nedra now dissolved into free-flowing sobs. Tears poured down her tawny cheeks. Ariel put an arm around the shaking shoulders. "I won't never be a lady! No man will ever want me!" Nedra bawled.

Why would Nedra weep over such an unlikely statement? So young, so pretty beneath all the layers of costume. Ariel made a rash promise. "I'll find you a man! In fact, I know exactly the right one for you, Nedra. Why, this is so brilliant I'll have to hang up my shingle as matchmaker!" Gently she wiped away Nedra's tears. "Here's the name for you to remember: Mitch Galway. He wants to be a fine gentleman just the way you want to be a lady."

"Mitch Galway?" Nedra tried the name. "An Irishman?"

"Oh, yes! And a good man, too. Well, a bit of a gambler and horseracer—"

"Oh, that's okay," insisted Nedra, quick to forgive. "What does he look like?"

"He's blond and sturdy, like a fine golden Palomino. His eyes are cerulean blue with long, long lashes. Oh, Nedra, just wait until you see Mitch's eyes—they used to turn me shaky inside just looking at them!"

Nedra looked at her curiously, so Ariel did not mention the time Mitch had kissed her. She hurriedly talked of other matters. "Now, all we have to do is get to Virginia City. Mitch is a railroading man. I'll make a proper introduction."

Ariel felt a trifle silly promising Mitch to Nedra. Mitch might not take to the colorful gypsy girl. But if not Mitch, then someone else; someone who would enjoy Nedra's spontaneity, charm and humor.

The girls left the music room and walked out into the chill afternoon, ready for the required exercise period. "Tell my fortune again, Nedra," said Ariel, dreamily. "Tell me again that Traver's all right and I'll see him soon."

But Nedra was out of sorts now. "Ariel, you're mooning like a lovesick calf!"

Ariel sat on the rim of the tiled fountain. "Please!" She clasped her hands around her knees. "I'm losing him, Nedra. I'm losing the bright memories. His touch like smooth silk.

His taste like a clean, young sapling. His arms like steel bands around me." She realized that her feeling for Traver had turned from one of loss to one of anger. Where she had once known quick, sweet passion she now felt a cold barrier to loving again.

At that moment Cleo Burney's strong soprano rang across the gravel courtyard. "Ariel Cortland! Hurry, child. We must take the wagon and pick up the flour sacks at the auction house."

Ariel was taken by surprise. She had presumed she would have some warning when it was her turn to help. "Oh, drat!" she whispered to Nedra as Cleo trudged toward them. "I'd planned to look for a way to escape! I meant to take along my Hell's Candy certificates and Sonny Staidlaw's address." She looked up as Cleo approached. "Wait a minute. I'll need a jacket."

"You'll be warm enough when we start hefting fifty-pound bags, Ariel." Cleo fanned her face in anticipation of the task, appearing weary and strained beneath her ruddy complexion. "Hurry, we must complete the trip before dark."

Ariel complied, not about to miss a chance to travel beyond the gates. In the streets the traffic moved slowly. "So many wagons! And they're so big. All going down Market Street. What's happening, Cleo? A parade?"

"Everyone's heading for Knoblock's Auction House. First-of-the-month bid time. All the big supply trains outfit at Knoblock's for the trip over the Sierras. Freighting with ox and wagon is cheaper than the railroad." Cleo glanced at Ariel with maternal concern. "Please remember to behave like a lady. Mind your manners and don't speak to any muleskinners."

Ariel admired Cleo's skill in managing the horses as she jostled the team among buckboards, pack wagons and freighters. She waved to another woman handling a team. "Good afternoon, Wise Ada!"

A short, wiry woman returned the greeting. The little woman appeared ancient, made of equal parts of tobacco juice and leather clothing.

Ariel was impressed. "Is *she* a freighter?"

"And making quite a go of it, I hear," replied Cleo, puffing with effort as she climbed down from the buckboard. "Folks say Wise Ada thinks of ways to transport freight that nobody else even dreams about!" Cleo handed a stack of empty bushel baskets to Ariel. "Now, you may look around in the auction house while I'm bidding on potatoes. I'll call you when it's time to sack flour."

Inside, Ariel found Knoblock's a wonderland, brimming with people and noise, marvelous smells and two-story-tall shelves of goods. There was a vast amount of merchandise—and not just staples. Gaslights. Potted geraniums with bright red blooms. Brass ashtrays. Wool braided rugs, oak wine casks, snuff boxes, caper sauce, peppermints and salt-and-pepper sets. Bins on the walls held potatoes, onions, dried fruits and beef jerky. There were tanned furs in piles that reached nearly to the tile ceiling. Ariel moved between tiered shelves of worsted material for clothing.

As she was admiring a bolt of bright blue cloth, she heard a voice from the end of the aisle. A booming, masculine voice with unmistakable curling sounds on the end of sentences and a lilt like morning sunlight. She crept to the end of the fabrics, following the trail of words, " . . . and oh, yes, roll me a case of that packing powder if you would, sir."

Traver. There he stood, his back to her, readily identifiable by his flame-colored hair, jaunty leather cap and gray flannel jumper. She stood transfixed, remembering Nedra's prophecy.

She must attract his attention without gaining Cleo's. Ducking down behind the cloth bolts, she reached out a hand and tugged Traver's loose shirt tail.

He whirled, fists raised. Always ready to fight!

She smiled at him without making a sound, shaking her head with wonder that he was really alive and healthy! Oh, he'd not changed at all. The same green eyes bright as jade, the dark fringe of hair at his jumper neckline, the marvelously muscled arms. She whispered his name, motioning him to be quiet.

But there was no need to warn him silent. He was totally speechless. He stepped into the aisle, then with wide eyes and slightly parted lips, he spoke her name. He touched her hair slowly, then her cheeks and chin. "They told me you were dead, honey lass!" Then, without waiting for an explanation, he captured her to him in a thrilling embrace.

"Oh, Traver, Traver," she cried hoarsely, memorizing anew the strength of his hands, the heady scent of his body and the feel of his auburn hair against her cheek. Then she pulled back. "Who told you I was dead?"

"Putnam! That bastard was the first person I saw when I

reached Virginia City. He told me there had been mutiny the last night on the *Pallas Maru*. Said the Chinese killed you!"

"That terrible man!" Her indignation at Putnam boiled anew. "But Mitch should have set you straight. He could certainly have told you I was alive—though penned like a chick."

"I've not seen Mitch. The railroad starts on the outbound end. I'm working in the pits in Virginia City." He lowered his eyes and voice. "Ariel, it galls me to admit this, but I'm back working for Ricket Putnam."

"Oh, no! You mustn't! You and Mitch must both get away from that evil monster."

"He owns Virginia City, woman. If you work at all, you work for Putnam. He controls everything—mines, water, the rail contract, even the Chinese laundry!"

She accepted the inevitability of Putnam. "But you're getting rich, aren't you, Traver? Taking your wages in claims? Digging a fortune from the bare earth as you promised?"

"Hardly." He pulled her further into the dimness of the sheltered aisle. "You can't imagine the hardship of the Comstock." Hurt dimmed his green eyes. "Ariel . . . the last day on the ship . . . why did you stand for Mitch and against me?"

"It was a trick—which didn't work," she admitted. She didn't have time to spend on misunderstandings. "What's important is that you're here and I love you!" She gripped his arms tightly. "Darling, how did you make shore?"

He boasted, "I probably beat the *Pallas Maru*. Hailed land south at Monterey, went overland to the Washoe diggings." Again the frown of concern blotted his dark, rugged face. "Men don't last a winter on those barren slopes. Women can't take the heat of summer. Children? Better off not born! Nevada is nothing but sinkholes and alkali desert. The sooner I can push on to Texas, the better I'll like it!"

She stopped his recital about the glory of Texas. "I'll come to you, Traver. We'll be together in Virginia City."

"No. Don't try it." He smiled at her and smoothed back her hair. "It's enough for me to know you're safe. You'd best stay here until I get the wanderlust out of my system."

"You're telling me *not* to come to Nevada?"

"You don't understand, Ariel. Nothing in the mining district is simple. There are big companies now, not grubstake operations. Silver mining means shafts, blowers, Howland stamps, reduction mills down on Carson water. There's hardly a foot of ground for a man like myself to dig a shaft—coyote holes they're called."

"Perhaps a one-man hole is no good, but . . ." She leaned upward and whispered in his ear how she'd stolen back her Hell's Candy stock from Putnam's cabin. "You won't need to grub in a coyote hole, Traver. The Hell's Candy is where we'll dig!"

"I don't think your certificates are worth anything, Ariel. I've not seen or heard of any Hell's Candy mine. It must be shut down or abandoned or the name changed."

She was disappointed to hear the Hell's Candy wasn't a thriving operation. Worse, she was saddened Traver didn't automatically plan for them to be together. "Don't you want me to come?" she asked shyly. "Not even a little bit?"

He looked past her. "You'd be better off to make a new life, sweet ocean dove." He cleared his throat, fingers drumming nervously on his pants leg. "That's what I did when I thought you were dead."

She realized he was making an important confession. But she refused to accept it. Her cheeks flamed with humiliation. "So our love is over and done?" she accused him angrily. "How can you be so indifferent to me? How can you say all that remains of feeling between us is standing here whispering behind bolts of cloth!"

He didn't respond to her challenge, simply remained silent, shaking his head. She took courage. Oh, he really wanted her to come! And surely he still loved her! He was only attempting to spare her the hardships of a brutal land. "My own darling Traver, quit shaking that red hair of yours. Your head is bobbing no, but your eyes and heart are saying yes." She flung her arms around him. "Don't you remember the way we looked at each other the first time on the ferryboat? The words we said in the sea cave? The meeting of our bodies that was better than thunder?"

He flexed both fists and beat them against the thick roll of material.

"What's happened to you, Traver? Where is your wonderful sense of adventure?"

"I'm barely keeping body and soul together, darling. Oh, Ariel, dreams die so damned fast under the shadow of Sun Peak."

"And that's reason to give up dreams entirely? All of them? The Hell's Candy? And the dream of us?" She reached out and pulled him to her. She poured her soul into her kiss, blindly trying to overcome all his objections. His mouth was hard, then passionately soft as a moan escaped his lips. An uncontrollable flare of desire washed through him, sending a quiver of unsteadiness to his knees.

When she looked up at him, he grinned. She almost swooned with happiness. That tiny grin with the nonchalant toss of his auburn hair, the mischievous wrinkle around his eyelids, the green pupils flickering with their old tenacity—all these things said he wanted her to come to Virginia City in spite of himself!

Ariel heard Cleo calling her to help load the flour. She moved in a daze, barely brushing Traver's hand as she hurried to Cleo. Everything was all right. She had her answer. Traver wanted her. He wanted her to come. In spite of himself.

Chapter 9

For weeks afterward Ariel talked of nothing but her meeting with Traver. "He looked wonderful," she insisted to Nedra as the two girls sat in the fortress courtyard in the August twilight. "Maybe a bit thinner, but the same devilish grin and sparkling green eyes."

"So you've said," yawned Nedra. "At least a hundred times!" She was attempting embroidery, alternately stabbing the needle into her finger and tangling the threads. "I'll bet I could describe that red-haired ox in my sleep. And don't forget the rest of the story. He told you not to tag after him over the Sierras."

"But he doesn't mean it!"

"A man who says stay away usually means it."

"His reasons are flimsy!" pleaded Ariel, trying to convince herself. "He's embarrassed to be working for Ricket Putnam. And he said he might not want to stay in Nevada. He's the type who doesn't stay in one place."

"A man after my own heart," sighed Nedra. "Lord knows *I'm* certainly sick of staying in *this* one spot." She threw down the hopelessly tangled embroidery.

"Traver must stay in one spot long enough to make his fortune," Ariel insisted solemnly. She sat silent, wondering how anyone could win in a town tied exclusively to Putnam's power. She wondered how Mitch was faring. And if frail Po Fan had found his sister. On sudden impulse Ariel spread her hand in Nedra's lap. "Tell my fortune again. See if Traver and I will be rich and happy."

Nedra had time for only a brief glance at Ariel's palm when a noise at the gate distracted both women. A wagon's metal wheels screeched to a halt. The horses neighed loudly. The driver stood up, shouting, then drowned his shouts by beating a gong.

Ariel and Nedra ran toward the gate. "Who in the world can it be?" cried Ariel.

Now they were close enough to distinguish the man's shouts. "Open up! Ambulance wagon! Hurry! This girl's hurt!"

Cleo rushed from the fortress, keys at her waist, billy club in hand, already perspiring as she trundled rapidly across the gravel.

"Open this gate!" cried the driver again. "Hurry, if you want this girl alive!" He stood upright in the driver's seat, looked over his shoulder and cursed. "For chrissakes, they're after us!"

To Cleo's credit, she did not stop to ask who or why about anything. She rattled the great wad of keys, the gate swung inward and the driver cracked his whip at the horses. It occurred to Ariel that she could easily have run away, but once again, when opportunity had arrived, she'd been without her Hell's Candy papers or Staidlaw's address. She made a silent vow to keep her valuables with her at all times.

The gates had barely been fastened back in place before two other wagons arrived. Metal wheels scraped against the curbing, causing sparks. The drivers were Oriental, flinging curses and threats in a dialect Ariel could not understand. Ariel whispered to Nedra, "Why would anyone chase an ambulance wagon? It must be someone very important."

"More fanfare than our arrivals, eh?" giggled Nedra.

Outside the gates the pursuers pounded and shoved. They threw loose stones into the courtyard, shouted and hammered at the padlock. Ariel laughed. "Look at that, will you? They're trying to beat their way *in* while we've been frantic to get out!"

"They're certainly hellbent on getting the girl in the wagon," agreed Nedra. "Let's find out who she is."

Hurrying to the canvas flaps at the rear of the ambulance, Ariel and Nedra peeked in to where Cleo was tending the new arrival. "Oh, no!" cried Nedra, recoiling in horror. Ariel stared at a young Oriental girl. She was in her mid-teens, as delicate as a budding flower, wearing a tight black cap pulled low across her olive forehead. She lay in a heap of bloody bandages, her arms stuck out stiffly from wet-slick redness.

Ariel swallowed hard and started to climb into the wagon to help Cleo. Suddenly the Chinese girl sat up. She smiled, lowered her arms and began to peel away the bandages. "Don't worry," she said pleasantly, in clear English. "It's only stage makeup—crimson capsules crushed with ginseng."

"What! You're not bleeding? Not hurt?" gasped Ariel, both relieved and confused.

The girl untangled herself from the pile of red sheeting, then stood up. Obviously she was not injured. Delicate, yes, but strong and quite graceful. She stood erect in a clean, two-piece, black pajama suit, bowed to Cleo, Ariel and the wagon driver as if she'd finished a performance. Then she began to giggle, thrilled to have pulled off such a stunt.

Ariel had been completely taken in by the act. Now she retreated. Speaking to Nedra, Ariel explained, "She staged it all. Very dramatic. And very real—especially those wagons following her."

The driver glanced around. "That part was too damned real!" he growled. "We nearly got caught by the tong boys!"

Ariel watched the driver's hand shaking as he attempted to light a cigar.

After he'd succeeded in calming himself with quick puffs on the cigar, she asked him, "Who is this young actress you've brought us?"

He shrugged. "A smart girl. And brave. The Hip Yee tong was all set to sell her inland. She took the fee, then ordered this ambulance wagon. When I arrived, she pretended to slit her wrists." He shivered with repulsion. "Aaagh—those bloody sheets! Damned good thing she paid me well to bring her here. I'll tell you, ma'am, I made racetrack speed when I seen them tong boys topping the hill!" He shook his head, smoothing bristly hair back into place. "Too bad the girl won't be safe here. A tong is a gang that never sleeps."

"She'll be safe with Cleo," said Ariel. "No one gets through this fortress!"

"The tong will be back. They'll get her," insisted the driver.

"Why should they?"

"'Cause they sold her as a whore. Two thousand they got

for her. That's a fancy price. A tong's not likely to write off that kind of investment. And don't forget there's some customer waiting who thinks he's bought himself a tasty fresh chinaberry. Bah, that girl would give some man a stomach ache!"

Ariel watched as Cleo escorted the tiny girl from the ambulance. The other girls gathered around. The Chinese actress avidly pantomimed the whole escape. Her movements were fluid and dancelike, her face marvelously expressive. Obviously she thrived on an audience; now she had a rapt one.

The driver complained, "I need to get this team cooled down and watered. Think someone can open these gates? The street's all clear now."

Ariel nodded and went to fetch Cleo and the keys. The newcomer had finished her performance. Now Nedra and the other girls were introducing themselves. Ariel joined the group after telling Cleo about the driver. A smart girl. And brave. Certainly that much was true. Ariel tried to remember the proper forms of Chinese greeting, but she'd forgotten most of what Po Fan had taught her aboard the *Pallas Maru*.

"Congratulations," said Ariel as she gave her name. "You're very talented—and very courageous."

"Thank you," replied the girl. "I have had to learn. I came to this land to perform at the World's Fair, but when I reached Seattle I was forced into a cattle car and shipped to San Francisco."

Ariel gasped; the story was familiar. Po Fan's sister! She grabbed the girl by the shoulders. "Is your name Su Lin? Is your village Wang Toi? Do you have a brother named Po Fan?"

The girl's dark eyes widened, then a happy chatter of questions poured forth. Yes, Po Fan was her brother! There was a quick exchange of information, Ariel giving the story of the *Pallas Maru,* Su Lin revealing how girls recruited as dancers had been kidnapped and made into whores.

"Your brother helped me," said Ariel. "He brought me food when I was hiding."

"Were *you* escaping a tong?" wondered Su Lin.

"What's a tong?" blurted Nedra, stepping into the conversation.

Su Lin explained carefully, head erect, eyes taking in the surroundings. "Tongs are like a guild. A labor union. A group of craftsmen. Some are artisans. But some are enforcers—

hatchet sons. The Hip Yee deals in prostitution." Su Lin shivered, as delicate as a butterfly about to be blown away in a strong wind. "They attempted to sell me to a thin, hawklike man who especially fancies young Oriental girls. He is a man who keeps girls for his railroad workers, but he intended to keep me for himself."

"Was his name Ricket Putnam?" cried Ariel.

"Yes! How did you know?"

Su Lin was exactly the type of graceful young woman Putnam favored. She smiled. "He once tried to sell me to a Hawaiian chieftain."

"But we both escaped him," laughed Su Lin. She took Ariel's hands. "Please—tell me of my brother."

"He has gone to Virginia City to work on the railroad. But his intention was to find you."

"Then I must go to Virginia City," said Su Lin.

Ariel knew the motives were proper, but the practical obstacles were stupendous. "In the first place, dear Cleo Burney won't let you leave here. Second, if the tong is after you, how could you be safe? Third, Virginia City is where Ricket Putnam lives."

Su Lin's courage and high spirits were not dampened. "I will have no trouble evading Putnam. I often go about in the disguise of a young boy. When I find my brother, we will simply fade into the Chinese community. As for the tongs, there are good ones and bad ones. If I can get to Nevada, I'll be safe. It is only the Hip Yee I have to fear."

"Then it's settled," said Nedra, taking the lead in organizing their futures. "We all want to go to Virginia City. Su Lin must find her brother. Ariel will seek Traver. And as for me—" she laughed gaily. "Ariel has promised me a fine gentleman when we arrive at the Comstock." She moaned and grimaced. "Right now I'd settle for a bearded fat man, if he had the key to those gates."

"Our chance will come," promised Ariel. "But we must be ready. Twice I missed escaping because I wasn't prepared. We must stay ready constantly." She smiled at Nedra's eager, devious face and Su Lin's dark bright eyes. "Su Lin, you must stay alert and healthy. Nedra, you must keep your wits about you. I will sew a vest with padded pockets so my stock certificates will always be available. Each one of us must keep her valuables with her at all times."

Nedra snorted. "Between the three of us, we haven't enough valuables to feed us for a day!"

Ariel added a new thought. "Don't forget my friend in San Francisco. A powerful man with a great house. I'm certain he will help us." She was slightly disappointed neither friend wanted to ask more questions about Sonny Staidlaw. She added, "Or, if we need aid, we can go to the police."

Su Lin and Nedra exchanged frightened looks. "No police!" they cried in unison.

"They're Irish," explained Su Lin. "They hate Chinese."

Ariel remembered the morning on the Embarcadero when the Irish policeman had baited the new immigrants. "No police, then." Mentally she added, perhaps no help from Sonny Staidlaw. She sighed at the future's mountain of obstacles. But she now had two friends. Brave girls. And smart. Together, they'd be able to dare the world.

Chapter 10

The tong threats began. A torn Buddha effigy, stabbed with a toothpick and smeared with foul-smelling grease, arrived in a package addressed to Su Lin. A letter came, saying that mandarin soldiers would harm her family in the Celestial Kingdom. Men marched outside Cleo's gates, holding red flags high in the air. Su Lin would not translate the threats painted in secret characters, but her almond skin turned pale and her eyes brooded.

Ariel took pride in Cleo's staunch defense of Su Lin. "I've dealt with guilds before," said Cleo. "The Triad Society and the Society of Heaven and Earth had real power in China. There they opposed the Manchus. In America they've become corrupt and fierce. But they'll not bother Cleo Burney's girls!" Despite feeling warmly toward Cleo, Ariel still worked on an escape plan. She sewed a vest with padded pockets to hold the Hell's Candy certificates. Sometimes she wore the garment atop her blouse, sometimes underneath.

But still no opportunity to escape arose. As Ariel helped Cleo in the storeroom, they talked about Su Lin and the tong. "How long will they pursue her?" Ariel asked.

Cleo, for all her idealism, was quite knowledgeable about the seamier side of San Francisco. "A month or so is standard. But Su Lin's a special case. Most girls come over thinking they have jobs. They borrow passage money from the tong—six hundred forty dollars. The girls arrive in America to find the jobs are fictitious. The loans are paid back by prostitution."

"Slavery."

"Roundabout. The tongs assess a girl four years indebtedness. Plus an extra month for every ten days she is ill." Cleo placed a basket of apples on a high shelf, huffing with the effort of lifting the heavy load. "The tongs keep accurate records. They know how long Su Lin's been gone."

"They'll keep trying to recapture her, then?"

Cleo's answer was muffled. Ariel turned to look at her and was shocked to see Cleo with arms outstretched and a silent, roundly opened mouth. Deep pain was etched on Cleo's face. Then she suddenly staggered, knocking over a bushel of potatoes.

"Cleo!" Ariel ran forward, grabbing Cleo's arms as the woman crumpled to the storeroom floor. Eyes fluttering as if they couldn't stop the lids from beating a frantic message for help, Cleo clutched her chest. Her skin turned ashen. "Help!" called Ariel. She cradled the stricken woman's head tenderly in her lap. By now Cleo was nearly unconscious. "Oh, Cleo, you were so good to me! So good to us all," cried Ariel, tears breaking through the dam of fear.

Cleo gave a faint gasp and slumped. Ariel called again for help, already knowing it would do no good.

Cleo Burney's funeral was held in the gravel courtyard, the hearse waiting outside the gates. The September twilight was cool and drizzly. Ariel, Nedra and Su Lin stood together with a thin canvas over their heads. The extra warmth of the padded vest around Ariel's chest was comforting.

When the service was over, the gates creaked open, admitting the wagon. The coffin was lifted in, the mourners filed past. Ariel and Nedra paused and walked on. Su Lin stopped for a moment. There was rustling in the covered section of the wagon. Then shouts. Two Chinese men leaped forward, seized Su Lin and dragged her into the wagon. The coffin was dumped on the gravel and the wagon lurched forward toward the open gates.

After a moment of confusion, Ariel didn't hesitate. "Kidnappers!" she shouted. "The tong!" She leaped onto the tailgate board of the wagon. Nedra ran alongside, then boosted herself aboard as the wagon rolled into the street.

The wagon rattled, shook and bumped, threatening to toss Ariel and Nedra back onto the street. They clambered toward the covered compartment. Inside, they found Su Lin, held with arms behind her, guarded by a young Oriental. In addition, a fat, almost white-skinned Chinese man sat on a folding stool, holding a pistol. He pointed the gun at Ariel and Nedra. "Sit down, ladies. No bribes. No barter. Simply be seated." He enunciated clearly, punctuating his commands with the pistol.

Ariel and Nedra sat crosslegged on the bouncing wagon floor.

When the wagon lurched to a halt, Ariel heard noises of confusion. Shouts and the nickering of horses. The young driver poked his head into the interior and explained to the fat man. "Friday night riot . . . the Dupont Gai is blocked."

"We will walk from here," nodded the pale, fleshy Chinese, indicating that Ariel, Nedra and Su Lin should have their wrists tied together with ropes. He smiled at the girls. "The Hip Yee tongmaster sent me for one. I have returned with three. Perhaps a reward will be mine."

The women were herded into the street. Loud pedestrians, Caucasian and Oriental, thronged the sidewalks, stalls and roadway. Jostled through the crowd, Ariel tried to spot landmarks or an escape route. Most of the signs were in Chinese characters, but a few were written in English. Blind Annie's Cellar was an opium den which catered to whites, promising "Pipes and Lamps Always Convenient." Another stall offered five taels of opium for eight dollars, insisting the product was the Patna variety from India, which would give the user neither skin rashes nor headaches.

"The joss house," Su Lin whispered as they were bustled under a canopied walkway. Red columns decorated the façade of the two-story building and a spiral tower adorned the sloping tile roof. Inside the door a market was in full operation, and odors of incense, eggs, fish and cabbage filled the air. As they were led down one set of stairs, Ariel knew they were passing an opium den. She glimpsed the walls black with smoke, the narrow cots and lamps. One hunched Oriental reached for a pellet, placing it at the end of the wire. Then he set it on fire, applied the bowl to the lamp and smoked.

At the bottom of the stairs, narrow passages led in all directions. Ariel tried to keep track of the maze of turns as they proceeded through the tunnel. The women were shoved into a single barred cell, one of many at the end of the tunnel.

The walls were peeling gray plaster, the floor clapboard. Su Lin pointed to a tray in the corner. "We are to be auctioned." The girls went nearer, inspecting the pile of garments and cosmetics. "It is traditional for a girl on the block to wear rice powder on her face. She must part her hair sideways over the crown and pull it behind the ears. The damask jackets and black pajama pants are required, too."

Nedra picked up a quilted jacket, then dropped it. "Not me," she vowed. "Don't look like the proper outfit for a highborn lady like me!"

The soft-bellied man with the desolate eyes stood outside the cell. He clapped his hands and spoke to Su Lin in Chinese. She whispered, "He is a eunuch. The inspector."

The man's voice turned soft like his flesh. "Su Lin, come here." She obeyed. He ran his hands over her body as if preening a bird's feathers. "You were sold as a virgin. Then you ran away. Are you intact?"

She nodded yes.

The eunuch lectured her. "It was severe loss of face for the tongmaster to have to return the buyer's fee to Ricket Putnam. Yet this night is fortuitous for you. You have returned, and your buyer is once again in town."

"What! Ricket Putnam's here?" burst out Ariel. She rushed to the bars.

"You know the man, too?" inquired the inspector with a slobbery smile.

Ariel shrank back and did not answer.

"The man often enjoys a day at the bay," the eunuch explained. "He refreshes himself at the opium den, selects new girls for the Sierras and settles his accounts. We will deliver Su Lin to him as agreed, provided she is up to standards." He unlocked the cell door, then motioned Su Lin into the dim hallway.

Su Lin managed to look dignified through the humiliating process of inspection. She stood erect, head held high, looking the man straight in the face. When she'd dropped the black pajama trousers, he whacked her thin buttocks with the back of his fleshy hand. He forcibly turned her to the wall, then yanked away the undergarment. Ariel could see blue veins quivering in Su Lin's thin legs, but her trim, muscled calves held steady.

"Squat," commanded the eunuch.

Su Lin obeyed, eyes focused on one spot of the ceiling.

The eunuch bent to examine the fragile girl. Ariel averted her eyes. In a moment she heard a whimper from Su Lin, then a grunt of satisfaction from the eunuch. He announced, "Su Lin, it will take a bonanza king with a long rod to break you! He'll get his money's worth."

There were noises from above ground as the inspector ordered the Chinese girl to get dressed again. Ariel detected the sound of rocks hitting brick, bottles breaking, shouts and cursing. "What's going on in the streets?" she asked.

"Usual Friday night mayhem. Paddy versus Chink," grumbled the eunuch. He locked Su Lin back into the cell. "Now I'll send for Putnam. He can appraise you two foreign demons himself."

Ariel pressed her ear to the outside wall. "I hear shouting close by. Gunfire. Breaking glass." The building shook.

Ariel hid her face as uncertain footsteps echoed along the maze. Then Putnam appeared, alone, the cell key held carelessly in his left hand. Stuporous, he leaned against the far recess. He massaged his temples, eyes unfocused. He was navigating poorly after his visit to the opium parlor.

Ariel whispered to Nedra and Su Lin, "When he comes over here, grab the key."

But Putnam stayed against the far corridor wall. Once he moved toward the cell, hands grabbing for the bars and missing. After crashing into the iron, he righted himself and moved back to sturdier ground. He tilted his head as if unsure whether the world lay horizontal or vertical. "Come to the bars," he ordered. "Let's see the merchandise."

Nedra faced him while Ariel stayed in the shadows. Putnam peered at the gypsy girl with wavering eyes. Apparently he was pleased, despite his haze. "Dark. Dark lady. Blue-black eyes and hair. The *Chileños* will like you, *señorita.*"

"I'm a grand lady," Nedra retorted. "Not a Spanish tart!"

"A *fancy* lady," he corrected, snickering. "Take off your clothes." He strained to make out the shape in the corner of the cell. "You, there. You, too—off with those clothes. Toss 'em out here."

Ariel crouched, pretending not to hear. Putnam growled his impatience. "Such false modesty! I'm not interested in your naked flesh at the moment. I only want to make sure you're not concealing weapons." He moved slightly closer to the cell, but not within reach. "You—the blonde in the corner. Move along, there. Toss out that blue vest."

Ignoring the order would only cause more trouble. Reluctantly Ariel shed the vest, making careful movements to avoid rustling the papers sewn inside the lining. Perhaps Putnam, in his bleary condition, wouldn't notice the irregular hand-stitching or the pockets which formed inside pouches. She handed the vest to Nedra, who offered it through the bars to Putnam.

He ran his hands over it, wadding it in half. The parchment inside crackled noisily. "What's in it?"

Nedra spoke rapidly. "Paper. Something to cut the foggy chills of this city."

Putnam shivered as if a sudden foggy chill had attacked him. "Certainly noisy papers." He doubled the vest again. "What kind of papers?"

"Private papers," hinted Nedra.

"Newspapers?"

She shook her head.

He asked, "Letter-writing papers? Tobacco papers?"

"Toilet papers!" Nedra exclaimed valiantly.

Putnam guffawed, frowning as if the laughter hurt his head. At that moment there were shouts close by in the tunnels. A sharp smell of smoke swept across the corridor. Footsteps echoed on the staircases in the maze. Putnam looked around, then moved down three steps, the padded vest still in his hands.

Ariel panicked at the thought of fire sweeping the locked cells. Should she call to Putnam? Reveal herself? The smoke smell grew stronger, perfumed with the sweet odor of joss sticks.

Inhaling the smoke seemed to rouse Putnam. He retreated from the stairway back toward the cell. The three girls moved closer to the bars. As he bent forward to peer into the cell again, Nedra and Ariel nodded at each other and thrust their arms through the bars, grabbing Putnam and crashing his head against the iron. He moaned, slumped downward and struggled only momentarily. Su Lin's quick fingers were already searching his pockets as Nedra's strong hands gripped him by the throat.

The key! In an instant Su Lin had the metal in her hand and had wrapped her slender arms around the outside of the bars. She unlocked the cell as dense smoke fumes filled the corridor. For an instant Ariel faced a terrible decision: here was her chance to lock Putnam into the cell and leave him to burn!

But even as she was debating the morality of such an action, Su Lin and Nedra grabbed her arms and started for the stairs. They left Putnam in the hallway, on his hands and knees, dazed but conscious.

As they emerged around the last twist, coughing, eyes watering, lungs faltering, Ariel remembered her padded vest. Too late now. She could not go back down into the barracoon! It would mean sure death. Perhaps Putnam won't discover what's actually inside the vest, she thought. Or perhaps Putnam and the Hell's Candy will go up in smoke together tonight.

The girls were now on the main floor of the joss house. The patterned dragon carpet was aflame at the edge. The front windows were broken, the red columns swaying, the litter of stones and glass extending far into the street. The battle seemed to center in the alleyway now. No one paid any attention to the three women running through the smoky lobby and into the Dupont Gai.

Once in the street, Nedra shouted, "Where are we going?"

"This way," cried Ariel, heading uphill as if to take refuge on higher ground. They ran three blocks, the crowds of shouting men thinning out, the smell of smoke and open market stalls left behind. Exhausted, they stopped. "Does anyone know where we are?" panted Ariel.

The women surveyed the street. Brownstone residence fronts. Small storefronts with produce stalls. "The only place in this town I can identify is Cleo Burney's," admitted Ariel.

"And the joss house for me," agreed Su Lin.

"The bawdy houses on the embarcadero," grumbled Nedra.

Ariel smiled calmly. "Then there is only one thing to do." She smoothed everyone's rumpled clothing and straightened their hair, feeling as motherly as tidy Cleo. "We're reasonably presentable. We'll pay a late evening call on Sonny Staidlaw."

Chapter 11

The Staidlaw mansion was easy to find, courtesy of directions from a horse trolley conductor. Yet when Ariel stood outside the gates at midnight, she felt intimidated. It was a huge house! There were Greek columns on the gray granite façade, and imposing windows on all three stories. The outside was forbiddingly ornate, not what she'd expected at all. She'd thought the mansion where her mother had taught the Staidlaw children would be sleek and somber. Suddenly Ariel felt timid about intruding on her mother's past.

But Nedra was entranced and not shy at all. "Hurry up and ring the bell," she urged. Then, as Ariel hung back, Nedra punched the chime.

The soft tones echoed within the house, and the heavy metal door swung open. Ariel's eager glance took in the enormous gilded entry hall, its ceiling decorated with clusters of white marble grapes.

A white-haired woman wearing a white apron stood in the soft glow which emanated from the gas chandelier. She was short and had a large bosom which seemed to keep her off balance. She tilted forward dangerously from the top of her body. "May I help you?" she asked, peering skeptically at the ragged trio.

"I've come to see Mr. Staidlaw," Ariel said in a small voice.

"And who might you be?" the woman asked. "I am Irene Haskell, the housekeeper. Mr. Staidlaw is not here. He is en route from Europe—which you would know if you read the newspapers." Her tone implied that none of the young women could read. She also seemed to doubt they had names. She patted her white, precise curls and locked her fingers together over her waist, letting the young women know she had no intention of admitting them.

Ariel did not know what to say next. "When do you expect Mr. Staidlaw?" she asked uncertainly.

"Within the week. But it's hard to say if he will headquarter here or at the ranch on the Palo Alto Road." She leaned forward, top-heavy to the point of having to readjust her footing. She confided in a low voice, "It is my opinion he'll stay at the ranch. He is so fond of those polo ponies!" She smiled with the fond indulgence of a long-time housekeeper who knows the master's habits better than he does himself. "Shall I tell him you called, miss?" She appraised Ariel a moment longer, adding, "I presume you have no calling card."

Ariel gave her name, knowing it would mean nothing to Sonny Staidlaw. Housekeeper Irene Haskell nodded, then disappeared inside the mansion, softly closing the heavy door.

Nedra sat down disgustedly outside the gates. "Now what? Are you going to propose we hike to Virginia City?"

"No," Ariel responded instantly. "I propose we hike to Palo Alto! Sonny Staidlaw was kind to my mother. I believe if he were here now and knew of my circumstances, he'd do me a favor."

"What kind of favor?" questioned Su Lin in a tone that indicated her wariness of any man's favors.

Ariel chose her words carefully. "I believe Staidlaw would loan us horses."

"Horse-stealing!" Nedra approved enthusiastically.

"I said a loan," Ariel reiterated sharply. "We shall have to walk to Palo Alto. But if we set a good pace, we can be there by dawn."

It was well past daylight when they reached the estate, identifying it by the black initials S.M.S. branded at intervals into the white wooden fence. "Beautiful," Ariel breathed, admiring the green rolling hills and wide meadows. "The grass isn't as lush, but it reminds me of Hawaii." A polo practice ring stood between low adobe barns.

As they crawled beneath a wire fence, Su Lin held back, frowning. "I don't know how to ride a horse," she admitted.

"You'll learn, Su Lin. You have to," Ariel told her.

Borrowing the horses proved to be incredibly simple. Ariel, Nedra and Su Lin took turns walking into the unguarded stable, lifting the stall bar and escorting out a horse. Riding the ponies proved more difficult. In the open the animals lurched and skittered. Ariel was the only skilled horsewoman. Her spirited mare reminded her of Mitch's Arabian stallion and the wonderful ride they'd taken on Lanavi.

Ariel longed to gallop and feel the wind in her hair, but the other girls had to be coaxed aboard. Nedra made a good show of sitting sideways on a blanket, acting like a lady on her way to a picnic. Su Lin was hopeless, alternately terrified and shrill. Ariel finally led the horse, instructing Su Lin to hold the animal's mane and be quiet.

As they rode along the dirt road, Ariel realized she'd make no progress toward Nevada with such a caravan. When they reached the village, she signaled a halt at the first livery stable. Ariel hailed a glum man busy at his blacksmith's forge. "How much will you give us for these three fine horses?"

He didn't look up as he wiped his hands on a leather apron. "You're on the dodge," he pronounced.

Ariel remained silent, not wanting to lie, but not wanting to get caught or return the horses, either.

The blacksmith's face was without expression as he said, "One twenty-dollar gold piece each, no questions asked. Plus a pigsticker for each of you from my own forge."

"A pigsticker?" questioned Ariel, not sure she wanted one.

"A knife," said the man dourly, moving closer to look at the horses.

"A dagger!" breathed Nedra happily, opening and closing her hand as if eager to hold a sharp knife in it.

Su Lin was the most openly relieved. "A gold piece for each of us and a dagger would get us to Virginia City faster than these . . . beasts!"

Ariel nodded. "Sold."

The blacksmith agreed. "You're not the first folks to try hightailing it out of Californy on Staidlaw's ponies." He moved to the shop where he counted out the coins and knives. "Staidlaw pays me double to buy back his horses!" He laughed heartily. "Where you pretty young horsethieves headed?"

Nedra brandished her dagger threateningly, riled at being called a thief. Ariel moved in front of her, answering the question. "We're headed for Virginia City, Nevada. Will the gold pieces pay for train fare?"

"Cost you those coins and more," the blacksmith informed them. "But if you're set on seeing the Washoe, you might talk to Wise Ada. She's packing down at the woodyard for a trip over the Sierras. Maybe you could work for her."

"Wise Ada?" Ariel tried to remember where she'd heard the name before. "Oh, yes! I saw that woman at the auction warehouse. She has her own freight team and wagon, doesn't she?"

The blacksmith nodded. "She's a *jehu*—a whip, a driver. Right now she's sporting a fifteen-hundred-dollar Abbott-Downing rig with red paint, and yellow wheels, pulled by oxen. Carries mail, baggage, freight and folks for ten cents a mile, with forty pounds of luggage free. No tellin' what Wise Ada will do! She has ideas for traveling around on God's earth that nobody else ever had!"

"She's at the woodyard?" asked Ariel. "We'll have a visit with her!"

They thanked the blacksmith and followed his directions to the woodyard. On the way Nedra flipped her gold piece, catching it in the air. "A grand lady like me needs a proper hat," she chimed. She veered off towards a millinery shop as if pulled by unseen hands.

Ariel sighed at such impractical notions. Then she moved ahead to find Wise Ada. It was not hard. The old woman stood in the woodyard, cracking a whip above the heads of a double yoke of oxen. "G—long! H—up!" She was no more than five feet tall, but bursting with authority and energy. Her coarse gray hair was cropped short, and her weathered face was permanently singed by sun and lined by wind.

Ariel hailed her. "Haloo, there! Wise Ada? A word with you, if you please."

The woman swung her whip in an arc. "That's me—Wise Ada. Ada from Decatur, county seat of Wise. Wise County, Texas, that is. Proud to meet you and proud to greet you. State your business." Her speech was made without stopping for breath.

"Are you hiring freighters?" Su Lin asked in a sweet, musical voice.

Wise Ada looked astonished, but stifled her outright laugh. She climbed down from the ox team, dusted her leather chaps and looked doubtfully at Ariel and Su Lin. "Freighters, are ye? Well, a good freightmaster makes eight miles a day. I make ten. I'm going to Nevada—sure as I'm also going to hell someday! This trip I'm taking only what sells, namely hundred-pound bags of leaf tobaccy and hundred-gallon barrels of rye whiskey." She shucked off gloves, then fumbled in her denim shirt pocket for a plug of tobacco. "You girls strong enough to tote hundred-pound barrels and boxes?"

Before the conversation could continue, Nedra came running across the woodyard, calling, "Look here! See what I found!"

All eyes turned toward her in alarmed fascination. Nedra now resembled an outlandish bird. She had a new feathered hat, plus an emerald green feather boa over her shoulders. Fringe and lace dripped from the edges of a bright blue Persian shawl. She'd probably spent her whole twenty dollars. As she came up to Ariel, she announced, "Now I'm ready to meet that fancy Irish gambler you promised me!"

Ariel despaired of making a lady of Nedra. And it was a cinch Mitch Galway would shy away from such a garish young woman.

Wise Ada snapped her fingers, then laughed. "I've figured it out! You girls are whores! Looking to cross the Sierras with a freighter as don't want his transporting charges in free feels of feminine flesh!"

"Watch your language!" sniffed Nedra. "I'm no strumpet! I'm a grand and highborn lady!" She wrestled the dagger from her waistband. "Swear you're sorry, you old crone!"

"I'll swear I'm amazed," laughed Wise Ada. "How's that?"

Ariel liked the old woman's intelligence and tact, as well as her native wit. "Can we sign on, Wise Ada?"

The wiry woman spat tobacco juice. "Bankroll you a blanket and beans. Which of you can handle a gun? Who's good with an axe?"

Nedra waved the knife. "I can handle this fair," she promised.

Su Lin offered, "I can sing and dance. Tumble and do acrobatics. At night, when we camp, I can perform. Men will pitch pennies to watch."

"I can tell fortunes!" added Nedra.

"God in heaven!" cried Wise Ada. "This is going to be

Wise Ada's traveling circus! A Chinese clown and a strutting fortune teller!" She turned to Ariel. "What's your trick, girlie?"

Ariel now felt unprepared to work with a freighter. "I was educated to be a teacher. Not much use here. But I can ride well. And I'll work hard for you, Wise Ada, if you'll teach me useful things—the things I'll need to know to make a go of life in the Washoe."

Wise Ada offered advice immediately. "Learn to play poker with a straight face. Learn that a washbowl's for sifting stream gravel and not for rinsing dishes. Learn to fight like a man and live like a dog." She thought a moment. "You're big on book learning, you say? Then you can trade me reading and ciphering lessons. I've a hankering to know things out of books concerning transportin' conveyances. There's a twist in my brain that says railroads is only the beginning of this country's moving about. Freighting with ox and wagon is about past. Engines, tunnels, balloons, sleeping cars—all that's coming. And mark my words, someday man will fly through the air!"

Nedra was unimpressed. "What'd be the good of that! Fly through the air? Pshaw, you're daft, Ada, not wise, talking like that!"

Wise Ada took no offense. Ariel was eager to strike a bargain and offered her hand. "When do we pull out for Nevada?"

"Be several days till I get the cargo all assembled," said Wise Ada, giving Ariel's hand a hearty shake. "In the meantime you and me will have some of them book lessons."

For the next three days they camped in the woodyard. Su Lin built a platform and attracted crowds of curious onlookers at night with her performances of "Butterfly on a Crimson Lotus" and "Dance of the Regal Firefly." Nedra soon earned back her twenty dollars and more by telling fortunes. Nedra reverted to living in a wagon as easily as if she'd never stopped. Each night Ariel fretted to Wise Ada, "I'm not earning my keep."

"Tonight you can," said Wise Ada. With a shy look on her wrinkled face, Wise Ada produced a leatherbound book from her satchel.

Ariel was astonished at the title. "You want me to read to you about submarines?"

"Yeah, them little cigar-shaped boats that move underwater."

"But why submarines? You're headed for the mountains with a wagon!"

"You never know how I'll be getting around next! Ariel, I'm a veteran of the Old Whiskey Trail from Coffeyville through Indian Territory. I've run the Kaw River to the Missouri on a barge. Caravaned into Santa Fe across the Cimarron cutoff. Did the Pike's Peak trip in fifty-eight and came out busted." She tapped her pipe on the underside of the wagon seat. "I'm here to tell you—rattlesnakes, gunslingers and bunco artists are the same this world over!"

Ariel didn't open the submarine book. "Tell me about Virginia City, Ada!"

"All hell breaks loose there every Saturday. At noon the railroads and the mines meet their payrolls. By two the payrolls have met the poker tables and horseraces. There's one young railroading fellow up there who's made quite a name for himself with a black stallion."

"Mitch Galway!" Ariel pronounced his name with eagerness. So he was making a name for himself, but he was spending too much time racing his black horse. He probably spent too much money on pretty clothes, too. "That man is so flashy on the outside, it's hard to see he's solid as granite beneath," Ariel sniffed.

"Why lecture me!" complained Ada. "Why does Mister Galway's name set you to fuming and blushing? Envy? Or shame?"

Ariel stayed silent, remembering the time Mitch had kissed her and made her tremble with sweetness. But she hadn't forgiven him for leaving her in Cleo's fortress.

"Never mind," sympathized Wise Ada. "Tell me why *you're* so hellbent on setting out over Geiger Grade into the roughest town in the West."

"Because it's not only the roughest, it's the richest!"

Ariel told Wise Ada the whole story. The Hell's Candy, the warning from Traver Loch to stay away, the duplicity of Ricket Putnam, the debacle of the padded vest with the certificates.

Wise Ada summed up, "So you don't know what happened to your papers? They could be with Putnam. Or lost in the joss house. Or in Virginny City with the old coot."

Ariel agreed. "I feel doubly bad about losing them—first, because Putnam is such an evil man. Second, that stock was my mother's gift to me. She earned it tutoring the children of Sonny Staidlaw."

"Staidlaw's a well-known fellow in these parts, Ariel. If you've lost papers he gave your ma, then he's the man to see about replacing them."

"He's on his way home from Europe."

"You should stay in San Francisco until you can see him." Ariel was unsure. "He may do nothing to help me."

"But Staidlaw's more of a chance than starting off to Virginia City where one man is your sworn enemy, a second has told you to stay away and a third sets you to trembling and turning pink."

Ariel could see the logic in Wise Ada's suggestions, but felt unwilling to abandon Nedra and Su Lin.

"Don't worry about your friends," insisted Ada. "They've got more native talent for getting along in a rough world than you do. I'll see them safe over the Sierras. We'll install Su Lin at China Camp with her brother. Her idea of a boy's disguise is good thinking. As for your gypsy friend, she's a born survivor."

"But I must go along and introduce Nedra to Mitch Galway," worried Ariel.

"God's help! You really *don't* like that Irish gambler!" cackled Ada. Merrily she whispered, "You better think again if you have visions of that butterfly gypsy settling down with a railroading engineer. Nedra's always going to have her wagon hitched to a distant star, not one set of tracks. She'll tell the fortunes of a thousand men and live in a hundred towns without ever calling any place home or any man husband."

Ariel smiled. "She's a lot like my man, Traver Loch. His idea of success is to be rich enough to keep a fast team hitched to a new wagon in case he wants to move on in the middle of the night." She reminisced fondly for a moment, hoping time had dulled the reasons for Traver's warning not to pursue him to Nevada.

Wise Ada called Su Lin and Nedra to the wagon for a conference. Both agreed Ariel must remain in San Francisco and talk to Staidlaw. Su Lin insisted Ariel should have her extra gold piece. And Nedra advised, "Use it to buy some decent clothes before you call on Mr. Staidlaw."

"I'll come to Virginia City as soon as I can," promised Ariel, hugging her friends. "I'll find you both!"

Back in San Francisco the next day, Ariel remembered their advice. She outfitted herself in a simple pastel pink cotton dress with looped skirt. There were tiny bright tassels along the fringes, but she rejected the bustle and horsehair

padding. She selected short white cotton gloves and a little
hat which perched perilously atop her smoothly woven blond
braid.

This time when Ariel stood at the impressive door of the
Staidlaw mansion, she felt more confident. The cheery, prim
housekeeper remembered her instantly. "Miss Cortland? So!
You've come back to call on Mr. Staidlaw?" She motioned
Ariel inside.

"I realize I have no appointment. But do you think Mr.
Staidlaw could spare me a few minutes of his time?" asked
Ariel.

"He arrived back only yesterday," confided Mrs. Haskell,
fluttering a hand across her mouth, tilting forward unevenly.
"Went to visit his ponies first thing, of course. Several of the
horses were stolen recently and only lately returned."

"That's too bad," murmured Ariel, smoothing down the
dress she'd bought with money earned from selling the horse
she'd stolen from Staidlaw. Feeling as guilty as a child caught
gulping an extra dessert, she changed the subject. "My
mother once tutored the Staidlaw children in this very house.
Her name was Leah. Leah Maguire Cortland."

Irene Haskell nodded her head. Obviously the name Leah
Maguire Cortland didn't register with her. "Those must have
been happy days, when the Staidlaw boys were young. This
house is so empty now—Mrs. Staidlaw dead these many
years, the boys grown, married and living in the East. I'm
sure it will be pleasant for Mr. Staidlaw to see you. If you'll
wait here in the foyer, I'll tell him you're here."

Ariel walked up and down in the great entry hall, admiring
but slightly awed by the opulence. A white marble pedestal
held a bowl of ferns and daisies. Simple and classic, she
approved. But part of the decor was overdone. Heavy metal
mirrors gilded two walls. Embossed doweling, painted in
greens and yellows, outlined the doorways. Ornate silver
sconces adorned the walls. Their candles were unlit, the light
provided by the overhead gas chandelier.

She wondered which of the many doors led to the school-
room. Had her mother's personal quarters been on this floor?
Ariel imagined the beautiful young Leah at ease in the
elegance of this house. It seemed strange for an intelligent
and vibrant young woman to trade San Francisco's excitement
for the tropics. The Staidlaw home must have radiated
glamor, brilliance and power. Why would Leah opt for the
disgraced Elijah Cortland and the isolation of Lanavi?

Ariel shifted her mental gears back to the present as the doors to her right slid open on magnetic tracks. A man stepped forward, an elegant, formal man in his sixties with a businesslike briskness in his gait. He was poised but aloof. He wore an immaculate dinner jacket, muted dark trousers and French-cut shirt. The only touch of color was the burgundy cummerbund around his full stomach. Ruddy skin, dark hair and a full dark beard indicated a healthy, hearty and still-handsome man. He took her hand. "Now, what youngster is this?"

"I'm Ariel Cortland," she began, wondering where to start the story. "My mother was Leah Maguire."

She did not have to speak further. Sonny Staidlaw dropped his reserved cordiality as he grasped her face between his hands. "Leah's daughter! Yes, I see! You're very like her—a beautiful dark-eyed blonde!" He shook his head, laughing. "Oh, no one ever forgets that combination of jet eyes and moonlit hair. Truly, you are your mother's image."

"Everyone who knew us always commented on how much alike we looked." She smiled.

"I'm sure," he said admiringly. The first hint of nostalgia crept into his voice. "First there's the bright hair and dark eyes, then the tone of voice, husky with energy and wit, then the way you talk with your hands in motion and head tossed back."

"Mr. Staidlaw, I fear I may have done wrong in coming to see you. Both my parents are dead. Your name is one of the few ties I have to my mother's past. And the stocks she earned in your employ are my only legacy." She apologized again for coming to call without an appointment. "I wish I had come to see you properly dressed and presented."

"Yes," he said abruptly. "It would be interesting to see how much beauty is hidden beneath that tasseled fringe and cotton flouncing." He rang a bell pull by the sliding door. Mrs. Haskell glided into the room instantly as if she'd been just on the other side of the door.

"Please direct Miss Cortland to the camellia suite," Staidlaw ordered. He turned toward Ariel, smiling. "You can stay in your mother's rooms. You'll find her things in good order."

"My mother's things? In good order? Why, that was twenty years ago! Why would you keep—"

"Twenty-one years ago. A little over that," he interrupted, then turned and left the room.

Bewildered Ariel followed Mrs. Haskell. Stairs took a full measure of courage for the housekeeper, the top-heavy half of her body threatening to keel her over.

Ariel tried to question the prim, short woman. "He said my mother's things are still in her room! After twenty-one years! Why? Is he . . . eccentric?"

"Of course. All men of power and wealth are entitled to their eccentricities." Mrs. Haskell negotiated the last set of stairs, then unlocked the camellia suite.

Ariel walked inside, wondering what possessions her mother might have left behind in this elegant house. Pastel blue wallpaper with bright pink flowers bloomed on the walls. There was a bedroom with adjoining sitting room, both with bay windows which jutted outward from inviting leather window seats. Everything seemed in order, as if the mistress of the rooms had merely stepped out. A cloisonné pitcher sat on a marble-topped dresser. There was a Chinese fan in a gossamer vase, textbooks in a leather binding case. In the armoire Ariel found floral chemises and petticoats with satin bindings, ball gowns and expensive lace daydresses. The garments were inappropriate for a young teacher, she thought, and much too expensive for a woman earning a tutor's wage. "What use had my mother for ball gowns?" she wondered aloud.

Mrs. Haskell hesitated. "The Staidlaws gave many parties in those days."

Ariel held a dusky rose gown to her body, imagining how it would feel to dance in it. "Goodness! I can't imagine why Mr. Staidlaw has kept all these things!"

"That's an excellent idea—not imagining too much," hinted the housekeeper. "Why not consider your good fortune in finding Mr. Staidlaw a kindly man, and not worry about the past?" She closed the door firmly, leaving Ariel alone with the questions.

Ariel avoided thinking of the mysteries of Leah's past. Happily she indulged herself, splashing on perfume, trying on the dusky rose dancing dress. It had a square neckline and silver threads spun through the bodice. The sleeves were short and puffy, with a bias skirt which hung in deep, inverted pleats. Ariel found white flocked stockings and black patent pumps for her feet, then tied a single white ribbon at her throat. She brushed her hair and left it loose over her shoulders.

When Mrs. Haskell brought a supper tray Ariel insisted she

couldn't eat a thing. The housekeeper's firm gaze immediately made Ariel pick up a cracker and eat it.

"Mr. Staidlaw wants you to join him in the billiard room," Mrs. Haskell said when Ariel had finished her meal. "Follow me."

To Ariel, the tour of the mansion was better than stepping into a castle. She examined three floors of finely outfitted rooms, full of framed mirrors, Italian paintings, silver moldings and beamed ceilings. A grand piano! Curio cabinets with treasures from every part of the world. Cupboards with silver serving trays, crystal wine goblets, leaded decanters. Heavy dark furniture, some in black lacquer with marble tops and Genoa parquetry designs.

The billiard room was on the ground level. Sonny Staidlaw stood by a rimmed table, a cue stick in his hand. He had changed to a smoking jacket of patterned velvet. The deep brown color enhanced his dark hair and beard. He took tortoiseshell framed eyeglasses from his pocket, which made him seem distinctly formal. Acknowledging her entrance with a slight nod of his head, he went on with the game.

"You have an elegant home, Mr. Staidlaw."

"Built by the mother lode. Gilded by the Comstock. I've never cared for this house, myself." He shot a ball into the corner pocket with a resounding snap of the stick. "This edifice—for it was rarely a home—has lacked life for many years. Since your mother left."

Ariel pondered his surprising words. He seemed sincere in saying he missed Leah. But twenty years! As far as Ariel knew, he'd never written her mother or attempted to find her after she left San Francisco.

Staidlaw crossed the room. "Ah, the dusky rose ball gown! I'm glad you've worn it. Leah looked equally beautiful in it."

"Then my mother attended your parties?"

"Certainly. And we danced." He held out his arms. "Like this." She rested her hand lightly on his shoulder. They made silent turns around the room.

Ariel imagined the past. Twenty years ago Leah would have been captivating. And Sonny Staidlaw, at forty, would have been at the height of his power and prestige. A feeling of warmth enveloped Ariel as she thought of the two dancing in the grand ballroom.

When the dance without music had ended, Ariel questioned Staidlaw about the Hell's Candy certificates. "I plan to go to Nevada and investigate the mine. It is my only real link with my mother—though you have provided another lovely one within this house."

"You are a young woman who likes to see things for yourself?" He smiled, but a cloud of dismay veiled his eyes. "Leah was like that. Going off to the tropics." He turned away, then added briskly, "I congratulate you on your ambition. But there's nothing to be seen of the Hell's Candy."

"What happened to it?"

"The easy silver was taken out in the late fifties. After the vein faulted, the mine was closed. Nowadays, it's only an abandoned, boarded-up hole in the ground. Unless you have in mind to reopen and dig deeper."

"I haven't thought that far ahead. I don't even know what you mean by the 'the vein faulted.'" She seated herself near the window, giving him full attention.

"Faulted means disappeared. Silver never follows a true course—much like love. Where the earth has cracked or buckled, a vein faults. Any place on earth where you find great riches of ore, you also find earthquake zones. In the Comstock the mountains wobble worse than a child's knees during a thunderstorm. The earth shifts constantly. No one knows when the silver veins move up, down, sideways or disappear entirely." He faced away from her. "It's no accident that the first three Comstock millionaires ended up a suicide, a crazed man and a cook in a poorhouse."

"When the silver vein faulted in the Hell's Candy, didn't you attempt to find it again?"

"We blasted in every direction. But we were at a depth where cave-ins begin. Did you know all Washoe sits on boiling water? If you dig deep enough, you may find silver, but you will certainly find hot water."

"Earthquakes, boiling water, cave-ins—I understand Virginia City's reputation for meanness now."

He leaned against the marble window sill. "I chased my share of legend around the lode. I've no interest in reopening the Hell's Candy." Suddenly he turned away and stared out into the foggy night. "I've no interest in reopening painful memories, either."

Painful memories? Of what? Or whom? Leah? He'd said little, yet Ariel sensed a dark mystery. She realized Staidlaw was staring at her. He said, "I see burning desire in your dark eyes, Ariel. You'll reopen Hell's Candy regardless of what I tell you."

"Would that be wrong? It's my mother's legacy to me. And from what you've said, the silver vein could still be there."

"It's undoubtedly there," he admitted. "With new methods of shoring the stopes, you might find it. Improved dynamite. Bigger pumps. Better stamps. Oh, indeed, you might yet find a bonanza."

She couldn't fathom the frustration in his eyes. "But you don't want me to try."

"I've paid my dues to Sun Peak." He took her fingers in a strong grip between both of his hands. "Ariel, the Sierra greed is like a fire. It took many years to burn out of me. I'll not risk starting the flames again."

Was he warning her to stay away? Or only speaking of long-ago disappointments which didn't involve her? Hadn't this lovely house been financed by such operations? "The Hell's Candy is my one stake for the future. I'd not ask you to be personally involved. But it would be so helpful if I could rely on you for advice. For example, are there ways of having stock certificates reissued? Mine have been lost."

"How did you lose them?"

"I was robbed." She told a quick version of her troubles with Ricket Putnam. "My certificates are in his possession, or they were destroyed by fire."

"Putnam! That nefarious beggar!" Staidlaw's eyes came to life. "So now he thinks to make trouble for the second generation! He will stop at nothing."

Suddenly Ariel remembered Elijah's warning: "Putnam can reopen wounds which began with your mother and me." Putnam, Leah, Staidlaw and Elijah were involved in ways she couldn't untangle.

Staidlaw warmed to the fight. "There are ways to outwit brigands whether they be highwaymen, stockbrokers, lawyers or vermin like Putnam."

"Then you *will* help me!"

"No. I'll not oppose you, but you must help yourself."

Ariel moved to the window, trying to sort out memories and ambitions. Staidlaw obviously had power. Charm and capability, too. Yet she felt a kind of tyranny about him. Had Leah felt this unreasoning strength? Had she left this house because of it? Why *had* he kept Leah's things for twenty years?

She listened as Staidlaw outlined plans. "Reopening Hell's Candy would be a gamble. Do you have the kind of high-stakes ambition it will take? The Comstock is like a poker game played for enormous stakes. Your first move must be to get into the game—on your own terms. Go to Virginia City. Ask Ricket Putnam to be your partner."

"Partner! He's my enemy! Surely you don't believe he'd give back my certificates for the asking!"

"Men do surprising things in the minefields. It's a game of stockboards and finance more than picks and shovels. Are you certain you can play in this gambler's game?"

She smiled, thinking Mitch Galway would have enough faith to take such risks. And Traver had promised to dig a fortune from the earth with his bare hands.

Staidlaw moved to the sideboard and poured whiskey into a shot glass. "In my day all one needed to succeed was a coyote hole, a broad-brimmed hat, red flannel shirt and two callused hands on a wide Ames shovel."

"My friend, Traver Loch, has a coyote hole," she said proudly.

"All he'll find for his backbreaking labor is a dab of dust."

"You sound as if you *hope* he'll fail!" she accused Staidlaw.

"I simply hope you and he will not repeat the mistakes of the past. Mistakes I made. Mistakes your mother made."

Suddenly Staidlaw was all business. "I have to travel to the East, but before I leave I'll determine the legal status of the Hell's Candy. You may have my remaining shares. With those, you can bluff Putnam into giving you financial backing."

"I can't take your shares," protested Ariel. "And I'm in no position to purchase them."

"They are a gift. Or, if you wish, consider them interest on a debt I owed your mother. A debt long past due."

She thanked him, wanting to shake his hand with fervent gratitude, knowing his offer came from deep emotion.

Staidlaw became quite hospitable, apparently finished with delicate maneuvers and painful memories. "While you are in San Francisco, consider this your residence. Mrs. Haskell will see to anything you need."

"Simply ring? Have the world served on a silver platter?" she asked ironically.

"You must dig the silver for your own platter," he laughed. "But I've warned you of the kind of game you're sitting down to play. Hold your cards until the other man has shown his. Hold your laugh till last."

"He who laughs last, laughs best? The philosophy is hardly original, Mr. Staidlaw." She watched his eyes, believing he had been a close-to-the-chest type of player who had taken immense risks. "I presume you were rewarded with your share of last laughs."

"Many of my laughs were at other people's expense," he acknowledged bitterly. "To succeed, you must be bold. Your actions are often justified, but they rarely make you loved. Be careful, my dear. Be especially careful of sunrise temptations."

"Sunrise temptations? How colorful! What are they?"

"A sunrise temptation is a time when your imagination runs wild. The moment when, after a long, dark night, the world suddenly turns cool and golden. It's an instant when you feel anything you do will turn out right. A moment when you'll risk everything. For you, Ariel, Hell's Candy is that kind of risk."

"Sunrise temptation," she repeated slowly, rolling the warm brilliant words off her tongue.

Staidlaw let his hand touch her hair. "I see an ache in your dark eyes. You want self-sufficiency as I did. You want love as your mother did. Don't let the sunrise stakes become a barrier in your life as they did in ours."

Chapter 12

Ariel spent the night in the camellia suite. Surrounded by Leah's clothes and books, Ariel felt close to her mother. Close to intrigue, too. She wondered about Leah and Sonny Staidlaw. Could they have been more than tutor and master of the house? She envisioned them dancing in the ballroom, Leah in the dusky rose gown, Staidlaw's dark beard nuzzling her mother's pewter-and-brass hair. The image of them laughing together seemed natural. Leah's head tilted back, her luminous dark eyes fastened on Staidlaw's handsome face.

Had the relationship had a darker side? Oh, for godsake, say the word, Ariel told herself. *Mistress.* She bit her lip as she thought, *Could my mother have been Sonny Staidlaw's mistress?* She giggled and looked around the bedroom. *There. I said it, and the walls didn't come crumbling down!* She imagined Leah and Sonny standing at the bay window, locked in each other's embrace. The image was forceful, compelling and, above all, believable. Perhaps Leah was *his* sunrise temptation, she thought. A brief, golden moment of risk; a time when, carried away, he lost judgment and control. She smiled, remembering Traver Loch as her sunrise temptation, the man for whom she'd risked everything. I must find Traver again! she vowed fervently.

She paced the room for more than an hour, then fell asleep crosswise on top of the bed. But her sleep was tormented with images far more vivid than the mere embrace she'd pictured at the window. It was a dream in which she saw Leah and Sonny engaged in lovemaking. And it was lovemaking, not seduction or resistance or bribery.

In the dream Ariel saw Staidlaw, dark and commanding. He entered the suite, scooped Leah into his arms and carried her to a corner of the bedroom. Leah smiled with delight. He devoured her mouth urgently; her response was open and joyous.

They fell together on the bed, wrestling each other for garments and kisses. Leah gave a tiny, involuntary flinch as he touched her bare breasts. He grew long and hard beneath her strokes. Kneeling above her, Sonny touched her hair, eyelids, lips, until she trembled with desire. Leah invited him by raising her body toward his. He slid inside with a rush like spring rain.

"Move with me," he commanded, dark beard nuzzled against Leah's ear. She secured her legs around his thighs, hooking her ankles into the back of his knees. They rocked like a swing pushed by the wind.

Leah seemed to retreat, nudging at Sonny with her hands, her legs stiffening outward. He said, "I'm too heavy. You're as dainty as these camellia blossoms on the walls." Without a word he lifted her, cushioning her body with wide hands placed beneath her hips. She leaned against the headboard, golden hair tossed back over naked shoulders. Face to face, they locked in an embrace, thighs rippling with tension.

Sonny leaned back slightly, using his hands to guide her to him. Her breasts swung against his chest and grew rosy, dark and taut.

Suddenly the man in the dream was transformed. He turned toward Ariel and his face was not Sonny Staidlaw's, but one which haunted her with longing. Eyes of deepest blue like the still waters of the ocean's tidal pool. Golden side-burns like the glint of sunlight on coral. A smile of desire and acceptance. Mitch! Even in her dream, Ariel felt a deep intake of breath.

"Kiss me, Ariel," demanded Mitch. She obeyed the command, opening her soul to him.

"Now we can never be apart," he murmured. "You and I are two sides of the same coin, two images from the same mirror."

Then the images dissolved again into Leah and Sonny. They stood, dark and shining, balanced forward, cupped and joined in bodily union. Leah moved against him willingly as the spasms broke through them both.

Ariel awoke, overwhelmed that her imagination had provided such intimate sights. The ache in her own flesh was exquisitely real. So vivid! Every detail of their bodies had seemed real, the smell of dampness, the noise of their ardent breathing. The dream vibrated in her mind as she sat upright in her mother's bed, a hand over her mouth. "It was *only* a dream!" she breathed.

She glanced at the window, sunlight streaming through in diffused diamond patterns. The camellias sparkled as if an overnight rain had refreshed them.

Ariel dressed hurriedly, relieved the night was over. "I didn't mean to intrude," she told the ghosts in her mother's room. Ariel was now sure Leah and Sonny had been lovers. Strangely, it did not frighten her. There had been warmth and caring as well as passion in the dream.

At eight, Mrs. Haskell brought a breakfast tray. "Mr. Staidlaw's business in the East became pressing. He left this morning early, said he'd be gone several weeks."

Ariel exhaled relief. She'd feel uncomfortable facing Sonny Staidlaw after the vivid dream.

"Mr. Staidlaw left money and books for you."

"I'll put both to good use."

For a week Ariel studied the mining manuals, perused the financial sheets and delved into the history of the Hell's Candy. All the while she felt surrounded by the presence of both Leah and Sonny. They trailed her to the ballroom, lingered in the bedroom, went with her to the study.

She tried to keep her mind on diamond drills and hoisting cages and the newest method of shoring. She memorized the names of the mines on Sun Peak, how deep they went and how far the laterals branched. She learned the problem was not finding silver so much as getting the metal into usable form.

When she had learned as much as she could from the books and papers, Ariel left the elegant mansion, with its sad and secret past, for the uncivilized but promising Nevada frontier.

At last! The Wells Fargo stage from Reno to Virginia City! She settled into the swaying carriage, thinking how primitive it seemed after the plush transcontinental train. The railroad had whisked her along at the phenomenal speed of thirty miles an hour, through granite-streaked mountains and snow-topped peaks, through switchbacks and tunnels where she could see the front end of the train crawling ahead around ledges like a great snake.

Now she sat at attention, taking note of the barren landscape south of Reno, the greens and tans of the foothills giving way to gray plateaus. Dry, cracked marshlands stood bleached in the sun. Sinkholes littered the desert like giants' footprints. Sagebrush, with its crisp, spiced scent, was the only vegetation which thrived in the harsh landscape.

A dapper gentleman sat across from her in the coach. He wore a dark blue walking suit, white vest and gray hat. Occasionally he would lick the ends of his curly brown mustache, looking like a kitten playing with its whiskers. He attempted a conversation. "Your first trip to Virginia City, miss?"

She was not anxious to talk. As she neared Virginia City, her worries had increased. What would Traver say when she appeared so unexpectedly? And how could she say a civil hello to Mitch after dreaming so intimately of him? Would Nedra and Su Lin be glad to see her? Would she have the courage and skill to deal with Putnam?

The man took it upon himself to keep up a one-sided conversation. "'Tis a wild spirit that's beneath the Nevada earth! You'd be better off staying away from the Comstock, miss."

She laughed. "Why is everyone so intent on warning me away? All the while they're hurrying to get there!" The tawny hills to the west flattened into treeless knolls. A lone jackrabbit sat by a cholla cactus. The heat rose with the dust, turning her braid limp. She had dressed too warmly, wearing a short walking skirt with two layers of crinolettes. She could feel her cambric petticoat with the pink satin ribbon sticking to her body. The red silk shirt with black braid and black velvet tie felt as heavy as damask. "Is it always this hot?"

"Often hotter than Hades! In the Washoe we have the usual four seasons, plus a fifth."

"Which is?"

"Claim-jumping season. When the weather is too wet or too cold to dig, the miners take out after the railroaders. The rail gang insults China Camp. That leads to mayhem and open warfare. Gangs dig through to each other's shafts, throw smudge pots, start fires, sabotage timbers, cut cables."

"I can think of two men who will be in the thick of any fights," Ariel mused. "One's a railroad man. The other— well, he's working a coyote hole at the moment, but he's promised to dig a fortune from the earth with his bare hands!" She hoped she'd sounded knowledgeable using such terms as "coyote hole."

The dapper man licked his mustache. "More power to your fellow and his digging. But grinding his way into a granite mountain with a pick and shovel is like spanking a giant with an egg beater." He leaned back and watched the grimly barren countryside. "You'll likely find him living in a rag shanty with his calico shirt for a windbreak and a couple of pine boughs for protection." Shifting position, the man removed a small card from his inner suit pocket. "When he makes his fortune, however, perhaps he'll need my services." He extended the card. "I am William Bondese, attorney-at-law."

Immediately Ariel was on her guard. Hadn't Sonny Staidlaw warned her about stockbrokers, bankers and lawyers? She barely glanced at the card as she took it, then busied herself scanning the scenery. The wind was rising, scattering dust devils along the uphill grade. Far in the distance she spotted a timber camp, some raggedy tents in a gully and several tall smokestacks descending from a single mountainside. "Are we nearly there?"

Mr. Bondese replied, "That's the woodchoppers' camp to the left, with the sawmill at the top of One Tree Hill. The lumber camp provides the ties for the new tracks of the Virginia and Truckee line. The tents in the dry wash at the bottom of the hill are China Camp."

She pressed her face to the isinglass window as they neared the flimsy shacktown of canvas and timber. Up close China Camp looked tattered and unsanitary. Laundry hung from pegs and tree limbs. A crude trolley of water buckets ran to a stream at the bottom of the gully. Outdoor charcoal burners emitted thin blue smoke into the haze of overheated desert air. "I have friends here," she announced.

"What! In China Camp?" Attorney Bondese trimmed his amazement with fatherly advice. "Then you'd best let them be *former* friends. No white man sets foot in China Camp. And no Chinaman comes to Virginia City unless it's on Putnam's orders."

Again Ariel had an inkling of Putnam's power. She said nothing, but vowed to find a way to see Po Fan and Su Lin.

She realized the lawyer was continuing to talk, so she paid attention, hoping to learn things which would help her in the town.

"As soon as we're over the divide, you'll see the city," he assured her. "And you'll meet the Washoe Zephyr."

Before she could ask for a definition of Washoe Zephyr, the wagon topped the last rise. A momentous gust of wind shook the carriage frame. Ariel's starched traveling bonnet lifted from atop her braid. "The Washoe Zephyr blows like the tropical tradewinds," she cried.

"Only stronger."

"Oh! Now I see the town!" The city lay at angles on red-pocked hills. The houses were made of unpainted, weathered lumber. A few greasewood and ash trees broke the monotony. Far up the slopes of Sun Peak, little houses perched like bird nests.

Mr. Bondese leaned toward her and gave a lawyer's appraisal. "Desolate damned town. Temporary. But with the audacity to call itself a city. Tracks and smokestacks. Mountains no goat in his right mind would try to climb. Nothing grows. No human goes back of Sun Peak except the Basque and his sheep."

"Where are the silver mines?" she asked impatiently.

"Right in front of you, clinging to the mountainside. The one furthest up Sun Peak is the old Ophir Works. Then down the hill stands every famous name you've ever heard—Gould and Curry, Hale and Norcross, Con Virginia, the Kentuck, Crown Point, Yellow Jacket—"

"Which one was the Hell's Candy?"

Attorney Bondese hurriedly concealed his shock at hearing the name by fumbling in his pockets for matches and pipe. He countered with a different question. "You have an interest in the Hell's Candy, miss?"

Two could play the game of secrecy. She smiled at the lawyer and spoke not a word.

He offered, "This is quite a coincidence. I've been in Reno filing papers to reopen the Hell's Candy. News travels fast, I guess."

"You must work for Ricket Putnam!" She scowled.

He nodded. "*Everyone* in Virginia City works for Ricket Putnam."

It was her turn to nod. But her agreement was not acceptance. If Putnam planned to reopen the mine, it meant he had her stock. She would make him cut her in. Tomorrow she'd confront him and, as Staidlaw had shrewdly suggested, she'd make certain Putnam did the financing.

Now the carriage rolled into the crowded streets. Would she spot Traver among the bustling throngs of pedestrians, horses, wagons and delivery carts? She bid William Bondese a curt farewell as she alighted from the Wells Fargo stage. Instantly she assessed that ninety-five percent of Virginia City was male. Most were attired in flannel shirts, denim trousers and beards. Such a hairy bunch! The men clustered around her as if she were some foreign flower. "Carry your bags, ma'am?" "Staying at the hotel, miss? Let me show you the way." Several were more forthright. "Married, mum?" One wagged a small chamois bag in front of her face. "Nuggets," he proclaimed. "Give you three for all night."

As she was declining all offers, Mr. Bondese pointed out the International Hotel.

"Thank you," she told him. "But I'll be staying with friends." Nevertheless, she took note of the five-story hotel. If she didn't find Traver or Nedra or Wise Ada by evening, perhaps she'd best stay at the International.

She picked up her leather satchel, shooing away the crowd of curious men. "Get away! I'm taken!" she scolded them. Reluctantly they fell back. She navigated the streets, choking on the dust which covered everything. A few nice wooden homes lay on the highest hillside lanes. The central street, B Street, was lined with stockbrokers' offices. As she walked downhill, the boarding houses and shops grew dingier. At the bottom of the hill sat the red light district, saloons and monte parlors. She passed Piper's Opera at B and Union, peering inside at the huge curtain painted with a scene of Lake Tahoe at sunset. She thought of Su Lin's theatrical abilities. Too bad no Chinese were allowed in town. Perhaps someday, when Putnam wasn't so firmly in control, Su Lin would perform at Piper's.

She passed mining-supply stores and saloons, saloons and saloons! Where were ordinary establishments, such as clean boarding houses and meat markets and bakeries? Plain water cost five cents a glass! The newest novelty being hawked in the streets was a hydraulic nozzle to wash soil away from pay dirt. What a city—so intent on finding, collecting and spending silver!

Her attention was diverted toward a narrow alleyway at C Street. A circle of men stood at the end. Coarse laughter rose and echoed between the buildings. The men formed a human barricade to something she couldn't see. But she heard a dog yelping and a child crying. The noises were all the more alarming and pitiful contrasted with the joking of the men. Angry that anyone should annoy a child or an animal, Ariel marched down the alley.

Approaching, she heard the thud of a heavy stone. The child cried in fear. The dog emitted distressed barks. She edged into the circle, pushing the men aside. Startled, then instantly furious, she discovered the crowd was tossing rocks at an emaciated black wolfhound and a cowering Chinese child.

"Stop this!" she cried boldly. Only then did she gasp. The skinny, frightened Chinese boy—was it Po Fan, her friend from the *Pallas Maru?* "Po Fan!" she cried. But the boy didn't look up, merely shielded his face in his arms against flying rocks.

"Stop this!" she cried again.

The men ignored her. "Get out of here!" they threatened the boy. "No Chinese in Virginia City!" They tossed pebbles at the quivering, lean wolfhound, who howled and trembled.

What cruelty! Ariel grabbed the arm of the man nearest her. "Stop it!"

"Step aside, ma'am. We tend to skunks in this town and don't make no stink about it!"

"Leave that child alone! The dog, too!" She rushed inside the circle, spreading her skirt wide as defense against rocks. One man laughed uneasily at her rash action. A few sidled backward several steps. One drunk called out, "I'll wager on the girl against the dog." Two rocks struck her feet.

"Get away from here!" she ordered. "Right now!"

A man in a plaid shirt shouted at her. "This boy has no business in town! Everyone in Washoe knows their place and keeps to it! Paddys at Crown Point on the trestle, Chinks at China Camp. Leave decent men alone!"

"Decent men, indeed!" she scolded. She edged toward the dog, shielding Po Fan, who stayed crouched on his knees. The dog tried to position himself in an attack stance, though his haunches quivered. She faced the men. "Very well. Stone me, too!"

No one had the courage to bombard her. Muttering and cursing, the crowd dispersed, making threats and crude remarks.

She turned to Po Fan and the dog. Both were obvious victims of malnutrition. "Oh, Po Fan! What were you doing in town? It's so dangerous! And how is Su Lin?" The questions tumbled out while she put a comforting arm around the boy's shoulders.

He seemed too scared to answer. He barely nodded yes as she asked again if Su Lin was all right. Po Fan tried to pull away from her grasp. "I deliver to Putnam," was the only explanation he gave, then bolted and ran.

"Wait! Tell me what's going on!" she called, but by then the frightened child had disappeared.

Ariel sat on the wooden curb, wondering what Po Fan meant. A delivery to Putnam? Opium, probably. She kept her voice low as she spoke to the dog. He lay down at her feet, expectant and obedient. "Are you lost?" she asked him, not feeling silly for questioning him. She looked at the barren mountainsides, wondering how anything could survive. She put her hand out and stroked the dog's head, feeling he was a special animal because of his fine, pointed ears, firm jaws and well-bred outline. "One thing I know," she told him. "I can't leave you lying here hungry." She stood up and snapped her fingers. "Come along." The dog obeyed instantly.

She bought beef jerky at the first shop she passed. The dog gobbled the food, looking at her with steady, trusting eyes. "Oh dear, I've done it now, haven't I? I hope I can find Nedra and Wise Ada tonight. No hotel or boarding house will rent me a room if I am traveling with a dog!" She petted him again. "Don't worry. I won't leave you alone in this barbaric town!"

A man moved across the sidewalk on the other side of the street. He was no closer than twenty feet, but the dog tensed and growled. "Heaven help me!" she laughed. "Now, *I* have a protector!"

Which way to go? Nothing but prostitutes' cribs along D Street, modest frame residences on C, stockbrokers on B. She purchased a newspaper, thinking to look for stories of Traver, Mitch, Nedra or Putnam. The *Territorial Enterprise*'s front page held news of typhoid at China Camp. The last water had dried up in Carson Sink. Sheep were missing from the Basque outpost behind Mount Davidson. Ricket Putnam intended to raise rates on his pipeline of water to the thirsty town.

As she stood on the sidewalk scanning the paper, the front door of Molly's Hotel opened. A little spiral of dust whooshed inward from the street, then out strode big Mitch Galway. Handsome, golden Mitch! His merry blue eyes twinkling, his sturdy body clad in riding breeches, suede shirt and glossy black boots.

She called to him immediately. "Mitch! Mitch Galway!"

He looked up, spotted her and his mouth jerked in delighted surprise. "Ariel! Christ, I should have known no girls' home would hold you." He rushed toward her, arms open wide. The wolfhound sprang in front of Ariel, baring its teeth and growling at Mitch. He pulled back, frowning. Ariel snapped her fingers and the dog moved to her side, protective but silent.

Ariel then reached out to Mitch, meaning to give him a friendly hug. But before she knew it, she was wrapped securely in his arms. His muscled thighs and broad chest pressed against her. A disturbing warm tingle coursed through her. How bewildering that she couldn't spend ten seconds with Mitch without their tempers or passions becoming aroused.

They stood facing each other, talking excitedly. She noticed that men stepped aside for Mitch. Respect? Or did he represent power, being in charge of the railroad? Maybe he'd been racing his stallion again and had earned the town's admiration with his victories. A little spark of pride warmed her heart. But she lectured him about her first experience in Virginia City. "It's wrong, Mitch, to keep the Chinese penned at China Camp and not let them into town."

"Not my idea," he defended. "Putnam's."

"We both know Putnam is an evil man. But you're a much better man! Don't go along with everything Putnam suggests."

Mitch's blue eyes clouded with shame. "I don't pride myself on what I do. If I had my way, there'd be decent wages for laying track and an open town. But Putnam understands only brute force."

The mention of force reminded her of Traver. "Mitch, I've come all this way to find Traver. Do you know where he is?"

Mitch's disappointment showed in his pout. "You haven't come looking for me?" He teased a bit, with rolling laughter covering his hurt. "Haven't you learned to love me yet?"

"Let's not fight."

"Traver's the one to lecture about fighting, Ariel. He brawled with a guy last week, then hightailed it to the mountains. I imagine he's hiding out at his claim."

"Is he in trouble with the law?" she asked, dismayed.

"For fighting? Sweetheart, if they locked up every man in

Virginia City who used his fists, the streets would be bare and the mines empty. Traver's just laying low for a few days. Or else he's left the county entirely. He's not the staying type—and he still talks about Texas."

"He'll hurry back when he knows I'm here," she boasted, hoping it was true.

Mitch sighed. "Then I'll not speak ill of him, seeing your heart is set for him. But, Ariel, you ought to know he's not been pining for you."

She bowed her head, admitting, "Traver told me not to follow him here."

"That's between you and Traver." Mitch stepped back, as if to say he wouldn't tangle in his friends' personal affairs.

When Ariel looked up, unsure whether to thank Mitch or ignore him, she spotted a strange machine coming toward them on the wooden sidewalk. "Watch out!"

Mitch pulled her to the safety of the hotel doorway as the contraption rattled to a stop. It was made of loops of iron, a saddleseat, chain, large front wheel and smaller rear one. "Wise Ada!" called Mitch. "What are you riding today?"

The old woman steered the unwieldy machine to a halt, pedaling first forward, then back. Her wiry legs pumped as she maneuvered her conveyance to a full stop and hopped off. "This here is a cycle," she announced, beaming. "A bi-cycle. Transport of the future, sure as shootin'."

Ariel had immediate doubts about the bicycle's role in the future of transportation. But she was delighted to see Wise Ada. "How was your trip? Where's Nedra? Is Su Lin all right?"

Wise Ada related the adventures the women had shared in crossing the Sierras. "That gypsy friend of yours told enough fortunes to get half-rich! She bought my freight wagon."

"Nedra has taken up driving a freight wagon?" Ariel was amazed, though Nedra had once said she'd like to own a wagon.

Wise Ada laughed. "She hasn't taken to the open road— not yet, anyway. She's set herself up in the fortune-telling business."

"Where?" Ariel looked up and down the street, as if to find her friend.

"Over the divide at Gold Hill," said Wise Ada. "There ain't many women in Virginia City, but the ones that do live here think they're the angel guardians of virtue. Call themselves the Decency Committee. They raised a ruckus about

Nedra keeping shop in a wagon, so she moved over the hill."
Wise Ada cackled with glee. "Nedra didn't do much to help
her own case, either. Started things off by predicting an
earthquake would wipe the Decency Committee right off
their snooty hillside!"

Ariel, Mitch and Wise Ada all laughed. But Ariel remembered Sonny Staidlaw saying that where ore lay in the ground,
the earth was prone to earthquakes.

"Su Lin is fine," Wise Ada continued. "She slipped into
China Camp and Putnam never knew. As for me, I'm off to
investigate flume boats. Transport of the future, I reckon.
Say, Ariel, did you find your redhaired Scotsman?"

Ariel shook her head. "I haven't found him. Yet." She saw
Mitch look away abruptly, barely concealing his disappointment.

Wise Ada hugged Ariel. "Maybe you're better off without
him. Honey, any man as would ditch you ain't right in the
head." She dusted her hands against her leather chaps,
dispensing with men in general and Traver Loch in particular.

Turning to Mitch, Wise Ada asked, "Which horse you
recommending for Saturday, Mr. Galway?"

Mitch's eyes lit up at the mention of his passion. "Bet on
the medium-sized sorrel. And maybe ten bucks on the bay."

An idea struck Ariel. "Mitch, can you get your black
stallion from the stable? Could you take me over the divide to
Gold Hill, where my friend is? If Nedra has a wagon, I could
stay with her and keep my dog, too! Besides, I want you to
meet Nedra. She's a beautiful gypsy girl."

Wise Ada lifted her bushy gray eyebrows at the mention of
introductions between Mitch and Nedra. But she held her
counsel as the goodbyes were said. Ariel and Mitch walked to
the stable at the end of C Street.

"This horse is more beautiful every time I see him!"
praised Ariel as Mitch boosted her into the saddle. He swung
up behind her, burly arms around the outside of her shoulders, chest to back. He took the reins in one hand and
galloped the animal along the ridges of sunbaked quartz.
Ariel exulted in the rushing wind, the sagebrush smell of
desert and the closeness of Mitch as they raced into the wild
ravine which separated Virginia City from its suburb, Gold
Hill. For the first time since leaving Cleo Burney's care, Ariel
felt alive and free, ready to meet challenges and life. The
powerful animal beneath her moved with ease, Mitch's steady

arms around her offered assurance. Unconsciously she shifted deeper into his embrace.

Immediately she felt him tighten. She'd given the wrong impression. She turned her head to look at him, seeing the sparkle in his eyes. "Mitch, no—you've misread my—"

But he captured her against him tightly, murmuring, "I don't think so!" He held her to him until she could feel each muscle and sinew straining with the ache to envelop her completely. "It's like the night we rode the headlands," he said rapidly, catching his breath. "And neither you, I nor the stallion has forgotten!"

She felt the excitement, but was powerless to do anything about it. She tried to focus her thoughts on Traver, but there was no denying her attraction to Mitch. She scanned the landscape, trying to keep her mind on geography while her body reached for dangerous ground.

Mitch's closeness and scent brought her senses to a tingle. This isn't what I want, she told herself. I don't want to fall for a man like Mitch. For all his charm, wit and cleverness, he's too obvious in his desire. Better he should stay with horses and me with Traver! She fought the urge to whirl in his arms and kiss him passionately.

Mitch slowed the horse as Gold Hill came into sight. Then he bent and kissed the back of Ariel's neck. She jerked, then trembled. Damn him! When she peeked at him, there was a glow of triumph on his broad face. Sheer delight—at the kiss? at her quiver?—made his eyes deeply blue and crinkly with mischief. "You're contemptible," she pouted,

"Agreed," he laughed boisterously. "And you're marvelous!"

Ariel remembered her priorities. "Now, Mitch, when I introduce you to Nedra, see that you treat her as if she were a grand duchess. Be on your best gentlemanly behavior. Understand?"

"For heaven's sake, Ariel! No matchmaking! My passions are fast horses and slow-burning whiskey, in that order. I'd put any woman—besides you—a distant third."

"At least let Nedra tell your fortune," begged Ariel.

"What does she charge? I'd rather put my money on the nose of a nag, where it will do some good."

"Oh, behave yourself!" She laughed at him.

As they threaded the narrow paths of tents, wagons and lean-to wooden huts, Ariel hoped things might go smoothly for Nedra and Mitch, despite his avowed lack of interest. "There!" cried Ariel, spotting the former freight wagon. Nedra had covered the utilitarian freighter with gypsy decor. She'd painted a large hand on the canvas side. Lettering beneath it proclaimed, "I tell the truth." Perhaps as a result of harassment, she'd also scrawled, "I shoot to kill."

In front of the wagon Ariel saw a cluster of women wearing hats and gloves. "Look at all those customers! How wonderful for Nedra."

"Those aren't customers," drawled Mitch, pulling the stallion to a halt on a small hill fifty feet away. "They're trouble."

"What? But they look like a ladies' sewing circle."

"No. They're harpies! That's the self-appointed conscience of Washoe, the Decency Committee. They've been after me a time or two for racing my horse on Sunday. They take out after anyone who isn't good enough for them!"

"Even in Gold Hill?"

"Sure!" He mimicked a woman's voice. "The job of the Decency Committee is to wage war against all things which are disgusting to pure-minded observers!"

Ariel didn't doubt the snobbish ladies would rate Nedra disgusting. How cruel for these women to make trouble for a gypsy girl whose ambition was to be a lady!

Suddenly there was a shrill burst of yelling from the wagon. Nedra rushed through the front of the canvas opening, waving a frying pan. "Keeping a disorderly wagon, you say? I'll disorder you, you bunch of female vipers!"

Mitch nodded his head vigorously. "Good girl! You tell 'em, sweetie!"

Nedra clambered onto the seat of the wagon. "You'd accuse me of loose living? Me? A highborn and grand lady? It's *you* whose minds are in the gutters! You white-faced old cows!" She flung the frying pan in their direction, causing a twitter and scampering of women. "You just wait," Nedra warned. "There's an earthquake coming! You'll all be swallowed down into the bowels of the earth!"

As Nedra reached for more ammunition, the Decency Committee gave ground. The women edged away, plotting among themselves. Regardless of the battle's outcome, Nedra had won this skirmish.

As soon as the women left, a few men edged toward the wagon. They looked sheepish for not standing up to the committee. Ariel heard one man asking for advice about his claim. Another wanted to know if he should marry a certain reformed prostitute. Several didn't seem to care what Nedra told them. They simply liked her charming smile.

Mitch and Ariel dismounted and came forward. The girls greeted each other exuberantly. Then Ariel performed the proper introduction she had promised Nedra and Mitch.

Nedra smiled at Mitch. "Let me see your hand, Irish." Nedra pursed her full lips, ran a red tongue invitingly over them, then gazed long and deeply at Mitch. The fair face of Mitch Galway was no match for Nedra's dark beauty. He blushed like an adolescent and tried to withdraw his palm.

Nedra kept his hand firmly between her own. Her performance was magnificent. Ariel listened, absolutely fascinated as Nedra told his fortune.

Nedra leaned seductively toward Mitch. "You've been on a horse." She smiled and he smiled back. "And before that, you were at Molly's Hotel—mounted on a whore. One with long, smooth-shaven legs. And she had those slim, cool legs wrapped clear around your neck!"

Mitch turned bright red, tried to yank away his hand and cursed under his breath. "Hold still!" Nedra insisted. "I see more! You're building the railway trestle at Crown Point. Your claim to fame is your black stallion, your rugged determination and your intellect." She winked at him. "But I'd settle for your body alone." She leaned against him, pretending to remove a speck of dust from his suede shirt.

Ariel felt pangs of outright jealousy. Oh, why had she promised to introduce them!

Mitch broke the spell by clearing his throat and forcibly retrieving his hand. "I admire the way you stood up to the Decent Ladies," he commented.

Nedra laughed provocatively. "You'd really be impressed if I'd lost my temper! But I'm a lady."

"You're a harlot, I suspect," teased Mitch. "A wanton sparrow no decent Dubliner would pour brandy for!"

His reward was a fast slap across the face. As Nedra reared back to belt him again, he caught her arm and yanked her down from the wagon. With a quick turn, he grabbed her elbow and twisted her arm behind her. She screamed, began kicking and flailed with her other arm. Ariel was appalled. Mitch turned dark red from his efforts to control the wild gypsy. But suddenly he shoved her away and stalked to his stallion.

Ariel was near tears. Nedra and Mitch were a serious

mismatch. They'd argued, and they both had too much pride.

"I'm sorry—" Ariel began.

"You and your good deeds!" Nedra interrupted.

"Well, you certainly didn't help things, Nedra, with your infernal temper!"

"He shouldn't have insulted me!"

"Nedra, for once you are dead wrong! Mitch Galway is a fine man. But you must tame Iron Mitch with gentle words and soothing fortunes." She folded her arms as if teaching an obstinate student. "And about this earthquake business—really!"

"Oh, the earthquake's coming all right," countered Nedra. She smiled as if she possessed secret knowledge. "Ariel, do you know what I really saw in Mitch Galway's hand? Someday he'll *own* this town!"

"Better he than Ricket Putnam!" Ariel thought of the way Mitch had talked of taking a chance on a new land. "He'd make a good leader for a new state. He's a builder and a dreamer—when he isn't taking orders from Putnam."

"You're underestimating Mr. Galway," said Nedra. "I've heard he stands up to Putnam when matters are serious. He's quite his own man when the chips are down."

"Good," approved Ariel. She wondered how well she'd do when confronting Putnam. For the moment she continued giving advice. "Now, Nedra, you must try again with Mitch. Next time, please lower your voice. Sheathe those claws and act harmless. Your eyes are gorgeous, but let them be soft and big instead of narrow and slashing."

"Play shy? Submissive? How could I? He'd get the wrong impression!"

Ariel ignored her. "And we'll buy you a dress of silk and pastel lace instead of these wild scarves and bright shawls."

"Ugh! Too pale!"

"We'll put cologne on your hair."

"What!" Nedra patted her shaggy hair protectively. She looked pensive for a moment. "There's no use, Ariel. He's not the kind of man I could hold, even if I could catch him. Besides, his cap is set for someone else."

"Did you read that in his palm?"

"No. In his eyes." She gestured Ariel into the wagon. The dog lay down behind a wheel. "Now, how are *you*? When did you arrive? Have you found Traver Loch yet?"

Ariel steeled herself. "I can't find him! Mitch said he was in a fight and ran off to the mountains. Wise Ada thinks he's married a fat widow with a big claim." Ariel sat on a packing case and held out her hand. "Read my palm, Nedra. Tell me I'll find Traver soon."

Nedra laughed. "When did you start taking my powers so seriously? You'd better believe me about the earthquake then." She busied herself serving little pecan cakes and cinnamon tea. "Ariel, a man like Traver, who brawls and runs away, isn't the type for you. You and he are as bad a mismatch as Mitch and me."

"But I can't simply quit loving Traver!" She tossed her hair back and began to braid it. "Oh, why did he have to rush off to the mountains! He told me not to follow him, but I believed once I was here, he'd be pleased." She let her silent fear spill out. "Nedra, he told me to make a new life. He acted as if he'd already forgotten me! How could he do that?"

"You wonder how a man forgets so quickly?" Nedra's mouth sounded cottony. She touched her temples as if she had a headache. "Men are wonderful actors, Ariel. They put my gypsy instincts to shame. You thought because Traver was your first man, he'd stand in line forever for your kisses? Did you think because you were a virgin that somehow he'd be in your debt?"

"He *did* love me," insisted Ariel.

"Dream on, silly goose."

Ariel moaned. Was Nedra damning her for dreaming? For being young enough to believe her first love would be her last? She slumped on the wagon bunk, burying her head in the pillow. The Washoe Zephyr howled through the canvas slits. "Nedra, can I let my dog into the wagon? This airborne grit is strong enough to blind him."

Nedra called the dog. "I ain't such a highborn lady yet as to keep critters out of my place." She sat down and stroked the wolfhound's back. "Get some rest, Ariel. Things will look better tomorrow. I shouldn't have been so curt with you, I s'pose. Go ahead and dream of Traver, if it will make you feel better."

"I'll dream of Traver. Will you dream of Mitch? Didn't you like him even a little bit, Nedra?"

Nedra rubbed her elbow where Mitch had manhandled her. Then she shrugged. "Don't think for a minute I won't try for him. Don't think I won't try with all my heart, body and soul."

Chapter 13

Ariel wrote a letter to Sonny Staidlaw, assuring him of her safe arrival in Virginia City. Walking back to Virginia City from Gold Hill was rough, uphill work. More than once she wished for Mitch's speedy stallion. Crosswinds lifted gravel and dust into the air and threatened to topple her. The big dog walked at her side, scouting ahead with alert eyes.

The post box was in the Wells Fargo office. She ordered the dog to sit on the wooden sidewalk while she went inside. What an elegant office! Outside there was a carved façade with little unicorns at the top of the columns, inside marble sills and counters, a Turkish carpet on the floor. Clerks in vests worked and men intent on buying tickets and posting letters waited.

Suddenly she stopped, paralyzed with surprise. Another dog! Identical to the one she'd left outside. She glanced outside, reaffirming her dog was still there. Reassured she watched the dog in the office. Another spry, lean black wolfhound. The animal stood beside a man whose back was to Ariel. The man transacted business with the post clerk. She glimpsed a profile as he counted out silver coins. The man was of medium height, wearing a dark shirt and trousers, leather vest and a black beret pulled far forward across his face. His trousers were held by a wide black belt decorated with small, crescent-moon silver spikes.

Were the wolfhounds a matched pair? She moved to the man, touching his elbow. He faced her, startled. His appearance was like the wolfhounds'—razor lean, alert, dark sun-tanned face overlaying an olive complexion. His eyes were gray-flecked in contrast to his thick black hair.

"Come with me, sir," she said quietly. "I believe I have something which belongs to you."

"Pardon me?" He spoke in accented English with a soft inflection. His arm muscles tightened, his eyes took in everything before him. He made a small, graceful bow. "Perhaps you have confused me with an acquaintance. I am Pedro Ybarra, the Basque."

"Oh! The Basque!" She remembered Wise Ada and lawyer William Bondese telling of the sheepherder's outpost behind Mount Davidson. And the *Territorial Enterprise* had mentioned his missing sheep. But this man seemed no itinerant shepherd. His clothing was clean. He moved with steady assurance of manner. She smiled at him and pointed to the window. "Come and see."

He moved to the doorway, then gasped as he saw the other wolfhound. She saw the tiny ripple of delight which fluttered the hollow of his throat, the gleam in his lustrous eyes. He turned and gripped her hands in silent gratitude. Then, stepping outside, he called to the dog in a language she couldn't understand. The wolfhound came forward. Then, at a signal from the man, the dog greeted the Basque and the other wolfhound enthusiastically. There was a torrent of language from the man, a smooth, excited tumble of words which were unlike anything she'd ever studied. She racked her brain for some knowledge of a tongue with multiple "z" sounds. Italian? Spanish? This Basque language was totally new to her.

Finally Pedro Ybarra turned to her. "How did you find my dog?"

"We met yesterday when I arrived in Virginia City. I provided a small act of kindness and he became my protector."

"Then my praise is yours!" cried the Basque. "I thought this dog dead." He caressed both dogs' shoulders. "These wolfhounds are so valuable I had to smuggle them out of the Pyrenees when I came to this country two years ago."

She was pleased to find the dog's owner such a gracious man. She told how the dog had been mistreated.

"The filthy scum!" he lashed out. "I live apart in the mountains because my livelihood demands it. But I prefer solitude to life among such barbarians! I came to this land to work hard. But I do not expect others to steal from me, not my land, sheep or dogs. I'll not be used like dirt, nor shall I dig in it like the miners. May they open a Pandora's box!"

Ariel was charmed by the Basque's stance, his firm gaze and trained mind. "Do you never come down from the mountains?"

"Only when unavoidable. I am here today to send a letter to the Vizcaya Province Council. I have written home for a bride."

"How wonderful! You'll have a wife to share your hillsides, then." She felt like Pedro Ybarra's old friend and delighted in his future happiness. "Is she someone you knew before you came to America?"

"A stranger. I trust the council to send a woman who can share both joys and hardships in a strange land."

"When will she arrive?"

"Perhaps six months. It is a long voyage from the Bay of Biscay." He smiled shyly. "I admit I am anxious. I have built a house for her and bought fine linens and clothing. All will be ready when she arrives."

"And yet you have no idea who she will be?"

"No—" He hesitated and looked at her with flashing, happy eyes. "But I hope it will be someone like you, with youth and beauty."

She smiled at the compliment. Then, as if he realized he had omitted a propriety, he asked, "How can I repay you for returning my dog?"

"It is thanks enough to see you and the wolfhound happy together."

"These dogs are more than partners with me. They are trusted companions, more faithful than a compass, more steady than a rifle."

Ariel liked his poetic cadences. His eyes, too, appealed to her, in the way they addressed the world with piercing directness.

He kissed her fingertips in a warm, courtly gesture. "If you are ever lost, in danger or in need, come to my hillside. It will be my honor to provide sanctuary for you, as you have done for my companion."

"Thank you," she murmured, grateful for the generous offer.

After goodbyes, she posted her letter. Then she stiffened her spine and took a deep breath. She must now call on Ricket Putnam. Asking directions from the clerk, she discovered Putnam's office was on the second story of the Guardian Concert Hall, behind the hotel on C Street.

When she knocked on Putnam's door, there was silence. She knocked again, more forcefully. The door opened a scant six inches. "Mitch! What are you doing here?"

"I have business with Putnam," he said steadily. "What brings you here?" He looked cautious, as if he disapproved of her coming near Putnam.

"I have business with him as well," she said.

"He's indisposed." Mitch made no effort to open the door.

"Is he ill?"

"He's not receiving."

"Oh! Another opium binge?" She figured her accusations were correct when Mitch looked past her. She stepped around him into the office. "I hope someday Putnam overdoses himself and sleeps till eternity! In the meantime I must see him."

"You don't listen well—"

"And you don't hear well, Mitch! I'm going in there." She strode past double file cabinets, bookcases, a mahogany pigeonhole desk and two tall hat-trees. In the inner office she found Ricket Putnam seated at a low wicker table. Awake. Drinking hot broth. His eyes were dim and bloodshot.

Ariel got right down to business. "I know you intend to reopen the Hell's Candy. I want my interest."

Putnam looked at her dazedly. "You want to buy in?"

"No. I want you to return what is rightfully mine."

She looked to Mitch, hoping for support. He stood apart, trying to untangle the threads of the conversation. "Can you prove ownership, Ariel? That would help your case more than stomping in here and threatening," said Mitch.

She evaded his question. "I can prove all that's necessary."

Putnam finished his broth. His eyes narrowed as he watched her with calculating side glances. "Have you any idea of the status of Hell's Candy?"

"I intend to investigate this very day."

"It's a hole in the earth eight hundred feet deep, with fire, hot water and cave-ins waiting for anyone who pokes his nose down there. The timbers are rotted. Heat makes working more than fifteen-minute shifts unbearable. Work nude and sponge with ice water and you'll pass out after twenty."

Ariel studied him. "I see you've done considerable research, Putnam. You believe there's danger, but you must believe there's silver, also."

Mitch broke into the conversation. "Common sense says you'd both be smart to steer clear of Hell's Candy."

She wondered if Mitch were annoyed with her for pushing past him into this office. Here was her chance to back away. But, defiantly, she followed Staidlaw's advice. "Putnam, you must cut me into this mine for thirty-five percent. If not, I'll tie the Hell's Candy tighter than a corset. William Bondese's law office will have a new client before the sun sets."

Mitch snorted with disgust. "Neither of you fools can leave Hell's Candy alone!" He paced the room nervously while Ariel seated herself at the table with Putnam.

"I detest you, Ricket Putnam," she said calmly. "I shall never excuse or forgive the terrible things you've done to my father, Traver and me. But, to my everlasting regret, we must be partners—temporarily."

Putnam smiled without agreeing. "Let's consider the depth at which Hell's Candy might prove profitable before we draw any partnership agreements." He moved his chair closer to the table as if waiting for tasty crumbs to fall into his lap. "Ariel, I'll honor your claim on one condition: you must be a silent partner. Back off and leave the operations to me."

"If it's silence you want, you're mistaken in thinking you'll have it from me," she cried. "I intend to take a full and active part in all phases. You'll not find me knitting in some dim corner while you cheat me at the claims office, assay cage or stockboards!"

"Our mistrust is mutual," murmured Putnam, studying his yellowed fingernails. He turned to Mitch. "Bring those geologic strata maps." Mitch looked reluctant, but performed the errand. Putnam spoke to Ariel again. "Now, if we share the profit, we must share the risk. Frankly, past the eight-hundred-foot depth, we can expect every kind of natural hazard."

"And count on labor trouble as well," predicted Mitch gloomily. "When you hit a thousand feet down, there's a big drop in courage among workers."

Ariel agreed, glad for a chance to display some of her new knowledge. "Labor will be our number-one priority. Then timbering. Then water for the stamping mill."

"And what are you going to do about the earthquake your gypsy friend is predicting?" sneered Mitch.

Putnam dismissed Mitch with a wave of his hand. He turned to Ariel, fixing her with a stare. He appeared cool and reserved, simpering eyes deep in their lined sockets, lips gray and coiled. "What say you, Ariel? Do we go deeper?"

"Yes. Why shouldn't we?"

Putnam tapped fingertips together. "We can bleed the mine down another two hundred feet before the local labor will revolt. At that point we can set the timbering and drain whatever water has seeped in. If we've found silver, we'll hire new labor. If not, we can pay off five cents on the dollar and blast the damned hole shut."

Ariel was shocked. "You're a human leech! And as long as I have a vote, we'll take no risks with human life."

Putnam laughed. "My dear, save the tender nonsense and sentimental stories. Are we going down or not?"

She dealt a new proposition into the game. "My vote in this venture depends on the future I expect to have in Virginia City. When I am married to Traver Loch, he will also be a force to deal with."

"Traver Loch?" scoffed Putnam. "Married! My word of honor, Ariel, where did you get such a notion? He's nowhere around here, far as I know."

"I'll find him and I'll marry him!" Ariel promised. She saw Mitch cringe. Oh, impossible Mitch! Did he doubt her love for Traver? Immediately she turned her attention back to business. "Traver Loch is to be manager of the Hell's Candy."

Putnam stared. Mitch's silent surprise was indicated by upraised eyebrows. Then Putnam's eyes glowed with trickery. "You'd send Traver down into danger? You're hungry enough for silver to risk his life?"

Putnam was bluffing, she was certain. "No one knows whether death or riches lie ten feet deeper," she pointed out.

Pushing back his chair and rising abruptly, Putnam guffawed. "If that's all you want, we'll send for Attorney Bondese and have him draw the partnership agreement."

Now she was fearful. Putnam had no love for Traver. Hadn't he once set him adrift in a rowboat? Perhaps Putnam now saw another chance to dispose of Traver by sending him into danger. What if she couldn't find Traver? What if he didn't want to manage the mine? She must not turn coward now. This venture was her legacy, and she would see it through.

Steadily, she asked, "How deep can we go before we hit hot water?"

"No one knows," responded Putnam.

She looked to Mitch for a better answer. He gestured palms up. "Why look at me, Ariel? My game's track and trestle."

"At least you're honest, Mitch."

"Then I'll tell you one more thing honestly. I don't want any part of this! I don't know at what level tunneling in a mine becomes a lost cause. I don't know which way silver veins fault. Nor do I know when that gypsy's earthshake will hit and turn all hell loose under Sun Peak. Leave me out! You've been happy enough to run roughshod over me before—you, Putnam and Traver. Don't involve me now!" He stalked from the room, slamming the door behind him.

Ariel was unnerved by Mitch's display of temper. But she covered her turmoil with brisk questions to Putnam. "If we do hit water, what can be done?"

Putnam spread the geologic map. "Sutro's tunnel will tap the mountain at sixteen hundred feet and drain everything above that."

"But Sutro has four miles to go and another four million dollars to raise before he can proceed. By then we might be down to the three-thousand-foot level." She traced the myriad red and blue lines on the drawing. "There have to be ways through a water barrier."

"Rock you can bore. Sand you can shuttle. If the vein shifts, you shift with it. But water, hot water at that, is hazardous by its nature."

"Dam up the water?" she suggested.

"You don't know when it will break through, but it will eventually."

"Pump it out?"

"Pumps fail. The crew drowns."

"Drains, perhaps?"

"Makeshift, at best." He sighed. "Hell's Candy will be a silver-lined coffin if we tap the boiling water. Ah, that even sounds right—boiling water cooking the Devil's candy."

Ariel didn't join the joking. "I want a safe operation. That's why I want Traver. He's been in the tin trade. He knows about mining. He'll know what's a decent wage to pay and how much timber we'll need for honeycomb stopes."

Putnam looked at her with respect in his eyes. "Where did you learn of the Deidesheimer method?"

"I've put my time to good use, Putnam. I also know about ventilation, pumping and plumbing. We'll have watertight oak and metal doors which can stop either fire or water. We'll need twenty-four Howland rotary stamps and collecting pans."

"Your costs will go out of hand."

"We'll make them back in silver, seven times over!" She smiled confidently. "But it's sudden riches we want, not sudden ruin."

"Ariel, the silver madness has gripped you!" His voice was excited, too. He walked around the room, hands to his temples as if concentrating. "My success has always lain in having options. Alternatives. Today you've provided the best plan of all." He gave a gesture of acceptance. "The lady wins. We open the Hell's Candy and Traver Loch runs the show."

Now all she had to do was find him.

Chapter 14

Ariel and Putnam signed partnership papers at the end of the week. The meeting in William Bondese's office was interrupted by a brisk pounding of the outer door. Pedro Ybarra, the Basque, entered. He looked at everyone present, barely giving an anxious smile toward Ariel. "Which of you is the medical man? I was told I could find a physician here," said the Basque.

Putnam gave a curt nod. "I trained as a doctor, but do not practice."

"Have you medicines for the swelling disease? I discovered a man wandering in the high country. He is ill of the swollen glands. Though he is tall and robust, he has been weakened to the point—"

Ariel interrupted, "A tall, robust man in the hills? Is he a Scotsman? A giant with red hair and green eyes?" She ran to the Basque. "Oh, is his name Traver Loch?"

Pedro Ybarra seemed surprised at her quick questions. "The man has been in no condition to tell me his name. But your physical description is accurate."

"You've found him!" she cried. "We must go at once! Dear Basque, take me to him."

He looked doubtful. "It would be a hard trip for you. I left the man in a shelter far above my cabin. I do not think I should take you that high."

"You must! Traver is my intended!" She appealed to the Basque, hoping he would remember his own bride from far away.

He smiled. "It would be my pleasure to return something of value to you. You have already done as much for me."

They departed hastily, she taking only a small bag of necessities. In less than two hours they'd navigated the moors and pinnacles behind the city. As they crossed a ravine lined with craggy granite boulders, the two great wolfhounds came running to meet them. The dogs' graceful black shapes stood out against the magenta-purple of the sunset. "Can we reach Traver tonight?" she worried.

"If we stop at my cabin for supplies, supper and a fresh horse."

The cabin was disguised in the shelter of the mountain bluff. They were nearly to it before Ariel could distinguish it as a house. A narrow path between spruces and ridges brought them to the camouflaged entrance. Inside, the roof sloped with the natural tilt of the rock ledge, making a triangular, warm burrow like a cave.

"How lovely!" she exclaimed as she looked around at the dark carved furniture, a wooden chest with ribbed padding for a seat, and large woven baskets of potatoes, onions and squash. Strings of dried red and green peppers hung from the roof rafters. A wine barrel sat in the corner by the fireplace. Hams and bacons, strung in white nets, dangled from a pole. The bedroom consisted of a pole bed with cornshuck mattress and sheepskin coverlet. A single arched window faced west, revealing a breathtaking view of sunset, schist hills and sheer drop-off to the valley floor.

"Come, eat quickly," he called to her. He had set out a salad with vinegar and bright red tomatoes, a long loaf of bread, wine and cheese.

Ariel could not master drinking from the wineskin. "Here," he said helpfully. "Squeeze from the bottom with your left hand and keep your right hand on the skin's throat."

After she'd eaten a few rapid bites of cheese and bread, she asked, "Can we go on? Reach Traver soon?"

"I will bring sheepskin jackets against the night chill."

As he went to a tiny cupboard in the back of the cabin, she complimented him, "Your home is tidy and secure. Your bride will be delighted." She looked around at the little touches of luxury which he'd provided—a silver flute with neatly punched holes and curved lip rim, five silver goblets on the mantel.

He picked up one of the goblets. "In this land, silver. In Vizcaya they would be pewter. Many things are different here. Perhaps Zena will not like it."

"Zena? You already know your bride's name? So soon?"

He shrugged. "No, I have named her to suit myself, to make her seem more real."

She smiled at his admission of loneliness. From the outdoors echoed the deep sounds of the gourd-shaped bells on the Merino flock as they settled for the night.

Outside, she could no longer distinguish shapes. The surefooted Basque pony picked his way along the ledges as if he were a burro. The wolfhounds barked, running ahead and standing stiffly as if to point the way. The trail played out into gravel and hemlocks. Finally she spotted a tiny lean-to shelter of pine boughs and firs. "Traver? Traver, are you all right?" She began calling even before she'd dismounted from the horse.

She ran ahead to the shelter, bending down into the narrow opening. Traver was lying on his side, pale but conscious. She fell to her knees and clasped him around the neck. "Oh, darling! I've found you."

He threw back his head and roared with laughter. "Honey lass, you promised to chase me to the ends of the earth! You sure keep your promises!"

Her joy overflowed into happy tears. She hugged him closely, testing his strength with her embrace. What a man, she thought. He'd survived the climate, the continents and the seas. His body was whittled down to stone muscles. The green eyes were cloudy, an aftermath of high fever. But his lipline was firm, and his voice as distinctive as distant bells. She nuzzled against him, stroking his soft, bushy auburn hair. "You're all right! I'm so grateful."

"I'm all right in the head—" he began, then pulled back and propped himself up on his elbow. Angrily he raised his voice. "The mumps don't *kill* people, you know!"

She teased him, paying no attention to the frustration in his tone. "Why, you big overgrown ox! Having a childhood disease! And running off into the hills to be sick. Shame on you!"

He defended himself. "I was working my claim in the high

country. I had to flag it by the end of the month or lose it. That's the rule—two days a month on the premises or forfeit."

"Oh, darling, you can forget that silly claim now. Traver, the Hell's Candy is to reopen!" She couldn't resist telling him the good news. "*You* are to be the manager!"

He turned his face away. "I'll be no good to you, Ariel."

"Nonsense, darling! You'll be wonderful. Perfect. You'll manage the mine with all the skills you learned in the tin trade."

His voice turned hoarse. "No. That's not what I mean. I'll be no good to you in other ways. Oh, I can run the show at Hell's Candy, if that's what will please you. But . . . this sickness . . ." He exhaled as if to rid himself of the pain. "This sickness has left me worthless."

"What do you mean?" She tried to turn his head to look at her, but he remained obstinately facing the darkness.

"I'll be no good to you, Ariel. No good as a *man.*"

She crouched opposite him, stunned. "No good as a man?" She didn't fully understand, though she'd heard of such things happening to men who lay unattended. Surely this couldn't happen to Traver Loch!

"The Scottish lion has been penned up, honey lass. For good, I suppose."

Unsure how to comfort him, she timidly took his hand. "It doesn't matter."

He yanked away, eyes storming. "Don't talk like a bloody fool! What could matter more?"

Chastened by his fear, she leaned forward and touched his closed lids. Was he holding back tears? She stroked his stubbly chin, traced the outline of his auburn hair. "Don't let a disease frighten you, Traver." How could she tell him there were things in their life together which could become as important as sensual excitement? Their first attraction had been one brimming with physical enticement. But passion could give way to companionship. There could be power in working together, making the mine successful, nurturing their care of each other as well. But she could not form the proper words to soothe him.

She called to the Basque, "Pedro, come at once. We must move Traver to your cabin."

Then she stayed busy, making efforts to keep Traver comfortable. I'll be patient, she vowed. He must have time for healing.

When they laid Traver on the cornshuck mattress at the Basque's cabin, he clasped Ariel's hand tight to his chest. "If things don't work out—oh, Ariel, if I *can't* get well, then I wish I'd died in those mountains."

For three days afterward Ariel and the Basque kept a vigil as Traver's fever rose again, subsided and finally ended. His bodily anguish was not as severe as his spiritual torment. He sulked, cursed, shed silent tears, begged Ariel to stay, ordered her away.

At breakfast on the fourth morning Ariel talked to the Basque. "Is Traver's anger a good sign?"

"When we are wounded, we grow angry. He must heal his pride along with his body."

"Yes, I must help him regain his confidence. Perhaps running Hell's Candy will give him important work to do. Success with the mine will help him disregard the after-effects of this illness." She cleared away the dishes. "You have been most generous with your hospitality to both of us."

Pedro shrugged. "I've been glad for the companionship," he admitted. "It's been little enough between friends—a fire to warm by, a plate of mutton stew." He rose from the table, picked up a wooden staff worn smooth from handling and reached for his cloak. As he put on his beret, he said, "Walk out with me this morning, Ariel." His tone implied he had advice to give.

She followed him quickly, wrapping herself in the soft sheepskin jacket. He reached down into a storage bin at the side of the cabin and picked up an unusual tool. "What is that?" she asked.

"A *laya*. For cultivating. Come along, I'll show you my garden and the hot spring." After they'd walked in silence for fifty feet, he smiled at her. "Ariel, you're like a newborn lamb. Suddenly you're facing the broad daylight of a new world with Traver. I see fear in your eyes, confusion and worry at this transformation in him. You must relearn the world—that the earth is warm, the rains are sweet, the clouds are soft and giving."

Relearn the world. Or create a new one. She understood the need, but not the process of how to reach Traver. She followed the Basque along the pinnacle ledge, crossing the spine of the mountain and moving into the forested slope.

"Don't watch the path, Ariel. Look at the sunrise. See how gloriously the clouds move! The sky is gray one instant, the next it's puffed with pink, like a veil lifted from a bride's rosy cheeks."

She teased him gently, "You *are* anxious for your bride, aren't you? When I looked for a blanket in the wooden chest, I found the beautiful garments you've bought for her—the pastel blouse with lace, the pleated skirt, the red cashmere nightdress." She lowered her eyes, embarrassed she'd mentioned the nightgown.

But the Basque smiled proudly, dark eyes shining. "Perhaps Zena will not like these things. She will be a woman who has worn nothing but black dresses and hair coverings. She may think me foolish for buying red gowns, and she may loathe canned peaches and detest striped mattress tickings." He laughed. "It is not good to plan another's life—though I'm trying."

Ariel was aware of the truth in his statement. It was not proper to plan another's life. Was that what she was trying with Traver? She fell in step behind the Basque, a terrible lonely ache piercing her side. Give up Traver? Oh, she could not!

Pedro stopped at a small furrowed spot. "My garden. Dry now in autumn, but I prepared peppers, corn, gourds, turnips and onions. Most of the bounty is stored. So you see, it is no imposition for you and Traver to stay as long as you need." He pointed to a cavern walled off with boulders. "This is the hot spring."

She glanced at the spot where a low ridge rounded into a flat. It was strategically placed, like his cabin, to escape winter's tormenting winds.

She ran to inspect the bubbling mineral waters. The coppery water swirled against a granite ledge, trapped by earth and rocks. A deep pool steamed like swirling dry leaves crackling underfoot.

"I must go to my flock," said Pedro. "I have devoted less time than usual to the sheep."

She knew his kindly attentions to Traver and her accounted for his lost time. "Yes, please go on. Tonight I shall make a pudding and cook supper for you."

He looked happily surprised that she had any domestic skills. "Mutton chops and sweet potatoes then. And if you tie onions in a net, they will boil in the hot spring."

The Basque moved steadily into the sloping forest, while Ariel lingered in the clear morning air. The pool bubbled gently, steam rising like a mist and condensing like tears on the boulders. A bath! A place to wash her hair! Despite the crisp autumn morning, the sun felt warm within the granite walls of the springside. She slipped off her clothing and edged into the pool.

Luxury! The hot water covered her. She dipped her face into the steam, then stretched full length in the swirling waters. Ah, this was as wonderful as lying on the heated sand on Lanavi's shores. Hawaii—half a world away, half a lifetime past! A veil of tears rose unbidden across her eyes as she thought of the greenery and soft air.

She took a handful of coarse pumice rock and used it on her elbows and ankles. Looking down through the water at her body, she was pleased at the soft proportions. She moved across the pool, flexible, yielding to the current.

Suddenly she heard footsteps. A twig snapped. A pebble skimmed the surface of the pool. She ducked down. Another pebble lurched across the surface. Unafraid she glanced around. "Traver! I see you behind that boulder!"

He emerged, grinning, hands in pockets.

"Come on in," she urged him. "The water is as warm as the bay where we took our first swim."

His green eyes flashed over her outline. "Remember that first day when we played the silly game of shark and mermaid?" His affectionate smile encouraged her giggle. The aloofness left his body. He knelt at the side of the pool, trailing his hand in the steam.

She swam to the rim and clasped his hand between hers. Huddling in the heated water, she tugged gently on his fingers. He leaned forward and kissed her forehead, then licked his lips as if drinking her perfume. His tongue retraced the outline of his lips, as if seeking more.

Unmindful of modesty, she half-stood in the water, wearing the steam vapor like a veil across her shoulders and breasts. Timidly she put out her arms to him. A panicky thought engulfed her: what if he rejected her?

She hugged him tightly, laying her head tenderly across his shoulder. "Hold me, Traver. Oh, hold me and tell me we'll be all right. Tell me fever can't burn away the feelings we have for each other."

The sweet ache of need budded within her, need for assurance, need for yielding.

Traver exhaled softly and placed his hands over her damp shoulders. His eyes dark as jade, he murmured, "I've taken many chances in my life. If I ran up against something I couldn't fight and lick, I moved on. But this uncertainty of my strength stymies me, Ariel. I've no way to fight." His hands went limp at his sides.

She nestled against him, soft, wet and warm. Slowly his arms came up, rounded and encompassed her. He kissed the top of her hair. She could sense him flexing his stomach muscles. Encouraged anew, she sought his lips. Candidly she let her fingers creep downward from his waist.

He flinched, broke the embrace and bolted from the poolside.

"Traver! Darling, darling, don't you want to *try?*"

"Not and fail." He walked away, breaking into a run at the cliff top.

Ariel knew he was angry at himself. She called after him, "I was wrong! I'm sorry—"

"Sorry?" he shouted back. "I'll take insults from no man—and pity from no woman!"

She dressed haphazardly and hurried after him. As she caught up, she insisted, "Traver Loch, I don't believe you've heard one word I've said since I found you. I love you! I want us to be together. I want you to manage the Hell's Candy!"

He threw up both hands and faced her. "Stop it! No more of your interfering!" The anger on his features gave way to ferocity. "I can tend the mine if you wish. But think of it, Ariel. Even if I am officially the master of Hell's Candy, you will be the mistress of an empire! What do I do then? Walk three steps behind you? Turn my head while you consort with bonanza kings? Hold my peace while you find satisfaction with Mitch Galway?"

She was genuinely surprised. "Is that what's angering you? Your old, never-ending competition with Mitch?"

"Yes, Mitch," he repeated defiantly. "And every other man I'll see looking at you, wanting you and, eventually—despite yourself—possessing you!"

Traver sprang forward on the path like a darting buck. He flung back his head, leaped a boulder and braced himself far out over the precipice. The look on his face said he'd leap from the pinnacle before he'd let anyone approach.

When the Basque returned at dusk, he pointed at Traver. "How long has the wild goat been perched on the precipice?"

"All day," admitted Ariel. She tried to explain what had made Traver flee to the ledge.

But Pedro Ybarra understood without complicated explanations. "In Vizcaya it is tradition that young men leap through bonfires. It is a test of courage. At other times they run through the streets ahead of the bulls during *feria.*"

"But I feel I've driven Traver out onto the ledge," she sniffled.

"He is quite all right. Your young man is simply testing his courage." Pedro took the small silver flute from the mantel and played a haunting melody. Pursing his lips thoughtfully, he said, "Traver is not a careful man. He is used to harshness."

"He was harsh with me today, that's for sure. I'm so confused. I spent so many months longing for Traver, searching for him, hoping he wanted me. Now, when I believed I knew him fully—"

"We never know even *ourselves* fully," he interrupted. "That is why we leap through bonfires, touch the bull's horns and leap over pinnacles." Holding the flute with a wrist crooked like a scimitar, he played a soft, faraway tune. Next he sang a ballad of longing in a lovely tenor voice.

When he'd replaced the flute above the mantel, he moved close to her. They sat facing across the heavy plank table. "Ariel, in my country it is bad grace to inquire into matters not one's own. But we also honor the tradition of the *tertulia.*"

She raised her eyes, asking for a translation.

"A talking," he answered. "Of an evening, people gather. Not for cheap whiskey talk such as I hear in Virginia City. There I hear cowboys and gamblers and miners chattering constantly of how their hearts and brains are engaged. But you and I—tonight, perhaps we can speak openly."

"I trust your judgment, Pedro."

"Then I will be frank. I do not know either you or Traver beyond what I see on the surface. Yet, somehow, I sense you are strangers."

When she remained silent, the Basque continued. "He provokes challenge. I suppose that intrigued you at first."

She laughed cautiously. "But flattening people to the floor doesn't always solve things, I admit."

"Traver wants friends, but not commitments. He seeks devotion, yet his nature keeps him detached."

Ariel sat with hands locked in front of her, fingers tracing and retracing each knuckle. There was no tactful way to avoid hearing the truth.

"I wonder . . ." mused the Basque. "I wonder if you are

truly the woman for Traver. Ah, do not be offended. Your devotion is honest. Your loyalty is admirable. But I sense uncertainty."

Ariel moved to the single west window, focusing on faraway galaxies.

The Basque sighed. "I hope I have not created a barrier to our friendship with my direct speech."

She shook her head no. But how could she tell him how hard it was to give up a dream? She and Traver together! She'd hoped for their reunion so long— through the days on the *Pallas Maru,* the months at Cleo Burney's, while traveling to Virginia City. Was it all to be for nothing?

"I admire your struggle," said Pedro. He stood behind her, a comfort in the darkness. "Tomorrow I leave for the high country to bring down strays. I will be gone several days. Ariel, in the nights I am away, you must decide. First you must heal Traver's pride. His fear will not let him make the first move. It will be up to you."

"But how am I to do this?"

"In ancient Crete, young men found honor in leaping completely over the bulls. The Basques honor that custom when we dart into the streets to touch the horns. You must prove your valor by touching Traver." He nodded toward the storage chest of treasures. "I suggest you wear the red cashmere gown."

Tonight.

She must approach Traver. Ariel had always valued spontaneity. It seemed scandalous to plan so much in advance. But she bathed, scented her body with sandalwood perfume, brushed her hair and left it smoothed over her shoulders.

She watched Traver's every movement. He leaned to stoke the fire. The scent of sage filled the cabin. He leaned forward after putting away the poker, then stretched upward and yawned.

She slipped the red cashmere nightdress over her body. Walking toward him, she searched his eyes for clues. Jade green in Traver's eyes meant he was happy, olive meant restless, seagreen—anger. Tonight they appeared a peaceful emerald. She ran her hands over his shoulders and across his chest, brushing his mouth with a mere hint of a kiss.

He smiled and held her against him, the warmth of their bodies making the soft cashmere gown rise with static. "You're warm as embers," he murmured.

She held back delicately, fearing to push him in any direction he didn't want to go. *It is n t good to plan another's life.* She'd been too bold at the pool and it had infuriated him. Tonight she would use tact. Oh, but how glorious he looked standing in the merry firelight, long legs wide apart, the auburn ringlets on his chest tightly curled.

She leaned up on tiptoes and laid her hot cheek alongside his. He laughed contentedly, " 'Tis a fire we're making of our own, honey lass." He lifted her into his arms and walked to the bedstead.

She extended her arms to him in invitation. Accepting, he stretched alongside her on the bed. One arm cradled her throat, the other smoothed down the soft red material across her breasts. As he bent to kiss her, it was she who was now uncertain. She responded with tenderness, seeking him hesitantly. He lifted his lips and touched his hand to the hollow of her throat. "You make me spark and crackle inside, Ariel. But my shell stays cold. Damn! Why am I so selfish that I can't bear to give you up?"

"Don't give me up, Traver," she begged. "Give me time to know you again. Give me your sweetness. Your strength."

She rolled against him, sensing that though their bodies lay close, there was an emptiness between them. She felt far away, as if no matter how hard she ran, swam, dived or climbed, she could never fall into harmonious step with this man lying beside her.

He tugged at the drawstring tie of the red gown. The soft fabric fell from her breasts. Half-raised, he clasped her around the waist, kissing each nipple, circling with his tongue and taking them far into his mouth. Her skin seemed to magnify each movement; his agile tongue seemed to stab as well as excite.

There is a wall between us, she thought. An invisible, unscalable wall. She moved to accommodate his embrace, but the wall moved with them. An ache of longing swept through her, a longing for a discovery that would end her doubts.

She took comfort that her body was becoming aroused. "We must try," she whispered. "We must find what we once knew. . . ." She smiled into the darkness. "Better than thunder . . . do you remember?" The memory of the storm at sea helped her accept the sensations which were now coursing through her, helped her ignore the invisible wall.

Then Traver's kisses grew stronger, more demanding. She

felt something unleashed in him which he could not control. His body bucked, unfamiliar and desperate. Suddenly he buried his face in her hair. "There are ways," he muttered. "I'll not deny them to you."

Again it was she who held back. She tensed as he pinned her wrists above her head with one hand. The other probed between her thighs. Apprehensive, she tightened as he attempted to nudge her legs apart.

"Don't play coy with me," he insisted. He forced his mouth over hers. Then he moved downward, suckling at her breasts, stroking her stomach, burying his head against her mound. A moment later he licked. Astonished, she felt a faint flower of stimulation drift through her, arcing and curving along her backbone. She had not suspected fingers and tongues could do such tricks.

But it was not trickery she wanted! She wanted *union*—not the mere satisfaction of desire. Traver took a fingerful of scented lamp oil from the bedside lantern, finding new places to arouse her. He moved astraddle, sending widespread comets of sensation through her.

How quickly he'd turned the tables from partnership to dominance! Her body would not say no to the growing sensuality. But deep within, she worried. Yes, she was receiving pleasure from the gentle thrusts and delicate kisses, but this love was not comforting. This was not the lifeline which bound heart to heart. Could they ever recapture that? Or had it ever existed?

The room seemed undersea, full of dampness and green shadows as she felt the mysterious sparks widening out from her womb. Then she no longer regarded needs or feelings, caught up in a tightening ring of pleasure within herself. The blood in her veins constricted. The heartbeats speeded like a tiny trip-hammer. Her body danced with the same fluid freedom she'd felt in the hot spring.

After she collapsed against him, convulsive little shudders continued to dart. Surely Traver loved her deeply to give her such pleasure! I only need the chance to know him better, she consoled herself. Then, suddenly, out of the darkness, she heard him laughing.

Horrified that he would mock her, she tightened and rolled away from his touch. "No, no," he assured her with a playful swat at her backside. "I'm only laughing at myself! I set out to hurt you, Ariel. But with your pleasure, you taught me a great lesson."

She held her breath; now he would admit the need and partnership between them, the mutual confidence, the loyal concern.

His voice fell to a swagger. "Hell, even half of me is a better lover than most whole men!" He guffawed, riotously pleased.

She forced a chuckle, realizing the importance of his self-confidence. And, admittedly, he had satisfied her body. He'd known the twists and thrusts and manipulations to make her flesh respond. For him, that was enough. But it was a trade-off—self-confidence for satisfaction. For her, that would never be enough.

She lay awake, wide-eyed and staring into the fireplace embers. The dying fire. The dying love. So wretched to watch them go! Tonight had not been wrong, she thought, but her concern had been misplaced. Her courage had not been sinful, but erring. There had been passion, but not closeness, laughter, richness. She fought valiantly to right things in her mind. We'll work things through. We'll draw strength from the mine. We'll recover our balance. Yet it seemed her love, now unbalanced, might never again tilt into perfection with this man.

Chapter 15

"Let's go straight to Hell's Candy," urged Ariel as she and Traver arrived back in Virginia City. "I must learn that property from the top of the stack to the bottom of the stopes!"

Traver stiffened. "Tradition says women stay out of mines."

"Well, we'll just have to change that," she laughed. Normally she liked and upheld tradition. Now it was in her way. "Surely *you* don't think I'd be bad luck, do you, Traver?"

"You can go as far as the elevator entrance. If you step into the elevator, the other men will quit. That's the truth, Ariel. I can't run Hell's Candy without a crew, so you'll have to stay above ground."

She grudgingly gave ground—for the time being. "We must have labor," she admitted. "There're weeks, maybe months, of hauling and timbering before we actually begin mining. I'll be on good behavior."

"Don't get in my way," he warned. "You must give me free rein, Ariel. I need space."

Ariel understood this was not the time to press her rights. "I'll be patient," she promised.

"I'll live at the hotel," said Traver, avoiding her gaze. "You can live with your gypsy friend."

She nodded. This was not at all the plan she'd had when she'd arrived in Virginia City, but it was practical, and she had vowed patience.

The next weeks forced more patience than she'd imagined she possessed. The first snows topped the Sierras. The decorated wagon at Gold Hill became a windswept home. "Please, Nedra," begged Ariel. "Let's take rooms in town. There are several decent boarding houses. We'll freeze if we try to winter in this wagon!"

"I'll not part with my wagon!" insisted Nedra. "Never in my life do I want to be without a way to leave town in a hurry."

"You're as daft as Wise Ada and Traver about quick getaways."

"A compromise, then? We'll take rooms at Canada Sally's Boarding House on A Street. That's a proper address for a highborn lady like me. But on Saturdays I'll bring my wagon over from Gold Hill and tell fortunes."

"What about the Decency Committee?"

Nedra narrowed her violet eyes. "What about them?" she threatened. She put her plan into effect the next Saturday. She was met by a committee of unsmiling women, their black hats clamped tight against the wind, their faces grim.

The Decency Committee formed a blockade at the bottom of the hill on D Street. Nedra pouted. "Making me set up shop on this street? I ought to be allowed on B Street, at least—with those other grand liars and entertainers, the stockbrokers!"

Business was good most of the day. When Ariel helped close the wagon flaps late in the afternoon, Nedra counted over fifty dollars in coins. "Shall we go to Piper's Opera with the rest of the town now?" Nedra asked. "Everyone wants to see that magician who can carve ladies in half."

Ariel wasn't interested. "You could do as good an act as that magician! And Su Lin could do twice as well!" She clamped the cinch pin in place. "I don't know why this town thinks it's too good for Chinese to walk its streets. There's nothing here but sagebrush and dusty streets! Prices are going up as winter nears—sugar and coffee a dollar a pound, baking soda so scarce it goes for eight dollars a tin and pickles for eleven!"

Nedra touched up the art work on the side of the wagon.

"Su Lin can't come to town anyway," she offered. "Putnam might recognize her."

Ariel had a sudden idea. "Then let's go to China Camp! Yes, right now. Let's take the wagon and go visit Su Lin and Po Fan."

Nedra was dubious. "We might not be welcome."

But Ariel climbed into the wagon seat and reached for the reins.

China Camp lay three miles from town in the direction of the railroad's Crown Point trestle. It stood in a ravine which was a dry wash in fall, a twenty-foot snow drift in winter and a raging river in spring.

On this autumn Saturday Ariel and Nedra found the camp knee-deep in dust. A clatter of voices shook the desert air. Cabbage odors and charcoal smoke hung over the whole ravine. Pike stick weapons and laundry hung in trees, banners and ribbons and strange paper birds decorated laundry lines.

No one stopped them from entering the maze of tents and shanties after they'd parked the wagon. They found Su Lin and Po Fan's tent—a scrap of canvas hung from a pine branch, a charcoal brazier pot and cots. The quarters seemed so hopeless. Ariel sat silently after greeting her friends. Both Su Lin and Po Fan were thin, their eyes bright with hunger.

Nedra made a feeble attempt at humor. "One good thing about China Camp. You'll be safer here than in town when the big earthquake hits."

"Hush, Nedra!" scolded Ariel. "We need to find a place for Su Lin and Po Fan to be fed and sheltered, not shaken!"

"Oh, there's going to be an earthquake, all right," insisted Nedra. She solemnly touched the gold loop earrings in her ears as if giving the sign of truth. There was such drama in her wide violet eyes and outflung hands, Su Lin giggled, approving of the staging and theatrics.

Ariel changed the subject. "Su Lin, do you find time to practice your dances and gymnastics?"

"Certainly." Su Lin struck a limber pose.

Impulsively Ariel promised, "Oh, Su Lin, when I'm the newest bonanza queen on the hill, I'll buy Piper's Opera and you can dance there!"

Su Lin said humbly, "I wish I could come to town simply to buy the things we need. The only contact we have is when Po Fan is ordered to take Putnam's supplies."

"Supplies? Do you mean opium?"

Su Lin nodded. "He relies on China Camp, especially in

the winter when travel to the Bay is blocked." She smiled serenely, "There is talk among the elders. This winter will be the time to wean Ricket Putnam from his vices."

"Stop his supplies?" breathed Nedra, who apparently foresaw violence associated with such a move.

"Gradually," said Su Lin. "Bit by bit, we will withhold the *chandoo* he craves."

"You'll be setting up an earthquake all your own," predicted Nedra.

Ariel scolded, "Stop talking about earthquakes!"

Su Lin tried to smooth things over. "The Chinese say a dragon is asleep in the mountains. When he stirs and shakes his tail, he is only trying to get comfortable. It is every creature's right." She smiled. "See? We don't have to worry about earthquakes."

Po Fan spoke with the weariness of an old man. "Winter will be hard, quake or not. The railroad is closing down."

Ariel was startled. "Are they finished?" She had been so concerned with Traver and the Hell's Candy, she had lost track of the progress Mitch's crews were making.

"It's far from finished," explained Su Lin. "But the ravine with the trestle will fill with snow soon. Chinamen work mainly on the trestle. It's the highest and most dangerous work." She glanced around at the obvious suffering and poverty of the camp. "Things are bad now. If men lose work and cannot go into town for jobs, there will be trouble."

Ariel spoke up. "I'm certain Mitch Galway will try to keep the crews on. He wouldn't turn anyone out to starve."

Su Lin was uncertain. "It won't be his decision. There is already bickering in the local tongs. Last week the Yan Wo rolled a rock down on the wash tubs of the Sam Yap. Mitch was barely able to soothe the trouble."

No one laughed at the battle of the rival guilds. Trouble in China Camp meant trouble for the railroad, the mines and the city. Ariel was incensed at the injustice she saw all around her. As goodbyes were said, she promised, "I'll find a way to deal with Putnam. Mitch will help me, I know. And Traver is a strong force again." She hugged Po Fan's thin shoulders. "I'll see you have food this winter even if I have to smuggle it to China Camp myself!"

In the wagon Ariel continued to brood about the overwhelming problems. She couldn't stop winter snow from coming. Suddenly she realized Nedra was driving away from town. "The livery stable is the other way."

"I know. We're taking a detour. I want to visit the railroad. See how work is coming along on Crown Point trestle."

"Oh, you're just hoping to see Mitch Galway," laughed Ariel. "Nedra, have you made any progress with him?"

"Faith, he's hardly paid me a bit of attention. I need a new spell to take his attention away from his racehorse on Saturday nights!"

"He's not as big a gambler as he lets on," explained Ariel. "His philosophy is to take risks only when he has faith."

"I wish he'd risk something with me," laughed Nedra.

The wagon topped the hill. Crown Point trestle lay halfway across the ravine, like a huge wooden matchbox toy stuck out over a giant's ditch. "My stars! It's so much bigger than I'd imagined," exclaimed Ariel. The scaffolding reached ninety feet in the air. Gangs of Chinese moved over the construction like a parade of ants, toting buckets, carrying lumber, hauling sledgehammers.

She spotted Mitch. "Look! There he is on his black stallion." Mitch dismounted, took a swing with a sledgehammer, bent and showed how he wanted things done.

Nedra said softly, "Ah, he rides as smoothly as he dances. And he swings that hammer with the same kind of energy that flashes in his eyes."

"You really like him, don't you, Nedra?"

"For all the good it will do me!"

Mitch spotted the wagon and came galloping over. Up close Ariel could see that Mitch was thriving on the regimen of hard, outdoor labor.

She surveyed his handsome, sturdy frame and clean-cut jawline. He was building a reputation as something more than a hard taskmaster. He'd be known as a builder. A man who made things happen. A leader.

Proud Mitch! He acted as if he'd invented railways! "Look at that, ladies!" he crowed, pointing out the fine sections of trestle. "Those iron Howe trusses, that scaffolding and support towers! Look at that figure-eight loop we're starting. God, we've got a grade of a hundred twenty-nine feet to the mile coming up."

"It's wonderful, Mitch," Ariel complimented him.

"Ain't it, now!" he replied, grinning like a little boy with a new toy. "More than wonderful. It's a damned miracle! Fill and cut, bridge and tunnel. My boys pound spikes into rails, sure, but there's more to it than that. We're pounding civilization into a whole continent!"

Nedra tossed him a sultry smile, climbed down and took his arm, asking question after question. Ariel sat alone on the wagon seat, watching the trestle. There was something magnificent in Mitch's dreams. Both he and the railroads seemed here to stay.

Mitch and Nedra were walking back toward the wagon when he took her arm and pulled her to a stop. "Tell me, gypsy girl, how long till the snow shuts us down for winter?"

Nedra declined. "Weather prophecies aren't my line." She leaned against him slightly. "But if you'll come to town tonight, I'll try and see something nice for your future."

Mitch didn't accept the invitation. But he didn't decline. He smiled. Ariel felt a tingle of unwarranted jealousy burn her heart. She immediately stifled her feelings. Hadn't she introduced her friends on purpose?

Mitch called to Ariel. "How's Hell's Candy? Are you in operation yet?"

Ariel answered, "We're short of money, timber and patience. Not to mention labor."

"Use Chinese, like the railroad," Mitch said matter-of-factly.

"And *boo how doy?*" she flared.

"Speak English, woman!"

"Tongs. I know the tongs are competing for the jobs on the railroad, Mitch. I know you're barely keeping things smoothed over and that winter may lead to mayhem. Su Lin told me."

"I don't deny it. But as long as I'm taking orders from Putnam, I can't do more than try to keep Crown Point trestle going as long as possible. I'm just one vote."

She knew Mitch was hemmed in as badly as she where Ricket Putnam was concerned. She kept a restrained silence while Nedra cooed a long string of goodbyes to Mitch.

When the women were back on the road to town, Nedra turned to Ariel. "You didn't have to be so hard on Mitch." She looked over her shoulder to catch another glimpse of golden-haired Mitch on his black stallion. Dreamily she asked, "Do you think he will come to town tonight? Oh, what a fortune I have in mind for him! And what a fortune he will have in his fat pay envelope."

Suddenly Ariel didn't want Nedra anywhere near Mitch. "You'd take him for all he's worth! You're not right for each other."

"My, my, aren't you the touchy one!" Nedra laughed and ran her hands through her kinky, multicolored hair. "Well, I'm open to paying propositions from any well-toned gent in this territory. Including Mitch."

The silence grew more strained.

In the evening Ariel made a point of leaving the boarding house, so she wouldn't know if Mitch called on Nedra or not. Ariel hurried to the hotel where Traver always ate supper. As she entered the dining room full of wooden tables with checkered cloths, he waved to her. "Sit down. Weekly report's about done."

She pulled up a chair, keeping silent as he worked over the long columns of figures. One thing still galled Ariel. The taboo forbidding women in the mines. She hadn't pressed the issue, but she was never satisfied by descriptions. She asked Traver again, "What does it look like down there?"

"Dirty. Gray. Hard blue rock in hard brown rock. Air full of grit. Never enough light. Never enough air. Sweating bodies and suffocating earth. A delight of a job!" Suddenly he slumped forward, head on his arm.

"Traver! Are you sick?"

He shook his head no. "There was a little shake down there today. Did you feel it here in town?"

She tried to remember. "Perhaps a bit of a wobble." She'd noticed a slight vibration around noon.

"We had a few rocks knocking us on the head in Hell's Candy."

"But no one was hurt, were they?" she asked anxiously.

"No. But half a dozen men quit on the spot. I can't blame them. Nedra's earthquake talk has them expecting Sun Peak to collapse any minute."

"Why would grown men believe a gypsy's silly predictions? Oh, that Nedra! I'll give her a good talking-to for touting disaster!"

"Suppose she's right?" Traver shook his head as if *he* didn't believe it, but lesser men might.

"Don't tell me Nedra's done her hex on you, too!"

Traver pushed back his chair and walked around the dining room, returned and stood behind his seat. "We might do well to hold off the opening till spring. Wait for new pumps to arrive. The tremors will subside or the big shake will hit by spring. Let's wait and these problems will work out by themselves."

She understood his argument. But her heart had been set on getting the mine started this year. "Can't we try for operation by winter?" she pleaded.

"*I'm* not offering to quit," vowed Traver. "But if the shakes keep coming, I can't vouch for others. It takes powerful courage to make a man stick when his fellows pile out."

Once again Ariel was distressed she could not go down into the mine and see things for herself. She didn't want people in danger. But surely there were ways to be safe and stay on schedule.

Traver laughed as he closed the conversation. "Hell, what's a few quakes between friends in the Comstock?"

Ariel smiled. Come Monday morning, she'd be at Hell's Candy, by damn! It was time for superstition and legend to die. She'd go down, perform an inspection and reassure everyone that neither women in the underworks nor dragons asleep in the mountain meant harm.

She leaned across the table and caught Traver's hands. "You're doing a wonderful job with the mine," she praised him.

He looked at her, pleased with the compliment. For a moment she thought he might invite her to spend the night with him at the hotel. But then he gruffly disavowed any relationship beyond business.

She despaired of things ever coming to rights between them. If only he'd hold me—love me—kiss me, she longed. But she was no good at playing harlot.

She left him alone in the dining room, doing up the mine accounts, drinking endless cups of black coffee. Glancing back as she exited, she saw him look up at her with longing mixed with anger.

He's building up steam inside, she worried. When he finally explodes, it will make an earthquake seem tame.

Ariel kept a watchful eye on both Traver and the landscape during the weekend, alert to any tremors. All seemed calm. Monday morning she hurried to the elevator shaft of Hell's Candy. She peered downward, and saw only ordinary things: winches, cables and wires. Box cages carried men up and down. From here she could ascertain nothing of the inner workings. Engines rumbled. Hoists rose. Steam escaped lazily from the deeper shaft. But what was going on underneath? She looked out across the sage and juniper hills at the folded, crusted gullies. Everything was shale-colored in late autumn. But what color was Sun Peak on the *inside?* She smiled, imagining the dragon the Chinese believed within the mountain.

There was no question of Ariel descending. Traver refused the request. The foremen, the elevator operator, the superintendent and lines of blank-faced workers backed him up. But she came back each morning for two weeks, hoping he'd change his mind. On the first Saturday in November Traver came up from the shaft and showed her his lunch pail. It had a large dent in the side. "Falling rock?" she asked.

He nodded. "Dented by the dragon," he grumbled. "Every little shake makes the crew braver."

"Braver?"

"About quitting." He sighed. "You'd better go to town and tell Putnam to bring extra money for today's payroll. I think a good percentage of the men will want the balance due them."

"They're going to quit? How many?"

"About half would be my guess."

She was dismayed. The men's fears were real, she couldn't deny. Yet the pressing need to keep working was locked in her mind. The stakes are high, but the results will be worth it, she thought.

Traver was severe with her. "These men are hardly cowards, Ariel. It makes sense to fear things which need fearing." He handed her the dented lunch pail and signaled the elevator man he was ready to go back down.

Ariel was frightened. She went to Putnam and delivered the message. Putnam didn't comment, but she was relieved, later in the afternoon, when he came up the hill with bulging bank bags.

Ariel quizzed Putnam, "What will we do if *everyone* quits?"

"As always, for smart men, there are alternatives."

"Chinese?" She remembered Mitch's admonition, "Do as the railroads."

Traver joined the conversation. "Chinese!" He seemed startled at her naïveté. "John Chinaman works too cheap for the tastes of Virginia City. Chinks are fine for outside town at a dollar a day on the trestles. But four dollars a shift is steep wages in the mines. The whites aren't going to let you pay that kind of money to coolies."

The elevator bell rang, signaling the end of the shift. Men hastily formed a line at the paymaster's office. Their faces were flushed with happy relief that they'd lived to collect!

Money in hand, they rushed away from the elevators, not about to risk their necks again. The next group moved to the window, laughing, joking, slapping backs. They were much too jolly. It was clear, come Monday, they'd not return.

A light snow began, settling over the hillside with gusty brightness. Winter's arrived, thought Ariel, and we're still weeks away from opening the mine!

Suddenly she noticed a little knot of men at the bottom of the hill. They were screaming. Throwing hats into the air. Cheering. Racing toward town. She nudged Traver, who was helping close the payroll shack. "What's happened?"

He peered at the men. Some were racing to and fro as if confused. Most ran downhill toward town; a few straggled back toward the mines, shouting at the peak of their voices. The noise spread along the chain of stacks. The news reached Hell's Candy with ear-splitting force. "A big strike! Glory hole at the Annie Lynn! Dancing in the streets. Strike games! Races and faro! Crack-loo and Memphis dominoes! Specials in the D Street cribs—fifty cents off the going price for any girl!"

Within seconds the last of the employees had rushed down the mountainside to join the fun.

Putnam locked the payroll cage and pocketed his pistol.

Ariel asked, "How long will this mayhem last?"

"Until the whiskey runs out. Until the monte tables on the sidewalks fall down. Until the money's all changed hands a dozen times." Putnam put the bank bags over his saddle horn. "I'd not take unkindly to a bit of amusement myself." He rode away at a trot.

Ariel and Traver followed him down the hill. The merry-makers had turned Virginia City into a street carnival despite the softly falling snow. It was difficult to move through the streets. With barely an hour of celebrating under their belts, men were already asleep, drunk, in the empty water troughs. Stockbrokers had set up street corner auctions of mine shares. Games spilled out of the gaming parlors onto the boardwalk. Ariel heard Mitch's loud Irish voice yelling, "Start the race on B Street, circle the Ophir works. First man and beast across the threshold of the Bloody Bucket saloon wins!" Men ran for their horses.

"Wise Ada!" Ariel spotted her friend across a traffic jam of wagons, buggies, draycarts, mules and pedestrians. The old lady waved and held up a handful of large tickets. "What are they?" called Ariel, wondering what Wise Ada might be promoting.

Wise Ada was unable to cross the street, but she hollered, "I've rigged a tramway. Want to ride? Transport of the future, right as rain!" She pointed to a perilous contraption of wires, ropes and ore buckets which ran at a steep angle between the roof of the five-story International Hotel and the two-story bank building. Swarms of grown men snatched tickets for rides on the death-defying transportin' conveyance.

Ariel waved goodbye and moved along the sidewalk, wondering how the town could survive such an onslaught.

As they made their way past the Guardian Concert Hall, she spotted a small figure darting from the overhang of the entryway. Po Fan! Oh, what was he doing in town among such an unruly crowd! She raised her voice to shout to him, trying to make herself heard over the noise. "Po Fan! Here!"

The Chinese boy's face broke into a smile. He dashed across the street. At that instant a rider on a brown buckskin galloped around the corner at breakneck speed. The rider screamed a curse, and galloped away. Po Fan crumpled in the quartz roadbed.

Ariel and Traver rushed to the boy. Only a few people on the sidewalk bothered to notice who'd been trampled. Once they saw it was an Oriental, they went about their business.

Po Fan was lying twisted, his arms and legs stuck out of too-short pajamas. The left leg stuck out at an unnatural, oblique angle. Ariel cried, "His leg's broken!" She knelt on the streetbed, cradling Po Fan's head. He tried to smile. "Oh, I'm so sorry, so sorry," she repeated.

Traver knelt, kindly and strong, taking charge. "We're right outside Putnam's office. I can carry Po Fan that far." He stroked the boy's forehead. "This will hurt," he whispered gently.

Traver slid long arms beneath the matchstick child, lifting him carefully. Po Fan blinked rapidly but made no sound.

Ariel shoved people aside, ran upstairs and knocked at Putnam's door. "Open up!" cried Ariel, pounding harder.

When there was no answer, she turned the knob and barged inside. Putnam was seated at the low table with his opium lamp. Of course! That's why Po Fan had been in town.

She ran into the room. "Putnam, wake up! You must help us. A boy is hurt." Putnam was too far into his opium haze to respond. His features were so pallid he appeared covered with wax.

Traver entered, Po Fan in his arms. "This child's leg is broken. Putnam, you must set it."

Putnam glanced up. "No strike games go by without casualties."

Ariel was appalled. Was Putnam implying he'd let the leg go untreated? Surely he can put on splints, even in this condition, thought Ariel. Anything he does will be more professional than my amateur first aid. "Get up!" she demanded again. "Set this child's leg immediately."

Traver placed Po Fan on the couch. Putnam remained immobile. "Waste my time on a China boy?"

"You're responsible for his being in town, Putnam. It's your fault he was run over in the streets!" roared Traver.

Putnam folded his arms. "Chinese have their own ways. They'd not want my interference. If I prevent this boy from going to his ancestors, no one will thank me."

Ariel scowled. "Since when were you interested in Oriental customs? I want this child tended—promptly and properly."

"Ariel, you've never understood. Chinese are expendable."

Expendable. The word dizzied her. Everyone was expendable to Putnam—the young girls he abused, the labor in Hell's Candy, Mitch and the railroad. "No one need know you treated a Chinese, if that's what's bothering you," she snapped.

Traver stopped the battle with direct action. He pulled Putnam's pistol from its belt. "Children can't fight their own battles." He aimed the gun directly at Putnam's left temple. "Now, no one in the goddam town will know *why* you set this broken bone. But set it you will. Right now. And skillfully. If this boy has a limp, I'll see *you* have a permanent kink in your spine!" Traver handed Putnam a cloth. "Go to work."

Putnam raised his eyes at Ariel, as if to say, call off your dog. Traver clicked the safety catch of the pistol. Then Putnam inhaled sharply, rose and reached for his physician's bag.

It took Ariel half an hour to maneuver the livery rig close to the back door of the Guardian Concert Hall. Traver carried Po Fan to the wagon, settled him carefully in the splinted cast, then turned away. "Get in," insisted Ariel. "We must take him to China Camp."

"I'm not going. You can make it on your own," said Traver stubbornly, slouching and sticking his hands in his pockets. "I'm tired. Tired of fighting your battles. I'm going out and get drunk and fight with my fists." He turned away. "I loused things up in there."

"How can you talk like that! You were marvelous, Traver. Standing up to Putnam. So very gentle with Po Fan."

"My pulling a gun on Putnam was the same as slitting my throat. I won't have a job come Monday."

"You can't quit!" She wondered if he was using Putnam as an excuse. She tried reasoning with him. "Putnam won't remember anything when his haze wears off."

"I really don't care. I've been city-bound for weeks. I'm going upland and work my mountain claim."

"You can't go to the highlands! It's snowing!"

"I'm going." He turned toward the nearest saloon.

"You stubborn ox!" She'd have to deal with him later. Now she must take Po Fan to China Camp. She flicked the reins across the horse's back, hoping to jostle Po Fan as little as possible. She took side streets out of town and made good progress on the open road.

Within seconds of the time Ariel pulled the wagon through the arched bamboo gate at China Camp, the word had spread through the gully. Su Lin came running and settled Po Fan in the tent. "It is time to take matters out of Putnam's control," she said bitterly.

"You'll begin withholding opium?" Ariel asked.

"Diluting it at first. It must be subtle, so he cannot retaliate." She lifted her hands and pantomimed an accompaniment to her words. "It must be the way the butcher slices the pig—not by hacking at the whole animal, but deftly, tilting the blade quickly into the joints." She smiled and folded her arms. "My people will avenge Po Fan."

Su Lin's mysterious new strength unnerved Ariel. She rose to leave. "Sit down," ordered Su Lin with the force of an imperial empress. "We shall take tea." She poured the dark, bitter *oo-long* brew into fragile cups without handles. "The snows have begun. Now the trestle work will halt. Do you know what will be left of China Camp by spring? A heap of bones!" She banged delicate fists against the hot surface of the charcoal pot. "My people will starve."

"Your troubles are like mine, only in reverse," sympathized Ariel. "At Hell's Candy, we will have to close for lack of labor."

For an instant the two friends stared at each other. The obvious answer hung in the air, but neither dared to put it into words. Ariel spoke first, quietly and almost breathlessly. "It would defy tradition, of course, using Chinese in the mines."

"Tradition might yield in the face of starvation."

Ariel grew thoughtful. "I wonder, though, would men from China Camp dare to come to town and work in the Hell's Candy?"

"It would be better to fight for a job than fight each other for the few coins left at the railroad." Su Lin stood, regal and gracious. "How many workers will you need?"

"One hundred. Monday morning." The objections Putnam and Traver would surely raise made Ariel cautious. "Have them ready. Keep them here. I shall come to China Camp and personally lead them to work at Hell's Candy."

Chapter 16

Snow fell all weekend, and the strike games finally ended. Sunday morning at six, a slight tremor woke the town, setting off church bells. Ariel roused herself and called to Nedra, "All the Catholic miners in town will take that bell ringing as a sign from heaven to stay clear of the mines."

Nedra yawned and turned over to go back to sleep. "The Hell's Candy won't be the only one out of workers. All the big works up and down Sun Peak will have to close."

"Nedra, can you keep a secret?" Ariel was wide awake now and brimming with eagerness to talk. "The Hell's Candy won't have to close! When everyone else is shut down, we'll be going strong. I've made a deal with Su Lin. No one else knows about it. The Hell's Candy will have Chinese workers!"

Nedra sat upright, wide-eyed. "What will Traver say to that?"

"Oh, Traver's stalked off into the mountains!" pouted Ariel. He had actually made his threatened departure for the upland claim. "Why, Monday morning, Traver probably won't even show up! He'll be trapped in the mountains by all this snow."

Nedra pulled the covers over her chin. "You've gone loony,

my girl! I can see by your eyes you're worried about Traver *and* about the deal. I predict you'll have a sleepless night tonight."

Nedra's prophecy was all too true. At daylight Monday, Ariel hurried to China Camp, bundling herself in her winter coat and boots. Promptly at nine she took her place at the head of the rag-tag column and started the overland march to the Hell's Candy. The men trudged silently through the snow. Few had jackets. Most wore only thin cotton pajamas. Well, they'd be warm and cozy in the Hell's Candy. She started a song, an Australian ditty Traver had taught her. Soon the men joined in, singing in dozens of dialects.

As she led her army over the last hill, she saw three men at the entrance to the Hell's Candy. Surprised, she made out the figures of Traver, Mitch, and Putnam. Apparently they were preparing to shut the gates permanently. Triumphantly she called out, "Wait a moment, gentlemen! Don't be so hasty in giving up. Look! Workers in abundance."

Traver hurried forward to confront her, an astonished frown on his dark face. His red hair blew in the wind. "What have you done?"

She avoided a direct answer. "I see you're back," she said coolly.

"For the moment," he conceded. "Now, what the hell does this mean?"

"I've hired them."

"This isn't right," he argued. "The men who quit did so out of fear. Fear that may be justified. It's wrong to hire men who can't weigh their chances of danger."

"They understand," she insisted. She turned and spoke in Cantonese, "You want work?" The upraised arms and voices repeated, "Work! Work!" It was clear in any language they were willing to descend into Hell's Candy.

Traver wasn't convinced. "They don't understand! They believe in joss sticks and dragons and flowery kingdoms and celestial dynasties. They don't understand what might happen in a bad quake."

Again she stood up to his objections. "They understand starvation. They'll die waiting for the railroad to begin work again next spring."

Now Mitch Galway and Ricket Putnam walked over to the elevator cages where Ariel and Traver stood arguing. After listening a moment, Mitch supported Ariel's proposal.

"Personally," said Mitch, "I'd rather be roasting my ass in

Hell's Candy than freezing on the trestle. You damned well can't pound spikes into snowdrifts."

"Stay out of this, Galway!" roared Traver.

Finally, Putnam nodded. "All right, Traver. Put them to work."

Traver snorted. "I'm caught in a damned crossfire between you and Ariel! You're both attracted to Hell's Candy like rats to cheese. With you two in cahoots, I don't stand a chance. I'm odd man out in this deal."

"For once, you're right, Traver Loch," cried Ariel, realizing she was much too harsh. "You're acting like a coward because you're superstitious! Superstitious about Chinese in the mines. Superstitious about women going down. You're looking for excuses to quit and go wandering in the mountains. You've lost your courage!"

He said quietly, "I won't back down."

She'd have to take matters into her own hands then. She seized the hand rope and clanged the bell which started the morning shift.

The Chinese cheered. Putnam smiled with approval.

Mitch moved protectively toward Ariel, as if to defend her from Traver and Putnam both. Traver silently stared at Ariel for a long moment. His forehead wrinkled, his green eyes blazed and his face reddened. "I've not *lost* my courage," he muttered. "It seems I *sold* it!"

An uneasy peace hung over the town during December. The earth tremors continued, keeping the Caucasian miners off the job even though they voiced their resentment at the Chinese laboring in Hell's Candy. Traver stayed away entirely, and Ariel hoped he'd come back. She knew things ran more smoothly with him around. And she missed him terribly, with a dull ache inside that never went away.

On Saturday evening Ariel looked for Mitch at the stable. He was there, currying the black stallion, his face glowing with excitement.

"Won another race today, didn't you?" she asked.

He patted the stallion. "He never fails me." He smiled at Ariel. "And did you come all this way to congratulate me on my bad habits?"

"Mitch, I have a proposition for you."

"When did you take to propositioning men, Ariel my pet?" His golden laughter boomed through the barn.

"I want you to run the Hell's Candy. Be the manager." She

didn't allow him a chance to object. "You know how to handle the Chinese workers. And the railroad is all but shut down for the winter."

"Not me. I want nothing to do with Hell's Candy, Ariel." He softened his frown, adding, "Unless it's owning it!"

She was disappointed. He moved closer, tilted her chin up and, for a moment, she thought he might bend and kiss her. But he only looked deeply into her brown eyes and smiled. "I'll talk to Traver for you, however."

"Oh, Mitch, thank you! You *are* a good friend."

"Is that all?"

Ariel had begun to doubt her relationship with Traver. So many problems! But she didn't want to give Mitch false encouragement.

"Don't you see, Ariel? Haven't you figured out about you and Traver yet? You were so damned ready for a man—"

"Mitch! It's improper for you to say such things."

"I've never claimed to be proper." He grinned, combing the stallion with energetic strokes. "Traver's a battler, don't you understand?"

She could hardly deny that.

"But I'm a builder," he went on. "I'll build an empire out of this sagebrush and sand. And I won't do it by clawing and scratching or sticking my head in a hole in the ground."

She dared not think in Mitch's terms. "Have Traver come back," she begged. "Have him work the Hell's Candy. He can learn to stay in one place."

"I doubt it. It's a wonder you've held him this long. I'm amazed he hasn't hitched his wagon and gone to Texas." He threw down the curry comb and grabbed her shoulders. "No matter what you try, Ariel, someday you'll find yourself stranded—half of a two-horse rig."

"Don't you ever think of anything but horses!"

"Yes," he replied softly. "Sometimes—too often for my own good—I think of *you*." He drew her against him gently, holding her against his chest like a delicate bouquet. "I think of your sweet honey hair and moonlight voice and fiery lips."

The tenderness in his voice startled her. Then he bent to kiss her and she didn't shy away. His lips softened, applying only slight pressure, somehow all the more intimate for not being greedy. A quiver of response rippled through her, like a feather drawn across the nape of her neck. His lips brushed her cheeks, trailing little kisses down across her throat. She felt the gentle pressure of his hand against the small of her back, urging her toward him. How easy to melt into his embrace! How simple to deny him nothing and partake of his delight.

But she broke away and ran from the stable.

Mitch's voice boomed after her. "My God, Ariel! Who are you running from? Me? Or yourself!"

Ariel was surprised when Traver came back to the Hell's Candy. Mitch's good deed, she supposed. Mitch and Traver were a pair of ruffians who took turns being on good behavior. One was always bailing the other out of difficulty. Whatever the reason for peace on all fronts, she was appreciative. Even the earth went on good behavior. The tremors died away. The Chinese labored diligently. With hope balanced against pessimism, Ariel finally believed the Hell's Candy would open.

"December Twentieth! Hell's Candy Comes on Line," read the headline on the *Territorial Enterprise*. Ariel was up early, hurrying Nedra to get ready.

"We're expecting a crowd for the ribbon-cutting," Ariel said excitedly. She ran to the window of the boarding house room. "Look at them already! Everyone's heading uphill. The whole world will hear it when I ring the bell for the first official shift!"

"Damned fine crowd," mused Nedra, peering over Ariel's shoulder. "I'll take my wagon along. Tell a few fortunes."

"No earthquake predictions! Understand?" Ariel laughed goodnaturedly. Nothing could ruin this morning.

"Poor Nedra will be on good behavior," promised the gypsy. She was getting rich enough to be generous. Men with money in their fists seemed drawn to Nedra, and she made the most of it.

"I sent an invitation to Su Lin and Po Fan to be at Sun Peak and see the festivities," Ariel told Nedra as they drove up to the hillside. "Perhaps this will be the first crack in the town's armor against Chinese going downtown."

Nedra's wagon was quickly surrounded by miners eager to have their outstretched palms deciphered. Ariel hopped out, adjusted her wide-brimmed bonnet and started toward the stack.

Traver came through the crowd, smiling, ready to escort her to the platform. Then she saw him frown and point, so she turned, looking back at Nedra's wagon. Trouble. Oh, no, not today! Not the Decency Committee!

She took Traver's arm. "Couldn't they pick on poor Nedra some other time?"

"I suspect 'poor Nedra' can hold her own," he laughed. "But I'll go over, just in case." He arrived at the same time as the fuming, black-gloved delegation. Nedra listened to the complaints with a forced smile.

Ariel edged closer, wondering how Traver planned to handle the confrontation. Nedra stood up on the wagon seat as if to crack the reins and leave. But she didn't capitulate. Instead, she cracked the whip toward the tallest of the ladies. The woman screamed and jumped backwards.

Before Nedra could attack again, Traver stepped in front of her. "Tell my fortune, gypsy!" he ordered loudly, extending his hand.

Nedra appeared a bit taken back, as if she'd really have preferred to whip the black gloves off her adversary. But she also seemed to understand Traver's motives. She held his hand, stroking it with both of hers. "You expect trouble. And love it. You court danger. It is your destiny. You are a provoker, Traver Loch!"

Ariel was startled at the way Nedra now leaned provocatively toward Traver. And he responded with a puppy-dog grin!

The black-gloved lady adjusted her black hat and edged back for another round. "Young lady, you are creating a nuisance," she shouted at Nedra.

Traver looked sternly at Nedra. "Do you consider yourself a nuisance?" Then he leaned over and teased loudly, "Say yes and I'll hold your coat while you poke the livin' daylights out of that dried-up prune!"

Nedra roared with delight. What a pair Traver and Nedra made, thought Ariel. Both of them ready to go to fisticuffs with the world on a moment's notice!

Ariel intervened. "It's time to celebrate! We didn't come to referee any fights. Close up shop, Nedra. Come, Traver, it's time we got things started at the lifts."

Traver escorted her proudly up the hill. At the platform he handed her the bell rope. Without a moment's hesitation, she tugged. The bell resounded across the valley, ringing in each elevator cage. "At last! Hell's Candy is in business!"

A cheer went up from the crowd. The lines of workers prepared to go down. Traver doffed his hat, acknowledging the celebration. Then he stepped into the first cage to descend. Ariel stood peering after him, yearning to accompany him down into the depths.

Nedra came up to where Ariel stood and nudged her with a firm elbow. "Come on! Hurry. We have important errands."

"What's that?"

"We must go to the milliner's. And the seamstress."

"Why?"

"Ariel, don't be silly! With all the new money *you* are going to have, *we* need new dresses for New Year's!"

As Ariel put on her new gown of canary-yellow sateen, she was pleased with herself and the end of the year. There'd been no silver bonanza yet, but the town was in good spirits. The hotel was giving a ball and Daniel's French restaurant had ordered jeroboams of Moët et Chandon champagne.

"Ariel, you look lovely," praised Nedra.

Ariel accepted the compliment and was glad she could honestly repay one to her friend. "You, too, Nedra. You look beautiful in pale blue. It sets off the purple in your eyes and your dark hair. And the straight sleeves and embroidered muslin are quite ladylike." She hesitated a moment. "Perhaps you should take those feathers off the velvet neck ribbon."

"Trying to make a lady of me still?" laughed Nedra. But she removed the bright feathers and replaced them with a tiny spray of fresh violets at her throat.

When they entered the hotel, they discovered everyone had new clothes for the New Year's ball. Traver looked stunning, dark and elegant in Morocco leather shoes with cloth tops, a navy blue evening coat with gilt buttons, nankeen trousers and gaiters. He wore a stiff white collar beneath his clean-shaven chin. The auburn sideburns were slickly obedient, his eyes green and fresh as a meadow.

His welcome to the ladies was exuberant. "Ariel! Nedra! Come here and let me look at you! What a sight for sore eyes!" He clasped their hands, then glanced approvingly at Nedra. When the music began, he bowed and asked Nedra to dance. Oh, there were the makings of a gentleman in Traver and a lady in Nedra despite themselves, thought Ariel.

When the dining room doors were thrown open, they enjoyed a feast of duckling, corn pudding, champagne, Nesselrode pie and more champagne. Ariel noticed Putnam in the corner, entertaining two young girls. He lifted his glass in a toast toward Ariel; she averted her eyes. She looked for

Mitch. From Nedra's sly glances around the room, Ariel knew Nedra was looking for him, too. Then Nedra seemed to forget Mitch as she leaned back, filled with laughter at Traver's jokes.

There was a rustling at the door. Ariel looked up expectantly again. What a surprise! The Basque stood outlined by the lobby's gaslights. His long blue cloak was thrown back over one shoulder, his black beret pulled down almost to his eyebrows. Ariel jumped up and ran to him. "Pedro Ybarra! What a pleasant surprise. Please come and join us!"

She brought the Basque to the table and introduced him to Nedra. Traver greeted him warmly. The two men shook hands, clasping one atop the other, then Ariel urged Pedro to be seated. "Oh, Nedra, you must tell the Basque's fortune!" Ariel suggested.

Nedra held Pedro Ybarra's weathered hand. Her eyelids drooped as she concentrated, then she gazed with penetrating frankness at the man's face. "This is no ordinary hand I hold," she murmured. "It's luck written in your lines." She stopped abruptly.

"That's no fortune! Go on," urged Ariel. She nudged Traver to refill all the champagne glasses.

Nedra curtly dropped the Basque's hand. "Remember poor Nedra when you make your lucky strike in the mines."

Ariel was disappointed. "He's no miner—and you know it," she complained to Nedra.

Nedra leaned over and whispered, "You want the truth? It's luck in his lines, all right, but it's bad luck! There is something in his future he longs for. But he is not to have it. Something he desires will be lost. Something he has planned for and waited for."

Stunned, Ariel sat back. Too late, she saw the Basque had overheard. He rose abruptly, excused himself and hurried toward the door. Ariel ran after him. After trying to apologize to Pedro Ybarra and making no progress, Ariel sadly told him goodbye as he went out into the clear, cold night. As she turned back to the dining room, the orchestra began playing again. Nedra and Traver rose to dance, looking pleased with themselves. Nedra seemed to hesitate, as if waiting for Ariel's permission to dance with Traver. Then she smiled and moved into his arms, a spirited, happy look in her eyes.

As Ariel stood in the doorway, contemplating going home, she felt a tap on her shoulder. "May I have this dance?" inquired Mitch.

."Oh, Mitch, everything's going wrong tonight!" she cried.
He smiled and nodded. "Not everything. I've found you
waiting for me." He took her into his arms and they danced
apart from the crowded dining hall. Alone in the lobby, she
felt awkward at first and stiff in his embrace. He was elegantly
attired in newly polished black boots, striped trousers and a
cutaway jacket of softest wool. She closed her eyes, trying to
relax. It was good to feel Mitch's strong arms around her.

She lost her self-consciousness as he swept her around the
lobby. By the time the music ended, she was back in a party
mood. But Mitch didn't offer to dance with her again. He
escorted her back to the dining room and left her at her table.
This will be a good evening after all, she thought. We're all
good friends and can behave as such!

She saw Mitch dance with several of the married ladies.
Then, when she was dancing with Traver, she saw Mitch ask
Nedra to dance. They moved onto the floor with theatrical
flourishes, looking well-matched in each other's arms. "What
a pair!" she whispered to Traver.

He cocked his head sideways and didn't say anything. But
she noticed he kept an eye on Mitch and Nedra for the rest of
the number.

Things went smoothly until near midnight. Ariel excused
herself, visited the powder room and was returning to the
party when Mitch confronted her in the lobby. He held out
his arms silently for another dance. She started to avoid him,
then accepted his invitation.

They danced in silence, their arms barely touching.
"You're an elegant dancer, Mitch," she admitted, at ease in
his arms now.

He sighed. "It seems I've always known your arms around
me."

The implication hit her. He was correct. It was *his* arms
she'd felt she'd known forever! Her heart began to tremble,
her breath quickened. This wasn't right. She must break the
force between them before they acknowledged it.

He tightened his grip on her hand, then around her waist.
She could barely hear the music. Their bodies were so tense it
seemed as if lightning might jump from one to the other. She
tried to breathe deeply, but the odor of champagne and cigars
overpowered her.

The lights went out. "Happy New Year!" cried the crowds.
She felt Mitch's arms grasp her so completely she could
neither laugh, sigh nor breathe. His embrace seemed to

surround her wholly. Her whole world stopped. The music died away and fear welled up in the center of her being as she felt him bending to kiss her.

She clutched his neck, meaning to push him away. Instead, she clung to him, craving the feel of his lips against hers. In a gesture of giving, she abandoned the struggle and went limp in his arms.

His face grew heavy upon hers as he sought her mouth. She felt she would suffocate with sweetness as their warm lips melted together. She wished she were naked—without skin, even—so as to join with him completely. Every sound, smell, touch seemed magnified: his sharp breathing, his masculine scent, the brush of his fingertips across her cheek.

Taut as wire, she felt her breasts swelling. This revelation of love for Mitch was so startling, so compelling, she felt as if the world had changed size and shape. She struggled with her desire to renew the kiss. "This is an accident," she said huskily.

"This is fate," he replied, and brought his lips over hers in a kiss of great tenderness but overwhelming force.

Her arms tightened around his neck and her lips parted responsively to his probing tongue. Her legs parted slightly beneath the canary-yellow sateen dress. She could feel his whole body against hers, pressing, urging. He lifted his mouth from hers ever so slightly and sighed, "Now do you doubt the bonds that are meant to be between us?"

Then, as if nothing had happened, the lights came back on. It was January 1, 1870. Mitch took her arm and escorted her into the crowded dining room. He left her without another word.

The party moved outside for fireworks in the streets. She held tightly to Traver's arm, shaking her head in an effort to clear away the memory of Mitch's kiss. The quartz in the roadbed sparkled in the light of a new moon. The crisp night was invigorating, not cold enough to harden the bones, only turn the cheeks pink. The Sierra peaks stood coldly beautiful with their white tops stuck through gossamer clouds. As they moved down the sidewalk, she felt a small wobble in her ankles. She ignored it, thinking her dancing straps had caught a loose stone. Then, from the pressure of Traver's hand on her arm, she knew he'd felt it, too.

"What was it?" she asked.

"Nothing," he shrugged.

At that moment another small swelling of the ground tilted the sidewalk. They both stopped simultaneously. The brief tremor was accompanied by a low rumble, like far distant thunder.

People in the street stopped, turned their heads inquiringly at each other. Most noises subsided. It seemed someone had pulled the world to a halt unexpectedly. One lively voice called out, "Judgment Day!" Twitters of laughter chimed in the clear darkness. But no one moved.

The night took a long pause, then a slow undulation rocked the street, spread to the buildings. The noise sounded like someone clearing his throat in the next room. A long chord of rumbles died away, then a monotonous tone, like one note on a pipe organ, rose from the earth. "Is this it?" someone cried.

Now people were lifted from their paralysis. A drunk staggered from curb to curb. A couple began to polka. Some people rushed inside buildings, an equal number barreled out into the streets. The earth strained. Ariel felt the pressure beneath her feet. What should she look for? Cracks in the earth? Breaks in the street surface? "It's like there're ocean waves under us," she said, adjusting her footing.

Traver seemed slightly frightened. Perhaps he was only more aware. "We'd better keep a close watch. These walls may come tumbling down on our heads."

The next rumble of sound shot through the buildings like a crackle of gunfire. The tall roofline of the International Hotel bounced in sections. The hardpacked streets popped with sounds like twigs snapping. Chimneys shook, shingles flew and loose bricks tumbled. Traver grabbed her, dragging her along the sidewalk. "Take cover!" he cried hoarsely. "This is it!"

"Where should we go?"

"A basement!"

A moment later all the second-story windows along the storefronts flew upward. People began to cry out in fright. They panicked, not knowing whether to burrow or flee. The turmoil was more terrifying than the earthquake, thought Ariel as Traver pulled her through a dark doorway. Where was everyone taking refuge, she wondered. She prayed that Nedra, Mitch, the Basque, everyone would be all right.

Darkness cut off her view of the street. "Where are we?" A hard shake sent concussions through the walls. Her teeth chattered.

"We're in a storeroom, I think. Boegle's book store." She heard him groping in the dark, breathing heavily. "Get these crates down! They'll fall on us. Hurry up!"

A groaning noise rose. Sidewalks? Slipping away from the storefronts, she guessed. Suddenly she felt dizzy. She reached for Traver as repercussions shook the floor. "I can't get my footing." Each new vibration sent her heart into erratic flurries. To her horror, her hands shook uselessly when she tried to lift a crate.

Her eyes adjusted to the dimness. An animal fear had distorted Traver's features. His eyes were wide as if bewildered that the sturdy earth could collapse beneath him. He worked wildly, heaving, shoving, his body jerking as if he were a puppet yanked by invisible threads.

Above them boxes of stationery and rolls of brown paper swayed. She reached to stop the fall. The next instant the whole wall of shelves and stationery supplies came hurtling at their heads.

The noise turned to drum rolls. The floor shifted up and down like a seesaw. A large tilt sent Traver reeling backwards, a heavy crate of books in his arms. He crashed against her, sending them both sprawling on the floor. "Let me up!" she cried, afraid she would be buried. Ariel was terrified. "Let me out!" she screamed.

She panicked, clawing and howling. Was Traver crazy, too? He was butting crates with his head, shoving wildly with his arms, bringing more debris on top of them than he moved away. Why was he barricading the exit?

"Don't keep us here!" she cried, pounding his back with angry fists. Her skin was clammy, her heart pounded wildly.

He grabbed her wrists, then her shoulders, shaking her. Dust filled the basement. Crates bombarded them, making hollow noise in the darkness. She began to tremble violently, falling against Traver, struggling to break his grasp on her shoulders.

He clutched her tighter. His power was as terrifying as the earthquake's. His ragged gasping sounded like a battle cry, as if he were furious the world could turn upside down.

She slumped to the floor. Her cheek scraped a packing case. Traver fell atop her, strange sounds coming from his throat. She could hardly breathe. Worse, she felt entombed. Walled up. Strangled. The more she struggled to get up, the tighter he pinned her down. With frantic urgency, he dug for her body. He lifted her face, crushing his mouth over hers.

Traver placed her body straight between stacks of packing crates. At first she hoped he meant to shield her. Then she felt him moving atop her, running his hands through her hair, driving his mouth against hers in furious kisses. His voice carried through the darkness. "If I am to die, let it be in your arms!"

He smothered her throat with kisses. "Tell me you want me!" he demanded, ripping at the square neckline of the canary-yellow gown. With his other hand he yanked away his clothing, then swept down on her.

He tore away the skirt of her gown, crushing against her flesh with overpowering force.

He will crush me, she thought. The walls of the basement will crush him. The mountains will crush the town. The forces have been blocked too long. He needs release like the dragon under Sun Peak! Despite her understanding, she struggled. "Traver, don't do this! Not like this! Not to me!"

But his fury was savage as the earth's. For an instant he poised over her like a clock about to strike midnight. Then he took her.

Ariel writhed beneath him. He has no conscience! He recognizes only physical power, she thought desperately.

Then, suddenly, she heard the crash of heavy crates from above. The force between her legs exploded. She felt the searing hotness, the shudder of his body, the frantic spurting within her. Then there was stillness.

Traver moaned as the full force of the collapsing crates struck him. He rolled away from her and sprawled backward, unconscious.

She tried to crawl out from under the crates, stationery, books and debris. But she couldn't move. For a moment she lay still, weeping softly. Then, when she found her voice to call for help, she was shocked beyond all knowing by her words. "Help," she called. "Oh, for godsake, help me, Mitch!"

Chapter 17

Virginia City's troubles officially entered history as the New Year's Quake. Locally, everyone called it the Nedra Shake. Wise Ada made a fortune during January, carting away debris in her wide-bodied, open-sided mud wagon. "We were lucky," she insisted to all who would listen. "No avalanche. Only three small fires. No people swallowed up—only two dogs and a donkey. By all that's holy, this place was devilishly lucky." Wise Ada called to Ariel, who was painting the window sills of her room at the boarding house.

Ariel didn't reply to Wise Ada's speech about luck. There was damage enough, she thought sadly. Her mind once again went over the details of the earthquake, the assault and the aftermath. She remembered every terrifying second, while Traver seemed to remember nothing. She shook her head in anger and confusion, thinking how, after the quake, Traver had regained consciousness in the armory infirmary. He'd climbed out of bed, insisting he felt fine, then made straight for his mountain claim.

Perhaps he didn't remember, she consoled herself again. And perhaps that was for the best! But her body remembered. Her father had taught, "What we can't excuse, we must forgive." But no, this she could not forgive. She was horrified by her discovery of the fury and fear in Traver. She tried to forget Traver's violation, but she also knew the time was close when she must see him.

The confrontation came when she, Putnam and Traver met to discuss repairs to the Hell's Candy. Traver had returned from the mountains, complaining of the winter's coldness. He was anxious to go back to the heat of the mine. In Putnam's office he seemed cordial and conciliatory. He offered Ariel a chair, businesslike and courteous. He doesn't remember, she decided. Or, if he does, he can't admit it.

Traver spoke energetically, "Preliminary reports look good. We were lucky at Hell's Candy. There have been some rockslides and some shot holes filled with silt, but nothing that can't be carted out in wheelbarrows."

"Then we can reopen in days?" questioned Putnam.

"The only problem is if we find water when we get to the bottom of the shaft," Traver answered.

Putnam was hopeful. "The center of the quake was at the top of the Comstock. Reports say there's been more damage on the surface than beneath the earth."

Not to me, thought Ariel. My damage is inside. She shifted position in the chair, trying to rid herself of the uncomfortable, unsatisfied feeling of her own flesh. Why didn't her odd ailments subside? It had been a month. Even her monthly cycle was off schedule. But she presumed an earthquake that could dry up cows, start new springs and cause gout could disrupt internal chemistry as well. Or—she suddenly inhaled and covered her mouth with her hand. For the first time it occurred to her she might be pregnant.

She wasn't aware she'd made a noise until Putnam asked, "Yes? What is it?"

"Uh . . . how long until the shafts are cleared?"

"Three weeks," predicted Traver. "Possibly four."

"That's too long!" Ariel cried.

Putnam looked at her through narrowed eyes. "What has gotten into you that demands such hurry? You were the one who always urged safety and caution. So far, we've been lucky—"

"Everyone in Virginia City mouths that stupid refrain," she cut him off.

"Well, we *were* lucky," Traver insisted calmly. "Lucky the mine wasn't full of men. Lucky we didn't lose blowers or elevators. And if you're smart, you'll not push too hard now."

"We must reopen at once," she persisted.

"Not until I personally inspect every stope." Traver said with authority. He seemed the only man in the Comstock who had *gained* strength from the earthquake. "We'll not open until I say it's safe. A quake can make things fall inward. Someone must check every watertight door at the very deepest levels."

Putnam asked Traver, "Is the timber usable?"

"Yes. And the ventilation shafts work. Water's the question. Is the bottom of Hell's Candy dry? Or six feet under? By and large, as I say, we've been damned lucky—"

"Don't you dare say that again!" interrupted Ariel. "Don't talk to me about luck! Oh, don't talk to me at all!"

"What's gotten into you, Ariel?" Traver asked. "There's two feet of hot water at the Kentuck. And they're over their knees in the Hale and Norcross at the eighteen-hundred-foot level."

"But it's dry in Hell's Candy!" she shouted. "The matter is simple. Go back to work! Tomorrow. Full shifts."

"No. No shifts until I've made my inspection," challenged Traver.

"Then do it, for godsake! You've spent weeks at your silly claim, stumbling around the mountains like some stupid bear! And now you're moaning about a little dampness in the pits. I've half a mind to fire you, Traver Loch! Find myself a manager who can get things squared away and the digging started!"

Putnam and Traver were both shocked by her fit of temper. "I've never seen you throw a tantrum. Are you sure you're well?" Putnam inquired.

But Traver wasted no time on her troubles, real or imagined. He said quietly, "I'll go down on Sunday. Alone. There'll be no one around to make any fuss. No one to sway my judgment." He stood opposite Ariel, glaring. "When you have my report, then you can hire whomever you please to manage your affairs! I'll be long gone to Texas, I assure you, madam!" He whirled and stalked from the room, slamming the door behind him.

Ariel sobbed, hands over face, back rigid against the stiff chair. She was aware Putnam was watching her, uncomprehending. "Why did you tear into Traver like that?" he questioned. "What's happened between you two? You've goaded the man into a dangerous situation, Ariel. Why? Do you *want* him down in the mine alone?" He thought a moment, pacing with measured footsteps. "Ah! Perhaps you have some alternatives? Perhaps you believe there *is* boiling water at the bottom of Hell's Candy? If those flimsy oak plugs break loose, Traver will be cooked alive. Is that what you're after? A well-planned accident?"

She stood up, not bothering to excuse herself. She knew the stories of the tragic Darlington flood when men had been boiled alive in the mine. For all her problems, she must not put Traver in danger. She would go to the mine on Sunday morning and tell him not to go down.

Her courage faltered when Sunday morning arrived, but she hiked up the hill. Traver had already arrived. He seemed surprised to see her, but didn't speak. He straightened the wire elevator cage. The morning sun shone on his leather cap and his suspender buckles glinted. "Don't go down," she said, not meeting his eyes.

He was silent, fingering the clasp on the elevator cage.

"Don't go down," she repeated.

"I'll take no undue chances."

"No! I forbid it! Oh, Traver, aren't you afraid? *I'm* afraid. I admit it. I don't want you to go down there!"

He smiled at her. "I'll do nothing reckless," he said softly. He seemed to see her anew, reached out and touched her braid. She thought she might swoon with the sweetness she felt coming back between them. He laughed. "I've done many *foolish* things, Ariel, but nothing *reckless* since that tropical afternoon on Lanavi when I dived off a cliff to rescue a girl who didn't need saving."

Tears brimmed on her lashes. She felt an overwhelming desire to recapture that innocence between them. She wanted desperately to tell him she might be pregnant, but before she could form the words, he reached for the elevator.

He stepped inside, fastened the simple clamp and nodded to the watchman. The man, who was the only other employee on the premises, unreeled the cable line from the drum. The box lurched into darkness.

Ariel stood petrified on the platform. She held her arms close to her sides as if that might protect them both. The cable squeaked as it played out from the drum. Steady scraping and clanking noises rose from the shaft. The winch whined and rasped.

Patience. She would force herself not to worry. She looked at the hillsides. Patterns of snow and sunlight glistened like crystal chandeliers. The town's newly shingled rooftops stood bright against the horizon. She faced the mountains. How was the Basque finding the winter? Did he spend lonely nights making new gifts for his bride? She peered at Geiger Grade Road, wondering if snow still blocked the passes to Reno. Would Wise Ada be able to make the coast in her new mud wagon? How was Sonny Staidlaw this winter?

Finally, when she couldn't stand not looking, she peered into the mouth of Hell's Candy. Faint noise. Then silence. Silence is worse, she thought, straining eyes and ears as the minutes passed.

Then the noise of winches resumed. Finally the elevator cage returned. "Empty!" she cried. "It's empty! Oh, dear God in heaven!" The wire box shuddered to a halt above ground. "Traver must be in trouble! Quick, lower me down!" She reached for the gate latch.

The watchman cringed. "Women in the mine be a hex."

She ignored him. Delay could mean tragedy.

He made no move to stop her as Ariel jumped onto the tiny cage elevator. "Lower me!" she shouted.

"You oughtn't to go down, miss—"

"Shut up! Get to the winches!"

He ran to the control drum. She crouched. A lurch. The bottom seemed to drop away and her knees buckled. Daylight flickered and disappeared. She hunched in the flimsy cage as it rocked and swayed. The box was nothing more than a square of metal laced with chicken wire and a snap-spring latch. Perspiration dotted her forehead as the speed of descent increased. At hundred-foot intervals she saw hooded lamps flashing past, like locomotive lights on a siding. "Dear God," she prayed aloud, "let the lights be on at the lowest level."

The bucket began to slow. "Traver?" she shouted. Her voice bounced back at her from the hard rock walls. The lift slowed to a creaking, swaying halt. She heard a humming sound. She tried to get her bearings. A cavern-room, fifty feet wide, with Davy lamps strung at fifteen-foot intervals. Separate tunnels led away from the main room. Six, seven, eight tunnels! Which one had Traver taken? She unlatched the cage door and jumped out, shouting his name, bombarded by the echoes.

As her feet touched the rock floor, she thought the humming noise grew louder. It was more a buzzing now. Or something rushing. *Water!* The unmistakable surge of rushing water. "Traver! Traver, where are you?"

She had hardly screamed her question before the words

bounced along the vault and were reflected back into the surge of floodwaters. The water swooshed in from the third tunnel to her right. In the gray underground light, the water looked silvery, streaked with foam. The tide spread out quickly over the cavern floor, washing against the pale blue rock walls with a hiss. As the first drops hit her feet, she was relieved to find the temperature was warm, not boiling.

The lamps swayed in the brackets. She fought the impulse to scream mindlessly, clamber into the basket and yank the cord to be pulled upward. She flailed through the water toward the tunnel. How far did the tunnel go? At what angle? Ariel tried to remember the plans she had studied. How much water could rush into the cavern? Could Traver be at some higher level? How long would the lamps burn and the elevator run?

The water continued to surge, making miniature waves against the confined walls. Part of an oak door came floating along. The brass fittings were still in place, but the hinges were wrenched apart. And there, beneath the lower hinge! A piece of red plaid material. Traver's shirt!

She rushed down the tunnelway, the churning water reaching nearly to her calves. "Traver!" She stumbled, and righted herself as the water sucked at her knees. She inched forward through the warm underground river. The water swirled, rushing round and round in the narrow tunnel.

Then she spotted Traver. Trapped. She saw instantly what had happened. He'd tested the oak pin on the door. Two planks had remained fastened. The rest of the door had sheared away, throwing him back against the rock walls. The trapped water had torn the door from its hinges, taking part of his shirt in the process. Traver's unconscious body had shifted sideways behind the remaining planks. One arm looped through the murky water into the tunnel opening. Water swirled over his chest.

She rushed to him. How to free him? She couldn't pull away the remaining door sections. Certainly she couldn't swing it shut against the pouring tide. There were no tools to unhinge it. Her only hope was to drag him under it before the water rose over his head and drowned him.

She dived for his legs, grasping them securely, and tugged with all her strength. Nothing. She tried again, staying under water until her lungs threatened to burst.

The third time down she shifted the door frame momentarily. Traver's arm slid downward. Bracing her shoulder into the wood, she shoved. The water pushed back against her. What if she simply yanked? Would she break his neck in the process? She balanced against the jutted rock outcropping of the wall. With a great effort, she heaved against the door. A gentle shift. The wood squeaked. She held her stance, gritting her teeth and straining with every muscle. An instant later the planking moved. Traver washed free!

She grabbed him around the chest, dragging rather than carrying him. The water, nearly to her waist now, helped float his body. She steered through the current with her free hand, forcing herself toward the main room. She was crying and panting with effort.

Around the tunnel bend, there were only a few more steps to the elevator cage. The slurping sounds of the flood ricocheted around the cavern.

It was easy to heave Traver's limp body into the cage. The water was nearly level with the floor of the basket. She scrambled inside and clanged the signal rope. Instantly the box lurched upward. She grabbed for the latch to fasten them inside. A sudden flash of darkness panicked her as the lights went out on the flooded lower level. In the black pit below, she could hear only the sounds of a trapped and angry sea.

"Traver," she whispered as she cradled him and knelt over him. There was no room to maneuver in the tiny cage. She couldn't examine his wounds except to feel a large lump on his skull. "Oh, Traver! Once you dived into unknown waters to rescue me! Now I've repaid you by saving you from the Hell's Candy."

Ariel and Nedra took turns sitting with Traver in the boarding house. He didn't appear badly hurt, but he hadn't regained consciousness after twenty-four hours. Putnam had been called. He came, shook his head and refused to make a diagnosis. Mitch called, hat in hand, and left, quiet and miserable.

At noon of the second day the women changed shifts again. Nedra went into the bedroom to sit at the bedside. A moment later she came flying out, shrieking. "Come quick! My stars in heaven, he's raving mad! Loony! Asking who I am! Asking who *he* is! My saints, he doesn't know his name from Adam!"

Ariel rushed into the bedroom. She ran to Traver, dismayed by the look on his face. His green eyes were wide open, darting back and forth from Nedra to Ariel to the window. He looked like a trapped wolf about to make a break. He flung the pillow, tossed the covers back and grabbed for his torn shirt.

Ariel's heart sank. She pinned his hands against his chest. Staring into his unfathomable eyes, she asked quietly, "Do you remember anything?"

"Of course I remember!" he snorted. "There was one hell of a flood!"

Oh, he did remember! Ariel went giddy with relief. "A flood indeed!" She repeated the story, clutching his hands. "Oh, Traver, Traver, thank God you've come back to me!" She wept, leaning against his chest.

"Traver?" He croaked the name, obviously trying it out. She drew back in alarm as he repeated the syllables. He looked at her steadily. "And you? Who are you? What is your name?"

She barely could whisper. "Ariel. I'm your . . . Ariel."

He smiled happily. "A good name for a pretty lass. It suits you—goes with your frothy hair and lovely dark eyes."

"Traver! You *must* remember! If you remember the flood, then you have a whole lifetime of memories dammed up behind that. You *must* recognize me. It's terribly important. We—that is, I—oh, please!"

She continued to ask him questions. He answered restlessly, "I'm sorry. I have no answers for you." In the next hours they discovered he could read. And write. But he didn't know what to write of his past. "I feel strong," he remarked. "The worst I've got are bruises on my ribs and one heck of a goose egg on the back of my skull."

He remembered nothing of his recent past. He scoffed at his nickname, the Scottish lion. He laughed aloud when she told him how he loved to fight, flexed his fists and stared at them in amazement.

"And you came to Nevada from the Sandwich Islands. And before that, you were in Australia," she told him.

"Quite a traveler I am!"

"And Texas, Traver. You always say your idea of heaven is moving to Texas."

The interrogation was interrupted by a knock at the boarding house door. Nedra answered the knock, then loudly shooed the caller away. "Get away with you, beggar boy!"

Suddenly there was a squeal from Nedra. Ariel hurried to see what the trouble might be. "Who is it?" she called as she went into the parlor. "Oh dear!" Ariel was almost taken in by the sight of the frail, hunchbacked beggar boy standing in the doorway. Then the boy reached up, shrugged off his hunch-back and Ariel recognized Su Lin. There was laughter from all three women.

After Su Lin had shed her props, she smiled. "How long ago it seems since we were all behind the safe walls of Cleo Burney's house."

"It seems I am back staring at a blank wall again," explained Ariel. "Traver does not recognize me."

"I hope Traver improves," sympathized Su Lin. "I am sorry for your troubles but I have come on behalf of my people. We must ask if you intend to hire a new manager. Will you drain the Hell's Candy? Will there be work for the Chinese again?"

Ariel was taken back by the questions. "I . . . I haven't had time to think! I haven't talked to Putnam, either. I'm sorry, I simply can't think about business yet."

"You must," pressed Su Lin. "Do you intend to drain the mine?"

"I don't know!"

Su Lin stood, folded her arms and spoke with quiet determination. "Decide soon, Ariel. The tongs are restless. The railroad is at a standstill. With the Hell's Candy shut down, the tongs may turn on the town itself."

"Is that a threat?" inquired Ariel, amazed. "Be practical. Would the Chinese return to work Hell's Candy? After an earthquake? After a flood?"

"Certainly! As I told you long ago, we recognize the dragon spirits within Sun Peak." She made dramatic gestures with her fingers and face, like an animal rolling about, attempting to get comfortable.

Ariel tried to contemplate business matters. Drain the lower level? It would take more money, new pumps. There'd be more lost time. Would it be worth it? She needed someone with expertise to advise her. "How I wish I could visit Sonny Staidlaw! He could help me. But I can't leave Traver! He needs me."

"I will stay with him," Nedra volunteered.

"You'd be wise to go to San Francisco anyway," Su Lin urged. "It is already known that you went down in Hell's Candy. Perhaps if you are gone a few days, the talk will fade."

"Only the watchman saw me descend," argued Ariel.

Nedra laughed bitterly. "Washoe gossip spreads faster than

prairie fire! You'll have every superstitious Comstocker plus the Decency Committee camped on your doorstep!"

Ariel had no trouble imagining the soft mutterings which would follow her around town. Little groups of men would gather on street corners and point. Chattering women would raise their hands to their foreheads and nod.

Su Lin encouraged her again. "You must go to see Staidlaw quickly. Find help. Putnam will take advantage of you if Traver can no longer work at the mine."

"I will fight Putnam on my own terms," Ariel told her.

"I will send herb broth and tea from China Camp," Su Lin announced. "Nedra and I together can care for Traver."

Nedra took up the planning. "I will use my gypsy powers to restore his memory." She presented a final argument. "Each new snowfall may block the passes through the Sierras. The transcontinental train from Reno to the Bay may not run much longer."

Ariel hesitated. "Let me talk to Traver again." She went into the bedroom. Traver was awake, dressed, standing at the window, staring.

"I'm remembering," he said. "The mine. The high country landmarks to my claim. The route to Crown Point."

"That's fine, Traver, but don't you remember anything about *people?*"

He looked past her as Nedra and Su Lin peeked in the door. "Hello there, girls. Come in! This young woman tells me I'm her man."

Ariel felt cold terror when she looked at this smiling stranger. She wanted to pound memory back into his skull by force. Shake him until his past rushed through bone, blood and spirit. Anger surged through her. Couldn't he sense what she and he had been to each other?

She knew she was better off in San Francisco than tearing her heart out and crying her eyes out in this bedroom. Damn you, she cursed as she left the room. Damn you, Traver Loch! Once I loved you! Now you've gone! Left me! Abandoned me as surely as if you'd drowned in the depths of Hell's Candy.

Chapter 18

The soft wind from Golden Gate Bay tickled Ariel's cheeks. How lovely to feel a gentle breeze after the howling Washoe Zephyr. The smell of fog and salt replaced the metallic odor of the mine slopes. Green hills were more to her liking than jagged peaks.

Irene Haskell took Ariel's unexpected appearance at the Staidlaw mansion in stride. "Come right in," she said in her prim, mellow voice. "The camellia suite is in order. Will you be staying the week?"

"A few days," answered Ariel, grateful to have access to the lovely house. Suddenly she felt healthier. It's the solidity of this home, she thought.

Inside Leah's room, with the pastel blue wallpaper blossoming with pink flowers, Ariel felt all her tensions released. "Oh, mother, I tried so hard to make a go of Hell's Candy! I wanted it so much as a link to you. Now, I feel as if I've come home empty-handed." Home. The Staidlaw mansion did feel comfortable this trip.

In the afternoon Ariel went shopping. Returning home, she spread her purchases on the bed and admired them. A plum-colored Foulard silk dress with the prestigious "City of Paris" store label sewn in the gusset seam. A little woven net for her hair. A popular *en tout cas* parasol with embroidered daisies on the inside lining. What luxuries!

She ate supper alone, disappointed that Sonny Staidlaw had another commitment. But the supper itself was marvelous—fresh crab from the bay, little green grapes in a wine sauce, scalloped potatoes and mint tea. What an improvement over Virginia City's staple menu of sourdough bread and beans!

Again, at breakfast, she was sorry to find Staidlaw had departed. Perhaps I remind him too much of mother, she thought. "Mrs. Haskell, do you think Mr. Staidlaw doesn't care to see me?"

"Not at all. He's a busy man. He left a message for you, asking that you join him for lunch at the Garden Court." She smiled proprietarily, as if it were only natural she should have the news before Ariel. "The carriage will be here at eleven."

The surrey was prompt and so was Ariel. But she was disappointed when the driver halted the carriage in front of a gray granite edifice which seemed more like a fortress than a garden courtyard. "This is the restaurant?"

"This is the Bank of the West. Mr. *Staidlaw's* Bank of the West," the driver said, repeating the name for emphasis.

She studied the imposing building. *Seven* stories tall! Amazing! And such power in the carved façade and white columns. Impressed, she alighted from the carriage and walked inside the marble lobby. She could see the broad staircase with patterned blue carpet on the risers and teller's cages with bronzed bars and mahogany fittings for pens and ink.

San Francisco was where the real power lay! Not in barren, dirty outposts like Virginia City. Not with men who actually ran machinery or shoveled ore. Men like Sonny Staidlaw controlled the railroads, shipping lines, and Comstock mines from their paneled offices.

Charming and courtly, Sonny Staidlaw came from his office, shook hands and escorted her proudly through his domain.

There were questions and compliments about the Bank of the West. Then Staidlaw tucked her arm through his and escorted her down the broad staircase. Ariel caught a glimpse of them in the baroque gilded mirroring. Was this the handsome image Leah and Sonny had presented twenty years ago? People in the lobby turned to look at them. Ariel felt gracious at Staidlaw's side.

In the carriage he asked, "Did you take my advice, Ariel? Play your cards close to the chest in the Comstock? Did you have the last laugh? Avoid the sunrise temptation?"

"I hope you are well-stocked with sympathy," she laughed. "When I tell you all my troubles, you will have to send out for more."

"One of the worst things I remember about Washoe is its barrenness. I think lunch at the Garden Court will please you."

They entered the restaurant. The beauty of the indoor arboretum sent Ariel's senses reeling. "Wonderful!" she breathed as they walked to a dining table placed among palms, ferns and blooming azaleas. The ceiling of domed greenhouse glass had open skylights. On the tile floor sat large pots of blooming periwinkles, rose moss, zinnias and marigolds. The rich aroma of tropical blooms—ginger, bird of paradise and plumeria—filled the room. "I haven't seen such greenery since Lanavi!"

She sat down, busy thoughts filtering through her delight. Things would be better in San Francisco. A smart woman could make a fortune here. How could things not be better here? Where they had restaurants and clean air and green, growing plants! Where she could live in a substantial house!

When they were seated Staidlaw ordered salmon and fresh asparagus. Fresh asparagus! Oh, things would be much, much better in San Francisco.

"How did things go with the Hell's Candy, Ariel?"

"Every move I made was wrong. I've had to do things on the spur of the moment." She told him everything that had happened. "I need time to back off and try to think clearly. That's why I've come to San Francisco. It may be time for me to give up trying to make Hell's Candy my link with my mother."

Staidlaw looked up abruptly at the mention of Leah. "Whatever you decide," he said casually. "Please stay as long as you wish." He smiled shyly. "But Hell's Candy is not her legacy—*you* are."

Ariel thanked him for his kindness, but before she could pursue the subject of his relationship with Leah, he began asking questions again.

"So your charming smiles weren't sufficient ammunition to bring about total capitulation of your enemies in the Washoe? Ariel, perhaps you need military strategy. You may have to cannonade Virginia City into submission!"

"Do you mean retreat? Is it time for me to give up the Hell's Candy?"

"Not at all. Dig in for the long fight. Camouflage your maneuvers. Counterattack."

She gave a mock salute, flattered he thought her capable of such grand battle plans. "Should I join the Sutro tunnel scheme? Can I get Bank of the West financial backing to drain the lower sections?"

"The backing is yours," he affirmed. "I told you that before. I honestly believe the biggest silver bonanza of all may still lie deep in the heart of the Sun Peak." He raised his glass in a toast to her. "The woman—or man—who gets there first will be wealthy as Croesus. Late arrivals won't find enough to pay for a drink on their way out of Virginia City."

"Then the time to press deeper is now."

"Spoken like a true general. I salute you!"

She wished she knew more about him. "You sound like a military commander."

"It has been my style of conducting business." He sat back in his chair, studying her with wistful eyes. "But such a method hardly works for affairs of the heart. I wish all my casualties had been on the field of business!"

Ariel saw an opening. Here was her chance to ask about her mother. But Staidlaw continued to barricade himself behind talk of business. "Always hold the high ground. That's a cardinal rule in campaigning."

Very well. She would find out about Leah and Staidlaw another time. She turned her attention to Hell's Candy. "Hold the higher tunnels. Drain the lower. Right?"

"Correct."

"I have one more matter to discuss. It is more a confession than a business plan. I broke the taboo against women in the mines. The talk is making the rounds that I have a done a terrible thing in going down in the Hell's Candy."

He laughed and patted her hand. "And you will, no doubt, do more 'terrible' things in the name of opening that mine." He smiled confidently. "No harm will come of your adventure. The tradition was long overdue to be broken. Why, I'll wager within a year you'll see touring ladies donning dusters and going down to explore the stopes. Some bonanza queen —maybe you, Ariel—will point to a line of blue silver and say, 'Order Tiffany's to make me a silver service from this very vein!'"

She joined in his laughter. What faith he had in her! She

felt happier than she had in months. Perhaps she would spend
a few extra days at the Bay, stroll along Fremont and Maiden
Lane, admire the new fashions and inhale the balmy air.
Perhaps she would visit a physician. She thanked Staidlaw
with a lump in her throat. "I know your hopes for my success
are sincere. I'm very grateful." This man understood her
desire to succeed in a man's world. Staidlaw was the mentor
her own father had never been.

As they dined, she confided more and more in Staidlaw,
telling him of her adventures with Traver, Nedra, Su Lin,
Mitch, Wise Ada and Putnam.

He seemed to revel in the stories of youthful energy.
Finally he proposed, "Why not bring your friends to San
Francisco, Ariel? Enjoy the big house. Put it to good use with
parties. Find a doctor to cure Traver's loss of memory."

She shook her head no. Her business, friends and obliga-
tions all remained in Virginia City. But she asked the
question she feared most. "What if Traver doesn't get well?
What if he never remembers me?"

Staidlaw turned thoughtful, his brow furrowed deeply.
Finally he spoke. "This country is a great mix of color. Noise.
Excitement. Energy. It fascinates me—this country's energy. New people in a new land are not afraid to try any
damned thing that pops into their heads. Like Wise Ada
and her transport schemes. The secret of America's energy
isn't magic. It's astonishingly simple. We invent precision machinery with interchangeable parts that will work on any
track, any locomotive, any mine shaft. Bearings and alloys
and brass that will bend. *Tolerance.* That's what does it. And
that's what this country teaches anyone who will listen."

"It hasn't taught Traver tolerance. Not for himself. Not for
me."

"From what you've told me, Ariel, Traver doesn't expect
tolerance from others and isn't open to admitting it in
himself."

"But we have an obligation to each other!"

"Ariel, don't sell yourself cheap for what you mistakenly
consider an obligation. Even if Traver does remember you,
you have every right to a man who can equal you in
intelligence and authority. Traver *may* be that man. But from
your description of him, I'd guess your ambitions far exceed
his."

She laughed. "I'd like to own San Francisco. He'd like to
strike out for Texas."

"It sounds as if you will both need all the tolerance you can muster. I don't doubt your concern for Traver. But it seems more *concern* than passion."

Before she could defend her conflicting emotions about Traver, a messenger arrived with a telegram for Staidlaw. He flipped open the envelope and tipped the boy. Unfolding the yellow paper with one hand, he glanced at the message. "It concerns you, Ariel."

"What has happened?"

He read the message, watching her eyes for reaction. "Traver is gone."

"Traver gone!" She echoed the words as she grabbed for the message. "*Gone?* What does that mean? Is he dead? Gone from the boarding house? Or Virginia City?" She stood up in consternation, dropping the linen napkin to the tiled floor.

"We can wire for more information," he said, gesturing for the messenger to return. He pulled a pocket watch from his jacket. "Or you can make the afternoon train if you hurry."

"The train," she said as she reached for her parasol. "I must return at once."

Nedra repeated the explanation. "He disappeared."

"When did he leave?" demanded Ariel, moving away from the Wells Fargo office into Virginia City's B Street. "What did he say? Where did he go?" She gave Nedra no time to answer. "Did he wander off without taking his things? Did he go on purpose? Oh, Nedra, if this is one of your gypsy tricks, I'll—"

"Hardly!" huffed Nedra. "A six-foot-tall, flaming-haired Scotsman spirited out of sight by mysterious forces? Hardly, indeed! I'm a seeress, not a magician."

Ariel accused her friend again. "But maybe you *let* him escape."

Nedra looked as concerned as if she'd let newborn pups tumble from a cardboard box. "You can't believe I sent him away," she said quietly. "I'm worried sick about him, Ariel. He can't take care of himself."

"Not in those mountains, especially," nodded Ariel, glancing toward the snowy Sierras.

"Why do you think he's gone to the peaks?"

"He thought he remembered the directions to his claim. Of all the things to remember—"

Nedra sighed. "Then let's ask Su Lin to send trackers from

China Camp. The tong have ways of finding people who have been gone for years."

"I don't think trackers will do much good," Ariel said doubtfully. "Try it if you wish. I'll make inquiries here in town. He couldn't simply disappear!" She left Nedra and made her way through the streets, stopping people to ask if they'd seen Traver. She checked at the hotel, the boarding house and the saloons. No one had seen him leave town. No one knew his whereabouts.

Dispirited, she rested in the International Hotel lobby. There were other matters to be faced. Putnam, for one. She must see him immediately or risk his making decisions without her. She needed courage to confront Putnam and ordered a glass of brandy in the dining room. Warmed, she went directly to the Guardian Concert Hall.

Putnam answered the knock, appearing unusually meek. His shirt was open at the neck, revealing loose folds of gray skin. He's old, she thought, slightly surprised. His eyes were dim, watery and creased. His hands toyed restlessly with a string on the frayed cuff. Events are taking a toll on him, too, she thought. His face looked so composed it was almost lifeless. She thought of him as having no nerve endings, had never known him to stroke his chin nervously or slap his knee in merriment.

"Are you awake?" she asked. "Or in a trance?"

"I am having difficulties," he answered. She realized the opium lamp was unlit, and hoped China Camp had carried out the threat to cut off his supply.

He smiled coldly. "I have alternatives, of course, as a smart man always does." He picked up a bottle of dark liquid. "Less enjoyable, but an option. I have had to become an eater."

Ariel seated herself on the floral couch. She had no time for Putnam's opium habits now. "I have come to ask you two questions. Number one: is Traver's amnesia permanent?"

"There is no answer to that question." His glance went to the wall of medical books. Was he looking for an answer? Or was his gaze so dim he was merely retreating? Or did he know more than he was admitting? Perhaps he even knew where Traver was! Perhaps Putnam had *sent* Traver away. She'd suspect him of any duplicity.

"Do you know Traver's whereabouts?" she asked.

He countered with a wave of his hand. "I don't believe that was the second question you intended to ask."

Indeed, it had not been. She summoned her courage. "I

have felt unusual for some time." She chose her words with care. "For six weeks—since the New Year's earthquake—I have had tenderness, swelling and a plague of little ailments."

"And you're asking for my diagnosis?"

She turned away. "I have no need of your services. I believe I am pregnant."

"You may have no need of my services," he repeated in a calculating manner, "but you will certainly need a name for your child." He rubbed his hands together slowly. "Are my assumptions correct? Traver Loch is long and far gone. He's probably stumbled down an abandoned mine shaft by now. Or perhaps he's halfway to Texas. Or maybe he climbed over the peaks into another valley and started a new life. Whatever the reason, he *chose* to leave you."

The words stung like pinpricks. "He didn't remember me. He didn't know I was pregnant."

"Which still leaves you in the position I mentioned earlier. You need a name for the child." He chuckled with treachery.

As always, she sensed Putnam maneuvering. If she left town, he'd be sole master of Hell's Candy. But if she stayed, she'd have to provide for the child she would bear.

He pressed his point. "This town often forgets names. Sometimes faces. But never sins." He went on smoothly, his voice silver steel. "Perhaps we could find you a husband, temporarily. There are several men who would follow my orders and marry you."

"Perhaps," she admitted. "But *I* will not follow your orders."

"Then what will you do with your bastard?"

Bastard. Hateful word, but precisely the term the town would use behind her back—and to the child's face. Putnam's phrase echoed in her mind: "Traver *chose* to leave you." Marry another man? She needed time to think. She rose and headed for the door.

"Ariel, I have a man in mind who'd not blink twice at playing the gallant for you. He'd give the child a name and swallow his pride enough to bide by another man's rules."

She stopped by the door, tense as a coiled spring.

"Ariel, think about it. Your only option for remaining in Virginia City is to marry. And your best option is to marry Mitch Galway."

Chapter 19

Marry Mitch. The words whirled in Ariel's mind all week. She hardly dared think of the implications. On Saturday night, as Nedra dressed lavishly for dinner at the hotel, Ariel asked, "Do you have a date with Mitch?"

"Don't I wish!" burbled Nedra, tying ribbons in her dark hair. "No, but Mitch will be there and I'll keep trying. That impossible Irishman!"

Ariel busied herself in the corner of the room, discreetly watching Nedra. The gypsy continued to adorn herself, looping layers of gold chains around her long neck. Many of the necklaces had been favors from gentlemen who remembered Nedra when they made their lucky strikes. Nedra put henna powder on her lips to redden them, charcoal around her eyelids to darken them, rouge on her cheeks until she had a bright, wanton look.

Ariel offered some unasked for advice. "Nedra, if you want Mitch to notice you, tone down your costume a bit."

"He notices me, all right. But it's lust instead of love. I might as well be one of the tarts on D Street." Nedra stuck a hairpiece of feathers atop her ribboned coiffure.

Ariel lay down on the bed, despondent. Traver gone by his own choice. Nedra still attempting to corral Mitch. If Ariel married Mitch it would solve her problem, but she was too wary of Putnam to act at his suggestion.

Nedra came to the bedside. "What's wrong, Ariel? You're in low spirits tonight. Is it because of Traver?"

Ariel appreciated Nedra's concern. She had a sudden need to confide in her friend. "I'm thinking of Traver, that's true. Oh, Nedra . . . do you realize . . . I'm carrying his child! I'm sure of it!"

A wave of surprise washed over Nedra's face, immediately replaced by a delighted smile. "A baby! How wonderful!" She ran her hands through her ribbons and feathers, then reached out to hug Ariel. Then the obvious complications struck her. "What will you do?" She bit her lips in consternation, sat down on the bed and held Ariel's hands.

"I don't know," admitted Ariel. "But I'll not have Traver's child bear the stigma of being a bastard."

"Will you go away? Have the baby somewhere else? I'm certain Mr. Staidlaw would let you come to San Francisco."

"I must stay in Virginia City if I'm to have any say-so in the Hell's Candy. Putnam would like nothing better than for me to pack my bags and head for the Bay."

Nedra was silent a moment, then looked away. Her voice was low. "Putnam could abort you. He knows how—"

"I couldn't harm a child of my flesh and Traver's blood."

"There are quiet, gypsy ways."

"Stop it!" Ariel shuddered. "I'll not consider it."

"Ariel, are you certain you're pregnant?"

"Why?"

"Because I haven't suspected," answered Nedra. "I usually spot such things," she boasted.

Ariel shut her eyes, remembering the hardness of the basement bookstore floor, the world and all its packing crates crashing down around them. The shattering thrusts of Traver's wildness. Of all the nights we were together, she thought, why should I conceive during the one of cruelty? "Oh, Nedra, where can Traver be? Could I find him in time?"

Nedra gave no answers because she had none. She held Ariel gently and let her own tears mingle with Ariel's soft sobs.

Ariel spoke quietly. "I realize I can't expect Traver to return." She took a deep breath, stifling a new sniffle. "I'm thinking of marrying."

"Marrying! But, how? Who?"

Ariel turned her head aside. "Putnam suggested I marry Mitch Galway!" She forced a laugh. "Can you imagine that? I realize Mitch is indebted to Putnam, but he can hardly manipulate Mitch's personal life!"

Nedra seated herself at the dresser and started to repair her makeup before answering. "I think Mitch would consent. In fact, as much as I hate to admit it, I believe Mitch would jump at *any* chance to have you, Ariel."

"It's not that simple. I couldn't just grab Mitch."

Nedra sighed. "You wouldn't be taking him from me, if that's what's bothering you. I've never had him. Sad, but true enough. You promised me Mitch before we ever came to Virginia City, but that's as close to magic as I've come. Don't get me wrong, Ariel. I'd love to have that big, handsome Irish gambler!"

"He's far more than simply a good-looking horseracer."

"Yes, and I'd love to have him, Ariel, because I'd *love* him! You either don't love him or won't admit it. So, you're only planning to *use* him."

"Oh, Nedra, I wonder if he'll have *me!*"

"You will have to ask him that! But the situation is simple. Traver is gone. Mitch is available. There's no room for misdirected sympathy for any of us in this!" Nedra's voice was usually warm and excited, but now she spoke in firm, controlled tones. "We both know Mitch and I never were a good match. I'm more like Traver. I don't want to be tied down. Or the Basque. I like being alone in the mountains. Actually, I've been thinking, when it comes spring, I might move on. Oh, you don't have to worry about Nedra! There're plenty of fish in the sea for me!" She finished her face-painting, and sat back to survey her efforts. "And if you're worried about Mitch accepting your proposal, make it a paying one. Offer him some shares of Hell's Candy."

Ariel ran to embrace her friend. "Oh, Nedra, the wonder of all this is that you wouldn't fight and claw to the bitter end for Mitch."

"If I thought it would change things, I might. But it won't." Nedra swept grandly out of the room. She called to Ariel. "Hurry up. Get your cape and boots on. You have a proposal to make."

Ariel lost courage in the corridor of Mitch's lodgings. The rooms appeared dark. Maybe Mitch isn't home yet, she hoped. She barely knocked, her fist shaking, then stepped back into the shadows.

Mitch opened the latch, peered into the hall and gave a delighted chuckle when he spotted her. "Step into my lair, little spider lurking in the dark. We'll spin a web of delight."

Startled by his words, she entered, immediately spotting a half-empty gin bottle on his parlor table. Then she looked at him closely. Glorious Mitch—his white cotton shirt tied up with wide bands, his muscles shifting as he moved. His golden hair fell askew over his wide forehead and his cerulean eyes were like the sea off Lanavi. He moved directly to the table and bottle. "Join me in a drink?"

She nodded, hoping it would steady her nerves.

He turned his back to her as he poured the clear liquid. "I hear you're in need of a husband."

Obviously he'd talked to Putnam. Did that account for his half-empty bottle and being alone on Saturday night? How could she talk to him if he was senseless? "Mitch, are you drunk?"

"I hope so," he said with melancholy. "Otherwise I've wasted half a bottle of good gin."

She picked up her glass and drank it hurriedly. The burning liquid seared her throat. "Mitch," she said, "I want to get married."

"Bully for you." He walked away from her and sprawled on the damask couch.

"I want *you* to marry me, Mitch."

"Pick on some other mother's son," he grumbled without looking at her. "Dammit, Ariel. I'd be a ninny to consider marriage to you! Don't think for a moment I don't realize this is Putnam's idea and not yours. Well, marriage to you would be a hell of a hardship for me." He managed to get up from the couch. "You'd get a name for your child. But what would be in it for me?"

She faced him directly. "Half my shares of the Hell's Candy," she said evenly.

"What! You'd part with some of that famous inheritance?"

"Famous folly, it seems." She opened the parlor window. Mitch came and stood beside her, looking out at the night which was lightly dusted by powdery snow.

He breathed deeply, then said, "Let's try again. What is it you want, Ariel?"

"I want us to get married. A paper marriage. A relationship of convenience. For your trouble, I'd pay you in mining stock—half my shares."

"A paper agreement? Some kind of free ride for you?"

"Not entirely. We could live here, if you'd like. I'd keep your house."

"But not share my bed?"

"No."

He leaned out the open window and inhaled sharply. He rubbed his temples with both thumbs, as if trying to figure things out. "I can't pretend to know why you'd opt for this way out of your troubles, Ariel. But I know it's not for love of me." He moved to a linen-covered armchair, leaving her alone at the window. A dry laugh broke his moody silence. "I went around like a sick calf for nearly a year, convinced I was in love with you. If you'll recall, my dear, you've rejected my advances across islands, oceans and continents!"

She remembered precisely the looks, touches, kisses.

He continued. "Now, you show up in the dead of night, asking my hand in marriage!"

A flash of insight told Ariel that Iron Mitch Galway, for all his bluster, wanted to be courted! She moved behind his chair, putting her hands around his neck, liking the strength and firmness and warmth of touching him.

But he pushed her away, and moved to close the window. "No need for soft stroking fingers and batting eyelashes. Say out the conditions of your offer straight and clear. No haggling. No bartering. No pretending you think more of me than anything else you might bid on at the butcher's!"

She felt sorry for him. Sorry for them both. Why must the situation be so coldblooded? Yet she couldn't compound the misery by sudden declarations of false love. "Marry me, Mitch. After the child is born and christened, you'll have your freedom and half the Hell's Candy."

"I'd rather have all of you and none of the mine," he told her. His eyes darted over her body. "You honestly believe the two of us could live here in a paper marriage? They way I feel about you, Ariel—" He broke off. "What makes you think I'd keep such an unworkable bargain?"

"That's the price tag for us both."

Normally Mitch's face was uncluttered and simple to read. Now she saw a mixture of feelings. There was fear of himself, her, Putnam, and disgust with the whole idea. She pressed for his acceptance. "You'd like owning half my shares, wouldn't you? It would give you a way to pay off Putnam. Be free of him."

"Sure and for faith, I'd like a way out of Putnam's grasp!" he agreed. "I'd like owning all the works on Sun Peak for that matter. This whole mining district! All the Virginia and Truckee trackage from here to Reno!" He stood, hands expansively listing his dreams. "Throw in the brokerage houses on B Street while you're at it. The horses in the Sierra canyons. How about a branch of the Bank of the West? Don't think I lack ambition, Ariel. But I will marry for love, not some damned paper shares to pay for a paper marriage!"

She went to the Franklin stove and warmed her hands. Mitch's eyes reflected the fight going on in his mind. "Mitch, we're not strangers. And Lord knows we've caused each other hard times. But I believe we could live together in some semblance of harmony. We'd only have a temporary arrangement. But I'd do my part. You deserve a decent homelife."

He chuckled. "You'd make pot roast on Mondays?"

She held out her hands to him. "If I didn't think you'd offer me protection and trust, as well as the use of your name, I'd not approach you."

"But you'd make no promises except paper."

"I'd tell you no lies, either."

"Then let me tell *you* a certain truth, Ariel. Your offer is appealing. I swell with pride thinking of you as my wife—even in name only. I imagine us strolling the sidewalks, you on my arm, me the envy of every man in Virginia City!"

"Mitch, I'd try hard to please you," she promised. "Tell me the things you like."

He grinned. "I like freshly laundered white shirts. Buttered popcorn and a cozy fire on Sunday afternoons. And little chocolate chickens at Easter time."

"Chocolate chickens!"

"I like the smell of cobbler shops. Mittens made of rag wool. Frisky, black dogs. Puppet shows."

"Oh, you do like some of the quaintest things!"

"One of the things I *don't* like is a sham marriage."

She panicked. He was going to turn her down! "Please, Mitch, just keep things simple. Say yes, and let's be done with it."

"Keep things simple? Wouldn't that be nice! Call in some man of iron, someone who doesn't make mistakes, doesn't have feelings for you. Someone who doesn't have doubts.

Now, that would be simple—much easier than calling for me, a mere mortal human." He sat down disconsolately on the couch, patting the place beside him. "Sit here with me."

She moved cautiously, perching at the far end.

Instantly he was angry. "Goddam! I see exactly how far your trust and admiration go! First you smile and stroke my neck, urging me closer. Now you spit at me to keep away. I see how marriage would be. First you'd tease me to come to you, then laugh as you knocked my knees out from under me!"

Chastened she scooted halfway toward him. What a struggle it would be to keep Mitch's virility at bay for months! She didn't trust herself all that much, either.

She leaned against his arm, stroking the flounces of the soft cotton shirt. She teased him softly. "What a lot of Irish blarney. Come, now, make up your mind. Here I've proposed to you and you've beat around the bush. What are you—some half-witted girl hiding behind a lace handkerchief? Let's hear your answer, sir! Yes or no?"

"Hold on a minute. Why demand frankness from me? There's coyness written all over your golden skin! Every little toss of your shining hair shouts trickery. And in those lovely brown eyes, I read every kind of scheme." He reached for her and held her close. "I hear all the words you're *not* saying, Ariel. At this moment, with your eyes, you're saying, 'Yes, go ahead and kiss me—but not too deeply.' With your ruby lips, you're telling me, 'Yes, hold me—but not too closely.'"

She was surprised at the depth of his feelings. She felt cheap because his accusations were true.

"Do you know what else I hear from this whole proposal? You've announced to the world that I'm worth a few months of your time drying dishes and ironing shirts. But you've also shouted 'As a *man*, Mitch Galway, you are worth nothing to me!'"

"Don't, Mitch! Don't humiliate us both," she begged. He looked so forlorn she had an intense desire to throw herself into his arms. But she only put her face in her hands whispering, "Marry me, Mitch."

He pulled her hands away gently, kissed her tenderly on the forehead. She sighed softly. Mitch pulled her tightly to him, no longer tender but masterful. He kissed her fully, holding her so close her ribs ached. His mouth and hands controlled her until she felt all her senses blur and yield. Her breasts pushed against his chest, her lips opened and accepted him. Blood rushed to her cheeks, turning them fiery hot. But inside, she felt cold disappointment in herself. Was her memory of Traver so weak that any man's kisses could stimulate her?

Suddenly Mitch released her, slammed his fist against the couch pillow and whispered hoarsely, "God! How it galls me! I'll give you all my love and half my pillow and still not possess you!"

She knew by his admission that the matter was settled. She sighed and touched her lips, which were continuing to tingle.

He noticed her gesture. With a merry wink, he said, "If you should change your mind, Mrs. Galway, I daresay we could have a house full of kids in no time!"

Chapter 20

Mitch wrote his name on the marriage license slowly, adding extra scrolls and flourishes as if wanting the world to take due note. Ariel's hand shook when she held the pen. She felt both a bride and a traitor.

But she knew they looked, outwardly, like any happy couple. Mitch wore his navy blue suit, the shirt with pearl studs and a striped ribbon for his watch fob. Ariel's costume consisted of a chocolate brown moire gown covered by a matching half-cape. Mitch had presented her with a diamond. "Just for show," he assured her. "Not a ring. You can wear it on a chain around your neck, or in a locket bracelet. Please?"

"Thank you, Mitch." What loyalty and friendship! She hardly dared think the words but they came unbidden—what love!

"I want all the trimmings," declared Mitch after the ceremony. At the restaurant Chef Daniel himself prepared sage hen, carrots in brown sugar sauce and apple crêpes. Then on to Piper's Opera, where Mitch made a show of doffing his hat and bowing to half the population, grandly escorting Ariel to her seat.

"It's been a lovely evening," she told him as they walked back to his lodgings.

"Too bad this is the end of the festivities," he teased.

She squeezed his arm. "I do thank you for marrying me." She felt so much better! Physically, ever since settling matters with Mitch, her body had behaved. Maybe everything's getting back to normal after the earthquake, she thought. She glanced at the storefronts which had been repaired. The courthouse clock was keeping accurate time again. It just took a while for things to right themselves, she decided.

The night seemed joyous, not forbidding, as they returned to Mitch's home. He hesitated on the threshold, as if wanting to carry out the tradition of lifting the bride. Courteously, he opened the door and ushered her inside.

Earlier in the day they'd moved many of Ariel's things to Mitch's rooms. Now she felt quite at home. There was a certain ease between them, a comfort. In Mitch's presence she never felt nervous, never nibbled a fingernail or tensed like a cat whose fur has been rubbed the wrong way. She vowed to observe all the niceties of domestic life. She couldn't bring herself to call it a marriage, even in her mind. But she'd work hard at making it a thriving arrangement.

She took off her cape and sat down, taking up a piece of needlepoint. Mitch sat opposite her, smiling.

"I never knew your full name was Ariel Melinda Cortland. Before today, I mean. Now, it's Ariel Melinda Cortland Galway!"

"And Mitchell Walter Regis Galway!"

He moved his chair closer and put a tentative hand on her knee, stopping the busy scissors and yarn. By mutual accord they looked shyly at each other. Ariel was first to glance away. He patted her knee. "It's all right, darling. Getting married—contrary to popular thought—doesn't have to extinguish our friendship." He stood abruptly. "How about some tea and muffins before we go to bed?"

"No, no! I'm quite full from the dinner at Daniel's and the champagne."

"Then let's go to bed. How do you like to sleep?"

"Alone."

"I've had to pitch cots since schooldays. Now there's one decent bed in this place and we shall share it. Besides, while I've promised not to touch you, I'm looking forward to waking up next to another warm body these winter mornings."

Mitch's forthright declaration made the sleeping arrangement more welcome. She put on a long blue flannel nightgown and brought an armload of books to bed with her. "I always read until I get sleepy," she told him. He did not raise his head from the pillow where he lay face down. She could see the long, firm silhouette his body made beneath the covers. "Will having the lamp on bother you?"

"Yes." He smirked. "Do you mind if I smoke cigars in bed?"

"Yes!" She tensed. "You shall have to get used to the lamp," she sputtered. Then she laughed. "Oh, Mitch, it's certainly for the best that we married—now we can argue."

She left the lamp on, deposited the books across her pillow and pulled back the quilt. "Oh, my God! You're naked as a jaybird!"

"My body will never darken the inside of a church door or a pair of pajamas." He rolled on his side, away from her. "It's your idea to keep the lights on."

She maneuvered onto her half of the bed, curled up with her back to his, holding her book out over the empty space between mattress and wall. She read for hours, without seeing the words, until the muscles of her arm ached. Surely he was asleep by now! She let the book close, tucking it next to her pillow. She barely let her head touch the goosedown before her eyes closed.

Instantly she felt Mitch above her. Her eyes flew open, her hands coming up to flail at him. Then, to her astonishment, she saw his hand move to turn off the bedside oil lamp. His eyes were studying her face with tenderness. She shut her eyes quickly, embarrassed she had almost lashed out at him.

She felt him lean over her, extinguish the lamp and move back. For a moment she felt him hovering, then the merest wisp of a kiss brushed her ear. From close beside her, she felt his warm breath in the darkness. Then he whispered, "Good night, missus. If you work half as hard at caring for me as you do at reading books, I honestly believe you could learn to love me."

A warm thrill encompassed her—a warmth which, if she stirred, would become a furnace. She must be on guard constantly, or she *would* learn to love him.

He was making it terribly easy.

Their domestic life ran smoothly, with only two sore spots: Ariel's reading in bed and Mitch's habit of dressing in his best clothes after dinner and leaving the house.

Where did he go! Ariel was too proud to ask and too curious not to wonder. For a month he'd not skipped a night of going out. Did he seek the company of prostitutes? Could he be seeing Nedra?

Left at home alone, Ariel put on her long flannel gown, climbed into bed and read until she fell asleep. She smiled as she thought how goodnatured Mitch's complaining had become. He often growled, "Damn! I can't squeeze a spot to sleep among all these volumes!" But he showed his good humor by bringing her a new volume of Dickens. Sometimes she caught him reading over her shoulder, a smile on his face.

Usually, when he returned, she was fast asleep. One night, in the hours of darkness, she rolled against him. She came awake slowly, completely comfortable with his arm over her back, the gown slipped up around her thighs. Their legs were cupped. She was terrified to move and rouse him. Terrified to hear them breathing so perfectly in time together. Terrified to find how well they meshed physically.

She went out the next day and bought a pair of head-to-toe, footed, one-piece muslin pajamas. Mitch roared with laughter. That night he made a grand show of coming to the bed by turning his back and walking backward. "My eyes are shut, too!" he growled. "Look here! Both hands over my face as well."

"Stop it! You embarrass me more than if I were naked between silk sheets!"

"Ha! Pull my other leg a while! You've no interest in such frivolities!"

They laughed together and she playfully threw a book at him. When he caught it, she saw his eyes had suddenly gone somber.

"Ariel, I've considered framing our marriage license and tacking it out in the hallway for all to see."

"That would look foolish!"

"Once I wanted to hide it under the mattress."

"Mitch Galway!"

"I've given up, though. There's been no marriage in your heart. Not with these damned footed pajamas and making a bookcase of our bed."

"You understood this was to be a paper arrangement."

"Yes. And they don't grant licenses for the kind of love I want from a real wife!" He pushed a stack of books toward her. "You've made up the rules of this game. But don't for a moment confuse this charade with what might have been between us!" His eyes blazed defiance. He would love her in spite of herself.

After that he made a point of staying out nights until long after she fell asleep. And, true to his word, he never touched her.

Ariel felt jealous when Mitch went out each evening without her.

Tonight, as she watched him preparing to leave, the anger boiled through her. He had washed and shaved and stood before the mirror, a towel around his waist. He dabbed some cologne behind his neck and rubbed a little more in his hand, sniffed, touched it lightly to his scalp. Grinning, he wiped his hands on the towel.

She watched him surreptitiously. His spine stood straight, rows of vertebrae marching downward to the point the towel covered his lean buttocks. She never tired of watching him shave, though she was careful not to let him see her observing him.

She knew many intimate things about Mitch. Too much rosemary and bay leaf on the chicken upset his stomach. He ate jelly on his biscuits, but no butter. The stable hay made his eyes itch when the weather was cold.

When he finished dressing, he looked the part of a dandy eager for a night on the town. Whistling, he smoothed the cuffs of the white shirt she'd ironed. The striped trousers held a sharp crease where she'd pressed them. His boots, which she'd shined, had a high gloss. He looked glorious! And now he was set to go off and leave her again! Jealousy burned like a Hawaiian firebrand through her. "Mitch, why don't you stay home tonight?"

"With you absent?"

"What! I'm right here," she protested.

"Maybe in body, Ariel. But your heart isn't in this house and your spirit isn't in this marriage." He grabbed her wrist; his blue eyes riveted her with yearning. "Don't you understand? I can't stay in the same room with you." He molded her against him, both arms around her now. "Don't flutter those dusky eyes at me! Don't drive me mad tossing your hair against my chest."

Ariel knew if she moved, the long coil of passion between them would unwind. Any motion would start an avalanche of sensuality which could only end in bed. But how could she force such control of her body? She *liked* Mitch's arms locked behind her back, pressing her spine. She liked the feel of her breasts held high and tight against his soft shirtfront. She liked his thighs pressed against hers.

He looked at her intently, his voice husky. "Tell me again you want me to stay home with you." He repeated the sentence in sections, giving each a distinctive emphasis. "Tell me you want me. To stay home. With you."

She broke the tension by breaking from his grasp. "No, no! Go on!" She waved him toward the door.

They were interrupted by a knock at the door. Ariel was glad for the excuse to remove herself from the overpowering anger and passion which tormented her. Answering the knock she was shocked to find Su Lin hiding in the shadowed hallway. "Come in! Why are you here? It's too dangerous for you!"

Su Lin's winter wrap consisted of only a thinly quilted blue jacket with a dragon motif on the sleeve. "I cannot stay. Only a moment. But I bring news. Trackers from the tong have found Traver!"

"You've found him! Is he alive?"

Su Lin took Ariel's hands. Ariel assumed the worst. "God, no! He's dead?"

"No," said Su Lin. "But you may wish he were."

"Of course not! If he's alive, I have hope! Quick, tell me everything!"

"Traver is alive."

"And well," added Ariel, hopefully.

"Alive and well," confirmed Su Lin. "And living with a woman."

Ariel gasped, "He never remembered me!" From the corner of her eye she saw Mitch standing rigid by the couch.

Su Lin bowed her head. "That is the worst part, Ariel. Now, when it is too late, Traver has remembered you fully."

"Where is he?" She turned to Mitch. "Oh, hurry to the stable and saddle a horse for me! I must go to him!"

Ariel saw her quick enthusiasm had hurt Mitch. "Don't be jealous," she pleaded. "There's no time for hurt feelings." She turned back to Su Lin. "Now, where is Traver?"

"He is working with the sawmill gang. Living at One Tree Hill with his woman."

"His woman." Ariel repeated the words.

"She is only a young girl," explained Su Lin. "A child, really—only sixteen. Her name is Mina Mae."

"Does Traver know about . . . Mitch?"

"Traver is aware you, too, have taken a mate."

"I must go to him at once."

Now Mitch's brusque baritone boomed through the air. "No! I forbid you to go!"

"But I must see him! Tell him everything! Now that he remembers—"

Mitch interrupted again. "Can't you see that Traver's following his own nature? He's jilted you twice!"

"I only want to talk to him," she insisted.

"Don't insult my intelligence!" Mitch threw both arms up in fury. "Oh hell! If you can't see anything else, don't you at least see it breaks my heart every time you run after him?"

"But, Mitch—please! I owe it to Traver."

"Then let me out of here! Get me a bottle of cheap whiskey and a hot deck of cards!" He stomped toward the door, shooting back the final insult, "And a warmhearted gypsy girl to sit on my lap!"

Ariel did not allow herself to unravel. If she did, she might well run after Mitch. She turned to Su Lin. "Quick, give me directions to the sawmill."

Su Lin would not. "Traver did not ask to see you. He did not talk of returning to Virginia City under any circumstances. He said only, 'I've made a bad bargain, but I'll stick to it.'"

"Oh, surely we're not all meant to be so unhappy! Traver can't refuse to see me—especially when he understands how much is at stake."

"He considers himself bound to another woman."

"He's not responsible for things which happened before his memory returned!" Ariel dismissed Su Lin. When the Chinese girl had disappeared into the dark hallway, Ariel grabbed Mitch's best leather jacket. She braided her hair and wound it around her neck like a warm muffler. Hitching up her riding britches with a leather belt and pulling on thick gloves, she headed for the stable.

Chapter 21

The timber roads were snowpacked, easy going for the black stallion. At sunrise Ariel spotted One Tree Hill. Below the sawmill a few tents and hovels dotted the snowy landscape.

Uphill, behind the farthest cabin, she spotted a giant of a man moving to a wagon. It was Traver, loading cordwood with his strong hands. The snow came to his boot tops. He was dressed in a sailcloth windbreaker and wore a corduroy cap with earflaps over his auburn hair. He moved back to the porch of the lean-to shack, picked up a bundle and placed it under the wagon seat.

Ariel spurred Mitch's stallion through the loose snow. At the top of the hill she tied the horse to a branch of a pine tree, then pounded on the flimsy plywood door of the cabin. A girl peeked out the door. She was a small waif with pale skin, frail arms and sadly hungry gray eyes. "Yes'm?" she inquired in a timid voice.

Ariel couldn't speak. Poverty had taken a great toll on the fragile girl. Traver came bounding to the doorway. The three stood silent a moment.

Traver broke the silence. "Let's all go inside," he said.

"Yes'm, please do! Come in me house." Mina Mae chirped, parroting Traver's words as if they were absolute law. She held his arm politely as a semblance of introductions was made.

"And . . . uh . . ." concluded Traver, "This is Mina Mae . . . my . . . uh . . . fiancée."

Ariel gulped, fighting to keep herself from fleeing this horrible cabin. Mina Mae served a brew that passed for coffee, insisting Traver take the cracked cup and Ariel have the good one. Ariel understood: two teacups, one cracked. Not even enough coffee to make a pot. Barely enough food to exist.

As the three made small talk about the winter weather, Ariel observed how Mina Mae hung on every word Traver uttered. And Traver seemed considerate, helping her take the used cups to the sink, telling her quietly to finish packing her things. "Mina Mae will be staying with her folks in Eureka till spring thaw. It's too cold up here on One Tree Hill," he explained. He smiled at her affectionately, as if Mina Mae were a docile kitten.

When Traver went outside to see Mina Mae off in the wagon, Ariel peeked through the cabin cracks at them. He was extraordinarily gentle, handing her the reins, putting his hands over hers, cradling her head against his shoulder. He loves this shy, obedient girl! marveled Ariel. I've never seen him so tenderly affectionate. How could she tell him her news?

Traver kissed Mina Mae. He clucked to the horse and the skinny mare moved down the Sawmill Road. Traver turned back to the cabin, shaking. From cold? Or fear of facing her? Ariel wondered.

Ariel gave him no chance to start a discussion. The moment he entered the kitchen, she spoke first. "Traver, when you remembered me, did it worry you?"

He shook snow from his shoulders, shaking his head no at the same time. "It's a bad bargain I've made," he said, "asking anyone to share life on One Tree Hill. But I'll not back down from my end of it."

"But you are not the same man you were when you met her! You can't claim you found Mina Mae as the Traver Loch I knew!"

"No, but whoever that man was, he saw Mina Mae's good points."

"I don't doubt she's a lovely girl. But I have things to tell you which may make a vast difference."

Traver wrapped his jacket closer to his body as the wind

whistled through the cabin cracks. Ariel felt her teeth begin to chatter. "Come to town," she suggested. "This is ridiculous, working at the sawmill for six dollars a week, freezing yourself out here on One Tree Hill."

He didn't answer. He picked up a cold biscuit from the countertop. It was flecked with brown dots. "Wait," Ariel said as he started to eat it. "That doesn't look right."

"Weevils," he responded. He popped the brown biscuit into his mouth, obviously hungry enough to eat worms.

"Traver, for godsake! You can't live like this! Wind biting through your bones. Snow up to your collar! Bugs in your breakfast. Come back to Virginia City. Come back to work at the Hell's Candy."

He pulled a rough cedar chair around and sat down facing her. "I like it here."

"That's pure stubbornness!"

"No, it's hard work. Plain, hard, physical labor. And I like it. It's important to work with my hands."

"What's important about hauling timber? Work! Work! Work! Oh, you'd like nothing better than to be harnessed to a mule!" She turned away, knowing his remarks about hard work were true. He'd never backed away from the hardest tasks in the mine. But work was no reason to try to survive a Sierra winter. She softened her tones. "Please come back to town. I need you."

"Stop!" he ordered. His green eyes turned fierce and forbidding. "Why did you come here, Ariel? I didn't ask to see you. Did you expect to find me miserable? Did you want to hear that Mina Mae makes me unhappy? That my life on One Tree Hill is intolerable?"

She considered a moment, then spoke with trembling honesty. "Yes," she admitted humbly. "Those are precisely the things I wanted to hear."

"You have no right!"

"But I loved you, Traver," she cried blindly, "and now you must come back to me because—"

"Madness, Ariel! Sheer madness!"

She leaned against him, expecting him to push her away. But he rose, shielded her with his arms and patted her back softly. "Oh, honey lass, you simply don't understand."

"No, Traver!" she blazed. "It's you who doesn't understand!"

He silenced her with a hand across her lips. "For once— just once—listen to me! Hear me clearly. I mean to stay here on One Tree Hill. With Mina Mae. I don't want any more handouts from you—not white flour biscuits or jobs at the mine. And no more handouts from Mitch, either."

"What's Mitch to do with this?" she asked, freeing herself from his grasp.

"Mitch? Sure and a lot he's had to do with us both! He's bent over backward bailing us both out of jams." He smiled at the same time his jaw took on a bullying thrust. "I'm glad you married him, Ariel. He's a strong man and inclined to settling down."

She shook her head against Traver's words. How could this happen? The first man she'd loved wasn't the right one? She flung her arms around Traver, holding him tightly.

He stiffened at first, then met her upraised lips. His body trembled. "Ariel, have you no mercy? For either of us?" The dull throb of passion passed through his arms. His breathing turned ragged, the excited caress of his hands and mouth hovered over her body. "You're married," he whispered, as if to remind them both.

"Not really!" she whispered back. "It's only—" She stopped. No explanations were to be given. Traver had made it clear he was casting his lot, by choice, with Mina Mae and One Tree Hill. She could hardly disclose the predicament of her pregnancy and paper marriage now. *Not* telling him was a matter of her honor—like his fight to outlast the winter.

She fled from his embrace, dashing from the cabin, stumbling downhill in the snow and snatching the horse's reins from the tree limb.

She was uncertain how far she walked through the rising wind and swirling whiteness of new snow. She was unsure how many hours she had spent in the numbing landscape. She fell forward into a drift and lay cradled away from the wind, serenely content not to get up again. Warm, protected, she burrowed deeper into the snow. The horse whinnied, pulling her back to reality. She righted herself and trudged on.

Occasionally she spotted stumps, but no other distinguishing landmarks. Stumps. She must still be near the sawmill. Had she traveled in circles all this time? How long had it been?

She walked onward, trying to lead the horse, trying to keep going downhill. She felt sleepy now. She would rest. Sleep. The storm would end while she slept. She took another two steps, then tumbled when she tripped over something hidden in the snow. She felt a hot, bright pain in her stomach. Doubled over in the snow, the pain rippled through her like fire. She flailed the snow with one hand, searching for the object she'd tripped over. A stump! A sharp, splintered treetrunk. The rough edge protruded through the caked snow.

She sank into the snow, stifling the cascades of pain which still cut through her midsection. She knew she must not fall asleep. She must climb aboard the stallion or perish in the drift. She managed to kneel, and felt around in the snow until she found the reins. She lifted one foot, stretched up to the stirrup, yanked herself to a crouching position. Pain buckled her knees and a wave of nausea formed in her stomach.

She pushed herself upward toward the saddle, and finally managed to get aboard the stallion. Her head against the horse's mane, she tugged weakly at the reins.

Time was suspended, and Ariel drifted in and out of troubled sleep. Perhaps the horse would find his way back to the stable. Or perhaps Mitch would come looking for her. Or maybe Traver would seek her.

A noise awakened her. She blinked at a changed landscape. When had it stopped snowing? The sun was now so bright it hurt her eyes. Where was she? And why could she hear excited dogs barking loudly? She stared at the rocky pinnacle. She was far above the treeline. A solid blanket of snow covered the incline, broken only by two spirals of white rising into the air. Suddenly she uttered a tiny cry of joy. Steam! Smoke! She knew exactly where she was—the steam from the hot spring, the smoke from the Basque's cabin!

The wolfhounds' barking became louder as she neared the cabin. The horse moved as fast as he could on the treacherous, curving cliffside. The increased motion renewed the ache in her body, and there was a feeling of warmth and wetness between her legs.

She saw the cabin door open. The short, dark form of Pedro Ybarra stood outlined against the brilliant white of the snowscape. He made a startled gesture, then ran forward. She felt herself slipping from consciousness, but not before she had smiled at him and extended her arms in a gesture of supplication.

When Ariel awoke, her first sensation was that of glorious warmth. She stretched and inhaled deeply, catching the smells of the wool coverlet, the beeswax candle, the pine cone and sagebrush fire. Looking out the window, she saw it was snowing. The memory of her ordeal came flashing back. "Pedro! Where are you?"

Pedro Ybarra stepped into the alcove bedroom. "Here I am," he said quietly. He took her hand, gazing down with tender eyes and concerned smile. "Tell me what happened, Ariel."

"I was lost. In the snow. I fell. A stump. My stomach—oh, I've lost the baby, haven't I?"

"A child?" He shook his head. "What are you talking about?"

"I'm pregnant—or was—"

"You couldn't be!" he interrupted. He shook his head. "Ariel, I am nearly forty years old. I come from a family with nine sisters, not to mention a mother and two grandmothers. It's a culture where there are no mysteries about the workings of our bodies—men's or women's. I have been quite unembarrassed in caring for you. But there is no doubt in what I tell you now. You certainly are not pregnant."

How straightforward he was. And certain. But how could she have been mistaken for months! "I wasn't with child?"

"No."

"Not at all? Not ever? But how could this be? I was certain I had conceived—the night of the earthquake!" She asked him again. "Are you sure?"

"Absolutely. Perhaps the earthquake shocked your system," he theorized.

"I thought of that at first," she admitted. "But when things went on so long . . ." She was astonished her own body could play such a trick. No baby! After months of convincing herself, she now tried to believe the opposite.

"Didn't you once tell me you'd never lived through a true winter?" the Basque asked.

"Yes, but I never thought women conceived from being cold!"

He laughed. "Of course not. But many Basque girls who grow up in our sunny seashore regions have your same problem. When they move to the Pyrenees, their first winter often causes temporary interruptions." He patted her hand and pulled the sheepskin coverlet around her shoulders. "Ariel, you are young and healthy. You have a nasty gouge on your stomach, but that is the extent of your troubles."

Her sense of relief was mixed with anger. "No baby! I can hardly believe it. Then I needn't have married Mitch! I needn't have begged Traver to remember me! I needn't have given away half my Hell's Candy interest."

Once more the Basque reassured her. "It will take time for you to be at ease with what has happened. But remember this—your body did not betray you. Only your mind."

"Such deceit! And all from within myself!"

"I will leave you to rest now, Ariel." He left the alcove, returning at suppertime with a tray laden with hot mutton stew, which she downed ravenously. "Slow down," he admonished her with a chuckle. "I must feed you just enough and not let you overeat." He stood by the fireplace, looking pleased with himself. The two wolfhounds lay nose to nose at the door.

Ariel felt a rush of gratitude for Pedro. Without warning, she began to sob.

He moved closer, sat on the side of the bed and held her soothingly. "Let the tears flow. Warm food and a good cry will make you feel better."

"It seems you have a way of finding lost souls," she sniffled.

"You have found yourself, more than me finding you," he said. Ariel understood the double meaning of his words. "In a day or so I will go down the mountainside and see if the pass into town is unblocked. If so, we can make the trip into town together." He smiled happily. "It is time for me to be receiving word of the date to meet my bride."

"How wonderful!" She was pleased his long wait was nearly at an end. "In the spring you'll be meeting the ship in San Francisco! And then we will all dance at your wedding." She suddenly felt exhausted. "Perhaps I shall be going to San Francisco in the spring, too. Permanently. Life is so difficult on the Comstock. I'm too tired to keep on fighting Putnam. Too weak to engage in any more combat with Mitch or Traver."

"Your strength will return," he predicted.

The Basque was right. Day by day Ariel revived. On the fifth day Pedro Ybarra checked the passes. He returned with disturbing news. "I have been into the outskirts of town. Rumors say Mitch Galway is a wild man—drinking, gambling wildly, roaming the streets endlessly."

"Another temper tantrum!"

"I think it's more than temper," Pedro said. "I think he is sick with worry over *you.*"

"Me! No, he promised a binge simply because I went to talk to Traver."

"But you've been gone nearly a week. Perhaps he thinks you are lost in the mountains. Perhaps he thinks you are dead. Or that you have found Traver and stayed with him. It is hard for a man who believes he has lost the one he loves."

Despite Pedro's words, Ariel could see nothing but a spoiled child in Mitch's actions. "Drinking and gambling!" she stormed. "Was he carrying on with a gypsy girl, too?"

"They say he is making a grand show of courting Nedra. But his heart does not seem to be in it."

"I shall tell him plainly this afternoon: all bets are off. He can act the fool without *me* on his conscience. By tonight he'll be free as a sparrow. I shan't trouble Mitch Galway one day longer for the use of his name."

Chapter 22

Ariel let herself into Mitch's home. The parlor stood in disarray, the bed was unmade, her books heaped in piles on the carpet. In the kitchen she discovered Mitch. What was he doing home, scrambling eggs, at this hour of the afternoon?

When he saw her he nearly dropped his skillet. "Thank God you're back! Where the hell have you been all these days? I've been half-crazy with worry!"

"I've been staying at the Basque's," she said coldly. "Now I've come to pick up my belongings. I'm leaving."

He dropped the skillet into the sink, his eyes clouded with disappointment and confusion. "Leaving?"

"This entire marriage has been based on false premises."

"Hallelujah to that!" he muttered. "The woman finally speaks the truth."

"I'm not pregnant."

Instantly he was at her side. "Oh, Ariel . . . I'm so sorry!"

"No, no, I'm fine," she told him hurriedly. "It's only that I made wrong assumptions. I never was pregnant."

He shook his head. "Then I'm sorry again, darling."

"So now I must leave. There is no reason to continue our charade. I'll see you receive the half-interest in Hell's Candy I promised you."

Mitch turned and faced the mantel. His fingers drummed the plaster. "You want out of our agreement after I've kept my part of the bargain? That's hardly a fair exchange, Mrs. Galway."

"I told you I'd honor the agreement about the mining shares." She moved past him into the bedroom, looking atop the armoire for her valise.

His voice followed her like an explosion. "I told you all along—I don't give a merry damn about the Hell's Candy! But I do care about you. And I intend for you to stay here. We are two adults who took vows. The dishonor would be in breaking them now."

She reached for her satchel. "I know I've caused you trouble, Mitch. But I'll not bother you any longer."

He stood in the doorway. She could see the hurt in his eyes. His voice faltered. "Ariel, if you'll remember, this game was your idea. Now you want to throw down the cards and quit. Darling, have a little more faith. Stick it out. Your luck has changed. Traver is gone from your life for keeps. We can start over. Take the risk with me. I have faith we could make a go of it. Don't you?"

"Mitch, our arrangement was strictly on paper! You know that as well as I. And now it's over."

She opened the satchel and put it on the bureau. Her hands trembled as she opened a drawer and took out her lingerie.

Mitch advanced into the bedroom, muttering stubbornly. "I've kept my part of the bargain. My God, Ariel, don't you realize how hard it was to lie beside you night after night? I never let you whip me into a flame, though I was a glowing mass of coals. Now you breeze in here and announce you're skipping out. By damn, I've a mind to have a piece of you, even if I have to take it by force!"

She stood her ground. "It would be after one hell of a fight," she told him.

"You're primed for a battle," he tossed back. "And I'm in exactly the mood to oblige!"

He chased her once around the room, then grabbed her arms. She kicked. He circled her waist and lifted her from the floor. "Now, you can fight me or go along *with* me and make it pleasant for us both."

When she thrashed again in his arms, he dropped her on the bed. For a moment she lay still.

"Have you had enough fighting?" he asked. He stepped close to the bed, unbuttoning his shirt.

She raised herself as if to scramble off the bed. "Go ahead," he said coolly. "Race around the rooms like a filly first time on the track. Come back when you're exhausted. I'll wait for you."

She was convinced Mitch had passed some invisible stopping point. Any consequences she suffered now were a result of her own duplicity. But if she stayed on the bed, with Mitch beside her, she knew her resistance would crumble. She rolled over, ready to dart away.

He caught her lightly. "Don't you ever learn, darling? When I unearthed you from the hay on the *Pallas Maru* I had a pitchfork. Right now, I wish I had a board to paddle some sense into you!"

The memory of the shipboard scene sent her reeling. She'd held him close then, begging his help. And he'd been helping her ever since . . . paying for her keep at Cleo Burney's, running interference for her with Putnam and the tongs, offering to give another man's child his name.

She bowed her head, sudden tears springing to her eyes. If I don't leave this minute, I never will, she thought.

Mitch misunderstood the tears. Instantly he was cradling her tenderly. "Na, na, my pet. I'll let nothing hurt you!"

"But Mitch, this is the last thing I expected—"

"Easy, darling. This isn't a calamity. You know how long I've loved you, how much I've wanted you."

His gentle words touched her to the core. He kissed her hair, her throat, behind her ears. "Darling, you must know what you've done to me since the first time I saw you. I've felt like there was a snake wrapped around me, squeezing tighter and tighter. I've wanted you so bad it felt like the blood would boil in my veins. Every time you rolled against me in your sleep, I died, forcing myself not to touch you."

"Oh, Mitch!" She felt the tears streaming down her face. Every word, look, touch from him sent her senses whirling.

He leaned over her, brushing away the tears. Then he lay beside her, one hand cupping her waist. "I mean to kiss you now," he whispered.

She blinked. He bent downward. His hair tickled her cheeks. His long, silky eyelashes fluttered against her skin. In the dimness of the room he looked very powerful and determined. He rubbed his hands together as if to warm them, then slowly placed them at the outer edges of her breasts. As he caressed her, he lowered his lips until they met hers.

She didn't want to respond. It would be better for them both if she could lie taut and unfeeling. But her body was inches from capitulation and her soul urged her to give in to their union.

Such tenderness in his kiss! Perhaps he'd meant to capture her in cold fury, but now a fiery passion had melted them together. He caressed her again.

When he'd undressed Ariel and then himself, he rolled against her. Both inhaled deeply, the smell of their flesh like an exotic perfume that aroused them both. Their lips and tongues met, hot breath against cool skin.

Ariel arched against him, every inch of her throbbing with passion that begged to be satisfied. How could she have denied him and herself for so long? She admitted her need for him and kissed him deeply, more deeply than she had thought possible.

His mouth held hers while his hands brought her hips upward to meet him. Her arms reached around him and pulled him tightly against her. He bent to her breasts, tantalizing her anew until a rhythmic shivering enveloped her whole flesh. A fire spread through her body.

He entered her and her lips sought his furiously, consumed him with powerful desire. The truth of their love was clear now. Any night without Mitch would be too dark. Any road without him by her side would be too long. Any struggle without his help too wretched.

At the instant she perceived this their long struggle ended. She relaxed in the wonder that their desire could be so joyous. And she gave herself over to their love completely.

Her heart beat as if a torch had been lit within her chest. His whispered assurances of love echoed with the power of a waterfall.

Suddenly she was sobbing loudly. Mitch pulled back, a look of sharp pain on his fair face. She meant to reach out to him, but something held her back. The pain of the terrors she had survived since leaving Honolulu Academy demanded release. She could hold her tears back no longer. Mitch smoothed back her damp hair and caressed her cheeks. Ariel tried to speak, but the words stuck in her throat. She could do nothing but cry.

"All right," said Mitch. He rolled off the bed and picked up her valise. "I'll not try to hold you."

She couldn't look at him, but buried her face in her hands, her body wracked with sobs.

He began tossing her clothes into the valise. "I tried my damnedest. It didn't work. I'll not stop you from leaving. I'll not interfere when you see lawyer Bondese about the divorce. Sometimes finding the right *person* at the wrong *time* is as bad as finding the wrong person."

She found her voice and screamed his name as he left the room, but he did not turn back.

Ariel trusted no one. She moved into a private room at Canada Sally's and spoke to no one for a week. She couldn't comprehend what had gone wrong. Just as she was about to admit her love for Mitch, she'd lost him. Why had she been unable to speak through her sobs, to tell him that she loved him? She was afraid she would never love again.

Nedra came calling and would not go away. She stayed outside banging on the door until Ariel finally admitted her. "Why wouldn't you let me in, Ariel? And why are you living here again? Is it all over between you and Mitch?"

Ariel did not have the strength to explain. "Go away, Nedra. Leave me alone."

"You must still care for Mitch to be pining away like—"

"No! I don't care at all!" she lied.

Nedra smiled. "Then you won't mind if I try for him again?"

Ariel looked up in surprise.

Nedra shrugged. "You gave it your best shot and it apparently didn't work. So now it's my turn. Fair enough?"

Before Ariel could argue, explain or deny, Nedra assumed matters were settled. With a brisk shake of her curls, she smiled in triumph. "There's news of Traver, Ariel. It seems he's packed Mina Mae home for good and moved to his mountain claim. He thinks he's found pay dirt."

"I hope he has!" Ariel said, sincere in her wishes for Traver's good luck. "Anything that drags him away from One Tree Hill is a step in the right direction."

"There's news of Putnam, too," Nedra went on. "China Camp is withholding his opium. Even the liquid. He's talking of burning China Camp off the face of the earth!"

"What!" Ariel was astonished. Set fire to China Camp! "How can he even talk of such a thing!" Ariel envisioned the dry gully of tents and shanties set to the torch. "Fire is Putnam's favorite tool," she cried. "In Hawaii he burned the cane fields and killed my father."

Ariel got up and began to pace the room. "It's time I faced

the world again, Nedra. I've been in hiding too long. If I'd been taking care of my business as I ought, Putnam wouldn't be talking this way. I know it."

Nedra looked carefully at Ariel. "I'm sorry about Mitch, Ariel. But I'm glad to see you up and about." She smiled slyly and left the room.

During the next few days Ariel returned to her normal routine, letting Putnam know she was once more a force to be reckoned with. She buried the pain she felt in her heart when she saw Mitch and Nedra together—on the street, in the hotel dining room, on their way to Piper's Opera. They made a stunning couple, Mitch's golden coloring complementing Nedra's fiery darkness.

Ariel finally made an appointment with lawyer William Bondese who seemed not at all surprised to see her. He stood by his desk, his brown vest completely buttoned, his mustache tips shining as he licked them between sentences. "Mitch was here last week. Said to have things in order for you. He also said to tell you he understood."

"Understood what?" *She* didn't understand the situation; how could he?

Lawyer Bondese twisted his mustache tips around his little fingers. "I try not to intervene, except legally. But from Mitch's face and your nerves, I'd say you two need mutual forgiveness, not a divorce."

The breath caught in Ariel's throat. No, she'd not cry! But the shaken look on her face must have been obvious. Lawyer Bondese hastily produced a glass of water, a handkerchief and a pat on the back, as if to cover all possibilities. Finally he stood back, crossed his arms and sighed. "So, you love him after all?"

"How could I?"

"Stranger things happen constantly. I don't purport to be privy to what happened between you and Mitch. All I can see is that you're both torn up. Mitch looked like a dog who'd been half-choked. You act like a filly who's had her shins lashed."

"Mitch doesn't love me."

"So you you keep saying."

"And I don't love him."

"So he believes." Lawyer Bondese pulled a chair to his overflowing desktop. "Both of you have worked very hard to prove to me there's no love lost. So I shall simply follow directions and draw the papers." He smiled with paternal resignation. "There'll be no problem as you and Mitch are in complete agreement about not loving each other."

When Ariel fixed her signature to the legal documents, she felt as much a traitor as she had at the paper marriage ceremony. Lawyer Bondese buttoned and rebuttoned the same top two buttons on his vest. Finally he nodded and escorted Ariel to the door.

Leaving the law office, she first heard, then saw an altercation at the corner. Two men, surrounded by a crowd of curious onlookers. Two loud, angry men, one with his fists raised overhead. Traver Loch and Ricket Putnam!

Traver's voice carried half a block. "So, now when it looks like my claim will pay off, you have the gall to say I haven't clear title?"

"You were working for me at the time. By rights that claim is mine," responded Putnam in oily tones.

"Putnam, I'll give you twenty-four hours to see your lawyer! Have that title free and clear and in my name or I'll kill you!"

The townsfolk began to whisper among themselves. Few seemed to doubt Traver's temper or his physical ability to carry out his threat. Traver shouted again, "So help me God, I'll see you in the grave, Putnam! There's work to be done at my claim. But when I come back to town, it's free title or you're a dead man!"

Traver shook his fist and marched away defiantly. Ariel moved toward Putnam. He brushed his sleeve, as if Traver were insignificant. "That idiot is no danger to me. He won't come back to town. He'll simply keep going. Skip the country, now that the chips are down."

Ariel didn't think so. She'd seen Traver's ferocious temper before. "I think you'd better clear the title in Traver's name," she told Putnam. "And you'd better quit making threats of burning China Camp."

He didn't deny the ugly rumors. "If the Chinese persist in withholding my supplies, then I will use alternatives to persuade them. China Camp needs cleaning out. It's overpopulated. A good fire every so often makes labor cheap."

This man was insane! Worse, he had the ability to carry out his threats. She turned away, half hoping Traver would return to town and kill Putnam. How could she have done business with Putnam! Well, Traver had found the courage to break with him. She would, too. But first she must go to China

Camp and warn Su Lin. Perhaps no one else took Putnam's threats seriously, but Ariel remembered the holocaust on Lanavi.

Ariel went to the stables late in the morning. Entering, she heard voices. Putnam again! But this time his opponent was Mitch. Quickly she ducked into the shadows, not wanting to face Mitch in Putnam's presence.

The two men stood with their backs to her. She saw Mitch extend his hand to pat his black stallion's nose. Then he raised his fist at Putnam and punched the air. The horse, confused, pawed in agitation. "I've had enough, Putnam. You know that. I've already told you I'll not finish the trestle on your terms. What makes you think I'd do your bidding and destroy China Camp?"

"Be reasonable, Galway. You'd never be suspected. Why, folks around Virginia City look up to you. Reduce China Camp to ashes and I'll stay out of your way on the railroad."

"No! Putnam, you're a bloody leech! You've sucked this district dry. Now you're ready to roast the whole county. There's no way to control those Washoe Zephyrs. You'd burn everything from Tahoe to the Atlantic shore!"

Putnam had no concern for the damage he might cause. He continued to press Mitch. "I know you broke with me when you married Ariel. But now that she's out of your life, come back to work for me."

"Go to hell, Putnam. You promoted that marriage because you thought I'd get the mine and you'd get it from me. Haven't I made it clear? I'm a builder—not a raider or a pirate. Hell's Candy had nothing to do with my feelings for Ariel."

Ariel emerged from her hiding place, making plenty of noise to announce her presence. Though surprised, Mitch hurried toward her, took her arm, and turned away from Putnam. "I've avoided you," he began.

She motioned toward Putnam. She did not want to have an intimate discussion with Mitch in Putnam's presence.

"Never mind him, Ariel. It's more important to settle things between us. I was scared to see you. Flat out afraid. Hell, I was afraid to look at myself in the mirror! Afraid I'd see the kind of man you'd hate. Afraid I'd see the kind of man *I* hate!"

Ariel saw true remorse in his eyes. How she longed to tell him the fault had been hers! She dared not stand a moment longer looking into Mitch's azure eyes. Already her knees were threatening to buckle, her heart was bouncing as if it had torn loose from her chest, and her palms had turned damp. "Mitch, I must borrow your black stallion. I have an errand to do. I must go at once."

His eyebrows shot up as an angry frown swept his golden features. "Hellbent on chasing Traver one more time?"

Ariel's denial was cut off by Putnam's approach. Mitch backed away, steadied the horse, adjusted the saddle girth, held the stirrup and boosted her up. She longed to lean down and whisper a hurried explanation to Mitch. But she must not risk having Putnam know she was heading to China Camp.

She galloped all the way to the Chinese settlement. Surprised, she found the camp a beehive of activity. Men were marching in long columns, chanting and drilling in military formation. The younger men brandished weapons and pails. The rumor of burning had reached the shantytown long before Ariel.

Su Lin was cooking rice when Ariel found her. "Don't bother getting off that horse, Ariel." Su Lin did not even look up.

"I've come to warn—"

"We're aware." Su Lin blew on the charcoal embers. "This time my people will fight fire with fire."

"This is madness!" Ariel clambered off the horse.

Su Lin gave her no chance to speak. "Go to San Francisco, Ariel. No one in Washoe is going to be safe."

"Putnam must be stopped! Not by counter fires. You must help me, Su Lin! Talk to China Camp. Don't let them go on a rampage which will only bring more looting and killing!"

Su Lin dished rice into bowls. Po Fan began to eat hungrily. He hadn't gained an ounce since Ariel had met him a year ago on the *Pallas Maru*. Growing fat in a rich land was strictly a myth for this immigrant.

Su Lin caught Ariel's fond smile in Po Fan's direction. "Ariel, you have helped us before. Helped me when we escaped the barracoon. Helped Po Fan aboard ship and when he broke his leg."

"You helped me, too!" Ariel said eagerly. "You found Traver for me on One Tree Hill."

"But we cannot help each other this time. Putnam must be dealt with. You must excuse us. There are ceremonies." Po Fan tied a red sash around his thin waist. Su Lin picked up a hatchet with gleaming blade and tied a yellow streamer on the handle. Did they plan to stop fire with ceremonial weapons?

Ariel made one last plea. "Why not buy some time? Send Putnam some opium until your defenses are stronger."

Su Lin looked doubtful. "I will ask my people."

Ariel felt encouraged. When Su Lin and Po Fan returned from the ceremonies, they brought a bottle of dark liquid. Su Lin handed it to Ariel. "We will not deal with Putnam. We will let him deal with himself," she said mysteriously. "Give this to him and let him feed the fire in his brain."

Ariel took the bottle and put it in her pocket. This, at best, would only be temporary. Putnam would stop at nothing. She *must* break with him. Traver had done it. Mitch, too. Even the downtrodden residents of China Camp had the gumption to fight Putnam's threats. Where was *her* courage?

Immediately after arriving back in town, Ariel went to her lockbox at the Bank of the West. She removed her Hell's Candy ownership certificates, rolled them together in a neat parcel and concealed the papers in her jacket. Then she walked to the Guardian Concert Hall.

Chapter 23

"Putnam, I want to sell out."

"Why?"

She formed the words slowly, around the lump of sadness in her throat. "The mine was to be my link with my mother. But I cannot recapture her loving, lively spirit from a hole in the ground. Even if there is silver lurking deep in Hell's Candy, it cannot shine brightly enough to make me betray people and memories I love. People have been hurt in Hell's Candy. I've seen it destroying the values I cherished. Will you buy me out?"

"I'm more than delighted to do you the favor of buying you out." He attempted to rise from his lowslung leather chair.

She'd been so intent on delivering her message she only now realized how unkempt he appeared. The office was a mess, cabinet drawers open, files ransacked. The opium lamp sat unused in the corner, while empty *chandoo* bottles littered the desk and window sill. The shades were drawn against the sunlight, which hurt his weak eyes. A tray of surgical instruments lay on the desk, along with an open medical text.

"I want to sell, but there are several conditions. Traver is to have his claim free and clear. Mitch is to have complete control of the railroad. There is to be no trouble at China Camp and the Chinese are to be allowed in town."

Putnam uttered a profane curse. "Never! You go too far, Ariel."

Swiftly she took the bottle of dark liquid from her jacket. She held it toward him, saying nothing.

"Opium!" he cried. His hands grasped the air, clawing toward the bottle. "Oh, Ariel, my dear, I owe you many thanks."

Silently she set the bottle on his desk by the tray of surgical knives.

His lips seemed like paraffin as he maneuvered to the desk, unsteadily opened the drawer and took out a spoon. He downed a brimming spoonful of the dark opiate. He sighed deeply and sagged into a crouch against the furniture, perspiring heavily.

She was afraid he might pass out. "I've brought the ownership certificates," she reminded him. "I want a receipt from you, as well as a written promise about the other matters I mentioned."

"Yes, yes," he breathed dreamily. He fondled the bottle of *chandoo* in his hands. Seating himself at the desk, he unscrewed the lid and held the bottle to his lips, swallowing another draught. "We've been at odds too long, Ariel. I see you are really my friend. By all means, fill in the receipt and I'll gladly sign it."

Ariel's suspicions were aroused. He was too agreeable. She rummaged in the clutter of the desktop, shoving the sharp surgeon's tools to one side. She found paper and pen and began writing. While she was busy, he fumbled again for the spoon and the opiate bottle. He moaned, long and low, when he'd finished.

She hurried with her writing, fearing he'd become too drowsy to sign. Pushing the papers in front of him, she smoothed them and handed him the pen.

Instead of signing, he leaned back in the chair. His voice sounded as if he were speaking through fog. "Hell's Candy has been Devil's bait for both of us. You were as addicted to that mine as I am to this opiate." He shivered and drew his knees upward.

"Sign here," she urged.

"I'm as eager as you," he mumbled. He reached for the pen. She had to turn it in his fingers as he attempted to write with the wrong end. Perspiration ran down his forehead. He scrawled his name, one letter at a time, and the date.

"Done!" she cried, vastly relieved.

"Not a minute too soon," he croaked. "Indeed, I *have* done you a favor. I've prevented you from being a terribly rich woman! I went down in the mine this morning, after I saw you at the stable. And do you know what I found? There's not another three feet of boring till we hit the silver vein!"

"I don't believe you!"

"I haven't broadcast the news, of course. The flood in the lower levels saved years of work. The water, as it drained, washed away chert and quartz. Now Hell's Candy will finally pay off." He flung a disdainful look of triumph in her direction. "For *me!*"

Suddenly he rose, wobbly but determined. He reached for one of the sharp knives in the medical tray. She backed up, uncertain what he meant to do with the instrument.

He turned toward her, cackling a wild laugh. Did he mean to attack her? She retreated another step, clutching her jacket around her. "Leave me alone," she warned. "You have your *chandoo*. You have the mine. Stay away!"

"But I don't have control of Traver, Mitch and China Camp with you around," he growled. "And now that you know of the silver, you might go back on your agreement." He brandished the knife, the blade gleaming in the subdued light. "This is one contract that calls for no witnesses!"

She threw herself against him, trying to wrench the knife from his grasp. She pinned one arm against his chest, pushing him backward with the other.

His raised arm jerked, came down in a swift motion, then was pushed upward obliquely by her grasp. The blade nicked his throat, like the dainty prick of a sharp sewing needle. His eyes bulged in surprise. Then the knife dropped to the floor.

She turned to flee. He let out a deafening roar. She saw his arms flail, then he collapsed. Blood rushed from the wound in his throat.

She stopped, horrified. He reared backward on his knees, then pitched forward. A single, blue bubble formed in his mouth.

Panicky, she started again for the door. Should she send help? What had happened? Surely that tiny nick on his neck hadn't killed him!

Suddenly she heard footsteps outside the office. She leaned back to examine Putnam again. His head drooped against the desk. His eyes had disappeared into the sockets. His right leg jerked convulsively.

The footsteps outside the office halted. There was a knock at the door. She stood paralyzed. Should she answer? Or flee? If no one answered, perhaps the caller would go away. She held herself perfectly still, hardly daring to breathe.

The knock sounded again, louder and more insistent. She knew she'd left the outer door unlocked.

After a moment of indecision, she sprang toward the shaded window. Carefully she maneuvered the shade to shield her, then unlatched the catch and raised the glass. A second later she swung out onto the balcony.

Ariel lowered herself from the second floor balcony, grateful there was no one on the street at the moment. She smoothed down her skirt and vest, and walked down the street, forcing herself not to hurry. Oh, dear, she still had the stock certificates—and she'd forgotten the signed receipt. Cautiously she increased her pace. The person knocking at Putnam's door had probably entered by now.

Ariel hurried in the direction of Nedra's wagon, knowing her friend would be telling fortunes this afternoon. Barging into the wagon, Ariel interrupted a fortune in progress. The irate customer was sent away with a promise of a double fortune another time. Ariel climbed behind the canvas flaps and closed them tightly. "Nedra! I may have killed Ricket Putnam!"

"God's nightgown!" cried Nedra. "Wait. You *have* killed him? Or only think you might have?"

"I . . . I . . ."

At Ariel's hesitation Nedra jumped to her own conclusions. "Traver killed him! Didn't he? You're establishing an alibi for Traver!"

"No, no, I did it! Traver's at his mountain claim—"

"I saw him on the streets not an hour ago."

"God help him! I must find him at once. When people find Putnam, they will surely accuse Traver. Oh, why did he make such loud threats last week!"

"Tell me everything. And quickly," demanded Nedra.

Ariel complied.

"You climbed down from the balcony? Did anyone see you?"

"Not that I know of."

"You must go away. Quickly. But you must *not* see Traver. When Putnam's death is discovered, Traver will be able to say truthfully he hasn't been there and hasn't seen you."

Ariel was too distraught to think matters through. "But perhaps I should—"

"Go! Take the back streets from town and then climb to the Basque's mountain hideaway." Nedra issued directions, taking complete charge. "I will find Traver. Spirit him out of town and back to his claim. Here, take my shawl and sunbonnet. Go quickly!" She practically shoved Ariel from the wagon.

Nedra's plan seemed sensible, but there was no time to examine it from every standpoint. Ariel threw the striped muslin shawl around her shoulders, darted down the alleyway and ran.

The wolfhounds came racing to meet her. The Basque raised his staff and threw back his blue cloak and hurried along the pinnacle to greet her.

She was out of breath when she spoke. "I need a place to hide."

"It is yours." He did not question what had sent her to him but took her to the cabin, fed her mutton stew and played the silver flute to cheer her.

As he replaced the musical instrument on the mantel, he asked softly, "Why are you here?"

"I fought with a man."

"Was he your enemy?"

"It was Ricket Putnam. I think I killed him."

"By all that's holy, if you did not succeed, I shall do it for you!"

Ariel was deeply touched by his unstinting support. "Bless you, dear Basque, for your understanding."

He took her shoulders, gazing deep into her eyes. "I'm glad you came here, Ariel. Glad you thought enough of me to seek refuge in my hills. But I'm sorry it is trouble which always leads you to my door." He took her hand. "Come, let's walk to the hot spring. It will restore you."

Walking along the trail, Ariel explained her decision to be done with Hell's Candy. She swept her hand across the landscape. "Pedro, you are correct in living above the mines. Here the air is clean. You are able to live in peace."

His glance was serene. "I love the jagged peaks, the sigh of the mineral spring, the grass on the windy plateau." Suddenly

both he and the wolfhounds tensed. He pointed to a small
figure on the faraway canyon rim. "Did someone follow you,
Ariel? A man on horseback is hurrying this way."

"Perhaps it's Traver," she reasoned. "Nedra was to find
him. Maybe he's come here instead of returning to his claim."
She squinted at the rider, worried about what might have
happened in town when Putnam was discovered.

The horse picked its way along the ledge. When it emerged
from the fir stand, she distinguished both horse and rider.
"The black stallion! Mitch!"

Mitch spurred the stallion along the upland trail. Ariel and
the Basque moved down to meet them.

"Ariel! You must come at once!" cried Mitch as he reined
the stallion to a halt in the clearing. "The town has turned
against Traver."

"Traver! What has he done now?"

Mitch's voice rang through the canyon like a shot. "You
killed Putnam. But Traver's taken the blame. He's been
arrested. Nedra told me where to find you and why you ran
away."

She clutched the horse's reins. "What's happened? Traver
was nowhere near! I told Nedra. She said she'd send Traver
back to the mountains."

"Oh, Traver and Nedra never had time to make any such
plans. Traver was found inside Putnam's office—kneeling
over the body!"

"The knock on the door!" She clapped her hand over her
mouth. "But Traver didn't do anything! He couldn't have!"

"I believe that," Mitch said sharply. "Nedra believes that.
You and Traver certainly know that. But the rest of the town
remembers only that Traver vowed to kill Putnam. And now
Putnam's a corpse and Traver's in custody. There's talk of a
lynch mob. An impromptu hanging. That's why I've come to
fetch you."

Blood rushed to her temples, making them pound. "A
hanging!"

"There's no way to control a mob. You'd better come with
me, Ariel—if you care at all about Traver. If not, then before
morning, Traver's corpse is likely to be laid alongside Putnam's."

She didn't hesitate. "Of course I'll come! But I don't
understand how the town could turn on Traver! I'd think the
town would raise a cheer for the person who rid them of
Ricket Putnam!"

The Basque spoke firmly. "Putnam was far from loved. But he kept order. Everyone knew what to expect from him. His influence was evil, but it was sure."

"Now there is chaos," agreed Mitch. "Frankly, I don't know whether people will believe you or not. But it's your right to try."

Mitch extended his powerful arm and helped her onto the horse. Then they were off, racing like the mountain clouds. She sat rigid, careful to protect the papers in her jacket. They galloped down the cliffside, through the canyon flats, along the ridgebacks still covered with snow. What could she do if there was a mob? Would anyone listen? Would anyone care that she was defending herself when the knife had cut Putnam? She shouted against the wind, holding Mitch tightly. "I can hardly understand how Putnam died! The cut was so tiny! No larger than a shaving nick."

"I suppose a small prick on the jugular vein could mortally wound a man," Mitch conceded. Suddenly he reined the horse and pointed to the valley. "The mob! Heading across the ridgeback."

The entire town seemed to be stretched out in single file, moving hurriedly along the lower slopes of Sun Peak.

"Oh, hurry, Mitch!" As the horse galloped over the incline, nausea rose in Ariel's stomach. She knew how a mob refused to think. She'd seen the grown men of Virginia City pelt a hungry wolfhound and Chinese child for sport.

The crowd milled around the railroad supply yard. "They've got logging chains! And they're heading for Crown Point ravine. The trestle! They're going to hang Traver from the trestle," cried Mitch, spurring the stallion.

She envisioned the half-completed wooden trestle arching high above the valley. "Do you see Traver?"

"Far back! Blindfolded."

She spotted him, hands tied behind him, being led along with a rope around his neck. The first of the mob reached the trestle. Young men edged out, testing the woodworks to see if they'd bear the weight. The logging chains were thrown over and looped.

Mitch urged the horse to dizzying speed, covering the mile. Even before they reached the crowd, Ariel was yelling, "Stop this! Stop! He didn't do it!"

Mitch pulled the horse to a trot, forcing their way deeper into the throng. Ariel cried, "Stop! Listen to me! Wait till you hear what I say!"

The noisy mob paid little attention. She shouted, "Traver didn't kill Putnam!" The few who had turned their heads her direction lost interest. One attempted to nudge the horse out of the way.

"Stop, Mitch. Let me stand up." Mitch halted the horse. She clambered to her feet, holding onto Mitch's sturdy shoulders for balance. "Look here! I'm the one you should have in custody! You can't hang an innocent man!"

The crowd hissed and guffawed. "Move on! Get out of the way!" someone shouted.

Aghast, she tried again. "Aren't you interested in justice?" Her words fell on deaf ears. The logging chains clanked together as they were adjusted over the wooden tie ends.

Ariel swung down and ran to the end of the trestle. Mitch tried to distract the mob. "Ho, there!" he shouted. "This trestle is property of the Virginia and Truckee line! No private use of the property!" A murmur of dissent shot through the crowd, then laughter.

Ariel fought her way to face the crowd. She waved her arms and screamed for attention. The mob shoved back, impatiently hustling Traver along the span to the end of the trestle. "Stop this! Leave him alone. Oh, what can I say to make you stop?"

Suddenly she knew the answer to her question. She would give them Hell's Candy! She shrugged off the jacket. "Wait! I have something for you! All of you!" She held the jacket with one hand, quickly reaching into the pocket for the certificates. She unrolled the stack of papers, holding them aloft. "Look!"

The people nearest her turned sullenly quiet, staring at her hands. They began to elbow each other. The word circulated through the crowd, people pointing and nodding.

"Here! Take it!" she cried triumphantly. "It's the stock to the Hell's Candy! It could be worth thousands. Putnam said the Hell's Candy is about ready to break open! Please, take it! But give me Traver. He's innocent! Leave him alone."

There were frowns and murmurs, a smile here and there. She waved the stock certificates. "Worthless to me! Perhaps a fortune to you! Who wants them?"

A loud voice inquired, "You'd sell out for this redhaired varmint?" He turned to the crowd. "I say, let her!"

A shouting match broke out, some men yelling approval, others intent on a hanging.

Then Mitch took charge. "Hand me some of those certificates, Ariel! I want my fair share!'' He grabbed greedily, with both hands. She understood his action was to spur the crowd to join in. He urged the others to follow his example. His action unleashed a mad scramble for the papers. Ariel flung the stocks high in the air. The crowd surged to meet them, men pawing, leaping and clobbering each other.

She rushed to Traver, grabbing the rope from his neck and the blindfold from his eyes. No one opposed her. Everyone was intent on the scramble for the Hell's Candy stocks. When she pulled the blindfold from his eyes, he blinked in confusion. Oh, those eyes! Hollow, sea-green and gaping. He stared at her as if he had suddenly been blinded. Those eyes she had once loved! Now they looked as if his soul had flown away. She collapsed against him, horrified anew.

He looked at the logging chain dangling at the end of the trestle. "Too damned close for comfort," he muttered. Then he said coldly, "You bought me."

"Yes!" she breathed, thrilled the gamble had worked. "I've bought our freedom, Traver! Oh, it's freedom for all of us! You, me, Mitch, the whole town—we've gotten free of Putnam *and* the Hell's Candy!"

Traver's usually animated voice was now a monotone. "I'm not so sure." As she untied his hands, he said, "This town lives on blood. This may not be the end of anything. They turned on me. Now they may well howl for *your* blood—and you have nothing left to barter."

Anxiously she watched his eyes, waiting for them to warm and brighten. But his face did not change.

A short man in a khaki shirt and a battered felt hat pushed through the crowd. "Missy, I'm the law in the county, though I ain't had much luck enforcing it of late." He smiled in a tired, kindly way as he laid a callused hand on her shoulder. "You sort of complicated doings this afternoon, confessing and waving that stock around. I'd best hold you for a hearing. It ain't too bad. We use the dressing rooms of Piper's Opera for cells for the ladies." He stood only as tall as Ariel, with wisps of cornshuck hair sticking out from under his hat. "The circuit judge will be along soon as spring thaw opens Geiger Grade. Probably be a formality, but you better come along till then."

Traver fell in step beside her as the sheriff motioned her to proceed toward town. She refused to be anything but proud! Hadn't she saved Traver? Weren't a few nights in Piper's Opera a technicality? Traver began muttering. She couldn't catch his words. The bizarre look in his eyes now alarmed her. He followed them to the opera house.

The little sheriff opened a dressing room at the end of the dusty backstage corridor. "Sort of pretty, huh? All them mirrors and lights and red flocked wallpaper." He nodded that she should go inside. To Traver he said, "You make your goodbyes quick and move along."

"Yes, I'm leaving," mumbled Traver. As Ariel started inside, he put out his hand. "Ariel, I'm leaving."

"Leaving!"

"Going away. Leaving Virginia City for good. Getting the hell out of the Washoe."

"Right now? Leaving me in jail? After what I—"

"Yes," he admitted, no trace of shame or pity in his jade eyes. He flexed his biceps as if eager to start new adventures.

"What about your mountain claim?"

"The Devil take it! Never produced ten cents of pay dirt!"

This didn't sound like the Traver Loch who had threatened to kill a man over the claim. "You'll have no trouble about the title, now," she reasoned. "With Putnam dead."

"Quit bribing me to stay in this hellish town!"

She stared at him. "I simply don't understand why you'd run away now!"

"You bought me off the end of that trestle, Ariel. But that doesn't mean you own me. I probably owe you something— to your way of thinking. But I'm leaving."

She shrank from him. Leaving wasn't a strong enough word. He was deserting her!

His shoulders stiffened as he turned away. "You gave away a fortune for me, Ariel. But I have to go, honey lass. I have to." And he didn't look back.

Chapter 24

The cheery, considerate little sheriff apologized each morning for keeping Ariel locked up. He often came in the afternoons to chat. "Double apologetic, ma'am," he told her on the tenth day. "It's a shame you can't be in on all the excitement."

"What excitement?" she asked.

The sheriff blushed. "It's the Hell's Candy, ma'am. Town's crazy. Men, women, dogs and babies are all down in the stopes, clawing their way toward the big bonanza."

To her surprise, Ariel heard herself laughing. "More power to them!" She could imagine the frantic dig for riches now that both she and Putnam were out of the way. She could wish others well, but the aftertaste of Hell's Candy in her own mouth was bitter. "One good thing—the tradition of barring women from the mines is a thing of the past."

"Yep. 'Bout the only people left in town have come calling on you. Visitin' time." He motioned toward the end of the hall.

Wise Ada, brandishing a cane and wearing a tall straw hat over her frizzled gray hair, came striding into the dressing room. "Ariel, I been out of touch. Now I hear this story of you taking a sharp instrument to Putnam's chicken-skin neck.

265

Well, your head is a blunt instrument for 'fessing up to such an affair!"

Ariel giggled. No one laid matters out for inspection as succinctly as Wise Ada. She hugged the wiry old woman.

Wise Ada produced a cigar and chewed the end. "You heard about the rumpus in the diggings? Sure no superstitions stopping women now. They're clawing their way down to bedrock with their fingernails!"

Ariel wondered if Hell's Candy would yield treasure to such a heavy-handed assault. "I bungled everything, Wise Ada. Fought for the wrong things. Stood by the wrong man."

"I heard. Traver hightailed across Forty-Mile Desert headed east so fast it seemed he'd invented a new transportin' system. By the way . . ." Wise Ada unfolded a scrap of paper from her leather shirt pocket. "What do you say to this new transportin' conveyance?"

Ariel squinted at a jumbled drawing of wires, winches and cables. "What are all those wires and clouds?"

"It's an aerial locomotive!" huffed Wise Ada. "That's balloon to you folks as hasn't any transportin' imagination."

"Pie in the sky for sure," teased Ariel.

"No, no. Ain't far in the distant future at all. I'm scrounging parts right here in Virginia City and I've toted in all the canvas and gas bags I'll need. The snow on the Sierras will keep this town trapped for another month. But I'll be up and on my way!"

The sheriff poked his head through the door. "Time's up, Ada! Move along. Ariel has two more visitors waiting—a matched and fancy pair!"

Wise Ada scurried away. Ariel leaned against the bars, straining to see the new callers. Mitch and Nedra! They entered, arm in arm, sweeping down the hallway in obviously new, store-bought finery. Nedra tripped along carrying a parasol and planting noisy kisses on Mitch's cheek.

Mitch wore a three-piece suit of worsted black wool which set off the golden coloring of his face and hair. Nedra's costume was stunningly bright, with a fuchsia silk striped bodice above a billowing green skirt. She kept a possessively tight grip on Mitch's arm.

Ariel felt herself turn hot and breathlessly jealous at Nedra's revolting performance. Damn! Why couldn't she find the room in her heart to wish them happiness? She forced herself to offer congratulations.

Nedra shook hands by merely touching, then flaunted the engagement ring on her fourth finger.

"Yes," acknowledged Ariel. "I thought that noisy smack on Mitch's cheek sounded like wedding bells."

During this exchange, Mitch stood silent. Ariel could tell he was embarrassed. She turned the conversation to business. "Mitch, how much of the Hell's Candy did you end up owning?"

"A tidy enough amount." He laughed. "Enough to make a decent wedding present for my bride." He patted Nedra's hand.

"But he bought me this ring with the bonus from the railroad," Nedra explained. "He's getting work done on the trestle even before the passes are fully unblocked. It's enough to put us on easy street."

"And enough to buy Piper's Opera," he laughed uneasily. "You're residing on my property, Ariel."

Ariel remembered a promise she once made. "You own this place now? Why, Mitch! Here's your chance to break tradition and do a good deed at the same time. Let Su Lin perform at Piper's!"

He was obviously startled, but not offended. "You think anyone would pay to see a Chinese dancer?"

"She's quite good. The dance of the Crimson Lotus and the Seven Fireflies is very exciting. It would be a gamble at first, I admit, but—"

"I gave up that gambling business!" he interrupted. "I'm such a fine upstanding citizen these days that folks are talking of me for mayor!" He grinned, half-proud, half-sheepish. He patted Nedra's arm. "This gypsy harlot and I intend to infiltrate Comstock society for sure!"

"Aw, go on!" laughed Nedra, clinging to Mitch's neck with both arms.

"This spitfire gal always wanted to be a highborn lady. Soon as we're settled—we're thinking of buying the Graves mansion on the hill—then she can tell the Decency Committee to go to hell."

Apparently the intention to buy the fancy house was news to Nedra. She looked taken back, then frowned. She elbowed Mitch. "You didn't tell me nothing about having to stay cooped up halfway on Sun Peak!"

He didn't take calmly to the elbowing. "Settle down and act like a lady," he ordered.

"Where do you get off insinuating I ain't *always* been a lady!" she spit back.

Mitch's eyes flashed, a cross between dismay and anger. "Hush, dear. Your clown act was fine for telling fortunes, but—"

"Clown? Spitfire? Harlot?" Nedra's violet eyes went blue-black. "Durn if I know where you get the high and mighty right to call me names! And speaking of living in a grand mansion—staying in one place all the time—I'd not live in a pig sty with the likes of you!"

Ariel closed her eyes, hearing Nedra's skirt swish down the hall, a counterpoint to her heavy steps.

Ariel looked up. Mitch stood bewildered. "I deserve better," he muttered, hands slouched in pockets. Suddenly he leaned against the bars and put his hands out to Ariel. "I *do* deserve better! I deserve *you*."

"Mitch Galway! How can you be so fickle? Two minutes ago you were draped over Nedra, cooing like a dove!"

He leaned closer, head down, hands strangling the bars. His voice was soft with laughter and longing. "Listen to me, Ariel. Marry me. Again. This time for real. The railroad people have given me full charge. You could be Mrs. Mitch Galway in style."

"You've gone berserk, Mitch."

He shook his head. "This time we'd be legitimate," he insisted. "I only regret I wasn't the one to dispose of Ricket Putnam." He looked at her intently. "Ariel, I still find it hard to believe you killed him. From what you've said, the nick under his chin was accidental and minor."

She didn't want to re-create the scene again. More than once she'd vowed to kill him. But it did seem extraordinary that a pinprick could be lethal.

Mitch spoke again. "I'm ashamed of all my sins. Sins of haste. Sins of outrage."

She knew he was now speaking of the two of them. Oh, but she'd committed her fair share of the sins of haste and outrage. For an instant she wanted to throw all sense of justice to the Devil. The quickest route to freedom and happiness would be to grab Mitch back from Nedra. But she must not consider such treachery.

Mitch pressed his case. "You know I'd take good care of you. I'm making investments—Piper's Opera, the Hell's Candy. I've even put money into Wise Ada's balloon scheme."

"Then your head is in the clouds, too." She pressed her fingertips against his. "Darling Mitch, I think you have a bad case of engagement jitters."

"Perhaps," he admitted with a forlorn sigh. "Perhaps I'll get over them. Deep down, I suppose I'll marry Nedra. *You* won't marry me. And *she* can certainly be counted on for a life of excitement."

He paced the corridor, talking more to himself than Ariel. "You heard Nedra objecting to the new house. I talk about settling down. She complains she'd rather have a new wagon. I talk about permanence. She wants to take off cross country."

Poor Mitch, so ripe for domesticity! Ariel remembered the evenings she'd propped against the pillows with a stack of books, Mitch peering over her shoulder. Would Mitch and Nedra have that kind of cozy intimacy? She tried to envision their future. Then she tried to imagine her own future. She couldn't think of living in the same town with Mitch and Nedra. San Francisco. She'd go there, of course. The moment the mountain passes opened.

"I'm tired of this personal talk, Mitch. It hurts us both. Tend to your own affairs. And no more moping around as if you were in love with me."

His response was bitter. "God help the fool who *does* love you!" Mitch straightened, pride stiffening his shoulders. His parting words struck her like a knife. "If you had only *tried,* Ariel, you might have learned to love me."

She averted her eyes. As he left, she vowed never to tell him exactly how much she did love him.

Ariel was surprised the next week when the sheriff announced, "You're free to go, ma'am. Mitch Galway came to my office yesterday and posted a personal bond for you. He's the real power in this town, now. Lucky for you he's your friend. Anyhow, you can do as you please, providing you're here when the circuit judge makes his rounds."

"In the meantime, I can go anywhere I wish?"

"Yep. Going to trudge after that wild Scotsman? Head across Forty-Mile Desert to the East?"

She shook her head no. She couldn't march into oblivion like Traver. He was probably in Texas by now. "I plan to go to the Bay."

"Then you'll not be going post-haste. Sleds and snowshoes

are moving over the Sierras, but nothing else. Geiger Grade is plugged tighter than a cork in a moonshine keg."

"No trains? No Wells Fargo?"

"Not even the telegraph. Last I heard, the transcontinental railroad was running between Reno and the coast. But you've nary a way to travel to Reno."

"Even the weather is conspiring to keep me here!" she lamented.

She finished signing the releases, then hurried toward her lodgings. Snow lay deep on the hillsides above the town. The March wind blew more like a banshee than a zephyr.

She detoured when she saw a crowd in the open field behind the Catholic church. Wise Ada was directing men as they spread loops of wire and canvas on the ground. Delighted, Ariel ran to the old woman. "Wise Ada! When will your balloon be finished?"

"Soon." Wise Ada nodded her head.

"Sell me a ticket! I want to go with you," Ariel begged.

"What! You're foolish enough to be my first customer, girlie? Jail's addled your brain, Ariel." Wise Ada pushed her straw hat back across her wrinkled forehead. She reconsidered for a moment. "Well, I need someone brave enough to take to the skies with me. The rest of this town has their noses stuck down in Hell's Candy most of the time." She clasped Ariel around the waist. "All right, then! It's you and me into the airy blue!"

"When?"

"Depends on hitting a springlike day with light breezes. We need enough warmth to float us plumb over Geiger Grade."

Ariel was disappointed they couldn't leave now while her courage was at its height. As she looked at the heaps of junk spread on the vacant lot, she grew worried. "Will you have control over where you fly us, Ada?"

"Partly," laughed Wise Ada. "Now, run along and don't worry. Wise Ada's airborne locomotive express will get off the ground!"

Ariel went to her rooms and packed her valise. It sat, ready, by the door for the next ten days. The whole town, by then, was wagering, scoffing, admiring and scorning the balloon as it lay like a huge sack on the ground.

Finally one morning Wise Ada banged on her door at dawn. Ariel grabbed her satchel and hurried to the lot. The day was cold, clear and windy. Ariel felt lightheaded as she tied her bonnet firmly beneath her chin. She wondered if she might lose her courage at the last moment. A huge crowd had gathered. Money was changing hands as bets were placed. Would the balloon fly? How far would they get before tumbling back to earth?

Nedra came rushing through the crowd. Fortunately, Mitch was not with her. Nedra hugged her and offered good wishes. "Aren't you scared? Oh, you brave, brave thing," she cooed.

"I probably will be scared," admitted Ariel. She looked with apprehension at the chaotic maze of wires, ropes, canvas and rubber. The hiss of the hot gas filling the loose bag was not comforting.

Wise Ada cut the goodbyes short. "Come aboard, girlie!"

Ariel hurried up the loading ramp into the basket. She stood at the rail, half hoping to spot Mitch at a discreet distance and catch a last glimpse of him.

Wise Ada asked who she was looking for. "Not still expecting Traver to come back, are you?"

"No, I was looking for—never mind."

Wise Ada studied her a minute. "Oh, ho! So you finally learned the difference between brawling boys and sturdy men?"

Ariel laughed and nodded.

"What separates men and boys ain't stupidity, Ariel. Most of 'em live long enough to ride out the confusion. They live through their mistakes. But once in a while a fellow shows up who sees beyond his mistakes and limitations. More than sees beyond. Grabs hold of the future like it was a golden ring. And it lifts him above the crowd like this balloon is going to lift us." Wise Ada finished her lecture and patted Ariel's back. "Mitch is a hell of a man. Has that spunk I was talking about. But he ain't your concern any longer. Now let's git!"

In moments the basket was steadied, the flimsy contrivances of wire and rope cast off. The loose bag dangled and bulged above them like an oversized lung.

Then, in a brief minute of suspension, they were moving upward! Shouts of "Farewell! Good luck! Safe journey!" reached them. There was a jolting bump and Ariel's heart skipped three beats. She grabbed the railing and looked up. They were soaring and she wasn't scared at all! It was thrilling, slipping away from the world. All those tiny people —watching, standing in a circle, growing smaller every moment. Ariel waved her bonnet. She felt like an angel on her way to a new, pure world.

Wise Ada grabbed her sash as she leaned out to see the town. "Stay put! You're offsetting weights port and starboard!" She adjusted ropes and pulleys. "Well, we sure put our noses in the air this time!"

"It's wonderful!" cried Ariel. The ride was smooth, no worse than a gently rocking boat. It was so grand, not being anchored to anything but air!

Ariel watched all of Virginia City laid out below her: the church with the broken spire, Flowery Hill Cemetery, the tumbledown shacks on D Street, the sinkholes in Forty-Mile Desert. She spotted the underpinnings of the Crown Point trestle and Sutro's tunnel poking through the snowpack.

The sun shone on the bald head of Sun Peak. "Take me up forever!" Ariel shouted, dizzy with delight. "Oh dear, I'm getting silly!" Her nostrils tingled in the cold air. Tears sizzled at her eyelids. "How fast are we going, Wise Ada?"

"Can't get a fix on it. But there's the far side of the ridges already. Forty mile an hour, maybe."

"How close to Reno can you take us?"

"Don't rightly know. Close, I'm sure."

The balloon came down gently on an alkali flat just outside Reno. Ariel piled out, ready to walk to town. The journey was cut short as nearly the entire population of Reno came rushing to meet the adventurers. Ariel smiled and answered questions as if she'd been transporting herself about in balloons for years.

After saying a heartfelt thanks and goodbye to Wise Ada, Ariel caught a ride to town on a farmer's wagon. She was in time for the afternoon transcontinental train. Before nightfall, she was knocking on the door at Sonny Staidlaw's mansion.

As she waited for the housekeeper to unfasten the heavy door, Ariel thought, I always return here when I'm unsure what to do next. I'm like a homing pigeon. She smiled to herself, sadly. This time I've flown high. But now I must come down to earth and look for a permanent roost.

Chapter 25

Irene Haskell's chubby face radiated relief. "At last, you're here! We sent for you nearly a week ago."

Ariel entered the house, confused by such a welcome.

"No matter," chattered the housekeeper. "You're in time."

"In time for what, Irene?" Ariel remembered the blocked passes and downed telegraph. "Has Mr. Staidlaw tried to send a message?"

"Mr. Staidlaw is terribly ill!"

"Of what?" cried Ariel, her distress evident.

"A lifetime of stressful living, if you ask me," Mrs. Haskell replied, taking Ariel's valise and leading the way to the camellia suite. "He sent for you. Said no matter what time of the day or night you arrived, he wanted to see you."

"He had faith I'd come?" questioned Ariel.

"You're here, aren't you?"

That was true. But she was here because of her own troubles, not Mr. Staidlaw's. She hurried to Leah's rooms, tidied up quickly and followed Mrs. Haskell to the cavernous master suite on the second floor.

Sonny Staidlaw was not resting in bed, covers to his pale chin, as Ariel had expected. He was reclining on a chaise longue, watching a sunset fog blot out the Berkeley hills. A quilt covered his legs. His fingers restlessly picked fuzz from the binding.

Ariel hurried to his side. He nodded at her, a weak smile plying his lips. "Fog covers the horizon like graveblankets cover a corpse."

Ominous words said in an ominous tone of voice. Now she sensed the odor of death in the room. His dark beard was matted, his eyes heavy with blood pooled beneath the rims. Overcome with sorrow, she took his hand. She was sorry for herself, too, that she would not have his counsel for the future.

He whispered, "Sit down, child," and he squeezed her hand. "Tell me how things went."

"Things went poorly. I lost the Hell's Candy."

"I'm glad it's gone!"

"In a way, I am, too. But I feel badly in that it was my mother's only legacy to me. And before that, it was your gift to her."

"My bribe to her."

She pulled a footstool close to the chaise and sat down. Ariel ached to learn the whole truth of her mother's connection to Sonny Staidlaw, but she hesitated. How could she bring more pain to the old man's dim eyes? She returned to her own story. "Besides losing the mine, I lost the man I loved. I realized I didn't love Traver when he turned his back on me and walked away across Forty-Mile Desert. Then it was too late to admit there was another man." She told most of the last month's events.

"So! You tried to buy Traver the way I tried to buy Leah."

Ariel paced the room, wishing she could present a spirited defense of Traver Loch or herself or Mitch. But all of them had proved a terribly human lot.

Staidlaw slowly lifted his legs from the daybed and walked to the window. "You think a certain young man has done you an injustice in walking away? I felt the same way when your mother left me to pursue her own life."

"Did Leah run away from you?"

"As fast as she could. And with good cause."

"What was my mother to you? Friend? Tutor? Lover? Mistress?"

"All those and more."

"That's no answer."

"Ariel. It was a different time. I had much less security. God help me, I had much less courage. There were considerations. A wife, children, social position, newly made business connections. Many things I had put a premium on in my struggle for success."

Ariel moved to the far window, watching the gray fog creep across the bay. The jigsaw puzzle pieces were finally dropping into place.

Staidlaw continued his explanation. "In our affair, your mother's and mine, there was far more dishonor on my part than hers."

Ariel was curious to know all the details. Here was a man who had been in a position to support a wife and a mistress. "With discretion, the affair could have gone on for years. What happened? Did your wife find out and banish my mother to Hawaii?"

"No."

"Then you ended it?"

"Leah ended it. Without explanation. She suddenly married Elijah Cortland and booked immediate passage for the Sandwich Islands. Now I realize her reasons. But I didn't know for certain until *you* walked in here twenty-one years later. You were the reason."

Surprised—and not surprised—Ariel felt tears sting her eyes. Sonny Staidlaw was her father. This old man, once handsome, once powerful, was her true parent. She turned her head aside, afraid she'd weep openly, equally afraid she might lash out at him with her fists. When she'd regained her composure, she moved to him, took his hands, put her cool cheek next to his fevered one. "Father."

His lips trembled and poured forth promises. "This house will be yours, Ariel. And the Bank of the West can make up for the Hell's Candy. Move into this mansion. Give lavish entertainments here at the bay. Hundreds of young men will court you. Soon you'll forget weaklings such as Traver Loch and Mitch Galway."

"Did you expect my mother to forget you?"

"In all honesty, I wished happiness for her."

And she could see that he wished happiness for his daughter. But there were angry ghosts in the camellia suite as well as loving ones.

"Can you forgive an old man, daughter?"

"But you ignored Leah all those years! Surely you suspected what made her leave."

"I carry my remorse to my grave. It must look to you as if I bought her honor for a few shares of Hell's Candy. You must understand this was not the case. There was great love between us. Your mother had the courage to walk away from me. Exactly as Traver Loch walked away from you after you gave up the Hell's Candy to save his life."

"But now you are trying to buy me," she insisted. "You've spent a lifetime simply ordering things done. Build a railroad. Open a mine. Create a bank. Now it seems as if you're ordering me to take up the name Staidlaw, and continue your reign from this mansion."

Before he could interrupt, she went on. "Father—how strange that name sounds! I am glad I know our true relationship. There's no doubt you would have been precisely the right, powerful father for me. But now is the wrong time. Buying me back to your side as you—"

"Slip one foot in the grave?" He laughed. His voice sounded hearty. "Don't make up your mind so quickly. I'm not used to rejection." He said the words lightly, but she knew rejection still caused him pain. "Think about your future tonight, Ariel. Think of all we've said."

She nodded agreement.

He smiled. "You're so like Leah. So proud, with your shining candlelight hair and commanding dark eyes. Very well. We'll talk no more tonight of the future or the past. But I should like to hear of your balloon trip and the circumstances which forced you to abandon the Hell's Candy."

Ariel talked until she saw the old man's eyes drooping with exhaustion. She planted a kiss on his cool cheek and made her way to the camellia suite. She had many things to think about.

Ariel spent the next day alone in her suite, wrestling with the past, trying to come to some decisions about the future. By evening, she was exhausted and ordered a carriage. A drive through the city would be refreshing.

Mrs. Haskell detained her in the entry hall. "Should you be going out alone?" worried the housekeeper.

Ariel begged the question courteously. "How is Mr. Staidlaw this evening?" she inquired.

"Somewhat improved. I believe his will to live is stronger now that you are here."

Ariel laughed. "I suspect his strength is more formidable than either of us imagines."

The housekeeper dipped her head against her large bosom. "He says you're his kin," she said shyly.

Ariel wondered if she should acknowledge her heritage. It

would be easy to claim that Mr. Staidlaw's illness had caused him to make rash statements. But she could not let this link with her mother slip back into the shadows as the Hell's Candy had. She lifted her head proudly. "I am Ariel Staidlaw."

Mrs. Haskell beamed at her. "He's been alone too long, Ariel. I am truly glad you are with him now."

The housekeeper excused herself, leaving Ariel alone to wait for the carriage. Ariel paced the grand entry hall. Could she live alone in this somber mansion? Could she restore light and life to these rooms?

She peeked into the downstairs rooms, so formal and cold. She tried to imagine Traver sitting at the head of the mahogany dining table, silver and crystal at his fingertips. But Traver would never be comfortable in such a setting. He would rather take his meals from a lunch pail in the open air.

For a moment she succumbed to the vision of Mitch singing along with the grand piano. She could hear his merry baritone laugh echoing in the hallway, joking, calling to children. Together they would ride the black stallion at the Palo Alto stables, or linger over a stack of books at the bedside table.

Oh, damn! Who was the sentimental one now? The carriage arrived and she rushed outdoors.

The driver was flustered by her choice of destination. "Chinatown, ma'am? The Dupont Gai is renamed Grant Avenue now. Cleo Burney's Home? Closed down, I hear. The embarcadero! At this time of the evening?"

Ariel insisted, wanting to visit the only familiar landmarks she knew. At the waterfront she spotted the haberdashery shop where she'd helped Mitch outfit himself. And there was the noisy fish house where they'd eaten lunch the day they'd arrived on the *Pallas Maru*. Again memories of Mitch haunted her. In every challenge, every danger, every trial, she'd relied on Mitch. Why did she find it so hard to admit she loved him? And why had she waited until it was too late to be honest with herself?

She watched the rows of ships at anchor, tethered to the wharf like nodding, grazing sheep. Suddenly the carriage passed an empty pier. A lone man stood at the end of the dock. He was barely visible in the fog, but Ariel recognized his beret, wide black belt and pleated chamarra cloak.

"The Basque! Come to claim his bride. Oh, stop the carriage!" Climbing down hastily, she hurried toward Pedro Ybarra. She laughed aloud as she ran toward the end of the pier. Oh, there *was* happiness left in the world! A bridegroom keeping a solemn vigil, waiting for his unknown bride to arrive with the morning tide.

He turned as she called to him. In the foggy glare of the gaslight, she read anguish on his face. His lips were pale and rigid, his black eyes devoid of emotion. "Pedro? Why are you standing here alone in the night? Oh, dearest Basque, what has happened?"

He leaned against the pier post, one hand to his face as if to shield himself from the fog. He drew a crumpled paper from his sheepskin vest. "All is lost. Lost. Lost at sea."

She took the message, read the scanty details of the ship's foundering and loss. A deeply felt moan escaped her lips. What a terrible loss! Not only the woman he desired, but all his dreams of her! Ariel's arms went out to comfort him. "How unfair," she murmured. "All you've worked for. All you've longed for." She remembered the lovely things he'd made for the unknown girl—the copper pots, silver goblets, the woolen shawl and the red cashmere nightgown.

She put her arm through his, tugging gently. "Come with me. We will mourn together."

"That is the worst part. I cannot grieve properly for a soul I never knew. I feel only emptiness." He took the silver flute from his pocket. "I must play a song of respect for the lost one. The soul makes a journey beyond. Music must accompany it."

She listened with tears in her eyes as the dirge floated off into the fog.

He did not resist as she led him to the carriage and took him to the Staidlaw mansion. "This will be my house," she said.

The Basque looked puzzled but did not ask for an explanation. They walked up to the front steps, and Pedro stopped to touch the granite columns and peer at the ornate façade. "It does not fit you, Ariel. No more than it would fit me." He repositioned his beret on his black hair. "It is a house of another time. Of other people. Of a family who was not always happy here."

Ariel was amazed at his sensitivity to the house. And she felt comforted by his presence. "You have suffered a great loss, Pedro, yet you are receptive to my feelings. I am glad you are here. I, too, have found this house cold."

She offered him food and wine and they shared a late supper. "We drank from a wineskin at my cabin in the peaks.

Now we lift crystal goblets at your mansion by the sea."
When he settled his glass on the embroidered cloth, he added
a warning. "Don't stay here, Ariel. This house is not good for
you."

"But I can't go back to Virginia City. I did everything
wrong in the Comstock."

He patted her hand across the table. "It will help us both to
talk." He smiled, encouraging her to begin.

"First I loved a man I hardly knew."

"Traver." He nodded, refilling their wine goblets.

"Then I married a man who loved me. But I refused to face
that fact until I'd hurt him. Now I have no one!"

"As I have no one," he reminded her. When she sought to
express her sorrow, he held up his hand. "It is all right. I will
have my hills, the hot spring, the starry nights. But, you,
Ariel—you must have more than a granite fortress at the
Bay."

The Basque was right. A house could not assuage the
loneliness she felt within herself. Nor could her new bond
with the dying Sonny Staidlaw.

"You could go back to Virginia City and begin anew," he
suggested. "Perhaps you could even win back Mitch. Old
desires, like banked fires, need little to be relit."

"I appreciate your concern. So many times you have given
me help when I needed it. I will think about returning to
Washoe, but I don't think I could face . . ." Her voice trailed
off. She could face the hardships, the barren landscape, even
the greed. But she couldn't face Mitch being married to
Nedra.

The Basque stood and drained his wine goblet. "You are a
woman who hungers and thirsts and loves deeply, Ariel.
Don't stifle that love of life by imprisoning yourself in San
Francisco."

She told him good night and had Mrs. Haskell prepare
quarters for him. Love of life. It had been her sole asset when
she'd first met Traver and Mitch. Now the flame flickered
low, brought nearly to extinction by circumstance, grief and
loneliness. If she stayed in San Francisco, would it go out
entirely?

When Ariel went down to breakfast, she found the Basque
standing by the open bay window. His beret was pulled down
across his forehead, the blue pleated cloak tossed back over
one shoulder.

Suddenly Ariel was exhausted. "What shall I do now? All alone in this big house?"

He responded with other questions. "Don't you miss the whistle of the Washoe Zephyr? The sagebrush canyons painted in pastels and movement? The sound of sheep on the hillsides?"

"Yes, I do."

"You'll always be a servant to this mansion."

"Couldn't you stay here a few more days? There are so many things to be settled."

"It is time for me to go."

Suddenly she wondered how he'd managed to travel to the Bay. "I came over Geiger Grade by balloon. Are the roads open now? The passes unlocked?"

"No. I walked out."

"Across Sun Peak? Why, that's impossible! How did you do it?"

"As a child I climbed the Pico de Aneto, the highest peak in the Pyrenees. I learned to find my direction from the stars, the winds, the sun and the shadows. When I came over Sun Peak, I led two horses—one for me and one for my bride. They are stabled in Reno. If we take the train there, we will have no trouble going home."

"Home to Washoe. I never thought I'd want to."

"You must go back, Ariel. Not to chase the past, but to face the future. You cannot hide from it in this house."

She hesitated. "But I can't face the memory of Traver deserting me. Or Mitch and Nedra getting married."

"You must."

"You don't understand," she said sharply. "Last night I thought of all the men who might share this house with me. There was only one equal to its challenge."

"Mitch Galway," he said without hesitation. "Yes. It is a good match, though neither of you will admit it."

"Will you wait while I tell Mister Staidlaw I'm leaving?" She smiled at her own formality. "I mean, my father."

A smile brightened his face. "I'll wait."

When Ariel got to Staidlaw's room she found him seated at his desk, fully dressed, working at some papers. Today he's better, she thought, noticing the trimmed beard, combed hair and high color in his cheeks. She stood quietly until he looked up from his task.

"Father . . ." She hesitated a moment, then crossed and

stood before him. "I'm glad to see you are stronger today. I am stronger, too. I feel I should go back to Virginia City."

He balanced his pen carefully over the inkwell and sighed in resignation. "I guessed I could not hold you. So we part in peace, daughter."

"I will come often to visit, father."

She leaned down to kiss his cheek. His hand, steady today, came up to touch her hair. His voice was compassionate, yet filled with longing. "Ariel, your mother left me long ago. Now I pray you are not repeating her actions."

She looked up, assuring him again she would come to see him often.

"No, that is not what I mean. I am speaking of your relationship with Traver and Mitch. You must not abandon them."

"It was the other way around," she explained. "Traver left with hardly a goodbye. Mitch has promised himself to Nedra."

"Yet I insist both men may have had your happiness in mind."

She shook her head. "The best I can say of them is that they are their own men. Traver Loch, for all his faults, had the courage to pursue his dream of being footloose. Mitch—" She stopped. She would not torture herself with thoughts of Mitch.

"I expect to live many more years," Staidlaw announced. "I should like to live long enough to see your children romping noisily through these lonely halls."

Such a human wish! And humble. She hoped he'd be granted his wish, but her own hopes for it were dim.

She went to the window, toying with the fluffy panels. "Last night," she admitted, "I tried to imagine the men I knew in this mansion. Only Mitch would fit in here."

"Don't you understand, my dear? Mitch Galway is a sunrise temptation for you—a man unique enough for you to take risks. Ariel, you have such a wonderful capacity to love. And to fight. Why don't you bring both qualities to bear on the man you love?"

"Fight for Mitch? Risk everything?" Ariel warmed to the idea. "Mitch only risks when he has faith. I'm not sure I could—"

Staidlaw laughed with paternal pride. "Ariel, dearest daughter, I have complete faith in you!"

Chapter 26

Ariel and the Basque rode the train to Reno. Spring avalanches sent little quakes of snow tumbling down onto the train. Each time the train entered a tunnel, Ariel shut her eyes and shuddered. This was worse than going down in the flooded Hell's Candy! She was happy to climb aboard the pony which Pedro Ybarra had stabled in Reno.

The Basque seemed equally pleased to be back on home ground. Descending into the valley behind Sun Peak, he pointed to a few blades of grass peeking through the snow and mud. "Spring will arrive in two weeks," he predicted. "Things will improve. The railroad will finish this year. Putnam is gone. China Camp will have work again."

Ariel decided to check on Su Lin and Po Fan. "We will part ways here," she told the Basque, thanking him for his kindnesses. "I can walk to town after I visit my friends."

Pedro countered, "No, please keep the pony. Stable him in town and ride him to my mountainside for a visit now and then." He looked at her with tenderness in his dark eyes. "Ariel, you were the one who shared my loss. You were like a soft and healing wind. I think there will be better times ahead for us both. Please honor me with a visit to my peaks occasionally."

She waved goodbye and watched as he cantered the sturdy

horse toward the pinnacles. Soon he was indistinguishable from the snow and firs.

At China Camp she was threading her way through the maze of tents when she heard her name called. Po Fan came running toward her, without the slightest limp in his leg. She hugged him. "Oh, you look marvelous! I'm so glad to see you well and—why, Po Fan, you're getting chubby! Is Su Lin here?"

The smiling boy chattered the happy news. Su Lin was performing at Piper's Opera, playing to packed houses. And the railroad work had expanded, bringing jobs to the residents of China Camp. Po Fan took a quick breath. "And the Irishman and the gypsy are getting married tomorrow!"

"How wonderful! Tomorrow." Ariel tried to hide the sinking feeling inside.

"I'm glad you won't miss it," Po Fan went on excitedly. "Both hotel bands will play in the streets. Invitations are nailed to all the telegraph poles, trees and fence posts in the Comstock. Mitch has sent for fireworks! And because Su Lin has been such a success at Piper's, Mitch has hired our Chinese dragon to dance in Virginia City! All the way from the courthouse on A Street to the end of D Street!"

"Good for Mitch! He's finally opened the town!"

"He's a fine man," Po Fan said soberly. "Remember on the *Pallas Maru?* Mitch always came to give special feed to his horse."

It was getting harder and harder for Ariel to remain composed. Po Fan babbled on. "And Mitch is giving the bride a special wedding present. He bought much of Hell's Candy with his railroad bonus."

Ariel winced as she realized she wouldn't mind Nedra having the mine—if *she* could have Mitch! Fight for him, Staidlaw had recommended. But how? Tomorrow he'd be married!

Po Fan leaned toward her indicating he had a secret to share. "It was clever how we disposed of Putnam, wasn't it?" he whispered.

"We?" She thought she might have misunderstood. *"Who* disposed of Putnam?"

"China Camp," he said knowingly.

"But I am the one accused," she explained patiently. "And before me, the town thought Traver did it. How was China Camp responsible? What are you telling me, Po Fan?"

The boy looked like he was about to cry. "I have told too much!" He darted pell-mell into the maze of tents.

Ariel rode into Virginia City, deeply absorbed in trying to figure out what Po Fan had meant. She hardly realized the town's streets were deserted. Why, this was the quietest she'd ever seen the town on Friday afternoon!

Starting toward the boarding house, she noticed a large gathering of people at Flowery Hill Cemetery. So that's where everyone had gone! She wondered who had died. Flowery Hill was misnamed, for there was not a flower or shrub on the whole place. From three blocks away she could hear noise. How unusual. A noisy funeral! She watched people milling about, heard their strained, confused voices. Something out of the ordinary was happening.

She dismounted and tethered the pony to the fence rail outside the K.K. Saloon. She'd walk down the hill and find out what was happening.

Suddenly Ariel spotted Wise Ada hurrying uphill, waving her arms and beckoning. "What's going on down there?" called Ariel.

"Hurry up! The fuss in the cemetery is over *you!*"

"Me? I'm alive and breathing, thank you all the same!"

"Come on, lady! It's your two favorite gents, having another tiff on your account. Mitch and Traver are—"

"Traver? *Traver!* What's he doing here? Why has he come back?"

"Showed up this morning for the express purpose of starting that shouting match you hear in Flowery Hill. He's attempting to dig up Ricket Putnam's remains!"

"My God in heaven! Whatever for?" Ariel ran downhill, Wise Ada keeping pace on short, wiry legs.

"What does Traver think he can prove by unearthing Putnam now?" Ariel wondered.

Wise Ada panted, "Claims he can prove the throat-pricking you applied didn't matter. Traver's been east to Salt Lake City and fetched a medical fellow. A new kind of doctor who pokes holes in the dead and says what made the deceased pass on."

Ariel could hardly comprehend the news. "Traver here! To prove me innocent!" Her heart beat in feather strokes. At the gate of the cemetery she spotted Mitch and Traver. Shouting and gesturing, they both had upraised fists. Ariel almost laughed. This was the exact pose they'd held when she'd first seen them on the Honolulu pier.

She pushed through the crowd. "Traver! Mitch! What's causing the fuss?"

She ran between them, shoving them apart like a referee. "Is it true, Traver? You might be able to prove me innocent?"

A shrill voice interrupted, "It ain't right to rob a grave!"

"I say Putnam stays put!" agreed another bystander.

Traver grasped his shovel and threatened the crowd. Ariel once again saw him as strong and masterful. "Why didn't you tell me where you were going?" she asked.

"I couldn't tell anyone what I had in mind. Least of all, you. Any suspicion of what I was up to and this town might have cremated the evidence."

Such cleverness! She'd always known he was forceful. Now she was grateful for the way he took charge. But why was Mitch opposing Traver? Surely Mitch wanted her cleared! She faced the crowd. They edged back as if they were children caught playing among the tombstones. "Stand back," she ordered. "All of you. That includes you, Mitch."

"Wait a minute," argued Traver. "Mitch isn't opposed. Our argument wasn't over Putnam." He cast a glance at Mitch, then at Ariel, as if to say the argument had concerned the two of them. Traver gestured to the crowd. "All right, folks. I mean to dig now." Then he lifted his shovel, pushing it down through the clay and sandstone gravel.

Ariel felt a thrill sweep through her. Hadn't Traver once vowed to dig a fortune from the earth with his bare hands? Clearing her name was much more valuable than mere silver!

Traver worked steadily, arm muscles bulging, auburn hair falling across his forehead. She went to his side, anxious to understand fully. "How can this prove I didn't kill Putnam?"

He continued shoveling as he answered. "Remember when I found Putnam? Hardly a minute after you'd left. I barely noticed that scratch on his throat. But I did see his half-empty bottle of dark liquid on the desk."

"The *chandoo*—his opium."

"Opium, all right. *Raw* opium. Uncooked and unfiltered. Pure poison."

"How could you tell?" she wondered.

"I spent so much time in the Orient I learned to recognize the distinctive smell."

"But . . . I can't understand why Putnam didn't notice the smell."

Mitch entered the conversation. "Putnam had lost most of his sense of smell—most addicts do. His nostrils deceived him. He was probably so eager for the opiate, he didn't notice anything wrong."

She agreed. "Yes, he took three doses." Now she knew China Camp had dealt with Putnam. The raw opium was no accident, but revenge.

Traver looked hesitantly at Mitch. "Spell me on this shovel, Galway." When Mitch nodded and went to work, Traver turned to Ariel. "I came back to clear myself as well as you, honey lass. This town heard me threaten Putnam. No one could be expected to believe he'd killed himself."

"But that's precisely what he did!" Ariel cried with relief.

Wise Ada took charge of the crowd. "Here, folks, let's all step back. Give the shovelers some room. Sheriff, let's have you up front. Doc—yes, you—the fellow from Salt Lake. Where will you do your work, sir?"

The tall, somber doctor clutched his medical bag and stepped forward. "It would be better if I could have adequate time and privacy. I'd appreciate it if you'd all stand back now."

Wise Ada seconded the motion, adding a practical suggestion. "Let's all adjourn to the hotel bar and await the outcome of this investigation."

"Hooray! Hip! Hip!" The townsfolk converged on the hotel as if strike games were getting underway. Traver and Ariel followed as soon as the coffin was exhumed. The sheriff and the doctor carted it away. Mitch faded away into the crowd.

As Traver and Ariel entered the hotel, a cheer went up. Glasses were raised. Traver hooked his arm through hers. He was exuberant and full of energy. "Well, honey lass! I guess we showed 'em!" He swung her around and kissed her on the cheek. For a moment she had the feeling he'd come back to claim her as well as exonerate her.

She must speak to him alone before things went any further. She took him aside to a quiet corner of the lobby. "Traver, how can I thank you! You've done so much for me. Without my knowledge. Without my asking for it." She felt immense gratitude welling up. But gratitude was not love. She now had the maturity to recognize that she must forget the tender tyranny of first love. She wished she had time to formulate a proper speech, to think of the words which wouldn't disappoint him.

He sensed her reticence. "Ariel, this is the first time I ever saw you tongue-tied!" He laughed. "Let me be the one to say it then. I came back to balance accounts. You bought my freedom from the lynch mob with Hell's Candy. Now I've returned the favor by clearing your name."

Trust Traver to plunge straight to the heart of matters.

"Ariel, there can't be anything more between us than balancing the books. There were always barriers between us, I admit." He cocked his head to one side, green eyes subdued. "The barriers are still there—not the least of which is the news that you're Ariel *Staidlaw*."

Shocked that news could travel so quickly, she asked, "How did you know that?"

"The whole town knows. Mitch and Nedra. Su Lin. Wise Ada. I don't know how they found out. When the dust settles, you'll not only be a free woman, you'll be a highstepping, powerful heiress."

Unsure what to say, she explained, "I can't stop Sonny Staidlaw from claiming me as his daughter. That's true enough. But, Traver, I mean to seek my own fortune, not rest on the laurels earned by my father. He offered me the big house in San Francisco. But I came back here of my accord. As you did. Oh, Traver, I'm so proud of you!"

She basked in his appreciative grin. "Will you stay here now, Traver? Work your claim?"

"No, thanks. There's buyers aplenty for that piece of ground. I'll outfit myself with a new wagon and a set of harnesses." He tossed his hair and his eyes began to twinkle. "You see, there's this intriguing range of hills beyond Forty-Mile Desert—"

She laughed. "Oh, Traver, it's taken me a long time to see I tried to tie you up. And it's taken me a long time to remove the chains from my own heart."

He held her hands fondly. "Do you realize from the time we met, we tried to outdo each other saving one another? I jumped off that ridiculous cliff to rescue you when you were the far better swimmer. Then you followed me down the flooded mine and up One Tree Hill when I was surviving quite nicely, thank you. Now we've saved each other for the last time." He looked out the window, studying the horizon as if eager to be gone. "I'm a wanderer at heart, Ariel. While *you*, eventually, like it or not—you'll end up in that fancy San Francisco mansion."

"I'll have no one to share it with!"

"Mitch?" Traver suggested the name shyly. "He's waited for you longer than most men would. Loved you stronger.

Stepped aside for us both when I know it galled him." He looked down at his oversized fists. "That's what he and I were sparring about at Flowery Hill. I told him I was putting things to rights for you and him to be together."

"But tomorrow's his wedding day!"

They were interrupted by shouts outside the lobby. Wise Ada led the procession of cheers. "Ariel! Traver! Come quick and hear the report." Then the doctor and the sheriff barged inside, motioning for quiet. There was a moment of tension. Ariel felt Traver grip her shoulders, supportive and strong.

The medical man spoke first. "The cut on the neck of the deceased did not bleed enough to cause death. The man died of accidental poisoning—an overdose of raw opium administered by his own hand." He cleared his throat and threw back his shoulders. "My profession is a new one, but it has already been tested in courts of law in the East. My word carries weight with the circuit judge."

A cheer echoed through the International Hotel. The sheriff announced, "Ricket Putnam is going back in the grave for keeps! As for you, Ariel, you can go and do as you please, no questions asked."

In the next moments Ariel was aware of handshakes, backslaps, hugs and a whirl of excited congratulations, admonitions and toasts. When she looked up again through the crowd, she saw Traver moving toward the exit. He was friendly, accepting handshakes and smiling, but he was moving intently toward new territory—as he would forever.

Chapter 27

Ariel was alone in her rooms, ready for bed, when there was a knock at the door. A very quiet knock. Timid and light, as befitted the midnight hour. "Who is it?" she called. She had thought the whole town was busy at the saloons, drinking toasts to tomorrow's wedding.

Ariel was even more shocked to hear Nedra's husky tones. "Let me in, Ariel! I've got to talk to you!"

Ariel ran to the door and unlocked it. Nedra barged in, her face flushed. "Why weren't you downtown at the parties?"

"I was too tired," Ariel lied. How desperately she wished she could toast Nedra's and Mitch's happiness. But it seemed less hypocritical to stay away, not to feed her own jealousy by seeing the couple linked arm in arm.

"Don't feel bad," sighed Nedra, flopping on the parlor couch. "You're not the only one to stay away! None of the Decency Committee ladies could find it in their hearts to wish me happiness. Oh, hell, they'll never accept me in this town!"

"Give them time, Nedra. They'll come around. Why, look at you. What a lovely change from shawls and ruffles." Ariel bestowed the highest praise she knew. "How ladylike!"

Nedra stood up, awkwardly pirouetting in her new outfit. Lace demurely outlined her dark throat. Her bias-cut skirt was pastel blue silk, the jacket had velvet cording of deeper blue. Dainty pearl earrings touched her lobes and a rope of pearls twice circled her throat. "A present from Mitch," Nedra said slowly, touching her pearls. She sounded less delighted than annoyed by the gift.

Ariel lowered her eyes and nodded.

"And he's giving me the Hell's Candy for a wedding present."

Ariel looked up, wondering why Nedra sounded so unhappy. Then Nedra exploded. "What do I want with a damned hole in the ground? A damned dark, dirty hole full of dirty rocks!"

"Nedra! What are you saying!" Ariel began to laugh. "Oh, you *are* full of pre-wedding jitters. Here, sit down. I'll make us some tea. No, better, I'll get us some brandy!"

Nedra sat down, working hard at not mussing her elegant clothes. "I'm getting more nervous every minute! It's not just the Decency Committee, Ariel. And it's not being gussied up like this."

"Then what is it?"

"I . . . I . . ." Nedra nibbled a long fingernail. "I don't know!"

Ariel poured out generous portions of brandy.

"Did you see Mitch today?" Nedra asked.

"Yes."

"And?"

"And he seemed very happy," admitted Ariel.

"Damn! Double damn! That Irish lunkhead hasn't got the sense God gave grasshoppers! He's so full of plans. He still wants to tie me down in that big house on the hill! Listen what he's bought so far. A walnut gaming table with his initials embossed on the leather top. White china candlesticks. Braided stair treads. A chiming clock. And a bench! For godsake, he's bought this bench to sit in the hallway. A bench with mahogany legs and peach velvet cushions!"

"What's wrong with all that, Nedra?" Ariel sipped her brandy. "After your years of living in a wagon with nothing but a cot and canvas, I'd think you'd appreciate some nice things."

"Oh, *you'd* see nothing wrong, I suppose," cried Nedra, gulping the brandy. "Oh, I just don't know!"

"Drink your brandy, Nedra." Ariel felt very old and wise. "Then go home and get some beauty sleep. You don't want dark circles under your eyes in the morning. Things will be all right, Nedra. You've wanted Mitch for a long time. And he's a fine man." That was as much blessing as Ariel could bestow. The points Nedra had made were all too true. Nedra and Mitch were too different, just as she and Traver had been too different.

"He's moving too fast," complained Nedra. "He's sold my wagon."

"Enough of this nonsense!" Ariel felt exasperated. Nedra was the one who had courted Mitch. "Remember how many times you offered yourself to him?"

Nedra put down her cup, twisting her ring thoughtfully. "Ariel, do you remember back at Cleo Burney's? You planted the idea with me that I was meant to have Mitch Galway. I've hung onto that idea since that day, hoping it would be the magical seed for my garden of happiness."

Ariel felt misty-eyed. "I think it can be," she said quietly. "I believe you'll blossom, Nedra. And you'll look back on these night-before nerves and laugh." She turned exuberant to avoid dissolving into tears. "Now calm down! You're as bad as Traver, I'll swear! Things will work out. Here, give me your hand. I'll tell *your* fortune!" Ariel grabbed the gypsy's long, slim fingers and turned the palm upward. "Now, for Traver, I see a new wagon and a map of Texas. For Mitch, I see a Chinese dragon and fireworks. For you—"

But Nedra yanked her hand away and stared down at it, fascinated. "My God! I never looked into my *own* hand! Never before!" She stood up, holding her palm inches from her eyes. "Oh, Ariel, thank you! I must hurry! There's so much to be done! Ariel, thank you! Thank you!" She rushed into the night.

Ariel awoke to the sound of firecrackers. The wedding day. She rolled over, unable to face reality. After hiding under the pillow and shedding silent tears, she went to the window and peeked out. Su Lin was leading the dragon dance. Ariel could not bear to watch the colorful fabric and metal giant weave through the streets. She wiped away her tears and went back to bed.

Some moments later there was a knock at her door. Ariel grabbed her black corduroy robe and opened the door. "Su Lin!" she cried, astonished. "What are you doing here?"

"I left Po Fan at the head of the dragon. He knows the ceremony as well as I."

"It's so good to see you in the open, without having to sneak in hallways or hide in shadows. I heard about your triumph at Piper's Opera."

"Please come to see me perform soon. I will have special seats reserved for you. I cannot stay and visit right now. I've only stopped to deliver this letter." She took a thin envelope from her quilted sleeve. "Traver asked me to give it to you. He left it last night as he pulled out on the road past China Camp."

Su Lin handed over the thin epistle and hurried back to join the noisy dragon.

Ariel opened the envelope. One sheet of foolscap. Three letters: G.T.T. She laughed. "Gone to Texas!" Then she noticed writing which showed through the thin paper from the reverse side. Turning it over, she gasped at the words, "Love to all, Traver and Nedra."

Traver *and* Nedra! They'd run off to Texas together! Ariel's feelings came in three distinct waves. First shock. Then horror. Then she realized that Traver and Nedra were suited to each other and a life on the open road. But, oh, poor Mitch! No matter how much sense it made for Nedra and Traver to run off together, it was unthinkably cruel to Mitch.

She could hear the crowd moving noisily through the streets on the way to the courthouse. Oh dear! She'd have to find Mitch and tell him. Was this the fortune Nedra had seen in her own palm? Abandoning Mitch? How could anyone do that! Glancing out the window, she spotted him. Laughing and jovial, in his fine English-cut suit, a wonderful smile on his golden face, he was shaking hands and urging the crowd to hurry. He made his way toward her boarding house. She waved at him from the window, anxious to attract his attention and stop his merry shenanigans.

He called to her. "Hurry up! Here it is my wedding day and you're dressed in mourning! Wear something pretty, Ariel!"

"Mitch, come in here!"

"That's hardly a proper invitation to a bridegroom! Come on, get dressed. Hurry—this is one party that won't wait!"

He wouldn't hear otherwise. She rushed to put on a pale lavender frock she'd brought from San Francisco. It had been her mother's. The pastel color contrasted with her dark brown eyes and set off the cool beiges and warm yellows of her hair.

Now Mitch was impatiently pounding the door. "Come on, woman!"

She rushed out. He was surrounded by a jolly crowd. Well-wishers were joking, jostling and singing. Mitch was handing out boutonnieres to all the men. "Come one, come all!" he cried loudly. "Everyone to the courthouse steps!" He grabbed her arm as she came near. "Step right this way, miss!" Jovially he announced, "I wouldn't get married without you there!"

She grabbed him by both wrists. Every second of dreadful delay added to the embarrassment. "Mitch! Stop! You can't get married at all!"

"Nonsense," he joked, heading uphill with the crowd. "I've got the license in my pocket, just waiting for the bride to sign her name. The judge is waiting to speak the words." He hurried her forward, barely shaking hands with folks as they moved along.

"Oh, Mitch," she begged him. "Please, listen! Something terrible has happened!" She wanted to spare him from the full impact of her announcement, but there was no time to be anything but frank. "Nedra and Traver have run off! To Texas! *Together!*"

She stood petrified, hands to her face, awaiting his reaction. She expected fury. She expected overwhelming sadness or angry curses. Of all the possible reactions, the one she least expected was laughter. But Mitch threw back his head and roared.

"You lunatic! Why are you laughing? Are you hysterical? I'm telling you Nedra has jilted you! She and Traver have run away together. And you stand there roaring as if it were a joke. Are you crazy with grief?"

"No, no! Only with relief! My God, Ariel—*I* knew they'd run off together! They came and told me last night. I thought I'd have to tell *you!*"

Now it was her turn for confusion. "But if you knew, why—" Suddenly she began to tremble.

Mitch pulled her up the steps to the courthouse. "Folks," he began, speaking to the crowd. "There's going to be a wedding here today. At least I hope there's going to be! The dragon's going to dance. I'm going to give my bride the Hell's Candy."

Ariel shook her head, backing away. This was too much. Too fast.

He grabbed her wrist. "Ariel, I love you. Will you marry me?"

She couldn't answer.

"Come on, girl! Find your voice. Speak up! I'm waiting—impatiently."

"Oh, Mitch! I simply can't. *We* can't! This is too unexpected."

He looked disappointed, then turned sideways and took off his top hat, using it to shield them from curious stares. "Ariel, darling, I've never felt powerless until this moment. Not even last night, when Traver and Nedra ran off. Now I'm helpless. Hell, I realize this was an awful gamble I took."

"Mitch, please. We both need more time."

Suddenly he was stern. "No. No more time. We spent all last winter baiting each other. I won't spend any more years without you. It's now or never." He drew her inside the dim courthouse corridor. "Darling, help me. You know I'm not shy. By God, give me a rail gang of half-wits, and I'll do my darnedest to lead them. Give me power to clear a forest, build a bridge, stake a road, and I'll not consider it a burden but a privilege. Give me responsibility for keeping food in a thousand Chinese bellies, and I'll not run. But, by damn, Ariel, give me some help right this minute, or I'm likely to trip over my own bootlaces!"

She was thrilled by the depth and intensity of his speech. It had that same spark of authority she'd always loved in him. The same mischievous energy which would give him the audacity to go on with the wedding without knowing if she'd agree. "Oh, Mitch, what a terrible risk you took—"

"Darling, you know I never take a risk unless I have faith. I have faith in you yet. I honestly believe, given time, you might still learn to love me."

She cut him off, "No! I can't!"

His blue eyes clouded. She quickly took his face in her hands. "My darling Mitch, I can't *learn* to love you. I always have."

Dear Reader:

Would you take a few moments to fill out this questionnaire and mail it to:

Richard Gallen Books/Questionnaire
8-10 West 36th St., New York, N.Y. 10018

1. What rating would you give *Sunrise Temptation?*
   □ excellent □ very good □ fair □ poor

2. What prompted you to buy this book? □ title
   □ front cover □ back cover □ friend's recommendation □ other (please specify) _____

3. Check off the elements you liked best:
   □ hero □ heroine □ other characters □ story
   □ setting □ ending □ love scenes

4. Were the love scenes □ too explicit
   □ not explicit enough □ just right

5. Any additional comments about the book?

   _____

6. Would you recommend this book to friends?
   □ yes □ no

7. Have you read other Richard Gallen romances? □ yes □ no

8. Do you plan to buy other Richard Gallen romances? □ yes □ no

9. What kind of romances do you enjoy reading?
   □ historical romance □ contemporary romance
   □ Regency romance □ light modern romance
   □ Gothic romance

10. Please check your general age group:
    □ under 25 □ 25-35 □ 35-45 □ 45-55 □ over 55

11. If you would like to receive a romance newsletter please fill in your name and address:

    _____
    _____
    _____